THE
HIDEOUT

Camilla Grebe was born near Stockholm and in the early part of her career wrote collaboratively with other authors. Her debut novel as a solo writer, *The Ice Beneath Her*, has been sold in 22 countries and topped several bestseller lists, including the UK, France, Italy and Sweden. It is also in development for film, with Daisy Ridley set to star. Her second book, *After She's Gone*, won the Best Swedish Crime Novel of the Year Award.

Also by Camilla Grebe
The Ice Beneath Her
After She's Gone

CAMILLA GREBE

THE HIDEOUT

ZAFFRE

Originally published in Sweden by Wahlström and Widstrand in 2018

First published in Great Britain in 2021 by Zaffre
by arrangement with Ahlander Agency, Sweden

ZAFFRE
4th Floor, Victoria House, Bloomsbury Square, London WC1B 4DA

A CIP catalogue record for this book is
available from the British Library.

PB ISBN: 978–1–83877–435–6
TPB ISBN: 978–1–83877–066–2

Also available as an ebook and audiobook
1 3 5 7 9 10 8 6 4 2

Typeset by IDSUK (Data Connection) Ltd
Printed and bound in Great Britain by Clays Ltd, Elcograf S.p.A.

Zaffre is an imprint of Bonnier Books UK
www.bonnierbooks.co.uk

Prologue
Manfred

We were an ordinary family. It was a morning like any other.

The kind you don't expect to remember. One of the many insignificant days you assign no particular weight to, because you think you know that it won't make much difference to your life. Just another day to deal with, to live through. To cope with and handle, like a form to be filled out and mailed before five o'clock.

Afsaneh got up first to give Nadja a bottle.

I heard her steps: light, tentative almost, as she snuck down the hall into the kitchen. As if she was tiptoeing across thin ice. Then the clatter, the rush of water from the tap and the slight bang as she placed the saucepan on the stove. Finally the rhythmic scratch of metal against metal as she whipped the formula into the water.

From my place in the bed – still warm from Afsaneh's body – I could hear Nadja whining and coughing from the nursery next door.

The sounds of a very ordinary family: of a woman, my young wife, perhaps too young – there were those who thought so anyway – and of my daughter. And the silence left by my three older children who'd moved out and my ex-wife who left here one spring morning not too different from this one, with a suitcase so heavy she never would have been able to carry it if she hadn't been so pissed off.

But I didn't think of any of that at the time, not as I lay there, drowsy from last night's dreams, in the warmth of the bed. It is only in hindsight that these small events take on weight and become significant.

It's only afterwards that all the trivialities of a life grow, develop teeth and chase you through the night.

It was just another morning like so many others. In addition, it was Nadja's third cold in as many weeks and both Afsaneh and I were tired of waking up in the night and soothing our beloved, but defiant, two-year-old.

We joked that Nadja became a baby again when she had a cold. And Afsaneh used to say that I had no one but myself to blame for deciding to start over again with another child and all the rest of it at over fifty.

Afsaneh cracked the door to the bedroom.

She carried Nadja on her hip and as she gently bent her knees and lifted Nadja to get a better grip, her robe slipped open baring one of her breasts, those beautiful breasts that had become mine against all odds.

She asked if I could stay home with the baby today, and I explained I had to go in to the station for a bit.

The station was police headquarters on Kungsholmen in Stockholm. The place I've worked for more than twenty years, the equivalent of my job, the salt mines. The place where I investigate murders and other serious crimes. Where I dealt with the very worst sides of humanity, the repulsive variants of human behaviour that the rest of the population needn't concern themselves with.

How could I think it was so important?

Let them kill each other, I think. Let them rape and beat each other. Let the drugs flood in and the suburbs burn like fireworks in the night. Just leave me out of all that bullshit.

I remember Afsaneh frowning when I said I had to work. She reminded me that it was Ascension Day, a bank holiday, and asked what I had to do that was so important. Then she patiently explained she'd promised to meet with one of her doctoral students, which she'd already mentioned to me twice during dinner last night.

We went on like that for a while.

We squabbled about who would stay home, as if that were important at all. We squabbled in that unreflecting, tiresome way I imagine most families do on perfectly ordinary mornings in a safe and prosperous country like Sweden.

After Afsaneh had gone off to meet her doctoral student, and Nadja was lying next to me in our wide bed, pressing her little runny nose against my cheek, it felt pretty good after all. Why did I need to go to the station today? The dead could wait until tomorrow, and most of my colleagues were off anyway.

I don't remember precisely, but I think I probably spent the morning tidying up the apartment. My knee was aching so badly, so I took a couple of Naproxen. Maybe I snuck in a couple of cigarettes under the extractor fan too. Nadja watched TV, and I had to turn up the volume to offset the noise from the roadworks outside on Karlavägen.

My elder daughter, Alba, called from Paris and asked to borrow money. I explained calmly but firmly that she would have to talk to her mother, because she'd already got an extra 3,000 from me this month. Besides, her siblings, Alexander and Stella, hadn't received anything at all. And it's important to be fair, right?

Fair, what a strange concept, in retrospect.

Eventually Nadja tired of the TV. She screamed and screamed, and I carried her around the apartment in a futile attempt to calm her down. Her little body was scalding hot, and I gave her Tylenol, even though Afsaneh didn't like it when I did that – another thing we often squabbled about. Afsaneh didn't think young children should take any medication unless they were dying.

Maybe Nadja was soothed by the Tylenol, maybe it was the sandwich I made for her that did the trick. Or maybe it was the roadworks outside the window that finally managed to distract her.

I lifted her up onto the windowsill in the living room, and she stood there for a long time seemingly fascinated by the digger that slowly ate its way into the road three floors below, while she licked butter off her sandwich and snot from her upper lip with her pointed little tongue. We talked about diggers and cars and trucks and motorcycles for a while. About all kinds of vehicles.

Nadja liked anything that had an engine and made a noise – Afsaneh and I had noticed that early on.

It must have been at that point Afsaneh called from the café.

I put a loudly protesting Nadja onto the floor and went out into the hall to talk undisturbed – the noise from the roadworks made the whole apartment vibrate.

Afsaneh asked how Nadja was feeling, and I said that she seemed fine, that she'd eaten a sandwich and it must not be that serious if she was eating and drinking.

Of course, I didn't mention the Tylenol.

As soon as we hung up, I immediately sensed that something was wrong. It was as if the air had thickened, as if it was pressing against me, a tactile warning of approaching danger. A moment later I realised that I was actually reacting to the *absence* of something.

It was quiet.

The construction workers had apparently taken a break, and the only thing I heard was my own breath.

I went out into the living room to look for Nadja, but the room was as empty as her bottle, which lay on the floor in the middle of a pool of juice, and the pile of toys she'd dragged out in the morning.

Maybe it was then that my concern awoke, that primitive instinct we all possess, the drive to protect our children from any harm.

Then I was blinded by a ray of sunshine, a sharp streak of light that shouldn't be there for the simple reason that the living-room windows were in the shade.

I turned towards the light, squinted and looked into the kitchen.

The window stood open, and the sun reflected off the glass.

Suddenly everything became clear to me: Afsaneh had cleaned the kitchen windows yesterday. She must have forgotten to put on the child lock. But Nadja couldn't have climbed up and opened the window. And *why* would she do such a thing?

The moment I formulated the question to myself, I knew why: the digger, the goddamn digger.

I ran towards the open window.

I ran because it was the only thing I could do. I ran because you have to, because you have no choice. You cannot let your child fall, die. If there is one thing in life you cannot do it is that.

Everything else you can get away with.

Outside, the sun's rays played in the sheer green of the trees and below the construction workers stood still, looking up at me with blank eyes. A couple of them ran towards our building with outstretched arms.

Nadja was hanging off the windowsill and the strange thing was that she was completely silent, just as I've heard that children who are drowning are.

Her little fingers clung on, and I threw myself at her because that's what you do. You throw yourself at your child, you go through fire and water.

You do everything you can and then a little more.

And I grabbed hold of her, I reached forward and felt her greasy little fingers slowly slide out of my hand. Slipped out of my grip like a bar of soap.

She fell.

My child fell to the street, and I couldn't stop it.

All I'd needed to do was to get there one second earlier, if I could just have got one step nearer while time seemed to stand still and the roar of the silence echoed in my ears.

In another life, in a parallel existence, I might have been able to save her.

But *my* child fell.

She fell from the third floor onto the street, and I couldn't do anything to stop it.

We were just a normal family.

It was a morning just like so many others, but afterwards nothing was ever the same.

PART I

The Escape

Arise, go to Nineveh, that great city, and cry out against it; for
their wickedness has come up before me. But Jonah arose up
to flee to Tarshish from the presence of the LORD.

Jonah 1: 2–3

Samuel

It took me exactly ten days to fuck up my life.

I'm staring out of the window.

From my room I can see a car park and beyond that the outlines of Långbro Hospital – a former mental institution that has been converted into luxury apartments.

At the moment dark clouds are gathered above the buildings. The pale green foliage contrasts against the violet clouds. The grass grows lush around the car park, but it is still fucking freezing, even though it's June 11th.

I can hear my mum cleaning up in the kitchen.

She is so annoying. By annoying I don't just mean that she's always nagging me to do things – find a job, go to the unemployment office, load the dishwasher, unload the dishwasher and on and on for fucking ever – but that she worries so much. And that worry eats at me, makes my whole body itch, like tiny ants crawling under my skin.

It's like she can't get it through her head that I'm an adult now.

I turned eighteen a month ago, but still she hovers around me like some kind of mother hen, demanding to know every step I take.

As if I were her goddamn cause in life.

It drives me crazy.

I think she'd feel a lot better too if she didn't keep on like that. If she let go, just a little bit. She's always talking about how much she's sacrificed for me – so why not get her own life now that she has the chance?

Alexandra, my girlfriend, or maybe the girl-I-sleep-with, says her mother is the same way, but that's a lie. Sirpa never follows Alexandra into the city, doesn't phone-stalk her friends or rummage through her pockets in search of weed or condoms.

Speaking of condoms: shouldn't Mum be happy if she finds condoms? Isn't that what all parents want: for their children to use protection? Because I assume that's her biggest fear, that I'll knock someone up and end up just like her.

A single parent.

Or a *singular* parent, as they like to say at Mum's church to make every welfare recipient feel included.

Mum and I live in a three-storey apartment building on Ellen Key's Street in Fruängen, a totally unremarkable suburb in southern Stockholm. It takes exactly nineteen minutes by train to get to the central station, and surely you can spare nineteen minutes of your life.

Right?

Nineteen minutes to the city and nineteen minutes home, that's thirty-eight minutes a day. If you make that trip every day, it's 13,870 minutes a year, or 230 hours, or just about ten days.

Ten days of your life wasted: it's not so insignificant after all.

A lot can happen in ten days, as you know.

The point is that it's important to make some calculations before drawing hasty conclusions, like nineteen minutes on the train not mattering.

Maths was the only thing I was ever really good at in school. Maybe Swedish too, when I was younger. Because I liked to read books. But I gave that up; you don't want to be seen on the train with a book in your hands.

Maths was different though. I never had to make an effort. I could see the numbers in my head and knew the answer long before the others had even reached for their calculators. And though I almost never went to lessons, my maths teacher still gave me an A for my final year of high school.

I guess he wanted to encourage me, but I dropped out of school anyway. I didn't really see the point in going.

A movement at the corner of my eye catches my attention. In the cage on the floor, the blackbird chick – almost not a chick anymore – leaps up. He roots around a little with his beak among the seed debris on the floor, pauses mid-movement, cocks his head to the side to look at me with yellow-rimmed button eyes.

The common blackbird, *Turdus merula*.

Well, there is actually one thing I'm good at besides maths, and that's identifying birds. I was absolutely fucking obsessed with birds when I was little, but I don't mess with that anymore.

It's way too geeky.

But when I found the blackbird in the skip, I just had to save it.

I look at the bird again. See its shiny black feathers and the bright yellow beak pecking at the floor.

I feed him seeds and small pieces of tallow. I've even taught him to eat out of my hand, like some kind of well-trained pet.

I hold my phone between my thumb and index finger. Check Snapchat.

Liam's posted a video of an exploding beer can. It looks almost like someone is shooting it, maybe with his air gun. Alexandra's sent me a picture of herself in bed. Even though her blanket is pulled up to her nose, I can see in her eyes that she's smiling. Small, hot pink hearts pulsate around her, a filter she added to the picture.

I open WhatsApp: nothing from Igor yet.

In fact I hope I never hear from him again. But unfortunately I fucked up, and now I'm going to have to pay the price.

Ten days.

That's how long it took to get caught in Igor's sticky net. As long as it takes to go back and forth to the city by train every day for a year.

But if I'm completely honest, it started much earlier. Mum always says that I lack good judgement and can't focus for longer than it takes to drink a glass of milk. She's never said it outright, but it's clear that she thinks I got it from my dad. Since I've never met him, I can't really say otherwise.

Mum, on the other hand, obviously has no such problems.

At least not when it comes to stalking me. She never loses her focus, never gives up.

She's like a fucking bloodhound.

The school psychologist sent me to the youth mental health services, and they sent me to a specialist. Some shrink bitch with sweaty hands, large silver jewellery, teeth so brown it looked like she'd been chewing shit.

I never liked her.

Especially not when she started going on about neuropsychiatric impairment. She said that even if I didn't qualify for a diagnosis, I struggled with attention and impulse control. I stopped listening at that very moment. Mum did too, because she didn't want to admit that there was anything wrong with me besides a bit of *bad judgement*.

A few months later, I read in a tabloid about a celebrity who said it felt good to finally have a diagnosis; that it explained so much. As if he wanted to be mental, as if the diagnosis was a nice leather jacket or a beautiful tattoo that he liked to show off.

How did I end up mixed up in this shit anyway?

Liam and I used to shoplift in the city. At first it was mostly just for fun. We pinched small things, like perfume or clothing. But we soon realised that if we took electronics – small hard drives, headphones, portable speakers – we could sell the stuff. Liam bought a booster bag – a backpack lined with several layers of aluminium foil – from Janne at the gym, and then all we had to do was duck the surveillance cameras, pull shit off the shelves, throw it into in the bag, get out of there, get back on the train and nineteen minutes later get off at Fruängen.

It was almost too easy.

We got really fucking good at it, we never got caught, but pretty soon Liam's mum's basement storage space started to fill up. It was also very labour intensive to sell all the stuff online. And my mum began to wonder why I had multiple mobile phones and always disappeared into my bedroom when I answered them.

So we started selling the stuff to a Chechen named Aslan, a really creepy guy with face tattoos who never smiled.

Aslan didn't pay very well, we only got a quarter of what we would get on eBay, but he bought it all in one go and never asked questions.

We used the money for drinks, trainers, weed and, now and then, a few grams of coke. One time we went to Stureplan and ate seafood like a pair of high rollers, but usually we just got stoned and watched a good movie.

We hung out at my house during the day and at Liam's at night because his mum worked the late shift at Huddinge Hospital.

We really didn't bother anyone.

The shops had insurance, so they got their money back. And we never stole anything from regular people, just from huge companies like Media Markt and Elgiganten, who try to trick people out of their money all day long.

We bought our weed and coke from a guy named Malte who hung out at the pool hall. Malte was tall, extremely skinny, had shaky hands and was uncommonly friendly, for a drug dealer.

I think it was Liam who asked him if we could pay with electronics. But Malte just rubbed his bony hands together, laughed so that the gold teeth in his mouth flashed and explained that wasn't his line of business. But, he said, if we wanted free weed we could help him with something else instead.

And that's how it happened. We started working for Malte a bit.

We soon realised that he was an important cog in the machine that supplied the people of Stockholm with weed and coke. In fact he was pretty close to the boss, Igor. So close that Liam sometimes used to call Malte Igor's bitch.

We laughed a lot about that.

The jobs we did for Malte were small, nothing all that illegal or anything.

We picked up and deposited packages in various places, or watched the phone when customers placed orders on WhatsApp. Even though all communication on the app was encrypted, Malte and his gang had developed mad codes for various products. When someone called and ordered 'pizza' it was my job to ask what kind they wanted. 'Capricciosa' was weed, for example, and 'Hawaiian' was coke. So if a customer wanted five 'Hawaiians', that meant five grams of coke.

The price for a gram of first-class coke is 800 kronor, so the pizza wasn't exactly cheap. But then again the customer also got their product delivered within half an hour, so we did offer high-level service.

We were *strictly old school*: coke, speed, weed, etc. Not a lot of prescription drugs and shit like that. And of course, we didn't sell heroin – that market belonged to the Gambians in Kungsträgården.

Sometimes Malte told us about the old days, when dealers stood around on the street slinging product like it was ice cream. And the cops had no trouble picking them up.

I laughed loudly.

I couldn't understand how people survived before the internet and apps.

I took to it all like a duck to water, but Liam was nervous and wanted to get out. In the end, he forced me to promise we'd stop working for Malte and I said yes, mostly to make him happy.

After a few months we weren't just swimming in weed, but in money. I quickly figured out I could never earn that much from a normal job.

Liam bought a used BMW from a guy in Bredäng and actually seemed happy for the first time in a long while. As for me, I didn't dare buy anything expensive, because Mum was already asking so many damn questions about where I got my new clothes and shoes and so on.

It was almost as if she could smell something was off.

One day I was called in to meet Malte's boss Igor, an enormous Russian with pumped-up muscles and a shaved head.

Igor was a legend for three reasons.

First, he drove a large part of Stockholm's drug trade.

Second, Liam claimed he got rid of three guys who stole from him by hog-tying them with cable ties and drowning them like kittens.

Third, he apparently wrote poetry and had published several books.

To be honest, I was a little flattered when Igor said he'd heard that I was doing a good job and asked if I wanted to help out with some other, slightly bigger stuff. I'd get paid well and if I continued to show promise there were many openings in the company.

Yeah, he actually called it 'the company'. As if he were running a real business.

He talked a lot about how the customer was always right, about how important it was to be honest with your buyers and always be 'service minded'.

It was almost as if he'd taken one of those courses organised by the Employment Service, the ones all about running real companies with VAT and overtime compensation and all that crap.

I said yes immediately. It was only as I was leaving that I started to have any doubts.

But by then it was too late.

Later that evening, Igor invited me to the company's Friday beer night. I don't know if it was a joke, but he actually called it an 'after work' thing.

We drank beer and played pool. That is, everyone except Igor, who apparently never touched a drop of alcohol, and who just sat at one end of the room watching us.

Liam wasn't there.

Later he told me that he'd received the same offer from Igor, but declined. He said I was fucking crazy, and that my life would be hell if I didn't start thinking before I did things.

Besides, I had promised him not to do anymore jobs for Igor and his bitch. And now I'd let him down. Blah blah blah.

That was exactly ten days ago.

The week after, I had to go around with Malte collecting debts from customers who'd been running up a tab. That's when I realised that the company's credit management was not exactly customer-oriented and that Malte was not quite the friendly dealer Liam and I had thought he was.

It went something like this: we knocked on the door at the customer's house, and if he or she opened, Malte explained we were there to collect the money they owed. Sometimes they actually paid and then we thanked them, told them to have a lovely evening and left like a couple of well-mannered Mormons.

Customers often told us that they had no money, but that they would pay us soon. If it was the first visit, we told them we'd be back in a week and that it was 'best for everyone involved if they paid up then', after which Malte carefully noted the visit on his phone, where he kept track of all debts.

But if it was the second or third visit, they got a beating.

I didn't know what happened on the fourth visit, but I suppose somebody other than Malte made that one, probably a real gangster was in charge of that department. Probably the same guy who'd helped Igor drown those guys. That is if the story was even true, because Liam talked a lot of bullshit.

My job was to keep the customers quiet and upright while Malte kicked and punched them like some kind of psycho. Though he usually threatened the girls with a knife; he pressed the shimmering blue serrated blade against the thin skin just below their eyes, scratched just a bit until they bled, and explained to them what ugly scars they'd end up with, while simultaneously pawing at their breasts.

Only once did Malte decide not to beat a person – a chick, of course – even though it was his second visit. It was a young woman with long red hair named Sabina. It was obvious as soon as Sabina opened the door that she and Malte knew each other, and that Malte was hot for her. They talked for so long that I started to get bored and asked if I could use the bathroom.

I could.

When I came back, I saw Malte give the girl a thin bundle of cash, instead of the other way around.

Just like that.

The girl looked pleased and promised to pay him back soon.

Just as she uttered those words, Malte noticed me. He grabbed my collar, pushed me against the wall and hissed in my ear.

'Not a word about this to anyone, do you understand? I'd be dead. And you too.'

I just nodded.

What did he think? That I was going to talk to Igor? That I was one of his bitches now?

But, like I said, the redhead was the only exception. Everyone else got a beating.

Many screamed. Some cried.

Huge guys with gorilla biceps and skull tattoos wailed like babies and begged for mercy. One guy threw up on my new Gucci trainers after Malte punched him in the stomach.

It was awful.

This wasn't just shoplifting from Media Markt or taking pizza orders that were really coke, but hurting people for real. I couldn't handle it. I know I've done some illegal shit, but I'm not a fucking monster.

I realised that first night that Igor's company probably wasn't for me.

But how do you quit a job like that?

In the end, I screwed up my courage and told Igor how it was, that I didn't like beating the shit out of people.

He nodded seriously and smiled. Leaned back in his chair so that his nice leather jacket squeaked. He then explained that this job wasn't for everyone, and that there were other things I could help with, if I was a little pussy who thought he was too good to get his hands dirty.

He sneered as he said that last bit, and I felt myself turning red with shame against my will.

But then Igor got serious again, told me he believed in diversity, and that people had different talents. If you want to build a strong organisation, you had to make use of various kinds of competencies.

Then he leaned forward and took out a package, about the size of a square of butter and wrapped in brown paper, and he threw it to me.

'Go to the industrial area on Monday night. Meet me outside the abandoned garage at nine. Not a minute later. Turn your phone off before you go there and take this package with you. This is important, do you understand? Your job will be to keep watch while I meet a customer. A fucking big customer. A distributor.'

He paused and seemed to be scrutinising me before he continued:

'That package contains samples of our product, so I don't need to explain to you how important it is not to lose it.'

I nodded and left Igor's office at the back of the pool hall full of both shame and relief. But mostly I felt relief: I wouldn't have to beat anyone up anymore and anything was better than that.

But now it's Sunday and the relief I felt in Igor's smoky office has slowly been replaced by a creeping discomfort.

I weigh the package in my hand and stare out of the window. The clouds above the old mental asylum have grown denser and a light rain has started to fall onto the car park. The asphalt is black and shiny, like the ice on a newly frozen and very deep lake.

The package isn't heavy; I'd guess it weighs about a hundred grams. During my short but intense career within the company, I've developed the ability to estimate the weight of small baggies and packages to perfection.

I'm almost as good at it as I am at doing calculations in my head.

One hundred grams. Probably coke. 800 kronor per gram. This means that the street price of this product is 80,000 kronor.

There's a knock. Reflexively I lay the package down on the table and turn to the door.

Mum comes in.

She looks tired.

Her long brown hair is streaked with grey and hangs onto her shoulders in worn curls. Her denim shirt is stretched tight over her breasts and a gold cross glitters at her throat. Her pressed khakis are so worn they've begun to fray at the bottom. She's holding a bag of rubbish in one hand.

'What are you up to?' she asks, her eyes roaming as she pushes a wisp of hair behind her ear. 'Are you doing anything right now? Or are you just sitting around and . . . I mean, that's OK too. If you're not doing anything, I mean.'

Mum always talks too much. It's as if her words tumble out of her mouth without passing through her brain first. Like a bird that's just escaped from a cage.

'Nothing,' I tell her, hoping she'll leave, because I can't stand to hear her bitch at me right now.

'Did you call Ingemar today? I really do think it would be good if you did. Called him, I mean.'

Ingemar was one of the elders in Mum's congregation. A man in his sixties with frizzy grey hair and thick red lips. He was always smiling, even when the pastor was talking about hell and eternal damnation. Ingemar owns a small chain of hot dog stands and always needed people, at least according to Mum.

But why would I grill hotdogs for, like, 90 kronor an hour when I can earn at least ten times that much with Igor?

'Nope. Haven't had time.'

Mum drops the bin bag. It falls to the floor with a wet thud.

'But Samuel, you *promised* me. What did you have to do that was so important?'

I don't answer her. What can I say? That I spent all day playing video games?

She takes a few steps towards me and crosses her arms over her chest. A wet, shiny stain starts to grow beneath the rubbish bag on the floor.

'We can't go on like this, Samuel. You have to take charge of your life at some point. You can't just sit around at home and . . . and . . .'

Her voice breaks and for once she is at a loss for words. I see her eyes slide over to the birdcage, and she shakes her head almost imperceptibly.

Then she freezes.

'What's this?'

She picks Igor's package up from the table.

'Give that to me,' I say, standing up and simultaneously realising that my rapid and forceful reaction has exposed me.

Mum shakes the package, as if she could hear what's inside.

'Give that to me, dammit!'

I reach for the brown package.

'Don't curse in my home,' my mother hisses.

And then:

'But . . . what is it?'

She backs away from me a few steps, but her eyes say it all. They don't look worried or angry, just disappointed.

As usual.

I am her greatest disappointment.

'Nothing,' I say.

'Well, then it won't matter if I take it. If it's nothing important. You won't care if I take it from you. Right?'

Mum fiddles with the package, examining it from every direction, as if it were a bomb. With trembling fingers she tears off the tape and rips open the paper. Finally the brown paper bursts and about twenty very small, transparent white plastic baggies fall onto the floor and land at her feet, like autumn leaves around a large tree.

'What in the world . . . ?'

'It's not what you think. It's . . .'

But I can find no good excuse, because what else would be stored in tiny baggies besides marching powder?

Mum rocks back and forth with her mouth open. Her eyes shining with tears.

'You get out of here, Samuel. I mean it.'

Her voice is calm, even though she looks like she's just seen a ghost in broad daylight.

'I . . .'

'*Out!*' she roars and then sinks down. Scrapes together the tiny baggies, goes over to the bin bag and pushes them down in among old milk cartons, shrimp skins and apple cores. Then she picks it up and goes out into the hall.

I stare at the wet stain on the floor and hear the door to the stairwell open. Then I hear the familiar, metallic sound of the rubbish chute opening and closing.

I hear steps and the apartment door closing.

'*Out!*' she screams again from the hall.

I grab my stuff, put it in my backpack, pull on my hoodie and head out into the hall.

'Get out of my house,' Mum hisses. 'And take this with you.'

She takes off the bracelet of colourful glass beads that I made for her in first grade and throws it on the floor. Then she leaves the room sobbing.

I pick up the bracelet – she's worn it as long as I can remember. Rub the glass beads between my fingers.

They are still warm.

Our front door key works on the rubbish room in the basement as well, and after coaxing it for a while the door opens with a whine. I take in the suffocating stench of rotting food, old nappies and sour wine.

Somewhere outside, I can hear the sound of a truck driving away.

I grope for the light switch along the concrete wall, find it, turn it and in the next moment the room is bathed in cold light.

The rubbish is gone.

New, empty bin bags hang neatly in the carousel. They flutter and rattle a little in the draught from the door.

My heart pounds in my chest and I rush up to the front door, open it and step out into the rain, just in time to see the rubbish truck drive away with 80,000 kronor's worth of coke.

It was never my fault.

I have always had poor impulse control, even the psychologist with shit teeth said it was so, and she should know.

I've never wanted to hurt anyone, even though Mum seems to think that I consciously try to sabotage her life.

We only shoplifted from huge corporations that were insured to the teeth, and we only sold weed and coke to consenting adults, customers, who had chosen to pay to get high.

Where there is a demand, there will be a market.

All we did was meet that demand in a way that was quick, efficient and even *service minded*.

And the collection work with Malte?

No, that's nothing I'm proud of, and if I could go back and choose again I would have said no when Igor asked me. But you can't go back. Time moves in only one direction. The fucking clock just keeps on ticking.

Seven thirty-six.

In exactly one day, one hour, and twenty-four minutes, I have to be in the industrial area.

I remember Igor's words.

'That package contains samples of our product, so I don't need to explain to you how important it is not to lose it.'

If I show up there without the package Igor will go insane. But if I don't show up at all I don't even want to contemplate what might happen. I suppose they'd send the gangster after me, the one in charge of the fourth meeting.

I sink down on my knees. Staring at the wet tarmac with my back to the wall.

The bracelet of glass beads glitters in the streetlights. Five of the beads have letters on them.

I blink a few times and read the familiar word.

MUMMY.

Pernilla

The rain drums against the window, and I can hear the truck's hydraulic lift as it retrieves the rubbish from our block of flats. A moment later, my thoughts are drowned out by the roar of the truck driving away.

Was I wrong to kick Samuel out?

It's not the first time – I've thrown him out twice in the last three months. But we've always reconciled quickly.

A little too quickly perhaps – my friends in the congregation say I'm too nice. That I have to maintain my boundaries and let go. That I can't take him back two hours after I've thrown him out.

I've tried to explain to them that the problem is that I don't know how best to help him. Should I be understanding? Make demands? Encourage those infrequent, but still regularly occurring occasions on which he does show some initiative, behaves like an adult and takes responsibility?

And deep inside, the inevitable guilt resides, like a tumour that grows every time Samuel does another stupid thing. With each year that passes by without him accepting Jesus in his heart.

Everything is my fault.

I clasp my hands and close my eyes. Say a short prayer.

Dear God. Make Samuel understand that you are carrying him. Take him under the shadow of your wings and show him the right path. And guide me so I can help him. And forgive. Forgive. Forgive me for everything. In Jesus' name. Amen.

I sink to the floor and place my hands on the cool linoleum. Let my eyes wander over the room.

Samuel's schedule is still taped to the fridge, though it's been months since he dropped out of high school. I printed it out at double the size and put it up so he wouldn't forget any of his classes. Tuesdays and Thursdays are marked with a pink pen. 'Remember your gym clothes!' I have written above them. Monday is marked with green. 'Note! First class at 08.05!' it says next to it. Jars of fish oil stand on the kitchen counter. One of the women in my Bible group swore they could get rid of even the most severe difficulties concentrating.

That and prayer, of course.

But Samuel didn't want to take the capsules. He claimed they stank of rotten fish, which may be true.

Everything is my fault. My past has caught up with me, my sin has come to light, once again.

I had a very happy childhood until I turned nine.

I grew up in a deeply religious family. My father, Bernt, was pastor at an evangelical church and my mother, Ingrid, a housewife. Mother and Father had wanted a large family, but had only one child, a fact for which I long tried to compensate by being the perfect daughter.

A daughter who was at least twice as good as all other daughters.

We lived in Huddinge, south of Stockholm, in a little yellow house next to Lake Trehörningen.

We were an ordinary family, had a Volvo, two golden retrievers – probably surrogates for the siblings who never arrived – and a large garden filled with fruit trees and berry bushes. I was very committed to the congregation from an early age, and always had the best grades in school.

But if my parents were proud of me, they never said so.

I suspect they felt I was just doing what was expected of me.

Father worked a lot – it was part of his role as pastor to always be available to the members of his congregation, and sometimes it seemed as if he were a curer of souls, a bank and the police in one.

There was always a great deal of commotion in our home – friends, members of the congregation in need of help and guidance, we all broke bread in our Spartan kitchen while the dogs sat wide-eyed and begged for scraps.

At that time, I took everything for granted, material goods, my loving family and, not least, my faith, which so many lack today. It was a blessing to receive all this happiness without reflecting on it, but also a sin, because I didn't understand what a gift it was, wasn't thankful for the Lord's grace.

One day when I was nine, I came home early from school and found my mum naked on the couch with a neighbour from down the street, the father of one of my classmates.

I can still remember the sun shining on their sweaty bodies, as they lay wrapped together on the mustard yellow corduroy couch. I remember how Mother's long, dark hair flowed over Jöns' chest and how his hand rested softly on her blushing buttock.

That was the last time I saw my mother.

The next morning she was gone.

Mother was beautiful, perhaps too beautiful for her own good. Also, she didn't want to obey Father.

The face of an angel and heart of a snake. A rebellious temptress, that's how Father spoke of her afterwards, and in the same vein he would refer often to the Ephesian letter, said to be written by Paul, during his captivity in Rome: 'Wives, be in subjection unto your own husbands, as unto the Lord.'

But Father wasn't a tyrant, even if it might sound that way. He loved Mother – even after she left us in a dark void.

Even though she abandoned Jesus and lived in sin until her death.

If Mother's disappearance was traumatic, that was nothing compared to the three years of silence that followed. Not a phone call, not a letter. Every birthday, I hoped Mother would contact me. I prayed intensely and longed for her to show up.

But she never came and on my thirteenth birthday she died in a car accident just a few miles from our home.

I stand up, take my phone and go into the bathroom. Rinse my face in cold water for a long time, then look at my image in the mirror. The frizzy brown hair, the frown wrinkles at the corners of my mouth, stomach and buttocks bulging out of too-tight pants. The red-rimmed eyes and mascara smeared beneath them.

Still, I see it, there's something in the eyes and cheekbones – I am my mother's daughter.

But I inherited more than just my mother's facial features. I inherited her urge for sin, the one that brooded in my mother's chest. Maybe she passed it to me in her milk like an invisible but deadly poison, masquerading as nourishment and love.

At least that's what my father said when I was eighteen years old and met Isaac Zimmermann.

Isaac was everything a good Christian was not. First of all, he wasn't a Christian, he was a Jew. That alone was catastrophic and shameful in my father's eyes. Secondly, he was five years older than me, an American, and a 'hippie musician'.

Father refused to let him set foot in our little yellow house.

But young and stupid as I was, I defied my father and continued seeing Isaac. I found him irresistible, his lanky body, his tattered clothes and his long, curly hair.

He looked almost like Jesus.

And I fell. I fell into the welcoming arms of ruin, and I liked it, because I didn't know better.

I thought my love for Isaac, my burning passion, would fill the void my mother had left. That it would heal the lasting wounds that still ravaged my soul.

But the only thing that happened was that I got pregnant.

Isaac wanted me to have an abortion, but that wasn't an option for me. Of course, that was in part because of my upbringing, all that talk about the sanctity of life, but more important was my complete conviction that I already loved the little being growing inside me. That I, who had already lost my mother, wouldn't lose my child as well. That I couldn't choose to abandon it as my mother had me.

The last thing I wanted was to be like *her*.

The face of an angel and heart of a snake.

Isaac got angry, left on tour to Värmland and wasn't back in touch for several weeks.

Then a letter arrived explaining that he wasn't ready to start a family, and that if I wanted to keep the child, I'd have to raise it myself.

And that's what happened.

After almost six months without any contact with my father, I returned to the little yellow house.

Eighteen years old and heavily pregnant.

If Father was ashamed, he didn't show it. And the congregation received me with open arms. Yes, I was a sinner, but I was ready to heal, to save my immortal soul before it was too late.

Only once did Father put it plainly: the apple does not fall far from the tree.

It was a stormy autumn evening and we were quarrelling, I don't actually remember about what, only that he raised his voice and proclaimed that I was just like my mother.

That I had the devil inside me.

And now I've passed that evil on to Samuel.

I've done everything in my power to make a good life for him. I have struggled to provide for us. I've never in all the years since Samuel was born treated myself to a holiday or started a new relationship – not because I didn't want to, but because Samuel was such a demanding child from day one. A child who sucked energy out of me like an insatiable black hole.

I've done everything.

And I have prayed.

But God has clearly decided that my trials are not over, and I must accept that.

I just don't know how I will find the strength.

It is said the Lord never gives us more than we can handle, but sometimes I wonder.

I wipe my face with a towel. It turns black with make-up and I throw it on the floor. Pick up my phone and write a short message. Asking Samuel to come home. Writing that I love him and that I'm sorry I lost my temper.

Then I sit down on the toilet to pee.

A screeching sound comes from Samuel's room. It must be that blackbird rooting around in its cage.

He can be responsible when he wants to. When it comes to someone or something he cares about.

Like a blackbird.

I delete the message and throw the phone on the floor.

It bounces a few times against the bathroom rug and lands next to the shower.

No, I think.

This time is different.

This time he's going to learn his lesson.

Manfred

We're sitting on either side of the bed, Afsaneh and I. Nadja is lying between us, surrounded by the machines that are keeping her alive. The electronics beep and sigh. One of her arms is in a large plaster cast, and from a little hole in her throat a hose runs that is connected to the machine that is breathing for her.

Around her are monitors that measure her heart rate, temperature, oxygen level and the pressure on her brain. There are so many machines it feels like we're on a spaceship.

Out in the corridor, I hear someone hurrying by, probably headed to another sick child.

At the head of the bed is Angelica, the intensive care physician, beside a small white table where a computer sits.

She's good. Everyone is good at the PICU – the paediatric intensive care unit – where we were moved after the first week in the neurointensive care unit. They care, not just for the children, but also for us, the families. They bring us food, coffee. They explain all that which cannot be explained. They hold our hands and wipe our tears.

I don't know how they do it.

Nadja is in a medically induced coma.

She suffered severe head injuries when she fell out of the window and the doctors have anaesthetised her to allow her brain time to recover. But no one knows yet if she will ever wake up again, or what kind of life she will wake up to.

It's been three weeks now.

I thought it would get easier with time; that the uncertainty would become easier to handle, but the opposite is true. With each passing day it becomes more painful to live in limbo.

I let go of Nadja's damp, warm hand and lean back in my chair. Look over at Afsaneh who is sitting hunched over across from me with her head in her hands and her elbows on her knees.

There is something symbolic, almost fateful, about how we are sitting, on either side of Nadja. I can't reach Afsaneh, and she can't reach me, even if she wanted to, because Nadja has come between us.

Her accident has come between us.

Just as it has at home.

Afsaneh and I barely speak to each other, and she no longer touches me.

Do I touch her?

I don't know. I don't remember.

There's so much I don't remember.

Days pass, like distant ships at sea, and I have lost my ability to reflect on them. There have been times when I have got up in the morning, sat down on the sofa in the living room, and hours have passed until I suddenly realise the sky is getting dark outside.

Time has ceased to exist. Everything has become just a long, painful wait for the day Nadja either wakes up or leaves us for good.

Afsaneh stretches out and massages her neck with one hand.

'I'm going to get a coffee,' she says without asking me if I want anything.

I don't respond. I just stare out of the window where the sun is shining in a clear blue sky and where the wind is playing in the treetops.

Angelica looks up at me from her place behind the computer.

'Would you like anything?' she asks. 'I was just about to head to the kitchen.'

'No thanks. I'm good.'

I'm never hungry anymore. I, who have always loved food, who have been fat since I was a teenager. I must have lost at least two stone in the last few weeks.

The most effective diet ever: living with a seriously ill child.

All you have to do is stop paying attention for a moment, just long enough for your child to fall out of a window, run out onto a road or fall into the water from a jetty.

Life takes a long time. Life is a tired old donkey.

But death is lightning-fast. Death only needs one second, one step, one breath. Death is a cobra, whose bite arrives without warning. I'll be buggered if it isn't faster than its own shadow, just like Lucky Luke.

The phone rings and I look at it uncomprehendingly before I answer.

'Manfred? It's Malin.'

It takes a second before I realise that the person on the other end of the line is my colleague Malin Brundin.

Malin, who usually works in Katrineholm, was part of the group that investigated the murders in Ormberg – one of the most infamous crimes in Sweden.

The investigation took a turn that changed Malin's life forever. It turned out that a relative of hers had kept a woman imprisoned in a cellar for many years, and that Malin was also the woman's child. In other words, the person Malin grew up with, whom she had called her mother all her life, was not her biological mother.

How do you survive a thing like that?

In fact, I'm surprised that she hasn't left the force and moved to Stockholm or some other big city, where she can more easily hide from the press or the curious.

Malin has taken a temporary position in Stockholm over the summer, on my advice. I think I had some dim notion that it might do her good to get out of Ormberg. That it might somehow heal the horrible wound that I imagine she carries.

'Hello,' I say.

'How's it going?' she asks.

How do you answer a question like that?

People are constantly asking me how I'm doing, but I have stopped answering it, because I don't have it in me to explain. Not just because it's painful, but because it takes too long. And besides, I don't really know what is going on with me, because I've stopped paying attention to that.

'Unchanged,' I say after a moment's hesitation.

'Um, we're just wondering if you're on your way, because we thought we'd get started now.'

Damn.

Then I remember.

I was supposed to start working again today. My sick leave is over and life – my working life in any case – has begun again.

'Damn, Malin, I'm sorry,' I begin. 'I must have got the days mixed up. I'm at the hospital with Nadja and I had completely forgotten . . .'

'That's fine,' she says so quickly that I suspect she was expecting that exact answer. 'You can come tomorrow if that's better.'

'No, no, I'll come in.'

There's a pause.

'Wait there instead,' Malin says. 'We have a new case. The body of a man washed ashore on an islet in Stockholm's southern archipelago. We are headed over to forensics in Solna in an hour. You can meet us there.'

She hesitates a bit but then continues.

'Right. You are already at Karolinska Hospital.'

The sun is beating down on the hot tarmac, there is no trace of yesterday's rain.

Malin stands outside the entrance to the brick building doing something on her phone. I drop the cigarette as discreetly as I can and go over to her. The long brown hair, the slim yet muscular body. The dark eyes squinting at the sun under well-defined brows and the slight hardness around the mouth – Malin looks the same. But her cheeks have become fuller, her hips rounder and the T-shirt is tight over her large belly.

Malin and Andreas are having a baby.

They worked together on the investigation in Ormberg and were at each other's throats the whole time. Argued about everything from immigration to social assistance and couldn't even agree on which restaurant to get lunch from.

And now they're bringing a new person into the world together.

It's unexpected to say the least.

'Are you *still* smoking on the sly?' Malin asks, raising an eyebrow and nodding to the butt on the ground.

I don't answer, just pat her on the shoulder.

Standing a short distance to the right of Malin is Gunnar Wijk, whose nickname is Letit.

I glance at him.

His beard is grey and straggly. The eyelids so heavy that they must obscure his sight behind those thin, wire-rimmed glasses. He has a potbelly beneath his short-sleeved shirt, and his polyester trousers are a little too short and expose his sock-less, slightly swollen ankles, above a pair of worn-out brown sandals.

Gunnar is a legend. He came from a real police family, a family that paid a high price for working on the force. But he's best known for being the biggest Casanova the Stockholm Police ever saw. An accomplished womaniser, who, it is generally agreed, could seduce anything with a pulse. And just as he was facing the moment of truth, when he was about to overcome the last resistance, he would deliver his widely known line: *Let it happen*.

Of course, it didn't take long for Gunnar's modus operandi to become known, and shortly after that, the jokers on the force had renamed him Let-it-happen. As the years went by, the nickname was shortened into the catchier Let-it, which over time became Letit.

I greet him. We haven't worked together before, but of course we know each other, though superficially.

He's actually supposed to be a decent cop, even if he's got a little grumpy with age. Those who know him best say he is at his most moody when not in the midst of a romance.

'What do we have?' I ask.

'A man in his twenties,' Letit says, stroking a hand over his beard. 'Found by a recreational fisherman yesterday.'

'And why are *we* here?'

The question is relevant. Suspicious deaths aren't usually investigated by the NOU – National Operations Unit.

'We believe the dead person may be connected to an ongoing investigation,' Malin says. 'In addition, the Stockholm Police are low on staff. They asked for assistance.'

'Do we know who the victim is?'

'Not sure,' she says while shading her eyes from the sun.

Her eyes slide over me.

I must look terrible. Unshowered, unshaven and unprepared. I'm as different from the old Manfred as it's possible to be.

He never would have shown up to work like this.

The old Manfred would have worn a dress shirt and a suit jacket with a vest. He would have a silk handkerchief in his breast pocket and smell like a perfume department.

The old Manfred would have worn polished Italian calf-skin shoes and an exclusive, but not too eye-catching, Rolex watch from the early '50s.

But the old Manfred is gone.

'Shall we?' Malin says and heads towards the entrance.

*

The medical examiner, Samira Khan, hugs me when she meets us at reception. Her body is so small and dainty it could belong to a child. Her long, shiny plait rests heavily between her shoulder blades.

'Look how skinny you've got,' she says and grabs onto my forearm.

And then, in a quieter voice:

'How is she?'

'They're keeping her sedated.'

Samira nods, smoothing the top of her green surgical scrubs.

'That's so the brain can heal in peace,' she says matter-of-factly. 'Listen. At that age children have an amazing ability to recover. And their brains are able compensate for loss of function in an incredible way.'

I nod. I've heard it all before.

We walk along the corridor towards the autopsy rooms.

'So you think you know who the dead man is?' Samira asks, looking up at Malin.

'We *think* it could be a Johannes Ahonen,' Letit says then stuffs *snus* under his upper lip. 'But that conclusion is based on Ahonen having the same tattoo as the one found on the body.'

Samira nods and says:

'We'll have to wait for the forensic odontologist's report and the DNA results before we can make a positive identification.'

Then she opens the door for us. The unmistakable, suffocating smell of death hits me, and I can see Malin grimace before she enters. Letit's expression, on the other hand, doesn't change a bit as he ambles into the room with his hands stuffed in his pockets.

'Shall we take a look?' Samira says, putting on a pair of glasses and a plastic apron and then leading us over to an autopsy table.

On the shiny, stainless steel surface lies the body of a man. It is bloated and discoloured. The skin has come loose in several places and looks more like thin grey-green plastic loosely draped over the bloated, whitish tissue.

Maybe it's because of my emotional imbalance – I'm not usually so affected by seeing dead people – but something inside me is tying itself into knots as I near the table. It is as if a cold hand is rooting around inside my chest in search of my heart. I think about how Nadja might end up on just such a table one day. And a second later – that the man on the table is actually someone's child too.

I close my eyes tightly.

'We're going to conduct the post-mortem this afternoon,' Samira says, spreading her fingers and snapping her gloves into place. 'But I thought you might want to take a look. Before, that is.'

She continues:

'As you probably know, the body was found wrapped neatly in a blanket, which was wrapped in an iron chain. When the tissues break down, gases, including methane and carbon dioxide, form in the abdomen and chest. This is why drowned bodies often float to the surface. In this case, the body had obviously been dumped deliberately, and someone tried to prevent it from floating up. But that doesn't automatically mean that he was killed. I cannot make a pronouncement on the cause of death until after the autopsy. But I can say that the body was subjected to severe external trauma and that both legs, the pelvis and the back have fractures and contusions.'

'And someone has cut off a hand,' Malin says, nodding to the body, which was missing the left hand.

'Can't be certain,' she says. 'Hands and feet tend to loosen on bodies that are in water for a long time. It could be spontaneous, caused by animals, or some other type of mechanical damage; for example, a boat propeller.'

Letit nods and wrinkles his bushy eyebrows.

'What is that white goo?' Malin asks.

Samira runs a finger over the waxy substance that covers parts of the body. Then rubs her fingers against each other.

'Adipocere, or wax. It's formed by the hydrolysis of fat when the body is in cold water for a long time.'

'Jesus,' Malin mumbles and squirms a little, but falls silent when she sees Letit's expression.

'When did he die?' Letit asks, making notes in his notebook.

'I'll get back to you on that,' says Samira, hesitating. 'There are many factors that affect how quickly a body breaks down in water: temperature, salinity and oxygen content, just to name a few. But my preliminary guess would be between one and two months ago. It takes a few weeks for the wax to start forming.'

'And the reason we think this is Johannes . . . ?' I ask.

'Ahonen,' Letit fills in.

Samira lifts one forearm so that a darker area on the skin becomes visible.

'Look here,' she says.

Letit leans forward. Malin does the same, but I can see that her eyes are on the door and her face paler than usual.

'A tattoo?' I ask.

'Yes,' Samira says.

'I can barely make out what it is,' Malin says.

'Don't you have eyes?' snorts Letit, who is still bent over the body, wiping a thumb and forefinger up and down his big nose. 'It's a bird.'

Samira nods.

'It's an eagle. Probably a white-tailed eagle, but could be a golden eagle. They are similar. Apparently, Johannes Ahonen has a tattoo like it.'

She goes to her desk, takes off her gloves and throws them in a yellow rubbish bin labelled HAZARDOUS WASTE. Then she flips through a folder of papers.

'Here,' she says, returning with a stack of photographs that she hands to me.

The first image depicts a tattoo of an eagle with the characteristic curved beak and wings extended backwards, as if it were just about to land or catch prey in its claws. The other shows a body wrapped in a chequered blanket. Round and round the blanket runs a heavy, rusty chain. Here and there seaweed hangs from the metal links.

'The image of the tattoo is an enlargement of a photo from Ahonen's Facebook profile,' Samira says.

'These days tattoos are like arseholes,' Letit mumbles, and shoves his chin forward so that his beard becomes even more prominent. 'Every bastard has one. Who knows how many have got this birdie on their arms?'

'Absolutely,' Samira says. 'That's your job to figure out. You can keep the pictures. I printed them out for you.'

'What do we know about Ahonen?' I ask.

'From Haninge,' Malin says. 'Twenty years old. Reported missing by his mother in March. Sentenced for possession of illegal weapons, drug possession and theft. The reason we are here today is that he's popped up in the investigation of Igor Ivanov, a thirty-year-old Swedish citizen, born in Kiev, Ukraine and living in Älvsjö. He's believed to control a large part of drug sales on the south side of the city. He's a bit of a legend, apparently. We have never succeeded in pinning anything on him, despite rumours saying he runs his organisation with an iron fist and actually killed some guys who tricked him out of money. But that could be bullshit, of course.'

I let out a low whistle.

'*Igor Ivanov*,' I say. 'Well, I'll be damned.'

At the same time, Malin puts a hand to her mouth, turns around and rushes from the room.

'Oh,' Samira says, glances at me quickly, then follows her.

Letit looks at me and pushes his glasses higher up his nose with his index finger.

'I was wondering how long it would take,' he says with poorly disguised triumph in his voice. 'Where do they find the investigators they send us these days? Pregnant women who are just a blink of an eye from giving birth probably shouldn't be dealing with autopsies.'

Samuel

The forest is submerged in darkness, but the summer sky is still light. The smell of wet soil and foliage rises from the narrow footpath.

My head is throbbing, and my body aches. I slept on the night bus, though I didn't end up getting much sleep. I mostly sat there wondering how the hell I was going to get Igor's package back, and at Hökarängen the bitch driving the bus threw me off.

I don't even dare contemplate what Igor is going to say when I tell him that his samples drove off in a rubbish truck.

I pull my phone out to distract myself.

No messages from Mum.

I feel a twinge in my chest.

She's never been pleased with me.

It doesn't matter what I do. She wasn't even happy the time I got an A in maths. Instead she started bitching about how I failed almost all of the other subjects. And once, when I gave her a Hermès bracelet, she went crazy and started screaming about how she had no intention of taking any stolen goods, and it was a deadly sin to steal, even though I had actually bought it.

I sigh and return to my mobile. Send a text to Jeanette, Alexandra's best friend.

She's so damn hot.

Long blonde hair and small firm breasts. Big mouth and tanned skin that looks soft. And it is soft, that much I know.

We've got something going on, Jeanette and I. What it is, I'm not really sure.

I really should stop it – she is Alexandra's friend after all. But on the other hand, I never promised Alexandra eternal faithfulness. On the contrary, I've explained to her that I'm not ready to be in a real relationship. That I'm not *there*, basically, as if love were a station that I haven't yet arrived at.

And Alexandra said that was OK, that she didn't want any commitment either.

So we meet and sleep with each other and sometimes it's really good. Almost like a porno or like we're in love for real.

I speed up and hear my phone ding.

It's Jeanette.

No messages now, it says on the display. I'm just about to text her back and ask why she's playing hard to get when I hear it: a branch snaps somewhere behind me in the woods.

I stop and turn, peer into the darkness between the slender birches, but see nothing but the light, spotted tree trunks and the outlines of bushes behind.

It must have been an animal.

Even though we only live nineteen minutes from the city, there are deer in this forest. Not to mention all the dog owners who walk here.

I keep going.

The woods thin out and I see low, box-shaped buildings built of concrete and corrugated metal spread out in front of me. I crawl through the hole in the fence and walk towards the old garage, which is at the edge of the industrial area.

In the dimness at the entrance I can just make out two figures: one broad and large, one long and lean.

Igor and Malte.

My stomach drops as I cross the tarmac area in front of the auto repair shop.

Igor nods briefly, and Malte grins, flashing his gold teeth in the dim light.

'Yo,' I say. 'Something happened. That package . . .'

I don't make it any further before Igor raises a hand as if he wants to push the words back into my mouth. Then he takes a few steps away to an old container covered with tags and graffiti dicks.

'Hello,' he says, smiling, but not at me.

I turn around and see two more guys approaching.

One is short and a bit chubby, looks he might be Latino, and is wearing a biker jacket and jeans. The other is as pale as an albino, with white hair, wearing a hoodie and jeans. He is carrying a duffle bag with 'Just do it' written on the side.

I sidle over to Malte, trying to get his attention, but he hushes me.

'The package,' I hiss. 'The product samples. They're gone.'

Malte freezes and slowly turns to face me. I see the terror in his eyes.

'What the hell?' he whispers.

'My mum took them.'

'Seriously?'

I look over at Igor and the two guys he's talking to. Igor gestures and the guys laugh out loud as if he just said something really funny. A second later, all three start walking towards me and Malte.

Sweat pours off my forehead and from my armpits, even though the evening air is cool and humid. I try thinking of Malte as Igor's butt boy to make myself less scared, but even that doesn't work.

'Fucking. Loser,' Malte whispers between his teeth and spits.

Igor's leather jacket squeaks as he approaches, and the light of a street lamp bounces off his shaved head.

'Samuel,' he says. 'Take the bag.'

The albino guy throws the bag at me, and I catch it. I don't know what it contains, but I assume it's not product, because Igor said we were meeting a buyer, a distributor.

It could be money, though Malte says Igor usually uses bitcoin when large sums are involved.

Igor meets my gaze. His eyes look like black marbles and his expression is unreadable.

'The samples,' he says briefly.

'I-I tried to tell you,' I stammer. 'They're gone. My mum took them.' For a moment there's silence.

Igor looks like he can't understand what I just said, as if I were speaking in a foreign language.

'*What the fuck?*' he says finally.

'And then she put them in the rubbish chute, and the truck left before I could fish them out and . . . But I thought I had to come anyway. And of course I will pay you back.'

I realise that I sound just like my mum and decide to shut up.

Anything is better than sounding like Mum.

But that mean voice, the one that sometimes chatters in my head, wakes up.

You're toast, you fucking loser.

Igor takes a few steps towards me and his jaw tightens, as if he's biting onto something that's hard and maybe a little bitter.

'No samples, no advance,' says the Latino guy and shrugs indifferently.

And just then, when everything is as fucked up as it can get, a text message dings in my pocket.

Igor fixes me with his eyes and closes his big hands into fists.

'Didn't I tell you to turn off your phone, you fucking retard?'

I close my eyes and wait for the blow, while holding the sports bag tightly. Then I hear a voice roaring behind me.

'Police! Hands up! Get down!'

When I open my eyes again, Igor and Malte are squatting down, as if they actually plan to do what the cops say.

The other guys are running towards the forest.

I don't know why, it's not some well-thought-out tactic or anything like that, but I start running in the opposite direction, along the bike path towards the old plant nursery. I run as fast as I can, still gripping the bag tightly; shame burning my skin like scalding water.

How could I be so fucking stupid?

Because you're a fucking idiot.

Igor asked me to do two things: bring the package and switch off my mobile.

I failed at both.

I truly am worthless. Everyone who has told me so – and many have – was obviously right.

Shots echo in the darkness, and I speed up. My legs dash forward with my heart slamming in my chest. I'm suddenly overcome by nausea shooting out of the pit of my stomach, and I have to stop. I grab a lamppost and am sick on the tarmac. Panting in exhaustion, then I turn around.

The forest behind me lies quiet and deserted.

I see no one approaching from any direction, no police, no dogs. And most importantly no Igor or Malte.

Is it possible? Could I have escaped?

I realise I should step out of the revealing light of the street lamp and I take a few steps into the woods. My chest aches, and I have a bitter taste in my mouth from the vomit.

Somewhere in the darkness I can just make out a familiar shape – the big boulder where Liam and I used to hide secret messages, pornographic pictures and sweets when we were little.

I go over to it. Lay the bag on top of the damp granite and open the zipper. Blink a few times while my eyes adjust to the darkness.

Rolls of hundred-kronor bills are scattered around inside the bag. It's impossible to say how much money it is, but it must be hundreds of thousands of kronor. Maybe more. There are at least twenty-five very thick rolls.

I take out a roll and flip through it quickly.

How many can there be? A hundred?

If there are a hundred in each roll and twenty-five rolls, that's a total of 250,000.

I feel a sense of vertigo.

What happens if the police arrest me while I have this bag with me?

Surely I'd go to prison.

I think for a moment. Then I gently pull the zipper closed again and squat down. Rummage beneath the branches, leaves, and earth until I reach the hollow space I know exists beneath the boulder. I stuff the bag in there, cover the opening, and then jog toward the car park.

Next to a rusty old Volvo stands Igor's shiny new black motorcycle – the one I've been able to borrow a few times and which my mum hates me riding.

I stare at the enamelled flame that winds over the petrol tank, while I consider.

Igor must have been arrested. Surely it can't hurt if I borrow his bike? It might even be a good thing – after all, then police can't seize it. So, in a way, I'm helping Igor if I move his motorcycle.

And if there's one thing I can do, it's hot-wire cars and motorcycles.

Alexandra opens the door after I ring the bell many times. And even then she keeps the chain on. Her eyes peer at me suspiciously through the opening.

'Go to hell,' she mutters through the gap.

I don't understand.

'What's got into you?' I ask.

Alexandra tries to pull the door closed again, but I pull it the other way. Only now do I see that her eyes are shiny and that she has streaks of mascara running down her cheeks, as if she's been crying. Her hair is tangled, and she's wearing a dirty T-shirt and pants.

'What happened?' I try.

'Did you have to hit on Jeanette? Is that your thing, humili-ating me?'

Her voice is thin. She lets go of the door and stands still, as if hesitating. I jerk the door a few times, but the chain holds.

'Damn. Baby – it didn't mean anything. Jeanette isn't . . . You're the one I like.'

'Sure,' she says sarcastically, but I hear the tears in her voice.

'Let me in, baby. That fucking maniac Igor is after me.'

I don't mention the police, because Alexandra hates that I'm involved in illegal things. She always says that she would rather I worked collecting train tickets and earned nothing than as a dealer.

Though I think that's a lie.

Without money I'd be a nobody. Neither Alexandra nor Jeanette would be interested in me.

Because I am nothing. I know nothing. And I have nothing.

That's the bitter truth and I might as well I face it.

Because that's exactly how it is. You're nothing. Nothing.

'You know,' she says quietly, but with unexpected calm, 'I'm tired of solving your problems. Grow up. And don't drag me into Igor's fucking shit.'

She closes the door, but opens it again almost immediately.

'And for fuck's sake, don't call me *baby*,' she sputters so that spit flies out of her mouth.

The door slams shut again, and I'm left standing there in the stairwell.

Manfred

A fsaneh is still deep asleep despite the fact that the alarm has gone off twice. Her long, dark hair flows over the pillow, and she snores lightly. On the bedside table sits the box of sleeping pills she got from her GP and a half-full glass of water. Next to the box is half a tablet that I know wasn't there when I went to bed last night.

She must have woken up in the night and taken another half of a pill.

In the distance, I hear the bells of Hedvig Eleonora Church chime seven times.

Besides that, all is quiet.

This silence is so strange.

I've lived surrounded by the sounds of children for so long. First the shrieks and laughter of my older children. Then, after they moved out and Nadja was born, shrieks, children's programmes and toys being dragged across the floor.

Now the only sounds are Afsaneh breathing, the door that leads to the inner courtyard of our apartment building, and the sound of steps crossing the cobblestones.

There is something very familiar about the unpleasant and intrusive presence of silence, and I recognise immediately why that is.

Aron.

It's like the silence after Aron.

I grew up in this part of Östermalm. No one would have guessed I'd turn out to be a police officer even in their wildest dreams. That's not the sort of thing you do when you come from an academic, haute bourgeois background.

It was understood that Aron and I would get a university education.

Of course, we were free to choose what we wanted to study, as long as we chose the law, medicine, or maybe economics. Art or literature were also acceptable, if you happened to be a bit soft and aesthetic.

Aron was my twin brother.

We were identical and almost impossible to tell apart, even for our own parents and friends.

But when we turned twelve, something happened. Aron didn't want to eat. He claimed he couldn't swallow. My parents took him to several doctors, all of whom stated that there was nothing physically wrong with him so the problem must be psychological.

The weeks went by, but Aron didn't get any better. He just wasted away, and I got fatter.

I guess I ate for two.

In the end, Aron was so skinny that his ribs stuck out like tent pegs under his tight skin and his knees resembled bumps on thin legs. He was so weak he could only sleep on our Svenskt Tenn sofa in our large living room, watch TV and drink soft drinks through a straw.

One night, Dad said enough was enough, resolutely lifted Aron off the big flowery sofa, carried him to the car and drove him to the hospital.

Aron never came home again.

What the doctors thought was a psychosomatic disorder turned out to be an aggressive tumour of the thyroid gland, which had grown into the oesophagus.

The cancer had spread and Aron died after two months.

And that's when the silence took over our apartment – the same silence as in our home now, with me and Afsaneh.

It's the silence that comes out of the void of someone you took for granted – a wounded, numb feeling of sadness and loss. And many years later, when my ex-wife Beatrice took the children and left me, that same silence and emptiness occurred.

It was the usual – she said I worked too much and took no responsibility for my family. What she didn't say was that she'd met a lawyer named Hasse. A man who moved in the right circles and had country homes in Torekov and Verbier. A man who could give her the life she'd always wanted. Beatrice was never cut out to be a cop's wife.

I can't say that I mourned the dissolution of our marriage, but it hurt to only see the kids every other week.

I have promised Afsaneh to never put my job above Nadja. Told her that this time things would be different.

I turn on my side, so that my back is to Afsaneh. On the floor behind my bedside table are a few red and blue Lego bricks, fragments of another life.

I hope I'll get the chance to be that present and loving dad. I hope it's not too late.

*

When I get to the office, Malin and Letit are sitting in front of the computer with a colleague of ours in his forties whom I don't recognise. He's lean and sinewy, like a marathon runner, and looks like he might be from southern Europe, or perhaps the Middle East.

The screen plays grainy footage from a car park.

I would guess it's from a surveillance camera. Suddenly one of the cars explodes and seconds later another one.

'Once more,' Letit says and the unknown colleague plays the film again.

Letit runs his hand over his straggly beard and pushes his lower jaw forward in a way that makes him look like a sly old fish lurking in the reeds.

'Stop,' he says, pointing at the screen.

'There. You see? The smoke is white, which means the explosive charge is made with gunpowder. I would guess some kind of home-made device, an IED, like a pipe bomb or a pressure cooker. Did you say those other cars were damaged?'

'Completely wrecked,' says the dark-haired man.

'We found splinters . . .'

'Splinters?'

Letit leans forward and squints at the screen.

'Then I'd put my money on a pressure cooker,' he continues. 'Then we have the fact that two explosions were triggered. The bombs must have been remote-controlled or on a timer. Any idiot can build a simple bomb, but this is something else. But talk to the bomb squad, they know it better.'

The man I don't recognise thanks Letit, stands up and slouches off towards the stairs with his USB stick in hand.

'Hey, Manfred,' Malin says from her chair and smiles. 'Did you know that Gunnar worked for forensics in the past?'

I shake my head.

'Pressure cooker?' I ask. 'Are they actually used for real?'

'Yep,' Letit says without changing his expression.

Then he nods at the computer where the smoke still rises from the car.

'It's sort of a special interest of mine,' he says, rubbing his nose. 'Film and image analysis, that is. But everyone finds explosive charges interesting.'

I don't say that I thought his special interest was women.

'Is it time?' Malin says.

'It is,' I say.

Johannes Ahonen's mother lives on the top floor of a high-rise building in central Jordbro, not far from the commuter train station.

We enter the building and call the lift. It's rundown, and swear words and obscenities are scratched into its green walls. The mirror that covers one wall is frosted, as if it had been polished with steel wool for years.

Visiting next of kin of the deceased is the absolute worst part of being a police officer. But it's also inevitable and important – not just so that we can investigate crimes, but so that these families know what happened to their relatives.

Though in this case, we're not even sure if the body found in the sea belongs to Johannes Ahonen.

Ahonen could be sitting somewhere drinking a beer. Ahonen might be in bed with a woman, in an apartment not far from here. Ahonen might not be dead at all, not swollen up in that cold room at the forensic pathology unit in Solna, his body covered in corpse wax.

Nevertheless, we're here to talk to his mother, because we don't have time to wait for the results of the DNA analysis. If we're unlucky it could take two weeks to get the results.

The lift comes to a halt with a little lurch. The doors slide open exposing a stairwell with speckled walls and a row of identical dark brown doors.

We step out – Letit goes to the right and Malin to the left. I myself stand in front of the lift doors, which close with a sigh behind me.

'Here,' says Letit, who has stopped at the door at the far-right corner.

Malin and I walk towards him while he rings the doorbell.

The angry ring is clearly audible through the door, and a few seconds later I hear steps approaching from inside. A moment later a short woman in her mid-forties opens the door. She has her bleached blonde hair swept up in a knot and she's wearing black jeans and a floral blouse.

'Tuula Ahonen?' Malin asks, flashing her police ID.

The woman nods and her eyes widen.

'Malin Brundin, I called earlier. Can we come in?'

She nods and takes a few steps back without uttering a word. The apartment is small, but neat and cosy. The sofa in the tiny living room is full of colourful throw pillows and on the walls hang framed posters of tropical beaches and sunsets.

Tuula gestures to the sofa.

'Take a seat. There is more room here than in the kitchen. Do you want something, coffee, tea?'

Her accent is so slight that it's almost imperceptible. If it hadn't been for the Finnish-sounding name, I probably wouldn't have noticed it at all.

'No thanks,' I say. 'We won't stay long.'

Malin and Tuula both sit down on a sheepskin-covered pouffe. I sit down next to Letit on the sofa. There's a stab in my knee, and I have to stand up for a second and breathe through the pain.

Tuula looks at me, her eyes shiny and glazed.

'Have you found him?'

'We don't know yet,' I say truthfully. 'So we'd like to ask you a few questions. If that's all right.'

Tuula shrugs and reaches for a pack of unfiltered Marlboro, taps out a cigarette and lights it.

'I've already talked to several of your colleagues,' she says quietly, takes a drag on her cigarette and stares out of the window.

Beyond the light green treetops, several tall buildings stand out silhouetted against a clear blue sky.

'We know,' Malin says. 'And we do apologise for that.'

Letit takes out a notepad and a pen and clears his throat.

'So Johannes disappeared in March?' he says.

Tuula shrugs again slightly, runs her hand through her harshly bleached hair and makes a face that's difficult to decipher. It almost looks like a smile, but it's a sad, slightly ironic smile.

'Yes, well . . .'

She draws out her words and continues:

'I wish I knew. Johannes was often away for days on end, sometimes weeks, without saying where he was. And he lived here sometimes and sometimes with his girlfriend, so it wasn't that easy to keep track of him. But I reported him missing at the end of March, and at that point I hadn't seen him since the beginning of March. So . . .'

She leaves the sentence unfinished and taps ash from her cigarette into a small silver ashtray. Then she silently examines her well-manicured nails.

'And neither you nor Johannes's girlfriend have heard from him since?' Letit asks.

Tuula shakes her head causing the knot on her crown to sway.

'No. Poor Bianca. And the baby is due in a month. Who knows if the child will ever meet his father?'

I remember now reading that Johannes's girlfriend was pregnant at the time of his disappearance.

'Johannes was convicted of illegal possession of weapons, drug possession and theft,' Letit says. 'And he spent six months in a juvenile detention centre when he was seventeen.'

'Well, you know that was three years ago,' Tuula interrupts and stamps the cigarette hard into the small pile of ash on the silver dish. 'I don't understand why you people keep bringing it up over and over. He's on the straight and narrow now.'

Then, without warning, she starts sobbing loudly.

Letit leans forward and lightly puts a hand on her arm.

'Tuula,' he says with authority.

Her arm trembles, as if she's just about to pull away from his touch. But then I see it.

Tuula's eyes meet his, she relaxes and her cheeks flush. For a second, everything is quiet, but you can't mistake the energy that darts between Tuula and Letit. Eyes locked, a touch that lasts far too long.

So it must be true, I think. All those stories about Letit, Inspector Let-it-happen.

Then the moment is over. They let go of each other, and Tuula's gaze falls to the floor.

'I'm just afraid you're not taking his disappearance seriously,' she sobs. 'That you might neglect the investigation because you think he's still a criminal.'

'We take Johannes's disappearance very seriously,' Letit says. 'That's why we're here. But we need to know how he spends his days. If he had any enemies. If he had any reason to . . .'

He seems to be searching for the right words.

'If he was . . . depressed,' he concludes.

Tuula nods earnestly and reaches for a white napkin next to the ashtray. Then she sniffs loudly and knots the napkin into a small ball. When she speaks again, her voice is raspy, as if she has a cold.

'He wasn't depressed. And he took care of himself. Sure, he was unemployed, lots of people are. But he wasn't doing anything illegal. I would have known.'

Malin meets my eyes and raises an eyebrow almost imperceptibly.

We often meet parents who can't or won't believe anything bad about their children.

'And you don't know if anyone threatened him?' I ask.

'*Threatened?* If anyone did it would've been me,' Tuula says with a dry laugh.

Then she smooths out the balled-up napkin and blows her nose again.

Letit stares at me from beneath those heavy eyelids, and I nod.

'On Saturday, the body of a young man was found on an islet in the southern archipelago,' he begins.

'Oh my God, *no*,' Tuula moans and crosses her arms over her chest.

Malin holds up her hand.

'We have no idea who it is yet,' she says slowly, emphasising every word. 'But the man who was found had a tattoo. We have a photo of it. Could we show you that picture?'

Tuula doesn't answer. Instead she rocks back and forth on the pouffe.

Malin looks at me helplessly, and when I nod once more she takes the photograph out of her bag. She hesitates a bit before adding:

'Now this is just a picture of a tattoo. Even if you do recognise it, that doesn't mean it's Johannes's body. Many people might have the same tattoo.'

Then Malin puts the photo on the glass coffee table and pushes it towards Tuula.

Tuula freezes mid-move. Extends a hand and runs it over the photo of the eagle tattoo.

'No,' she whispers. '*No.*'

Pernilla

Tuesday.

It's been almost two days since I threw him out, and I'm sick with worry. I got almost no sleep last night. I lie in my bed tossing and turning. Praying to God and checking my phone constantly to see if there was any message from Samuel.

Before I left home, I fed the blackbird. I thought it stared at me in an accusing sort of way.

I thought about texting Samuel, but decided not to.

Eighteen years old.

He's almost an adult now, even if his behaviour leaves much to be desired. If he doesn't learn his lesson now, when will he?

A large woman in a tracksuit pops up in front of the check-out with a shopping cart filled to the brim with ready meals.

I smile automatically, and she smiles back.

'Such great weather we're having,' she says.

'Yep, summer came again this year,' I say and nod. 'Though it was hard to believe it would. Or at least for me. Well, the spring wasn't exactly warm. But now the heat is here and . . .'

I fall silent when I hear my own meaningless chatter, and feel my cheeks turn red. The big woman opposite me just smiles.

I start to ring up her groceries, but stop mid-movement.

'You know it's two cheddars for ninety kronor this week,' I say. 'It's cheese week. So maybe you want to go get another one?'

'Thank you, I will,' she says, turns around and heads back towards the cheese shelf.

I like my new job.

I've only been working at the supermarket for three weeks, but I can already tell how much better it is compared to the part-time job I had in a school cafeteria at Huddinge high school. Meeting adults, usually nice people, during the day, people who don't throw food on the walls, scream, or angrily point out that the food tastes like crap.

I've even got to take a course and there are long-term opportunities for advancement. All the things I wasn't able to do for so many years are suddenly possible again, now that Samuel is, if not exactly settled, at least older and somewhat calmer.

Almost an adult.

Where did the years go?

Someone puts a hand on my shoulder, and I turn around.

It's Stina Svensson, the store manager. A woman in her sixties with vivid red hair, a sunbed tan and speckled skin.

'It's going well, I see,' she says and nods at me. 'You're good with customers, Pernilla. And that's important.'

'Thank you,' I answer, smile and can feel my cheeks flush.

Someone clears their throat, and I look away from Stina. But instead of the large woman I expected to see, there are two uniformed police officers.

'Pernilla Stenberg?' says the older of the two. A man in his fifties with the beginnings of a potbelly and grey, wavy hair.

'Yes?'

'We're with the police,' he says as if I didn't have eyes. 'We'd like to talk to you about your son, Samuel. Do you have a few minutes?'

My heart starts to pound in my chest.

'Nothing happened, did it?' I whisper and feel Stina gently squeeze my shoulder.

The police exchange a quick glance.

'He hasn't been in any accident,' the younger policeman says quickly and runs his hand over his goatee. 'Can we speak privately?'

We are inside the stockroom, surrounded by brown boxes that are stacked on top of each other into small towers. It's crowded and smells of damp cardboard and rotten fruit.

'Yesterday evening, at nine o'clock, your son was seen with a group of known criminals in an industrial area south of Fruängen,' the older police officer says, meeting my gaze.

'We have reason to suspect that these people are selling drugs and that your son may be involved in that business.'

'*Oh no*,' I whisper and lean forward. Take a deep breath and rest my hands on my knees for support. My head spins, and my ears are ringing.

What the police officers are saying hardly comes as shock. I may be old-fashioned, but I'm not stupid. I knew immediately what Samuel's little bags contained, and I've long thought he has seemed to have too much money on his hands. Of course, I have asked him where it comes from, but he has always claimed he has various extra jobs. And he says he buys his clothes at an outlet.

The police officer pats me awkwardly on the shoulder.

'Listen. Samuel is young. There is still time to intervene, to make a difference in his life. But we have to find him. Do you know where he is?'

I stand up and meet his gaze. Leaning against a stack of boxes, which sway alarmingly under my weight.

Then I shake my head.

'No. I threw him out on Sunday. I found something. Something that . . .'

For a moment, I consider lying, but that's a sin. If Samuel's done something illegal, he has to take his punishment and atone for his crime.

'I don't know,' I continue. 'It looked like white powder, packed in tiny, tiny plastic bags. I suspected it was some kind of drug, so I threw him out. And since then I haven't heard from him.'

Although I fight it, the tears still come. They stream down my cheeks, ruining the careful make-up I put on, to no avail, this morning in front of the bathroom mirror. The police officer takes no notice of my tears, but his voice is soft when he answers.

'What did you do with those bags?'

'Threw them away. With the rubbish.'

There's a pause, and I see the police looking at each other. They probably think I'm nuts. A nutty failure of a mother who couldn't manage the most basic thing in life: raising her own son to become a law-abiding citizen.

'OK,' says the older policeman. 'It's OK. They can't hurt anybody in the rubbish. When was this?'

'On Sunday, at half past seven. I think. You know, I didn't look at the clock right then, but I remember that I heard the rubbish truck not long after and that I was struck by the fact that it came so late. And on a Sunday. Rubbish collection hasn't been working at all this summer. There must be something with the keys to the properties. Apparently, they have . . .'

The older policeman clears his throat quietly – he's probably not interested in hearing about the rubbish collection in Fruängen.

'Do you have any idea where he may have gone? Could he be with a relative?'

'Samuel's father is dead,' I say briefly. 'And his grandfather is in the hospital. We don't have any other relatives.'

I feel a sting somewhere in the vicinity of my heart when I say that about my father.

He has cancer and is in a hospice. I've tried to get Samuel to come and visit him with me, explained that Grandpa Bernt doesn't have much time left, but Samuel doesn't want to.

I don't know if he's scared or just uninterested.

'Could he be with a friend?'

I shake my head.

'No. Well. Maybe. He has a friend. His name is Liam. Liam Lindgren. He lives on the same street as us, at number eight, I think. They've known each other since primary school. I remember when they started in Year One, they were like two peas in a pod. But I don't think he's sleeping there. They have so little room. And they have dogs too. I don't know if it's two or three. But it's more than one, I do know that. No, what am I saying? It's two. The big dog died this spring. There must have been something wrong with its stomach. Yes. Dogs have such sensitive stomachs.'

I fall silent.

Once again I'm reminded that I talk way too much and also about completely insignificant things which could hardly interest the police. They don't care about Liam's dogs.

The older policeman takes out a business card and presses it into my hand.

'Call if you hear from him. We want to help him, but we need to talk to him first.'

I nod and wipe my tears away with the back of my hand. Then I smooth my blouse and open the door to the shop.

The police head towards the exit and I stand at the entrance to the storeroom.

Stina and the fat woman are standing at the checkout staring at me.

Manfred

Malin's laptop pings, and she leans over it. Taps at the keyboard a few times, then leans even closer.

We've been sitting here for almost two hours, going through every bit of information we have on Johannes Ahonen. Malin has followed through on all the usual threads – contacted Ahonen's mobile phone provider, bank, and waded through various social media platforms to gather information and map out his friends and relatives.

'The medical examiner just emailed,' she says with a frown.

And a few seconds later:

'It's him. The dead man *is* Johannes Ahonen.'

'I could have told you that from the beginning,' Letit says. 'Let's see!'

He pulls Malin's laptop closer and reads the email while stroking his straggly beard.

'*Jesus fucking Christ*,' Malin mumbles and for a moment I'm transported back to our temporary office in the abandoned supermarket in Ormberg. To the cold snapping at my cheeks and a mighty spruce forest climbing up the steep slopes of Orm Mountain.

Jesus fucking Christ.

That was something Andreas always said. Maybe not so strange that Malin picked it up, now that they live together.

'Poor Tuula Ahonen,' Malin continues. 'Poor, poor woman.'

The image of Johannes's mother rocking back and forth, weeping, on the sheepskin pouffe in an apartment in Jordbro appears on my retina.

Yes, of course I'd hoped it was someone else.

You always do.

But Someone Else also has parents and friends, that's just the way it is.

We are sitting in the small conference room facing the park. The sun is low, and the park lies in the shade. Dog owners walk by, and I catch a glimpse of a group having a picnic in the grass on a large red blanket.

Malin and I exchange a glance without a word. But Letit won't let himself be rushed, he just continues to read the email from the medical examiner. Every now and then he hums and nods as if agreeing with something.

'Identified with the help of dental records,' he references. 'The DNA analysis is expected to be completed later this week, but it will obviously say the same thing. And they're done with the autopsy. The report arrives tomorrow, but the medical examiner says she still hasn't been able to establish a cause of death.'

Malin sighs deeply.

'But he was completely battered,' she says and crosses her wiry arms over her swelling belly.

Letit hums again.

'That's right. Almost every bone in his body had fractures, but they could have happened post-mortem. She writes here . . . she didn't find any bleeding in the surrounding tissues, so he must have been dead when all of his bones were crushed by something. She certainly likes to talk in riddles, our dear medical examiner.'

'So, what does she think happened?' Malin asks.

Letit snorts a laugh, as if Malin just said something really funny.

'You think she wrote that in this email, do you? No, my dear. Nowadays, you've got to drag information out of the fine ladies and gentlemen of forensic medicine. They're so damn scared to stick their necks out that I wonder if it wouldn't be better if we did the autopsies ourselves right here on this desk.'

Malin's eyes meet mine again, and she discreetly raises her brow.

'I'll read it out word by word for you now,' Letit says. 'It says here, the body was subjected to high-energy impact post-mortem. High-energy impact? What the hell does that mean? Can't people talk like human beings anymore?'

'High-energy impact,' says Malin. 'A car accident perhaps, or a boating accident, or maybe a fall from a great height.'

As soon as she says the sentence, I can see her grimace. Letit, who also picked up on her faux pas, stares down at the table and clears his throat.

'I'm sorry,' Malin says.

I don't answer, but I feel sorry for them both. They are so careful, so afraid to say anything that would bring Nadja to mind.

As if that makes any fucking difference.

As if I'm not already thinking about her all the time.

'So what now?' Malin asks.

'We have to wait for the final autopsy report, the DNA analysis and the forensic chemical examination,' Letit says with a sigh. 'The technicians aren't finished with their report either. God, how they dawdle these days. But wait a minute! They found skin fragments under Ahonen's nails. He may have scratched a possible killer.'

'Bingo,' Malin whispers and smiles broadly, as if the case were already solved. And sure, sometimes DNA technology works miracles. Sometimes you actually find a match in our register and you go pick up your suspect as easily as if you were grabbing a pizza.

'But they don't know if they'll be able to extract any usable DNA,' Letit clarifies. 'The body was in the water for a long time. So don't start celebrating yet, young lady.'

I turn toward Letit.

'You mentioned earlier that Johannes Ahonen had some connection to Igor Ivanov. Is that something we should investigate further?'

Letit nods.

'Of course. But the connection is pretty weak. When Ahonen was arrested just over three years ago, he was in possession of a large amount of cocaine. Nearly 200 grams. So clearly intended for resale. The guys at the investigative unit were pretty sure he bought the coke from a Malte Lindén, even though they had no concrete intelligence to back that up. And Malte Lindén works for Igor Ivanov. But this Igor Ivanov is in charge of most of the drug trade in southern Stockholm, so there's not one fucking buyer or dealer out there who doesn't have some connection to him. Therefore, we *won't* pass this on to the prosecutor, because then he'll pull our trousers down before we can say "house search". And then we'll end up with our arses roasted and not get anywhere.'

Letit takes off his glasses, sighs again and polishes them with his shirt.

'And Igor Ivanov and Malte Lindén?' Malin asks. 'Where are they? Can we at least talk to them?'

Letit smiles crookedly, puts his glasses back on and hums.

'Of course,' he says curtly. 'We can talk to them. But they won't *talk*, you should be clear on that.'

Then he stands up and straightens his ill-fitting shirt. Lopes off down the hallway in the direction of the common room.

'How the *hell* did he have so much success with the ladies?' Malin sighs. 'Honestly, he's a real fucking arsehole.'

'You're probably not in his target group,' I say with a glance at her swollen belly.

Malin smiles acerbically.

Then silence.

'How are things going with Andreas?' I ask.

'Good,' Malin says. 'Great, actually. Though of course he's a real country bumpkin.'

'Like you?'

Malin laughs.

'Exactly. I thought I was going to get out of there. Far away from Ormberg. That was the plan, anyway.'

'Sometimes life has other plans for us,' I note.

Malin looks at me for a long time but doesn't say anything.

'And what about your mother?' I ask, as gently as I can.

Malin's face closes and her eyes drop towards her belly.

'We're not in contact right now,' she mumbles.

'Maybe you should get in touch with her. You never know how long you will have with the people you love.'

Malin puts a hand on her belly, rubs it a bit, but says nothing.

When I get home, Afsaneh is sitting in the middle of the living-room floor with Nadja's Lego box between her legs, aimlessly picking through the colourful bits of plastic. She's in her underwear and one of my old shirts. Her hair hangs in lank curls in front of her face, and she doesn't react when I enter the room and turn on the light.

I put my briefcase on the floor and walk over to her. I squat down and put my hands on her shoulders.

'Afsaneh.'

She doesn't answer.

'Come,' I say. 'Let's go make some tea.'

'You didn't come to the hospital today,' she says pressing a yellow and a blue Lego together.

I sink to the floor next to her and put my arm around her shoulders. Take a deep breath.

'I had to go to a meeting. They needed me.'

Afsaneh pulls the pieces apart again.

'*Nadja* needed you.'

I don't agree with her.

An unconscious child doesn't need to have both parents by her bedside around the clock, that's just the way it is. Even though I wish our presence made some difference, that it helped her heal, still I don't truly believe that's the case.

But of course I can't say that to Afsaneh.

We grieve in different ways.

Afsaneh's grief is all-consuming and physical, like a force of nature, and she seems insatiable in her need to be physically close to Nadja. She talks about Nadja non-stop as well. And apparently, she has found some kind of online forum, for parents of sick children.

Maybe she hopes their pain will alleviate hers.

Personally, I feel more shut down. Cold, that is. As if I'm dead, though I'm fairly sure I'm not.

I do dream about Nadja's accident.

There are two types of dreams.

In the first, I run and run across the kitchen floor trying to reach her before she falls. But the floor somehow turns into a vast field. And the further I run, the more distant the window becomes, until it's just a tiny dot on the horizon.

In the second dream, I'm agile and fast, like I'm not past fifty, don't weigh 260 pounds and don't have terrible knees.

I cover the short distance between the living room and kitchen window in one leap, like a leopard. Grab Nadja's wrist and pull her in through the open window.

It's the second dream, of course, that's the truly cruel one, the one that hurts the most to wake up from.

All I needed was one more second, one more step.

One *fucking* step. You think God could have given me that.

But my child fell to the tarmac.

I stand up with difficulty. My knee aches, but I ignore the pain. Then I gently pull Afsaneh to her feet.

'I'm so sorry I didn't make it in time that day,' I say, taking her face in my hands and kissing her on both cheeks.

They're wet and taste of salt.

She nods and wraps her arms around me. Hugging me hard.

I don't know how long we stand like that, but in the end she says:

'Everything will be all right. It *has* to be all right.'

Then I follow her to bed. Give her a sleeping pill, fetch a glass of water and tuck her in as if she were a child.

I give her a kiss on the forehead too, like I always do when she's sad. She smiles with her eyes closed, already on her way to a merciful drugged sleep.

I walk over to the chair next to the window. Unbutton my shirt and drape it over the back of the chair. Take off my trousers and put them on the seat.

My clothes look wrinkled and sort of shapeless, just like my life these days.

I open the wardrobe and let my eyes slide over the clothes.

The suits from my favourite tailor, Norton & Sons, on Savile Row in London, hang in a neat row, as if waiting for me to pull myself together and take them out into the sunlight again.

The tailor has sewn countless suits, shirts and even sportswear, for emperors, kings and presidents. Lord Carnarvon himself was in Norton & Sons when he opened Tutankhamun's tomb in the Valley of the Kings in 1922. Whether or not he was wearing the famous tailor's work when he died the following year in Cairo, the result of an infected mosquito bite, isn't included in the story. But I can see him in front of me, lying on his deathbed, his face dripping with sweat, but still impeccably dressed in Harris Tweed with his moustache as perfectly groomed as usual.

I know I'm a geek, but I love all this – the history, the myths, the craftsmanship. It's about quality, about professionalism passed down from father to son for generations. About creating garments that can be worn for a lifetime. The very opposite of the consumer hysteria and disposable fashion of our time.

I run my hand over the sleeve of a jacket.

The wool fibres catch slightly beneath my fingertips.

This particular fabric comes from a textile factory in the Outer Hebrides. The same family has run the company for four generations and the patterns have been the same since the business started – adapting the fabrics to current fashions would be distasteful.

Just knowing that makes it worth it to travel all the way to London to order a suit.

I close the wardrobe.

It shuts with a heavy sigh. The doors close on my old life like the lid of a coffin. The only things that remain are my wrinkled trousers and equally crumpled shirt hanging on the back of the chair, and the feeling that my life is slipping through my hands.

Samuel

The tree branches form a winding pattern above me – as if hundreds of wood and leaf fingers were braided together to protect me from above.

It almost felt like lying in a tree fort. A magical tree house, not so different from the one Liam and I built in the park outside Långbro Hospital when we were little.

I sit up.

My back aches, and my body is stiff from the cold. The back of my hoodie and jeans are wet from the dew on the grass.

The sun is high and there's no wind. In front of me are rocky cliffs and beyond that the sea – blue and shining like a mirror. In the distance I can just make out a sailing boat that appears completely motionless, and some gulls sit on a rock out in the water.

Larus canus.

That means common gull. Long ago you weren't allowed to kill them because people believed that drowned fishermen were reborn as gulls.

There are other birds here as well. Yesterday I saw five female eiders swimming with at least ten ducklings in tow.

And goosander, herring gull and mute swan. Anyway, I think it was a mute swan, because its wings whistled when it flew by and the whooper swans fly silently.

It was Grandpa who taught me all that. That, and a lot of other stuff about nature. And then I basically became obsessed with birds. I learned everything there was to know about them and dreamed of having my own bird, but my mother said they were dirty and smelled bad.

And now, when I actually have a bird, the only thing I want is to let it go again.

Birds shouldn't be in cages.

I shiver.

It's cold, and my stomach is screaming for something to eat and drink. Something other than the piece of chocolate I chewed on before I fell asleep last night.

After Alexandra refused to let me in I went to Liam, but his mother was home. And she was really fucking pissed off when she opened the door. Even their little dogs seemed angry. She said that Liam wasn't there, and I should come back during the daytime, like a normal person.

I slept in Liam's basement storage. I didn't ask his mother's permission, why would I? I already had the key, and I wasn't hurting anyone.

When I woke up I texted Liam, explained the situation and asked if I could crash with him for a few days.

He wrote back and said it wouldn't work. The police had just visited him, and his mother was furious with him. She was threatening to turn off the Wi-Fi and throw him out. The cops must have come by while I was asleep.

I pointed out that it wouldn't matter if she shut off the Wi-Fi if she threw him out, but then he answered that I had nobody to blame but myself since I had chosen to work for that psychopath Igor even though I'd promised not to.

In other words, it was a very messed-up situation; I was in Liam's storage unit texting him while he was just a few floors up and had no idea where I was.

But I figured out something else from what Liam wrote.

The cops must have identified me at the industrial area: why else would they have come around asking about me? And that means the police know I work for Igor.

A cold shiver went down my spine when I realised that. That meant the cops probably had a file on me, with my picture and everything.

Just like on *CSI*.

After that I left town. Picked up Igor's bike, which I'd parked in the garage beneath Liam's house and drove as far as I could get, in a total panic, until the road ended and the sea began.

I'm trying to analyse my situation, look at it clearly, like it's a maths problem, and not my life gone to hell.

The police are searching for me.

Igor probably wants to kill me.

My mother has thrown me out.

Alexandra is generally acting like she's on the rag and thinks I'm an arsehole just for flirting a little with Jeanette. And Liam doesn't dare touch me with a ten-foot pole just because the cops came around asking a few questions.

Besides, I have no money.

I pick a cigarette butt up off the ground, brush away a few damp blades of grass and bring it to my mouth. Then I take out my lighter, flick the small metal wheel and take two deep drags before stamping the fag out again in the dewy grass.

I'm so fucked.

The only thing I can do now is try to lie low, but I have nowhere to go and I can't sleep outdoors forever and live on sun and ocean air, like a fucking dandelion.

I fiddle with the bracelet of glass beads. Turn the beads so that the letters are facing out.

MUMMY.

An image of my mother appears before me. Her greying brown hair and her anxious brown eyes. The gold cross that she always wears. The never-ending nagging about taking charge of my life, how everything will be fine if I just let Jesus into my heart.

I'm sorry but where was Jesus yesterday?

I'm just wondering.

I guess I should call her, but I don't dare. That would surely be the first thing the cops checked – if I've been in contact with her? Isn't that what all retarded idiots do: run straight home to their mothers to cry after a robbery or assault or failed drug deal?

I stand up. Brush the dirt and grass off my trousers, go over to a bush, pull down my fly and take a piss.

Even my cock is freezing. It's small and wrinkled and seems to want to crawl into itself, like an anxious little animal.

Maybe I can find some empty summer house.

Empty, at this time of year? Hard to imagine.

I zip back up and glance at Igor's bike which is parked further inside the bushes. The chrome and the black lacquer are shining in the sunlight that finds its way through the branches. The flames that wind around the petrol tank glow weakly.

I button my trousers with one hand while scrolling on my phone with the other. Check the map on Snapchat.

Liam is home. Alexandra looks to be with Jeanette. I feel a pang in my stomach when I imagine them sitting there talking shit about me. Alexandra bawling her eyes out and Jeanette comforting her.

There, there. Alexandra. Sweetie. I never would have slept with him. Just so you know. He's a loser.

I check Jeanette's Insta.

She's posted a picture of herself in a bikini standing in front of her hall mirror. She curves her back and pushes her bust forward. Pouts with her lips and runs one hand through her long hair.

Normally I would have been rock hard, but not today.

Three hundred and ninety idiots have liked the picture.

Jeanette has almost 2,000 followers on Instagram and posts at least five photos every day. Usually in a low-cut sweater, or with her puppy in her lap. Or ideally with the fucking dog squeezed between her tits, like a hamburger between two slices of bread.

That's why she's so popular.

I read my messages. One of Liam's friends emailed me a link to Twitch, where a guy has promised to live stream his own suicide. But when I click on the link I find nothing. Just when I'm about to try again, I hear a car coming down the road.

I step aside, into the bushes, so that I won't be visible, and wait for the car to pass. But it actually parks maybe twenty yards away.

One car door slams shut and then another.

I hear voices in the distance. Voices that sound strangely familiar.

'Where?' says one.

'Buggered if I know,' the other answers. 'But it must be around here somewhere.'

Through the dense foliage I see two men approaching. One is short, a little fat, and his jeans hang halfway down his hips. He looks vaguely familiar, like a distant relative you meet every Christmas, but only then.

The other is tall and hunched over. Thin light brown hair falls in wisps around his gaunt face and his T-shirt hangs like a sack over his skinny chest.

My heart stops, and I fall dead to the ground.

In any case, that's what it feels like, because the other guy is Malte, Igor's bitch.

'Check again!' Malte says, stopping to light a fag.

'OK,' says the other guy and takes something out of his jacket pocket.

Why isn't Malte in jail? And more importantly: how the hell did they find me?

The thoughts tumble around in my head, but a second later I have it.

The phone.

It must be the stupid fucking phone. I got it from Igor, and there's a lot of shit in it that I didn't download myself.

Who knows what that psychopath Igor installed on it? It would be just like him to spy on his own.

With trembling fingers I bring up the phone to turn it off, but it slides out of my hands and onto the ground.

I curse silently, squat down groping for it among the dirt and dry leaves. It burns where branches scratch against my cheeks, tearing the skin. The smell of damp soil and budding greenery tickles my nostrils.

Soon I feel the sun-warmed metal beneath my fingertips. Grab the phone and press the button on the side to turn it off.

It feels like an eternity before the display goes black.

I sit completely motionless. Observing Malte and the other guy as they stand in the grass by the side of the road and talk softly.

I hardly dare to breathe, I'm so fucking scared. Because if they find me, they'll beat the shit out of me.

Or worse.

I think of the guys Liam told me about. The ones who deceived Igor and were tied up with cable ties and drowned like kittens.

'. . . not . . . maybe later . . . the fucking signal . . . hungry . . .'

The words sail through the balmy morning air like lazy swallows, coming to me in fragments, like shards of something broken, waiting to be meaningfully reunited.

My legs ache, and I stand up carefully. But my sweater gets caught on a branch, and it breaks with a sharp pop.

'What was that?' Malte says.

'It sounded like . . .'

Malte looks around.

'Uh,' says the fat guy. 'Let's go. Gotta eat.'

Malte doesn't answer. He simply stretches and starts walking towards me with determined steps.

I stand completely still and do my best to control my breathing, but I'm still panting like I just ran a 100-metre sprint.

Malte is on the other side of the bushes now, a few yards from me at most.

He has his face turned towards my hiding place and for a second I'm sure he's seen me. But then he puts his hands to his crotch and opens his fly. Seconds later an arc of urine hits the ground.

My heart starts to beat more easily again, finds its rhythm. My panting wanes, and my shoulders relax.

Malte pulls up his zip and turns his back on me. The smell of his piss makes my stomach turn.

But my heart is easy.

The heart knows.

I made it this time.

I sit in the bushes for probably an hour after Malte and his fat friend have taken off. In the end, I decide that it's safer to go than to stay.

I take the bike, follow the coast south a few miles with the wind in my face. Swedish summer unfolds around me. The green is so intense that it looks almost unnatural, as if I was in a computer game and not out in the countryside. There is a smell of grass, manure and sea.

I don't know what I'm on my way to, just what I'm running away from.

Fear propels me on down a dusty country road, past pastures and red cottages with Stockholmers on holiday and farms with real farmers who drive real tractors and have real cows.

The road is getting narrower and I pass a sign. STUVSKÄR 2, it says, and a few minutes later I roll into a sleepy little harbour.

It's postcard beautiful.

The sea lies glimmering between smooth granite rocks. Red wooden buildings are clustered around a steamboat jetty. One house is a pub and another a small supermarket.

The road itself ends in front of those red houses. There's a bus stop in the lay-by, and to the left of it is a large car park, almost completely filled with cars. Next to the jetty is a petrol station, which according to the sign also sells boat accessories. A sign points the way to the marina, which is apparently some distance away.

Opposite the red houses there's an old yellow stone house. An ancient sign hangs above the door.

HARBOUR MASTER'S OFFICE, it reads.

Below the text, someone has hung a handwritten poster: *Local Museum & Library*.

A moment later I'm sitting in the so-called library. It's no bigger than my mother's apartment and apparently run by a local non-profit. At least that's what it said at the entrance.

The lady sitting at the counter gave me a strange look when I came in, as if I were obviously homeless, but she didn't say anything. She just nodded to me and pushed the glasses up a little further on her nose.

The sandwich I stole from the supermarket burbles around in my stomach, and I'm finally warm. Warm, fed, and sitting comfortably in an armchair in front of an old computer with a thick screen. The kind you couldn't even give away on FreeBay.

Along the walls the bookshelves are full of books about the archipelago and old nautical charts.

There's nothing to steal here – I checked as soon as I came in, of course.

I google Igor, but don't find anything, which is hardly strange since a) I don't know his last name and b) there's no reason for the police to release the names of people they've arrested. But I do find a small paragraph on the Söderort newspaper's website. It says that the police 'discharged their weapons at a group of suspects in connection with an arrest made on Monday evening in an industrial area outside Fruängen'.

It doesn't say much more than that, besides that fact that an internal investigation has begun, which is apparently 'routine'.

I search for 'Stuvskär' and 'rooms for rent'.

The computer thinks for a long time before showing me a blank screen.

I try 'Stuvskär' and 'help wanted', mostly out of curiosity, because I'm not really interested in working at all. Not in Stuvskär or anywhere else.

The computer buzzes, as if my request borders on the impossible. As if I asked how big the universe is or what the point of this shitty life really is.

But then I actually get a hit.

I click on the link and read the ad. Once and then another time, while I try to come up with a plan.

A family near Stuvskär is looking for a home help for their severely disabled teenage son. It is not a traditional home help job, because the parents do most of the main care themselves – more of a social role. The family is looking for someone who can keep their son company. Someone who can read aloud, play music and help around the house.

I close my eyes and think.

Of course, I have no desire to be a nanny to some retard in Stuvskär, but the thought of a warm bed and running water is so tempting. Maybe I could hide for a while, have a roof over my head, make some money until I can sort out all the shit I fell into?

Pernilla

'm sitting on the metro on my way to Fridhemsplan and the Stockholm nursing home.

One of the nurses called to tell me that my father had taken a turn for the worse and wanted to see me. Of course I was worried, but not too upset – it's not unusual for them to call when my father has a bad day.

Outside the train window light green treetops and overblown lilacs pass by. If the circumstances were different, I'm sure I would have enjoyed greenery and warm weather finally having arrived, but now it is what it is. My father is dying, and I haven't heard a peep from Samuel.

Three days.

He's been gone for three days without any contact, and it takes almost superhuman self-discipline for me not to contact him. We've never gone this long without being in touch before.

I close my eyes and feel the warmth of sun shining through the window onto my face and think about that day in May, eighteen years ago, when Samuel was born.

Father was in the hospital the whole time, pacing anxiously back and forth down the corridor outside my room like a nervous, expectant dad. In fact, one of the midwives actually thought he was my husband. Father laughed heartily over that later, but of course I thought it was extremely embarrassing.

I don't remember much of the birth itself, except that the pain was inhuman. But as soon as they put that tiny, slippery little body on my chest, pain was replaced by joy, and I knew I wanted to name my son Samuel.

Maybe it was because we'd just read that passage from the first Book of Samuel in my Bible class. That story about how God called to Samuel several times without him understanding. I guess it struck a chord with me, because Samuel had been chosen to hear God's voice, and also because I thought the message itself was so important in our time, when God's voice is so easily drowned by the flood of information from television, radio and advertising.

It pleased my father that I wanted to name the child Samuel, but his brow also furrowed. Maybe he thought it was a concession to Isaac; to Judaism, which troubled my father so much.

The train stops and I get off and change to the green line, the one that will take me to Fridhemsplan and to my father.

Samuel was a demanding child from the start. He screamed incessantly and my father and I took turns caring for him at night so I could get a few hours of sleep.

I didn't think much about it at the time. I just thought that was what it was like to have a baby. After all, I was only eighteen years old and knew nothing about infants. But in retrospect, I wonder if Samuel's difficulties had started already. If he inherited them from me. Impatience, an inability to adapt, being drawn to problems like a moth to a flame.

Just like my mother.

But I loved him unconditionally, and he loved me. Even though we weren't a normal family, a *real* family, still we had it good – Samuel, my father and me.

The real problems started in preschool. Samuel bit his classmates. Samuel refused to lie still during nap time. Samuel threw the food on the floor. And Samuel kicked the teacher on her leg.

Small children, small problems.

Over time, it got worse: cutting class, shoplifting, countless conversations with anxious teachers and upset parents.

Could I not teach my son some manners?

Surely it must be my fault; surely a normal parent would be able to control her difficult son? How hard could it be to raise a child?

At the same time, he was so sweet, so charming and so social. Had a big heart and lots of friends.

But the problems continued. And over the years, I became increasingly convinced that it was in fact some kind of original sin. That my mother's worst traits had been passed on to me, and through me to Samuel.

I remember my father's words.

The face of an angel and heart of a snake.

I close my eyes and listen to the train rattle as it makes its way through the tunnels beneath Stockholm. The air is cooler here, and I'm a bit chilly in just my thin summer blouse.

God has a plan for all of us, a purpose.

It's just a matter of understanding what it is, listening carefully when He calls to us, just like when He called to Samuel in the temple at Shiloh.

Maybe my mission is to help Samuel?

*

My father looks miserable.

He looks, if possible, even thinner than the last time I was here, and his skin and the whites of his eyes are yellow. His hair, which was always so thick, is long gone and a large red-black bruise spreads out across the back of the hand where the IV is attached.

I embrace him gently and pull out the visitor's chair so I can sit next to him.

My father is not afraid to die, and there is great comfort in that.

But I am afraid.

I don't know how I'll go on without him. He's the only family I have, apart from the church. He is the one I go to when I need advice, or if I'm sad, or need to borrow some money.

All these trials and tribulations.

As soon as the thought passes through my mind, I'm overcome by shame. How can I – healthy and strong – sit here feeling sorry for myself?

'Hello, my girl,' he says.

'Hi,' I say and gently take his hand. 'How are you feeling?'

'Not as bad as I look,' my father murmurs. 'Do you think you can raise the back of the bed a little?'

I stand up and pump the pedal under the bed to raise it.

Father grimaces in pain. He runs his tongue over his dry, chapped lips and small drops of sweat break out at his sunken temples.

'Thank you,' he says afterwards. 'How are you two?'

'OK,' I answer vaguely.

'I was wondering if you could go by the house this week and pick up my mail,' my father says, and ends the sentence by clearing his throat of phlegm.

'Of course.'

I hesitate for a moment, fiddling a little with the blanket over my father's legs, then decide to be honest and tell him about Samuel.

'I threw him out,' I say. 'Again. Yes, well. This wasn't the first time. That I've thrown him out. As you know.'

Father nods.

'He has to learn, Pernilla,' he whispers.

'That was three days ago. I haven't heard from him. I don't know, it just feels so hard. I don't know how to cope with . . .'

I leave the sentence unfinished and swallow a sob.

'You have to let him go in order for him to come back.'

Silence falls again, and I become aware of my father's laboured breathing.

'Can you let go of your child?' I ask. '*May* you let go your child? Who am I if I do that? *What* am I?'

'You have to. Promise me you'll not try to contact him.'

'But . . . then I'm no better than Mother.'

Father wheezes and the wheezing turns into a deep, rattling coughing fit. It sounds like his chest is full of pebbles.

The coughing fit subsides. Father sighs and closes his eyes.

'Pray for him instead,' he mumbles. 'That's the only thing you can do now.'

Manfred

Bianca Diaz lives in a neat apartment not so different from Tuula Ahonen's, except smaller, more sparsely furnished and located on the ground floor of a five-storey apartment building in central Jordbro.

She asks me and Letit to sit down at the kitchen table which only has two chairs, and then goes into the living room.

Through the doorway to the hall, I see a stroller wrapped in plastic parked next to the wall.

Letit follows my gaze, but the eyes behind his wire rims reveal no emotion.

'Need help?' I shout to Bianca.

Bianca enters, carrying a small stool.

'No,' she smiles, 'I'm pregnant. Not handicapped.'

Letit stands up.

'Sit here, love,' he says and takes the stool.

Bianca smiles, shrugs and obediently takes the chair.

I also sit down and try to ignore the pain in my knee.

Bianca Diaz is twenty years old, same as Johannes, but she looks much younger. Her hair is long and dyed a honey-brown shade that's lightest at the ends. Her body is thin, but her stomach is huge, as if she might give birth at any second, though I know she has a month left.

Something about her reminds me of Afsaneh when she was expecting Nadja, which causes a stab of pain in the region of my heart.

'I'm so sorry about Johannes,' I begin.

Bianca nods.

'Yeah. It sucks.'

Her voice sounds strangely matter of fact. She shows no emotion at all. It almost sounds as if she's remarking on a broken washing machine, or saying she's run out of milk.

'How are you doing?' I ask.

Bianca's dark eyes meet mine.

'I'm getting by,' she says. 'I've always had to do that. Of course. It's terrible he's dead. Really terrible. But he wasn't someone you could depend on. He was all over the place from the start. I've been working double shifts *and* studying to be a biomedical analyst the whole time we've been together. And what did Johannes do? Did he help? Did he contribute any money? No. I already knew when I got pregnant that I'd have to raise this child by myself. Besides, all he wanted to do was head for Brazil, because he had some friend who lived there.'

She looks down and puts her hand on her large belly. Runs her hand over the taut, knotty fabric of her sweater.

'Weren't you planning to raise the child together?' Letit asks.

Bianca shakes her head.

'Johannes absolutely did not want a kid,' she says and her eyes wander out of the window, where a large bush with pink flowers is visible. She purses her lips into a thin line and for the first time I sense something resembling pain in her face.

'So how did he react when you told him you were pregnant?' Letit asks.

'He got angry,' Bianca says calmly, still staring at the window. 'Very angry.'

A short pause.

Letit's light eyes meet mine.

'It's probably just as well that it turned out like this,' Bianca murmurs. 'I mean, not that he died, but that I have to take care of the child on my own. He would have just made a mess of it. He always did.'

'Do you know if Johannes was under any kind of threat?' Letit asks and makes a note on his pad.

Bianca frowns.

'Threat? No, I don't think he had any enemies. But he did borrow a huge amount of money from somebody. And he was stressed about it, because he couldn't pay it back.'

'Do you know who he borrowed money from?' I ask. 'Or the amount?'

'Not a clue. I was very careful not to get involved in his so-called business.'

I lean towards Bianca and meet her gaze. She doesn't waver an inch. Her eyes are shiny and her face serious, but also completely unsentimental.

'His mother says he's been on the straight and narrow lately,' I say softly. 'That he wasn't involved in drugs or anything criminal. That—'

Bianca interrupts me.

'Sorry,' she says and raises her hand. 'But Tuula is so fucking naive. She thinks he's practically a saint. But sure, I haven't seen him doing any drugs or anything like that. I definitely haven't. Then I would have dumped him right away. But *on the straight and narrow?*'

She rolls her eyes and makes air quotes when she says the last phrase.

'*No.* Johannes was many things, but on the straight and narrow was not fucking one of them.'

When we reach the street, Letit takes a deep breath, runs his hand over his beard and his expression turns melancholy.

'I feel for humanity,' he says. 'Love brings nothing but misery. Still, it can't be avoided.'

He adjusts his too short pants a little and ambles away towards the car with his back hunched.

Afsaneh hugs me tightly when I get to the hospital.

Since I'm actually working full-time now, I had decided to go there over lunch. It's mostly for Afsaneh's sake. I doubt Nadja would have much to say on the matter. After questioning Ahonen's girlfriend, Letit and I returned to the city. I dropped him off at the police station and then headed on to the hospital. On my way, I took the opportunity to call my older kids. Alba didn't answer, but I talked for a bit with Alexander and then with Stella. Told them how their little sister was doing and asked the usual questions.

They're worried, of course. Worried and sad, even though they're so much older than their half-sister, they've loved her from the first minute.

'Good,' Afsaneh murmurs in my ear. 'Really good that you're here.'

She takes a step back and smiles. Her back is straight, her eyes sparkle and her skin has a new glow.

'Did something happen?' I ask.

Afsaneh nods eagerly and takes my hands.

'They're going to Nadja wake up. The doctor said so. They will begin weaning her off the sedatives tomorrow.'

'They are?'

My voice is a whisper.

Afsaneh pulls me closer and hugs me again.

'We're going to get her back, Manfred. We'll get our Nadja back.'

Afsaneh's thin body trembles in my arms, and I don't dare say what I think. What the doctors have been trying to explain to us all along.

What happens when you open the box holding Schrödinger's cat?

Well, pretty soon it'll be clear to everyone if the cat is very dead or very alive. Clear that that strange territory – when the fucking cat is somehow both dead and alive – is just an academic construct.

And the same is true of our child.

Only after the powerful medication has been discontinued, only once the tubes and machines have been disconnected, will we know if we'll get our Nadja back or if she's gone forever.

Of course, it would be best if she woke up.

But even this is better than losing her completely, because I would rather have a child connected to tubes in the intensive care unit than no child at all. The equation is very simple and at the same time unbelievably cruel.

But it can be counted on, even death can be counted on.

We sit for a while beside Nadja's bed.

This time we sit on the same side of the bed, with our chairs so close together that I can feel the warmth of Afsaneh's body.

Nadja looks like she's asleep, despite all the tubes and machines. Her face is peaceful and her mouth half-open. On the cast on her arm, someone's drawn a tiny bird and a heart in red felt-tip pen.

I take a deep breath.

I have always had a hard time with hospitals.

Of course, it started when Aron got sick. He spent almost two months at the paediatric oncology ward before he died.

I was there every day.

For the first few weeks, Aron responded well to the treatment. He got stronger, and we slipped away to explore the ward, sometimes even going outside. Once we even went down into the culverts. We ran around down there – me first and Aron behind me, with his IV stand in hand.

But then he got too weak. He mostly lay in bed and slept. I couldn't even talk to him.

In the end, he just fell asleep.

That's how it happened, not very dramatic or remarkable. He'd been unconscious for several days and eventually his heart just gave up.

One second alive, the next dead.

Since then I've had a tough time with hospitals.

Maybe it's the smell, but it's odd, I have no problem at all with visiting the medical examiner or attending autopsies, and quite frankly, *that* stinks. But the smell of the hospital, that strange combination of detergent, urine and overcooked potatoes, that I can't stand.

It's like something inside me jams up, and I'm twelve again.
My phone vibrates in my jacket, and I take it out.
It's Malin.
'Sweetheart, I have to take this.'
'Sure,' Afsaneh responds quickly, much to my surprise.
She doesn't even sound annoyed.
I head out into the hallway and answer while groping for
my cigarettes in my pocket.
'Hey,' Malin says. 'Is everything OK?'
'Absolutely. I'm just at the hospital for a bit.'
'Well, something's happened. Another body's been found.
Wrapped in a sheet and wound with a chain. Can you meet
me at two?'

Samuel

The woman who meets me at the harbour reminds me of my mother. Only a little slimmer, and her hair is darker and hangs far down her back. Her skin is paler as well, and looks oddly translucent in the bright sunlight. There's a network of fine wrinkles around her eyes and she's wearing a T-shirt and jeans. Her smile is warm when she takes me by the hand.

'I'm Rachel,' she says, tilting her head a little to the side so that her long hair falls across one of her shoulders.

'I'm Samuel,' I say and think that she'd be good-looking if she weren't so old.

I had prepared what I was going to say, but as soon as I take her hand I forget everything, and my mouth dries up, like it's filled with sand.

'It's great that you could meet today,' she says. 'Shall we walk while we talk?'

We walk down the gravel road next to the harbour. There is a man on the dock, sitting smoking on a flatbed moped. I suppose he's waiting for the Waxholm company boat to Stuvskär.

A little girl is sitting on the flatbed, eating a half-melted ice cream. It drips down onto her shirt and then onto the ground.

The sun is warm, and the sky is high and blue, but as soon as we walk into the shade beneath the big trees next to the supermarket, the air turns cool and humid, like a cold breath.

'How old are you, Samuel?' Rachel asks, without sounding suspicious. In fact, she sounds curious, but in a good way. Not like my mother, who always assumes I'm hiding something terrible. As if I were building a bomb in secret, or watching some kind of paedo porn, as soon as her back was turned.

I tell her that I'm eighteen, recently 'took a break' from high school and that I'm looking for a job. Then we talk for a little while about what kind of work I've done in the past. And, OK, I'm exaggerating a bit at this point, saying I worked part-time at Media Markt, which is almost true, and that I've coached a boys' soccer team, which definitely has no connection to the truth.

After a while we arrive at a small headland.

Rachel points to one of the smooth rocks that extend out like a giant tongue into the sea.

'Come on!' she says, stepping over the ditch and heading through the tall grass without waiting for my answer.

I follow her and we sit down a few yards from the water.

The rock is warm from the sun and rough beneath my jeans. Every now and then the wind catches small, salty drops of water and throws them up at our feet. At one point a larger wave breaks, and we have to back up a couple of yards to avoid getting wet.

Empty beer cans are wedged into a crevice and an old ciga-rette butt rolls by, pushed by the light summer breeze. Seaweed floats in the foam next to the rock.

'Isn't it great?' Rachel says, and I nod and look out over the sea.

Yeah, sure, it's great, but it would be a hell of a lot greater if I had something to eat. I'm completely broke. I've shoplifted sandwiches from the supermarket twice. But there are limits to how many times I can get away with that.

Besides, they only have weird sandwiches with avocado, hummus and tofu.

'It's one of the biggest advantages of living out here,' Rachel continues. 'Being close to nature. The sea.'

She closes her eyes and turns her face towards the sun.

'So, why are you interested in the job?' she asks. 'I mean, there's not much going on out here. It might get pretty boring for a young guy like you.'

The question surprises me a little.

'I like it calm,' I answer hesitantly.

'Good,' Rachel says. 'That's good.'

Then she falls silent, and I'm struck by a thought: she might expect me to ask her something too; to act like I'm actually kind of interested in the so-called job.

'So what's wrong with your son?' I ask, picking up a small, flat stone and flicking it away.

It skips a few times across the water surface before disap-pearing into the blue depths.

'Jonas was in an accident almost two years ago and suffered a brain injury. He was in hospital for several months, but in the end Olle, my partner, and I decided to take him home. And that's when the circus began.'

Rachel falls silent and her mouth narrows.

'The circus?'

She nods.

'I think Jonas had ten different home aides in three months. It just wasn't working. And the council was not exactly cooperative. In the end, we decided to care for him ourselves.'

'You and Jonas's father?'

'Olle isn't Jonas's father, but he still helps as much as he can. We sold the apartment and bought the house out here. I quit my job as a pharmacist and started working remotely, as a project manager for a pharmaceutical company. Olle is a writer, so he has a fairly flexible job. But we need some help. We can't leave Jonas alone for too long. He's bedridden and suffers from epilepsy. We don't really know how conscious he is, though he does have moments of clarity. But we can't risk, for example, that he might fall out of bed or have a seizure when we're not there.'

Rachel must have seen my expression, because she puts a gentle hand on my arm.

'There's no need to worry. The job requires no medical training. It's mostly about keeping him company. Reading aloud. Playing music. And helping out around the house. The hours are ten to four, five days a week. But right now Olle is away, so it could be a little more. The salary is 15,000 a month, but that includes food and lodging.'

Food. Lodging.

Just the thought of a soft bed and a real, home-cooked meal makes the proposal sound attractive, even if the salary is fucking shit.

Fifteen thousand. That's what I used to earn in a week.

Six hours of work, five days a week, that's thirty hours a week. If an average month has four and a half working weeks, that's a total of 135 hours. This means an hourly wage of 111 kronor.

One hundred and eleven kronor, *seriously*?

But at the same time, I realise that it's probably not that bad. If they're paying off the books – which I suspect, but don't dare ask – then it's better than working at McDonald's.

'If you were to end up working for us, we can revisit the salary discussion after the first month,' Rachel adds as if sensing what I'm thinking. 'If everything works out, that is.'

I meet her gaze.

If everything works out.

Is she serious? Is she really offering me the job?

But in the next second she says:

'You'll send me your references too, right?'

I don't manage to get out an answer.

'Your boss at Media Markt, maybe?' she suggests.

I'm still sitting on the rocks long after Rachel has left. Looking out over the sea and watching the sun set among the clouds hovering above the horizon. The air gets cooler and I take the hoodie out of my bag, remove some blades of grass and a dead beetle and pull it over my head.

How am I going to get references? And do I even want the job?

I think of Rachel, her pale skin and long, dark hair. And then I think of food and the feeling of sleeping in a freshly made bed with smooth sheets and a real pillow instead of a damp, fucking lawn.

It's tempting.

But then a second image appears, me sitting on a stool feeding a drooling retard wearing an adult nappy with arms as crooked as the driftwood that lies wedged into the rocks below me.

No.

That would never work.

Besides: 111 kronor an hour? It's a freaking joke.

A *fucking* goddamn insult.

I take out my phone.

Part of me wants to turn it on and call my mum, but what if Malte finds me again? Even though I went through my phone and turned off every location service, I still don't feel safe.

I think about it, rubbing the metal between my thumb and forefinger.

If I just used it for a minute – could they really track me?

I turn on my mobile and check my messages.

No one has texted me since I left – not my mother, Alexandra or Liam.

It makes me immediately depressed.

That's how important I was to them. That's all I meant to them.

Suddenly the voice is there again, the evil voice.

You are nothing, Samuel. Don't you get how happy they are to be rid of you?

I check Instagram.

Jeanette has posted a picture of herself in a bikini. She holds her hand in front of her mouth. Her index finger and middle finger form a V which her tongue protrudes from.

Three hundred and eighty likes.

The phone dings, and I look at the display.

It's from Rachel:

Thank you for the lovely meeting today. If you're still interested, the job is yours! Let me know as soon as you've decided!

As I read the message, the phone dings again. The hairs on the back of my neck stand up when I see it's from Igor.

It says:

You are so fucking dead.

That's all.

I drop the phone as if it were on fire. It falls off the rock with a bang and slowly slides over the smooth stones towards the water.

I jump down and manage to grab it the moment before it sinks into the sea.

Damn.

I thought Igor was in jail. Did the cops let him go?

I look around me, as if expecting him to be hiding in the shadows behind the trees, but everything seems fine.

The gravel road is empty and deserted in the dusk. Milky strands of mist caress the trunks of the pine trees, winding around the ferns and sliding over the stones. The wind has died down, and the waves lick the rocks slowly and rhythmically. The air is damp and raw, like a puff from Grandpa's earth cellar.

Maybe I should contact Igor. Explain that I hid the money and took the bike to protect him, but I don't dare.

And what if he's not even the one who sent the message?
What if the cops are trying to draw me out?

Thoughts whirl around in my head. It feels like I'm stuck on a merry-go-round and can't get off.

I need time.

I have to find out what happened to Igor. And I have to figure out how to get myself out of this bullshit.

All the time in the world won't save you, loser.

I sink down on the rock and take out my phone. Hesitate for a second, shivering in the cold. Then I go to the message from Rachel and reply that I'll take the job.

Pernilla

We are sitting in a ring on the floor in the meeting room. Candles burn on the counter by the window and the walls are covered with crayon drawings from Genesis – colourful, imaginative interpretations of the move to Egypt, Pharaoh's dreams and of Joseph testing his eleven brothers.

Karl-Johan, the pastor, sits across from me, and around us children are gathered, all between nine and thirteen years old.

I love our congregation's child and youth activities.

The children are so much more open to God's message, so unabashedly curious and quick to learn. And Karl-Johan is good with them. I am too, for that matter – they would never dream of challenging my authority in the way Samuel always has.

I look at Karl-Johan. With his grey beard and stocky body, he looks like a storytelling uncle, much older than his forty-seven years.

As soon as the thought occurs to me, I feel a little ashamed – after all, we're not dealing with fairy tales here, this is the word of God, recorded directly in the Holy Scriptures.

Besides. I shouldn't be sitting here looking at the pastor's body.

'So,' says Karl-Johan and his eyes glide over the children, 'why did Job's wife tell him to curse God and die?'

Peter raises his hand in a flash, followed by Lily and Julia.

Karl-Johan nods at Julia, a pale and quiet girl with teeth that protrude so far she almost can't close her mouth. She's shy, and I know he wants to encourage her to take up more space in the group.

'Because . . . because . . . God had made him sick and stolen his donkeys and camels and killed his sheep. And his ten children,' she adds after a short pause.

Giggles erupt among the children.

'Well,' says Karl-Johan slowly. 'That's right, Julia, though it wasn't God, it was Satan who did that.'

'That's what I *meant*,' Julia says quickly with her cheeks burning.

Karl-Johan nods encouragingly.

'And what did Job do then?' he asks. 'Did he curse God?'

Julia shakes her head vehemently.

'No. He didn't want to. Though three false friends told him he'd lived a very bad life. And then God was happy and made him well and gave him new donkeys and camels. And ten new kids.'

Karl-Johan looks satisfied.

The giggling has stopped and the kids seem bored again. We have been working on the story of Job for almost an hour, and they aren't able to focus for much longer than that.

'Exactly,' Karl-Johan says. 'So what can we learn from this?'

'That if you are faithful to God you get . . . get . . . get . . .' Julia stutters.

'*Camels?*' James interjects, the group's clown. An overweight boy with loud red hair who always seems to be laughing.

More giggles.

Karl-Johan also smiles, in a way that I know he wouldn't have done if an adult had made a joke.

'If you are faithful to God, He will bless you too, and you will have eternal life,' he says with feeling.

The children fall silent and stare at him wide-eyed.

'I think we'll end there,' he says and smiles again. 'Before you go, Pernilla will hand out some information about the hike next week.'

He nods to me and I get up, straighten my skirt and reach for the stack of papers lying on the bench next to me.

'We'll meet outside the congregation hall at six in the morning,' I say. 'Here's a list of things you'll need to pack. Read it carefully so that you don't forget anything. There won't be any shops. In the forest, I mean. Where we're going.'

More giggles.

I start handing papers to the children and continue:

'According to the weather forecast, it'll be sunny and warm, but you never know, so don't forget rain gear. And arrive on time. The bus leaves at half past six.'

A low murmur spreads through the room as the children pick up their books and papers and get up off the floor.

'Wear durable clothes,' I continue. 'And good shoes. We'll be hiking a long distance, and I don't want any blisters this time.'

No one answers. The children are already walking towards the door.

'And *no* phones,' I call after them.

Karl-Johan smiles at me.

'Come and sit down for a bit,' he says and pats his big hand on the carpet.

The last child leaves the room, and the door closes again with a dull bang. The candles flicker in the draught of wind.

I walk over to Karl-Johan and sit down a few yards away from him.

'Aren't they great?' I say.

He nods and smiles. Then he raises an eyebrow and tilts his head.

'How's Bernt doing?' he asks.

I think of my father lying in the hospice, waiting for God to call him home. Of his unnaturally thin body and how his skin and the whites of his eyes have turned as yellow as daffodils.

'Not good,' I tell him truthfully.

Karl-Johan nods, his expression sad.

'We will pray for him,' he says, emphasising every word. And then:

'Is there anything else weighing on you, Pernilla? You seem a little, I don't know, *out of sorts.*'

I shake my head quickly.

'No. There's nothing else. I mean, I have a new job and all, which I like a lot. So. Everything's good. With me. At the new job. And in general. That is.'

He stares at me. And as if he's reading my mind, he continues:

'Something going on with Samuel again?'

I nod, close my eyes and feel tears burn on the back of my eyelids. Thinking of the blackbird sitting in its cage at home, staring at me with accusing eyes. And even though I have no intention of doing so, I tell him everything, about the strange little plastic bags, about kicking Samuel out and about the police visiting me.

As usual, the story becomes much longer and more elaborate than I intend it to be, but Karl-Johan listens patiently.

He's a good listener.

A much better listener than I'll ever be, since I mostly just go on and on, as if I wanted to talk people to death.

'Oh, Pernilla,' he says with a sigh when I'm done. 'Unfortunately, I can't say I'm surprised, but you should know that I'm convinced it will all work out for Samuel as soon as he opens his heart to God.'

I nod and wipe away a tear. Thinking of all the times I've sat here with Samuel and felt ashamed.

All I can say is that the congregation has been very patient with him.

When he was little he hit the other children and stole biscuits. Then it got worse. Much worse. At one point, he even started a fire in the garden with the hymn books.

But he didn't mean any harm by it.

He just had a hard time focusing, and he was full of mischief.

He had been using the hymn books to build a tower, a tower which quickly became a house. And of course a house needs lighting, which took the form of a candle.

In other words, he didn't mean to burn the books. But no one understood that. Instead his actions were taken to be a heathen act.

It was the same for him at school. The teacher sent him to the school nurse, who referred him to a psychologist.

She said Samuel obviously had problems with impulse control and attention. She thought he might grow out of it.

As for me, I went straight to our pastor.

Together we prayed for Samuel. We prayed and prayed and prayed, but God must have decided our trials weren't over, because Samuel did not improve.

On the contrary.

I close my eyes and fight back tears.

'The important thing now is not to let him come back,' the pastor says. 'He's an adult, Pernilla. He must be allowed to make his own mistakes. If you clean up after him every time he does something stupid, he'll never learn. Wait. Be confident. He'll come back when he's ready. And then we will be ready for him. Then *God* will be ready for him,' he adds emphatically.

I nod, but I can't get any words out, because the painful lump in my throat makes it impossible to speak. But I suppose the pastor is right. He's probably seen this a hundred times before. And he has helped Samuel and me so much. When Samuel stole from the collection, he agreed not to report it to the police and when we've been going through tough times, he's loaned us money. And I never would have been entrusted with running our child and youth activities, if it weren't for his warm recommendation.

'Do you promise me not to contact Samuel this time?' he says. 'Can you swear to that, Pernilla?'

'Yes,' I whisper and smile a little because he sounds just like my father.

Karl-Johan nods, looking satisfied. Then his eyes slide over me, from head to toe. As if I were a used car he's considering buying.

'Are you seeing anyone?' he asks, and tilts his head again.

I don't understand.

'What do you mean, seeing someone?'

Karl-Johan laughs softly.

'A man, I mean. You've been alone for a long time, even though you're so young.'

He pauses. His eyes caught somewhere at the level of my breasts.

'And beautiful,' he adds. 'You shouldn't be alone. That's not God's will.'

I am both surprised and embarrassed, because if I didn't know better I'd say he was hitting on me.

But that can't be the case.

Karl-Johan's been married to Maria for as long as I can remember. They're the perfect couple in every way, and they have the respect of the whole congregation.

No, I think. I'm imagining things.

'Do you think so?' I whisper.

Karl-Johan nods and smiles. Stretches out his hand and strokes me lightly across the cheek.

I shiver, but can't get one word past my lips. Me, who can never keep my mouth shut. I have apparently been struck dumb.

'We will have plenty of time to talk on the hike,' he says, popping one of those throat lozenges he always eats into his mouth and leaning forward.

'Well,' I say, leaning back a little to escape his touch, the discomfort expanding in my chest.

'Let us pray for Samuel,' he says and stands up. He smooths the wrinkles from his crumpled chinos and beckons me to follow him.

I stand up and follow him to the large wooden cross on the wall. Stare at Jesus' lean body, carefully carved in dark wood.

Karl-Johan takes a step back so that he ends up behind me and puts his hands on my shoulders.

'Do you believe me when I say everything will be fine?' he asks, massaging my shoulders lightly.

'Yes,' I whisper.

He lets his hands run down my arms, then takes a step closer so that he's embracing me from behind and puts his big fists over my clasped hands. Then he clasps his hands over mine.

The sudden closeness makes me uncomfortable, and my first impulse is to escape, to run out into the summer day and leave the pastor in here with Jesus on the cross.

But I can't do that. This is my pastor after all, the man in our congregation who is closest to God.

You can't take that lightly.

'God,' he begins. 'Thank you for Samuel, he is a gift. But it's not easy to be young these days, to be tempted and deceived by false gods.'

He pauses and presses himself closer to me so that his arms press against my breasts.

I feel sick and almost don't dare to breathe.

'Protect Samuel through these difficulties,' he continues. 'Light a candle in his heart and show him the way. Help him find peace within himself and follow Christ.'

Karl-Johan's stomach presses against my back. I can smell him clearly now, sweat and throat lozenges.

'In Jesus' name . . .'

He shifts a little onto one leg and presses his crotch against my butt, and then I feel it clearly – the erection pressing against my buttocks.

I free myself from his grip and take a few stumbling steps towards the wall. Grab the cross so as not to lose my balance.

'Stop!' I cry. 'Stop that . . .'

Then I can't figure out what to say. When I truly need words, they fail me. They don't stand in line waiting to defend me, they press somewhere in the back of my mind. I'm paralysed by respect for the pastor and the church and God and all that is holy.

The pastor has a naughty smile on his face, and it makes him look like a mischievous boy. But his eyes are bleary and follow me as I sidle towards the door.

'Stop *what*?' he says innocently.

'You, you,' I stammer. 'You touched me.'

But my words don't have the effect I expected.

Instead of retreating and apologising, he just shakes his head. The smile has disappeared, and his face has closed and turned hard.

He slowly shakes his head.

'But, Pernilla,' he says making it sound like an accusation. 'I would never . . .'

'But I felt it. I felt. You. That. When you . . .'

'Excuse me?' he says, raising his eyebrows. 'What did you think you felt?'

My face is hot, and I can't say the words, not in the house of God.

'Pernilla, I know you're out of balance,' the pastor continues in a sympathetic voice. 'It's easy to misinterpret situations. Especially when one has been alone for as long as you have. I would probably dream of closeness too, if I were in your situation. There is nothing strange about that. To the contrary, it is very human and absolutely nothing to be ashamed of.'

My face burns with shame.

'I'll report you,' I say.

'For *what*?' he asks, clasping his hands. 'Pernilla, all I've ever wanted is to help you and Samuel, in any way I can. You know that.'

He's right.

What would I say? That I *think* I felt his erection against my backside? Everyone would laugh at me, thinking I'm some love-sick bitch secretly fantasising about the pastor. Love-sick and ungrateful, because everyone knows how much he's done for us.

'Please,' he says. 'Do not let this misunderstanding come between us. Our work with the children is so important. Surely you enjoy this assignment?'

I take a few steps back as the breadth of his betrayal dawns on me. Because what he's really saying is that I need to stop arguing with him if I want to continue to be responsible for child and youth activities.

I turn around and leave the room. Do my best to walk calmly, as if I still have full control over my body, but I start running even before I get out.

A sense of loss spreads inside my chest.

It's as if he's taken something important from me – my faith in him, faith in the church, and perhaps even in God. Not to mention my dignity, of course. Though that's probably the least of my concerns in this context.

When I step out into the sun, I look down at my skirt hanging at an angle and pull it straight over my hips.

Maybe this is all my fault? Maybe I was dressed too pro-
vocatively and encouraged him.

The face of an angel and heart of a snake.

Maybe I'm just like my mother.

Manfred

We are out on the island of Ornö, in Stockholm's southern archipelago. The air is cool and damp, the rocks are cloaked in shadows, but the June sky is still light. The smell of sea and seaweed is potent. It's joined by another scent, the sweet, nauseating stench of death.

About fifty yards in front of us large floodlights and bags have been placed on the rocks. Two men in white overalls kneel beside a bundle.

A uniformed police officer comes over to us and introduces herself as Miriam. She says that the bundle, which had turned out to be a body, was found by a German tourist a few hours ago.

'He was lying in the water next to the rocks, but we lifted him out,' she explains.

A few feet away, her male colleague is talking on the phone.

'The medical examiner was here,' she adds. 'But the body has been methodically wrapped, so you can't see much. And she'd rather transport the whole . . . *package* . . . intact to forensic medicine. In any case, she said the person is probably male and has been dead for a while. So there was no need to do any closer examination at this time.'

I look out over the water that spreads out in front of us like black silk.

'What's out there?' I ask.

Miriam nods at the horizon.

'Some skerries and islets. But then it's just open sea. Estonia lies directly to the east and Finland to the north-east. And to the west . . .'

She pauses, nods in the direction of the mainland and then continues:

'Yes, in addition to Ornö you have Aspö and a number of other islands. The nearest town is Dalarö, to the north-west. You took the boat from there, right?'

I nod.

The technicians take a few flash photographs and for a second I'm blinded. See nothing but darkness. There's the distant sound of a motorboat heading out into the distance.

About fifty yards away, a group of people are talking quietly, probably curious islanders.

'Have you spoken to them?' I ask Miriam, pointing to the group.

She shakes her head.

'Do it,' I say. 'And get their names and contact information.'

'OK,' Miriam says, somewhat hesitantly. She turns and walks away towards the crowd.

'Shall we have a look?' Malin asks, nodding toward the body near the water.

'Yes, let's.'

We head down the gently sloping cliff, greet the technicians and squat next to the bundle.

In the brightness of the floodlights, the body is clearly visible under the wet white fabric. I can make out the contours of a shoulder and a hip. A coarse, rusty chain, which appears to be of the same type as the one used to sink Johannes Ahonen, is wrapped several times around the fabric. Seaweed and clay cover parts of the chain. In one place a hand protrudes from beneath the cloth.

I lean forward to get a better look.

The skin is wrinkled and has come loose at the wrist, which makes it look like the man is wearing a thin plastic glove.

I have seen enough drowning victims over the years to know that's common. In fact, the skin on the hands and feet sometimes slips off completely – like socks or gloves – after a few days in the water.

Miriam climbs down to us and stands with her eyes fixed on the water. She seems not to want to look directly at the body, and I can understand why. It takes years of practice to overcome the natural reflex to close your eyes in the face of death.

I turn toward her.

'The man who found the body?' I ask.

'A Heinz Schwarz,' she murmurs. 'Fifty-nine years old, lives in Hanover, here on holiday with his Italian boyfriend Silvio. Heinz was out by himself walking when he saw something in the water close to the rocks. He climbed down to see what it was, realised it was a body and called the emergency service.'

'And this Heinz?' I ask. 'How long had he been here, in the Stockholm archipelago?'

'They apparently arrived in Sweden yesterday. Planned to spend a week here. But now they're thinking of going home. I think he was quite shocked.'

One day in Sweden. Heinz and his Italian boyfriend could hardly have anything to do with the body ending up here, I think.

'I have taken his statement,' Miriam adds.

'Good,' I say and turn to Malin. 'What do you think?'

Malin nods.

'That this is connected,' she says and tucks a wisp of her long, dark hair behind her ear. 'Whoever dumped Ahonen, did this too.'

Afsaneh is awake when I get home.

She meets me in the hall and gives me a long hug. She's freshly showered, and her hair is still wet. My cheek gets wet, and drops land on my upper arm.

'Poor you,' she murmurs. 'It really got late.'

'It turned out that way.'

She pushes me away and frowns.

'Have you been smoking?'

'No,' I lie.

'Hmm,' she says suspiciously. 'Do you want tea and a sandwich?'

'Gladly,' I say and kiss her lightly on the forehead.

We go into the kitchen.

'Oh, I meant to say,' she says, stopping in the middle of the floor. 'I'm thinking of going to a couple of meetings next week.'

'Meetings? Have you joined AA?'

Afsaneh smiles dismissively.

'Very funny. Work meetings.'

I go still, my body aware that something important might be happening.

Afsaneh has been on sick leave ever since Nadja's accident.

'That's great,' I say.

'It's the Project,' she says. 'I'm actually curious about how it's going.'

The Project is an interdisciplinary research project that aims to investigate how new technology, especially the internet and social media, affects people. In addition to Afsaneh and her colleague Martin – who are both psychologists – the group includes doctors, neurobiologists and IT experts.

Since Afsaneh defended her thesis and was hired to her position at Stockholm University, her focus has been on the interaction between human and machine – primarily on vehicles like cars, boats and aeroplanes. But with the Project, her research has widened to include other areas as well.

'It's probably because I hang out so much online myself right now,' Afsaneh says, smiling uncertainly. 'It becomes so clear how the internet brings people together.'

'For better or worse,' I say.

Afsaneh shrugs.

'Maybe. But there is so much love out there, so much understanding. So many who share the same experiences and the same pain.'

'And so many loons.'

Afsaneh raises one of her perfectly shaped eyebrows as if she wants to let me know that I've overstepped, but that she's letting me off with a warning. Then she smiles again – not even my hostility to technology seems to throw her off balance today.

'Aren't you exaggerating just a little?'

'Maybe.'

Afsaneh lights candles and puts water on to boil for tea. I set the table.

Only when she puts down the teapot and the sandwiches she's made do I discover my mistake.

I've set the table for three.

At Nadja's place, I put a plate and a glass. I don't even remember doing it, it must have happened completely automatically.

I turn cold inside as I see Afsaneh's gaze flicker across the table.

'I'm sorry,' I say. 'I don't know what I was thinking. I'm so fucking tired. Afsaneh, I'm sorry!'

But Afsaneh's reaction isn't what I feared.

She doesn't shut down and start to cry. She walks over to me and takes me in her arms. Laughs and mumbles in my ear.

'Silly. It's fine. I'll clear it away later. And besides, she'll be home soon. Then we can set the table for three again.'

Her comment causes something to tighten inside my chest.

Yes, the doctors have started to phase out the medication, but it will take days for Nadja to wake up.

If she wakes up.

I don't dare contemplate what will happen if she doesn't. Where would Afsaneh's new-found energy and joy go then? What life awaits us if Nadja leaves us for good?

But Afsaneh doesn't seem to note my hesitation.

'You are so funny,' she says again and kisses me with hunger for the first time since it happened.

Since our child fell onto the hard tarmac.

PART II

The Storm

But the LORD sent out a great wind on the sea, and there was a mighty tempest on the sea, so that the ship was about to be broken up. The mariners were afraid; and every man cried out to his God.

Jonah 1: 4–5

Samuel

Rachel meets me at the harbour.

After she's parked her black Volvo, jumped out and said hello, she glances at my almost-empty backpack, and I sense what she's thinking.

Shouldn't someone who's moving into their new workplace be bringing a bit more stuff with them?

I pull on my backpack, and do my best not to look like somebody on the run from an insane Russian drug lord and who has spent the last several nights sleeping in a fucking bush.

She has her hair tied up in a knot today. A few dark wisps have escaped and hang down over her back. Otherwise, she looks just like she did yesterday. No make-up, dressed in a simple white dress shirt and an old pair of jeans.

'Well,' Rachel says and glances over at Igor's bike. 'You can follow me, then. It's not far, just a couple of miles. But be careful. The road is bad.'

I nod and climb on the motorcycle.

Rachel jumps into her car, starts it, and drives towards the main road. After a couple of hundred yards, she turns right on a gravel road so narrow that I probably wouldn't have discovered it if she wasn't right ahead of me.

We drive through a pine wood and then over a small bridge. The water is calm and shiny between the rocks. The summer breeze is warm, the sun blinding, so I'm forced to squint while Rachel makes her turns towards something. A second later, a couple of large potholes appear in the road and I just barely have time to swing around them.

She was right, the road sucks.

I slow down, increasing the distance between me and the Volvo.

The road winds its way through pinewoods and cliffs. The smell of conifers and soil is intense. Here and there stones have come loose from the cliffs and rolled down onto the road. I'm forced to zigzag between them and the potholes that seem to appear with increasing frequency.

At one point I see a gate, and beyond it a driveway, which I'm guessing leads to a house.

Then Rachel stops by a white picket fence. She parks the car on the grass next to the road, opens the driver's door and jumps out. Then she waves to me.

I park the bike a short distance from the car and walk over to her.

'Do you live on an island?' I ask.

She nods.

'Although it almost doesn't feel that way, because of the bridge. You used to have to make your way by boat from Stuvskär.'

She smiles a little and those fine wrinkles around her eyes appear again.

Fifty yards or so away, behind some puny pine trees, I can make out glimpses of Rachel's house – a white single-family home with green trim and shutters.

There are no other houses in sight.

'Do a lot of people live here?' I ask, looking around.

The only sounds to be heard are birds singing and a distant boat.

'No, we are one of two families who live here year-round. Plus a few summer homes.'

Rachel wrinkles her nose a bit when she says the last part, maybe she doesn't like the holidaymakers. As if she senses what I'm thinking she says:

'That came out wrong. We have a lot to thank the holiday people for. If it weren't for them we wouldn't have the ferry, the harbour pub or the supermarket. Have you been to the shop, by the way?'

I say yes, and think about the sandwiches I stole.

As soon as I think about food my stomach cramps up. Hunger kept me up last night. I even dreamed I was at McDonald's.

'It's very convenient to be able to pick up things we're out of there. But their offering is a bit unusual. Pomegranates, lobster, Wagyu beef. Not exactly what a family with children needs at 11.55 on a Tuesday. But I suppose that's what the owners of holiday homes want, they have a lot of money and exclusive tastes.'

Rachel starts to walk and I follow her. Her thin shirt flutters as she walks; she is backlit and I can see the outline of one of her breasts.

'It used to be different,' she adds. 'Stuvskär was a fishing outpost. Talk to any one of the elders in the village and they will tell you. People here caught cod and herring in nets and put out eel traps. Every family had a fish smoker where they burned juniper and sawdust. And they used everything, ate ide and stewed bream, fishes people throw back today.'

We walk through the gate and arrive in a garden with a lush green lawn, fruit trees in bloom and young rose bushes in a raised, oval-shaped flower bed in front of the entrance. Knotty lilacs with pale green, heart-shaped leaves and wind-blown blooms past their best huddle in the corners. The scent of grass tickles my nose and the lines from the lawnmower are so clear that I suspect Rachel mowed the lawn right before meeting me.

The building itself is old and charming, as if someone drove it here straight out of a story book on a big fucking truck. In front of the main door there are small steps that are almost completely hidden under a wheelchair-friendly ramp. On the front stairs are pots with pink flowers that I recognise.

I don't know what they're called but Mum has the same ones in her kitchen.

As soon as the thought is formed I feel the pain and I realise that I actually do miss her, even though she is incredibly annoying and stalks me.

Not this time though.

This time she hasn't even been in touch.

She's probably glad to be rid of you and all your fucking problems.

I ignore the cruel voice and let my gaze slide across the house.

There are wrought iron curlicued bars across the ground-floor windows. I glimpse lace curtains inside.

Rachel points at the ramp.

'Sometimes we take Jonas out. Usually onto the terrace which is on the other side of the house, facing the water. But we left the ramp in place. In case . . .'

She pauses and then adds in a low, frail voice.

'. . . in case he gets better.'

She walks up the steps and to the door, takes out a heavy bunch of keys and unlocks it.

'Welcome!' she says. 'Shall I give you a little tour?'

The entryway is reminiscent of something you'd see in an old film, with blue wainscoting on the walls and a floral edging at chest height. To the right there are hooks, with clothes hanging on them. There's a narrow grey table by the wall. On it there is a vase containing red roses that must be from the flower bed in the garden.

I take my trainers off and put them next to a large pair of men's boots. Then I follow Rachel into the kitchen, which is to the right of the entryway. It is large and painted a pale shade of yellow. There is a wood-burning stove as well as a modern stove with a black induction hob.

On the range there's a large enamel pot and a saucepan. It smells of meat and spices. I feel dizzy.

'There's stew,' Rachel says, as we pass the stove. 'I figured you might be hungry. You're welcome to have some food later. And feel free to help yourself out of the fridge and pantry.'

We continue through the kitchen and into a large room, painted white, with white sofas and armchairs. Shelves line the walls, stuffed with books and ornaments. Next to a framed photo I spot a blue glass bowl on a stem. It looks almost exactly like my mum's cake plate.

I go closer.

In the bowl there is a watch and a mobile phone shell with a weed leaf pattern.

Maybe Jonas was a fun guy before he went and got himself brain-damaged?

Rachel looks inquiringly at me.

'My mum has one just like it,' I say, pointing at the blue bowl.

Rachel nods but doesn't respond.

I lift my gaze from the glass bowl and take a few steps away.

Large casement windows and a pair of double doors cover the entire wall; beyond them the sea stretches out, blue and infinite in the morning sun.

In the distance I see some skerries and a lighthouse.

'*Wow*,' I say before I can catch myself, but Rachel just smiles like some kind of *Mona Lisa* reproduction and walks up to the windows.

I follow her.

As I get closer I notice the doors open onto a terrace. Rachel opens them and we step outside.

The terrace is large, I would say at least thirty square yards. Deckchairs and a seating area are arranged on the wooden deck, which is surrounded by a low white fence.

We go up to the fence and once again I catch my breath.

In front of me steep cliffs cascade into the sea. Saplings, heather and blueberry bushes grow in the crevices. A wooden staircase winds its way down along the precipice toward a jetty, at least sixty feet below us. Next to the jetty I can glimpse a boathouse behind some shrubs.

'As you can see we can't take Jonas down to the water,' Rachel says and I sense the pain in her voice. 'Not that it really matters. He wouldn't appreciate it anyway. But you can go down when you like. I usually take a morning swim. It's not exactly warm, but it is . . .'

She laughs a little before completing the sentence.

'OK.'

'Shall we keep going?' she asks and walks back into the living room.

I follow her.

Rachel points to a door.

'That's Olle's and my bedroom. Jonas's room is the next one along. There's a bathroom between the rooms, but I think it would be better if you use the one upstairs. Shall we take a look at your room before we say hi to Jonas?'

We go up a spiral staircase connecting the living room to the upstairs. The stairs lead into yet another room, also furnished with sofas and bookshelves. It is almost like a library.

Just as in the living room there are large casement windows facing the sea.

'The family room,' Rachel explains.

She points to a door:

'And that is Olle's study. His writer's den. It is usually locked when he's not in there writing.'

She turns to the other wall that has two doors which the bookshelf is built around.

'Your bedroom and bathroom,' she says, opening the door to the right.

The room is large and painted a blue-grey shade, the kind that Mum would've called dove grey. A double bed is made up with white sheets and big, fluffy pillows – like at a luxury hotel. It looks so comfy I want to lie down right away, but of course I don't. I shrug my backpack off my shoulders and put it next to the bed before we move on to the bathroom which is small and rundown, but neat and clean. The walls are covered in mustard-yellow tiles. A cracked mirror hangs over the basin and behind a plastic curtain patterned with dots there's a shower.

'Well then,' Rachel says, lingering a bit on the words, 'shall we go and say hello to Jonas?'

In the bed there is a guy my own age. He is pale and thin and has short brown hair. His features are pronounced, with sharp cheekbones and a large nose. The pale little pursed mouth looks like a worm somebody placed in the middle of his face. There's a thin tube coming out of his nose, attached to his cheek with some brown surgical tape.

Next to the bed there's a strange structure of metal with something that looks like a blue swing seat attached with black straps. I don't know what it is but guess it might be used for lifting Jonas out of the bed.

I look at him again.

If I didn't know that he was sick I would have assumed he was just sleeping, because he doesn't look anything like what I imagined – his arms aren't bent, he isn't drooling and shaking and he doesn't make weird noises.

Instead he just seems totally gone.

Completely fucking unconscious, like a zombie.

I look around the room.

There are crayon drawings on the walls of cars, zombie-Jonas must have made them when he was younger, because they look childish and the smiling people in the vehicles look almost like stick figures. Here and there are film posters. On a hook near the window there is a pair of football boots tied together by the laces and a small Hammarby team flag.

I feel uneasy.

Rachel goes up to the bed and sits on a stool. She gestures for me to sit down in a small granny chair on the other side.

'I brought it in here for you,' she says. 'So that you can sit comfortably. You will be spending a considerable amount of time in here.'

I sink into the chair and put my hands in my lap. Feel the anxiety rush in. Something about this room, this guy lying tucked in between the sheets looking almost like a doll, gives me serious panic.

What have I signed up for? Am I seriously going to sit here six hours a day for *111 kronor* an hour?

How could I be so fucking stupid?

Rachel strokes Jonas tenderly across his hairline.

'Samuel is here,' she murmurs. 'He will keep you company while I work.'

The guy does not react.

'He will read to you,' she says. 'And play music. That will be nice, won't it?'

Jonas still doesn't move at all, he just lies there, perfectly still with an expressionless face and his eyes closed. There is absolutely nothing to indicate that he can hear or understand her.

Rachel bends over and kisses his cheek. Points to the tube coming out of his nose.

'Jonas is tube-fed,' she says. 'But you don't need to worry about it. I take care of all that.'

Then she reaches for a tube of cream on the little bedside table and squeezes a greasy blob into her hand. Takes one of Jonas's hands and begins to rub the cream in.

Above the bedside table there is a calendar, on which someone, presumably Rachel, has crossed out each day in June up until today's date.

'His hands get terribly dry,' she says. 'I usually moisturise them once or so a day. And when I remember to I also put some lip balm on him.'

I glance over at the bedside table. There is a lone red rose in a vase, next to it lies a hairbrush and a tube of lip balm.

Rachel takes Jonas's other hand and moisturises that too. Slowly rubs the cream in, all the way out to the tips of the fingers.

'There,' she says, turned toward Jonas. 'Is that better?'

Jonas groans slightly and Rachel smiles.

'He knows you're here,' she says, slowly nodding her head.

The cramps in my belly are increasing, not just from hunger but from panic. I let my gaze wander across the room, from the posters and the drawings over to the far wall. There are shelves with jars of medicine, plastic bags, nitrile gloves and rolls of paper towel.

On a small table next to the shelves there is a photo of Rachel and a boy. They are smiling in the photo and there's a hint of a beach in the background. In another they are on a ski slope. There's a loudspeaker by the table with a book next to it.

'All you need to do is to keep Jonas company,' Rachel says and meets my gaze. 'Most of the time he is calm, but occasionally he will get restless or have seizures. If that happens I want you to get me immediately. Do you understand?'

I nod and try not to look down her cleavage where I can glimpse a breast.

I swallow, hard.

'It's as easy as that,' she says, and smiles.

I'm in the big bed with the fluffy pillows. It is exactly as comfortable as it looked. My belly is full of meat stew and potatoes and my skin is warm from the long, hot shower, but the only thing I can think about is how I need to get away from here as fast as possible.

Away from Rachel and zombie-Jonas, away from the rocks and the pines and the supermarket that sells hummus and lobster to tourists.

I look at the mobile, lying on the bedside table, all shiny silver and still like a dead fish.

It's incredibly annoying to not be able to use it.

Lying here in bed, completely cut off from the rest of the world, it is almost like not existing.

The world is in there, under the metallic shell. Life is in there.

Liam and Alexandra and Jeanette, Igor too, of course – no way around that. And Mum.

But all the other stuff – this house, the setting sun reflecting in the sea outside, Rachel, Jonas – that's not really real.

I try to come up with a plan.

I can stay here for a day or two. Maybe there is something of value in the house that I can steal before I leave, something I can sell on eBay so that I can lie low for a while.

The tiredness overwhelms me and I close my eyes.

In my mind's eye I see Mum. She smiles and the gold cross at her cleavage glitters as if illuminated by a bright light.

'You have to let Jesus into your heart, Samuel,' she whispers, bends over me and kisses me on the mouth, a bit too long for it to be comfortable.

When she stands up again her face is no longer hers, it is Rachel's.

Pernilla

The grass around the yellow wooden house almost reaches my knees and the borders are in full bloom.

I pull the rusty old gate shut behind me and walk up the gravel path to the entrance as I take my keys out of my pocket.

It is hot, really hot, and birdsong and the sound of buzzing bumblebees surrounds me.

I unlock the door and step into the familiar hall.

There's a slightly musty smell along with something that could be mould, but everything looks the way it used to. Father's shoes are lined up in two neat rows on the shelf and the clothes hang on identical hangers under the hat shelf.

I put the stack of mail and newspapers on the chest of drawers under the mirror. Leaf through the letters to see if anything looks urgent and tuck some bills into my bag.

I don't have Father's bank details, but I think they're in his green chest of drawers. I decide to see if I can find them. If not I guess I will have to pay the bills myself, even though I have almost no money left in my account.

Father would hate it if the bills weren't paid on time.

I kick my pumps off and go into the kitchen.

Everything looks as usual.

Through the window I can see the blue water on the lake glimmer in the sun. The tall rose bush, the one that should have been cut a long time ago, covers almost the entire right-hand side of the windowpane.

I go up to the fridge, expecting to find mouldy food, but it is empty and switched off. A faint scent of detergent hits me and when I run my finger over the glass shelf it is so clean that it almost squeaks when I touch it.

Father has already emptied the fridge and cleaned it.

I look around.

The oven door is open and the baking sheets are arranged on a gingham tea towel on the counter next to it. Next to them is an opened package of steel wool.

Typical Father, he has apparently already done the estate cleaning, so that I won't have to.

When I realise what trouble he has gone to for my sake I am immediately hit by a mix of grief and guilt. The feeling adds to my already subdued state of mind and I think of Samuel, who has vanished, and the pastor's breath against the back of my neck when he pressed up against me.

I move on into Father's bedroom.

The sun is shining in and it is hot, almost stifling. Small particles of dust float in the rectangle of light that cuts straight through the room; seemingly weightless they appear to strive up, up, up.

The double bed is neatly made and the big quilt that Mother made when I was little lies folded at the foot. There is a Bible on the bedside table, the 1917 translation, Father's favourite, although he uses newer translations in his sermons. Around it are medicine jars in various sizes.

I go up to the green chest of drawers by the window. Crouch down and pull out the top drawer.

Empty.

The next drawer is empty too, but when I pull out the bottom drawer I find a large brown envelope.

It says 'Pernilla' in Father's large, shaky handwriting.

I take the envelope and close the drawer. Go up to the bed and sit down, unsure of what to do. It is obviously intended for me, but I don't know what it is. Father might not want me to read it right now. On the other hand it might contain bank information and other practical details that I may need.

In the end my curiosity wins out and I open the carefully sealed envelope with my finger.

There are five letters inside, all unopened and addressed to me. I look at the postmarks. The oldest was sent a few days before my tenth birthday.

I open it carefully and fish out a brittle sheet of writing paper with yellow flowers in the right-hand corner.

Dearest Pernilla,

I hope that you are well and that you and Father are happy! As I wrote to you earlier I miss you very, very much and long to see you. Please ask Father when we can meet.

Now you are turning ten – a big day. I would have loved to celebrate it with you, but I know that you are well cared for by Father and the others in the congregation.

There is so much I would like to explain to you, but I think it is better to wait until we see each other. Some things take a while to understand, and this one of those things.

As I wrote before I want you to know that I love you very much and miss you every day, but your father and I simply could not live together.

It has nothing to do with you, my little bumblebee!

Now have a nice birthday, and I hope that we can see each other soon. I have sent you a gift in the mail as well.

If you would like to write me you can. The address is on the back of the envelope.

Lots of love and kisses,

Mum

My stomach contracts as if someone had punched me. I double over and have to hold on to the bed so as not to fall.

What is this?

Mother didn't want any contact with me; she chose not to be with me. And the few, distant relatives that I had on Mother's side did the same.

Did Mother send me letters?

Why did Father never mention that? Was his plan that I obtain these letters after he died?

The letter, the handwriting and the sunlight that paints the familiar old rag carpet in warm tones bring up memories that I have long since forgotten.

Mother's scent: a mix of cooking, sweat and perfume. Her long hair that she almost always wore up and the far too beautiful, almost doll-like face.

And that expression: *little bumblebee*.

When my eyes fall on those words again it is almost as if I can hear her voice, as if she is standing close to me, whispering in my ear.

Little bumblebee, dearest little bumblebee.

The tears come and I don't do anything to stop them. They run along my cheeks and down onto my neck.

I tear open the other letters and read them one by one.

The next three are a lot like the first. Mother wishes me a merry Christmas, congratulates me on my birthday, writes that she loves me and wants to see me. But in the last letter, written just a few weeks before she died, I sense an increased desperation and assertiveness. She asks why I haven't been in touch, even though she has written so many letters, even though she has sent presents and wants to see me. She asks if I am angry with her and intimates that Father may have something to do with that.

When I read the last lines I freeze, because I cannot believe it is true. I have to read the passage several times before I am certain I didn't get it wrong.

Pernilla, my dear little bumblebee, you are old enough that you ought to be able to handle the truth. Your father was a demanding and manipulative husband. His words hurt worse than his strikes and in the end I saw no other way out than to leave him. He made me promise not to seek you out and I agreed, stupidly. I needed the money he gave me. But now I will not obey him anymore. I will come and congratulate you on your thirteenth birthday!

I fall back into the soft bed holding the letter.

Is it possible? Did father *pay* her to stay away or is that another one of her lies? Because everybody in the neighbourhood knew that she was capable of lying – if you can cheat on your husband with a neighbour then you're comfortable with deceit.

Face like an angel, heart like a snake.

Then I go cold inside. Look at the letter again and try to digest what is in it.

I will come and congratulate you on your thirteenth birthday!

But that's when she died, on my thirteenth birthday. And at once I understand why she was out driving in the vicinity of our house.

She was on her way to see me.

I bury my head in the quilt and cry in a way that I have not since I was a child. It is as if all the feelings that have been buried in my chest dislodge, become a deluge, gush out of my eyes and nose and into Mother's old quilt in the form of tears and snot.

I am nine years old again and Mother is naked on the sofa with our neighbour.

I am thirteen and Mother has just been killed driving her car, a few miles away from here.

I am eighteen, single and heavily pregnant.

I am thirty-six and my father is dying, my son has disappeared and I have been let down by everyone I trusted.

Suddenly I miss Samuel so much it makes my heart ache. The sensation is so visceral, so physical that I groan as I lie there. Suddenly I am certain that it is wrong for me not to be in touch with him. All we have is each other and this is the only thing that matters.

I pull out my mobile and try to call him but it goes straight to his voicemail, as if his phone was off.

On my way home I try calling Samuel several times. When the train stops in Västertorp I text him, write that I love him and I want to hear from him.

I hit send and feel a strange sense of contentment from defying the well-meaning advice I have been given by the members of the congregation, by doing the exact opposite of what I promised the pastor and Father.

When the train stops at Fruängen the sky has begun to take on a deeper blue shade on the horizon.

I glance at my watch and hurry my steps. It is already late and I have a slot booked in the laundry room.

The evening air is warm and smells of dusty roads and lilacs in bloom.

My mobile dings and my heart leaps.

I pull my phone out of my pocket but it isn't Samuel, it is Stina, the manager at the shop asking if I can take an earlier shift tomorrow.

I answer that I can and walk towards the entrance, still filled with the realisation of how much I miss Samuel, how much I need him. It is as if all this with Mother and Father has set something in motion inside me, has made me re-evaluate what's really important in life.

When I press the switch in the stairwell to turn the lights on nothing happens. I press again and again but note that it must be broken and walk up the stairs while looking for my keys in my handbag.

Maybe it's because of the rattling of my keys that I at first don't hear the steps down the stairs from the floor above.

Maybe it's because I am thinking of Samuel.

Then everything happens fast.

Somebody grabs my arm. Hard.

I glimpse the silhouette of an enormous man with a shaved head and let out an involuntary scream.

The man tightens his grip as he hushes me.

'Are you Samuel's mum?' he hisses.

He has a very heavy accent. It sounds like he is from some Eastern European country, maybe Poland or some Baltic state.

'Yes,' I say with my heart in my throat. 'I am Samuel's mother.'

The grip on my arm loosens a little and the man straightens up.

'Where is he?'

'I don't know,' I say truthfully. 'I threw him out. Well, not literally, but I told him to leave. That is, we had a disagreement and . . . Well, Samuel hadn't really been behaving and . . . I thought it was best we take a *time out*. That is—'

The man lets go of my arm and slams the palm of his hand into the wall with such force that it makes me jump.

'*Where?*' he roars. 'Where is he now?'

'I don't know,' I whisper. 'I have tried messaging him and calling him but his phone is off and naturally now I am full of regret since none of this would have happened had I not thrown him out. Or, well, if I hadn't said that he couldn't—'

He interrupts me again: 'He has something that belongs to me.'

I don't answer, because I don't know what to say, but of course my mind immediately goes to the little plastic bags with white powder that I threw out.

The man grabs hold of my arm again, but not hard this time. It is more like he wants to make sure that he has my attention than that he wants to scare me.

'Tell him I was here,' he says, then he lets me go and walks toward the stairs.

'Yes,' I say.

And then: 'Who should I tell him it is?'

I regret the phrase the moment it leaves my mouth. Why did I say that? As if he were an ordinary person who had knocked on my door asking for Samuel, not a 'career criminal', as the police who visited me at work said.

'He knows who I am,' the man says without stopping or turning around.

His steps disappear down the stairs and I'm alone in the half-light.

Manfred

Malin puts her hand on my arm and I look up.

'Shall we leave? You wanted to go to the hospital afterwards?'

I nod and stuff the last of the Danish pastry into my mouth.

It is Saturday and we are working a half-day – there are no breaks in a murder investigation. But it is also D-Day – the day that the doctors are going to begin withdrawing Nadja's medication.

But it is not for her sake I am going to the hospital, it is for Afsaneh's.

I stand up and smooth my pink shirt, the one that is actually ironed.

Maybe that's a good sign.

Letit appears next to Malin. He looks at me and the lion-yellow silk kerchief sticking out of my jacket pocket catches his gaze.

'I see,' he says curtly, as if he just confirmed a suspicion.

Malin smiles and winks at me.

'Let's sit in the small conference room,' she says and disappears down the corridor with light steps.

If one doesn't see her belly it is difficult to believe she is pregnant, because she moves with the grace of a dancer.

We follow, enter the room and sit down around the white table.

I say that I have spoken to Manuel dos Santos, the prosecutor who is leading the preliminary investigation. The investigation has now been assigned the highest priority and police command has promised us more resources.

'He wants us to wait before speaking to the media, so mum's the word if anyone calls you,' I say. 'Malin, what have you got?'

Malin leafs through her papers.

'As you know the DNA analysis confirmed that the dead man is Johannes Ahonen.'

'I told you so back at forensics,' Letit grunts.

Malin pauses, blinks a few times and continues:

'And I have looked up Ahonen's mobile data and card transactions during the time before his disappearance. The last call from his mobile was outgoing, March 3rd. The call lasted ten minutes and fifteen seconds.'

'Do we know who he was calling?' I ask.

Malin nods. 'Bianca, the girlfriend. I am collating all the numbers he called over the past week. But I can already tell you most of his calls are to his mother, Tuula, followed by Bianca, and some of his friends who we have already been in touch with. But there are a couple of numbers for prepaid phones in there. They might be hard to trace.'

'And the credit card?' I ask.

'Was last used the same day, March 3rd, to shop at a petrol station in Jordbro. The purchase was . . .'

Malin pauses and lets her finger run down the page until she finds the number she is looking for.

'Forty-three kronor.'

'A hot dog?' I suggest.

'Snus,' Letit says holding up his own box.

'Correct,' Malin says. 'I checked. And there are no strange purchases or large withdrawals from the account during the last weeks of February or the beginning of March. Everything looks normal. On the surface at least.'

I stretch a bit, massaging my neck with one hand.

'And what about his circle of close friends?'

Malin nods slowly and stretches a bit so that her belly almost hits the table.

'I have spoken to three of his friends and to his cousin. They confirmed what the girlfriend told us. Nobody knew of any threat to Ahonen. And only one of them knew that Ahonen had borrowed money. But unfortunately not from whom. All he could say was that Ahonen was very stressed since he couldn't pay it back, and that he had tried to find yet another person to borrow from so that he could pay off the original debt.'

'Did he know how much it was?' I ask.

'A few hundred grand,' Malin answers. 'He couldn't specify further.'

'People have been murdered for a lot less,' Letit states dryly and glances at the whiteboard where a mugshot of Ahonen as a seventeen-year-old has been taped up.

Ahonen looks terrified, as if he knew even then what awaited him.

Other pictures are next to that photo, those of the swollen body, wrapped in a blanket and a chain as well as a map of the portion of the coast, where the place he was found is marked with a red 'x'.

'Are there any large deposits to the account?' I ask.

'You're thinking of the loan?' Malin says. 'I've gone back a year and I can't find any large transactions. Maybe he got it in cash?'

'Maybe,' I say. 'Did any of the people you spoke to have any idea of what might have happened to him?'

Malin shakes her head.

'Really, only one of the friends wanted to speculate, and that was the same guy who knew about the loan. He thought perhaps the person who had lent him money had killed him. If he was killed – we'll see what the forensic pathologist says.'

'The good forensic pathologist,' Letit snorts. 'I bet my balls she is too good to speculate on the cause of death.'

Malin continues, taking no notice of Letit:

'He also said that there is a gang of Somali youths who had a bone to pick with Ahonen, but he didn't seem to think they would have killed him. They're apparently pretty young, fifteen. I've asked the youth unit to look into them.'

'Good,' I say. 'And the fragments of skin under Ahonen's nails? Anything new from the forensic pathologists at NFC?'

Malin sighs.

'No. We will have to keep our fingers crossed that they can extract a usable DNA profile. I spoke to our adviser at the National Forensic Centre – who coordinates all our analyses – and she actually seemed hopeful. She said that even though the body had been in the water for a long time it had probably been in deep, cold, low-oxygenated conditions before the gas formation brought it to the surface and it washed ashore. And that increases the likelihood of them getting a profile.'

I consider what Malin has to say and my eyes land on the cinnamon buns on the table. I think of the Danish that is swimming around in my stomach and decide to abstain, because despite my appetite having returned at the same rate as Afsaneh's renewed hope for life, I have no desire to regain the two stone I have lost over the last month.

'And what about the other victim?' I ask.

Malin turns to me.

'Still unidentified,' she says. 'I have spoken to the forensic pathologist. She says she thinks we are dealing with a man between sixteen and eighteen years old. He has probably been in the water for about two weeks. The body was found on June 14th, so that would mean he was dumped somewhere at the turn of May into June. Cause of death has not been determined but the body had injuries similar to Ahonen's. Mainly we are talking about contusions and fractures on the left side of the body.'

'High-energy impact?' Letit asks.

'Exactly,' Malin says and gathers her long, dark hair in a loose bun at her neck. 'And these injuries were also inflicted post-mortem, so we can probably assume that the cases are connected. The technician also confirmed that the chain is identical to the one used to sink Ahonen. And the white fabric he was wrapped in was an ordinary sheet, bought at Ikea. Can likely be found in thousands of Swedish homes.'

'Have you compared the victim to lists of missing persons?' I ask.

'I'm in the process of doing that. There are maybe three possible people. I'll get back to you on that this afternoon.'

Malin looks at her notes to make sure she hasn't missed anything.

'There is one more thing,' she says. 'Victim number two had a nail in his right heel.'

'A nail?' Letit asks, leaning forward. 'What kind of nail?'

'A regular carpenter's nail,' Malin says. 'Two and a quarter inches, or fifty-six millimetres.'

'Did he step on a nail?' Letit asks, looking at Malin with fresh, almost benevolent interest.

'Well, no,' she says. 'It was deeply embedded in the calcaneus, the heel bone. Either someone shot him in the foot with a nail gun, or a hammer was used to drive it in.'

She pauses, then continues: 'And that was not post-mortem,' she says. 'Somebody drove a nail into his foot while he was alive.'

'Bloody hell,' Letit says, grimacing. '*Fuck*.'

I arrive at the hospital at the same time as Afsaneh.

I spot her at a distance as she approaches the entrance. She is wearing a red summer dress and the wind is playing in her long shiny hair as it falls over her shoulders.

When I take her into my arms there is a faint smell of cigarette smoke and the perfume I know that she likes, the one I bought her last Christmas at my favourite department store Le Bon Marché in Paris.

'Hey, you,' she says and kisses me on the mouth.

'Hey, you,' I answer and hold her long and hard.

Then she takes my hand and we walk to the PICU together on feet lighter than we have known in a long time.

I have spent considerably more time in hospitals than your average Swede, which probably should have cured this phobia.

But it hasn't.

As soon as I step through the revolving door my pulse quickens and something tightens in my chest. My breathing becomes laboured and the memories wash over me.

But today Aron is far away.

Afsaneh's laughter and the sun shining in through the large windows keeps him at bay.

Everything looks normal in Nadja's room, despite the fact that something crucial is about to happen, something that will forever change our lives.

We just don't know what the outcome will be.

I look at my daughter who is lying still in bed. She looks so desperately small and helpless amidst all the tubes and monitors. The little clamp that measures her oxygen levels is attached to her index finger as usual and I can still see the chipped pink nail polish on the other fingers.

The door opens and the doctor comes in.

It is Angelica again – we know all the intensive care doctors by now.

We chat for a while about the weather before she asks us to sit down in the visitors' chairs.

'We have begun decreasing the dosage of the sedative,' she says. 'But we have to decrease the other medication slowly.'

Afsaneh nods intently and I can't help wonder if she really understands the kind of turning point we are facing. If she has seriously considered that Nadja may not wake up at all. That there actually is a risk that our wonderful, spirited daughter could remain a vegetable.

'It could be days before we know if she will wake up,' Angelica continues. 'And it could be weeks or months before we know how well she will recover *if* she wakes up. But one thing is certain, she will *not* wake up today. It will take more time.'

'We know,' Afsaneh says and smiles. 'But we can wait.'

She pauses briefly and meets my gaze. Then continues: 'We have nothing but time.'

Samuel

When I wake up the sun is already high. There's a clatter of pots and pans from the first floor.

I look around and at first don't understand where I am. But then everything falls into place. Rachel. The white house with the green windows. And zombie-Jonas. His pale, waxen skin, the tube coming out of his nose like a long worm and that strange structure with the blue harness.

I'm really here.

It's completely fucking messed up.

But my body is content. My body is warm and full and hasn't woken me up once all night. My body feels very comfortable in the bed in the white house and has no objections whatsoever to me nannying a weirdo for 111 kronor an hour.

I reach for my mobile that is charging on the bedside table. Without thinking I turn it on, because it is as natural as drinking or taking a piss.

Half past eight.

Mum has sent me a text message.

She writes that she loves me and wants me to come home again.

I close my eyes and a warm feeling spreads in my chest. I touch the glass beads on the bracelet.

For a moment I contemplate answering her immediately, but instead I open Insta. Alexandra has posted pictures from some party. She is holding a glass of wine and pursing her lips. Her eyes are open wide and her lashes look unnaturally long, like spider legs reaching for the ceiling. In her slightly lowered gaze there is a hint of something bleary and provocative.

Fifty-seven likes.

Jeanette has posted a picture in which she is straddling a chair. Her skirt is short and pushed up her muscular thighs. I can glimpse the lace panties under the hem. She smiles and her mouth, shiny with lip gloss, reflects the light from the flash.

Two hundred and eleven likes.

Fucking slut.

Then I realise what I am doing and turn the mobile off – it mustn't be on under any circumstances.

In my mind's eye I see Igor's shaved head and Malte's thin pockmarked cheeks.

I get up slowly and go into the family room, then into the bathroom, where I take a piss and a long shower. When I am done I wrap the towel around my hips and go back to get dressed, but I end up standing in front of the large windows in the family room.

The view is enrapturing.

I really cannot find a better word. Enrapturing tends to be one of those words they like to use at Mum's church, and really I don't like those words, on principle.

Because they are God's words and he doesn't want anything to do with you.

But in this case the view happens to be precisely enrapturing.

The sea glimmers in the sun and the lighthouse is stark against the light blue morning sky. A soft haze rises from the water, partially obscuring the horizon.

I'm just about to enter my room when I see her.

Rachel is jogging down the long winding wooden staircase towards the water. She is wearing her long hair down and a blue bathrobe that is far too big.

Her steps are light. It almost looks as if she is dancing towards the edge of the cliff.

When she gets down she goes all the way out onto the jetty, so far that her toes are over the edge. Then she pulls a mobile out of her pocket and holds it up, as if she is taking a picture – first of the sea and then of herself. Then she puts the phone back in her pocket, drops the robe and dives into the water in one movement.

It takes me a couple of seconds to realise that she is naked.

I look around.

I do it reflexively, because I don't seriously think that there is anyone in here who can see me spying on Rachel.

When I turn to the water again I can't see anything. Not a ripple on the smooth surface. It is as if she was never there. But the bathrobe lying in a pile on the jetty tells me I wasn't dreaming.

Where did she go? What if she dived straight into a rock or something? Should I go down and look for her?

Just as I articulate the question to myself, Rachel's head emerges at least twenty yards from the jetty. With slow, smooth movements she begins a crawl swim to the shore. When she gets to the jetty she heaves herself up and sits on the edge for a while with her legs in the water.

I know that I should leave now, that I should disappear into my room and get dressed rather than stand here by the window looking at her like some kind of perv, but I can't. Something about her slender body and the way that she splashes her legs in the water has an almost hypnotic effect on me.

She gets up, still with her back to me – leans to the side and twists her long hair so that the water drips onto the jetty and forms a gleaming puddle.

Then she turns around and I see it.

She is beautiful.

She is so fucking beautiful.

Her breasts are full, her thighs are a bit rounder than Alexandra's, and between her legs there is a big bush of dark hair, the kind I've only seen in practically antique porn.

I swallow and feel myself getting hard even as I am overcome with throbbing shame.

For fuck's sake, she is as old as my mum.

I can't be standing here getting horny for a *forty-year-old*, whose freak of a son I am supposed to be taking care of.

For 111 fucking kronor an hour.

It is *beyond* fucking bizarre.

After breakfast Rachel follows me into zombie-Jonas's room and asks me to sit in the granny chair as she strokes his hair and explains that I'm here.

Just like yesterday Jonas is completely motionless in bed and doesn't seem to understand a thing. All that confirms that he is alive is the regular rise and fall of his chest and slight spasms in the fingers on one hand.

Rachel goes up to the table and gets the book that is lying next to a speaker, hands it to me and says: 'Read!'

Then she makes herself comfortable in the chair and reaches for the hand cream that is next to the vase with the rose. She slaps the tube against the palm of her hand several times before she gets anything. But in the end she succeeds and starts to massage Jonas's right hand.

'Read!' she says again.

At first I think I've misunderstood her — surely she isn't going to sit there listening to me as I read?

She looks amused when she meets my gaze.

'I was joking,' she says and lets out a quiet laugh. 'You don't need to read to me. I am just going to moisturise Jonas's hands, then I'm going to sit down and work. He had a hard night. I injected him with a sedative at five this morning, so he won't make any trouble.'

'OK,' I say and watch her as she smooths cream into the other hand.

Rachel is wearing a thin white summer singlet and the same worn jeans as yesterday. Her hair, which is still wet, is up in a tight bun at the back of her neck. Her face is smooth and without make-up.

Once again I am struck by how much she looks like my mother.

'There,' she says and stands up. 'You can begin reading by the bookmark, OK?'

'Sure,' I say and study the cover.

The book is called *The Sun Also Rises*, written by someone named Hemingway.

I have never heard of the book or the author, but dutifully open it at the page Rachel showed me and begin to read, slowly and very quietly.

At first it feels awkward and I stumble, but then it flows pretty well. I pause, leaf forward and back to understand the context.

The book is about an American in Paris, who mostly seems to hang out at nightclubs and bars with other rich expats who don't have jobs.

Reading about them makes me think a bit about Liam and me. We actually have some things in common with the characters in the novel, except that we have to steal stuff to afford not to work.

The American is in love with a divorced girl, but they can never have one another, since a battle wound has made the guy impotent. And that is about where I get tired of the book. Yeah, I get that it sucks to lose the use of your dick, but I don't want to read a whole book about it.

Besides the chick he is in love with seems pretty messed up.

I would have dumped her right away.

I put the book aside and look at Jonas.

He doesn't move a muscle.

I get up and stand closer, lean towards his ear.

'Hallo!'

No movement.

'*Halloo*, anybody home?' I try, a bit louder this time.

But zombie-Jonas just lies there looking as dead as a plastic-wrapped fish in the refrigerated counter at a supermarket.

Unease comes creeping like a furry spider.

I don't like this room. I don't like the drawings hanging on the walls, they remind me far too much of my own drawings that my mum has saved in a folder back in Fruängen. And the Hammarby team flag and the boots make me think of when I used to play in Älvsjö AIK in primary school.

I look at Jonas.

Once he was just like me, I think. If I'd been unlucky and fallen in front of a bus I could have been the one lying there in bed, forced to listen to some idiot reading aloud and having hand cream rubbed all over my goddamn body.

I look at the clock: almost eleven.

I get up and sneak into the bathroom that connects Rachel's and Jonas's rooms. It is big and white and has a hand-held shower with a very long hose. Maybe it's for washing Jonas when he is hanging in that weird blue harness.

Rachel must be working because I can clearly hear the tapping from her computer keyboard from her bedroom.

Tap, tap, tap. Tap-tap.

Sometimes it is quiet for a while, as if she is thinking about something, but then she begins to type again.

I think.

If I am quiet I can have a look around the house. Perhaps I can even find something of value, something I can sell.

I go back into Jonas's room and carefully close the door to the bathroom behind me.

'I'll be right there,' I mumble, without even glancing at the figure in the bed.

I don't even know why I say that; he doesn't understand anyway. But it feels decent somehow.

After all he is a human being, not a fish.

The kitchen is neat and has been cleaned up after breakfast; the crumbs have been wiped away and the dishes put into the dishwasher.

Next to the bread bin there is a stack of paper.

I leaf through it.

At the top there is a form from the Swedish Social Insurance Agency, headed 'Application for reimbursement for caregiver'. Somebody has attached a small pamphlet to the sheet with a paper clip: 'The law about support and service for certain disabled people, LSS – a digest for next of kin.'

I put the pages back and begin to go through the cabinets and drawers without really finding anything of interest. All I come across is worn china and old, mismatched cutlery.

'Can I help you find something?'

I turn around.

Rachel is standing in the doorway. Her smile is warm and her eyes are shining. She has a wallet in her hand.

'I . . . some water.'

'There is sparkling water in the fridge if you want it,' she says, then turns around and puts on a pair of clogs. 'I'm going to do some shopping, OK?'

I nod without answering.

I remain standing in the kitchen for a long time after Rachel leaves. Then I go to her bedroom.

The double bed is neatly made and on one bedside table there is a stack of books. Across from the bed there is a wardrobe made out of dark wood with two doors.

I open one of them.

Blouses, dresses and trousers hang on hangers. Below them shoes vie for space. Behind the other door hang men's shirts, a few pairs of chinos and some knitted sweaters.

Those must be her partner's clothes.

I go into the bathroom.

Above the sink there is a white medicine cabinet. The door slides open with a squeak when I push the gold-coloured knob.

There are two shelves in the cabinet. On the top shelf there are girly creams, a few bottles of perfume, a deodorant and a box of tampons. On the lower is an electric razor and a jar of hair wax.

I carefully close the door and look around.

There is a large metal cabinet next to one wall. It looks almost like a filing cabinet, of the kind one would find in an office.

I feel the handle.

Locked.

Carefully I feel around with my hand along the top edge of the cabinet, and *bingo*, there's a small key.

The key slides easily into the lock and I know it fits even before I've turned it.

My pulse quickens.

You don't lock a cabinet unless there is something important inside. You don't lock a cabinet full of toilet paper and toothpaste.

The door slides open and reveals shelves full of medicine. Pills, injection vials, needles and syringes.

My first reaction is disappointment, but then I look closer at the packaging. I vaguely recognise some of the names: Dexmedetomidine, Klonodine, Midazolam, Xanax, Klonopin, Stesolid and Fentanyl, 50 microgram/ml. injection fluid.

Wait a minute.

Fentanyl.

Even though Igor and Malte are strictly old school, I do know a thing or two about prescription drugs. They are hard currency on the street, after all, and are increasingly giving street drugs a run for their money. And Fentanyl is worth its weight in gold. Malte has told me how junkies cut up Fentanyl patches into tiny pieces and eat them.

I run my finger across the packages.

There are fourteen vials of Fentanyl on each shelf and there are three shelves – a total of forty-two vials. That's enough dope to knock out an entire fucking school class for weeks.

I think about it for a while, then I take three vials of Fentanyl and pocket them. They give off a dull clink as they slide into my pocket.

Will she notice that they're gone?

The neat rows of little glass vials filled with translucent fluid makes me suspect that she knows exactly how many she has. I sense that Rachel is a bit like me, that she can count.

On the shelf below, some empty vials lie randomly and I have an idea. I take a syringe out of its plastic cover and fill it with water from the tap. Then I put the needle through the thin rubber membrane on one of the empty vials and shoot the water into it.

When I pull the needle out the membrane closes up again. I lean forward and take a look at the thin rubber cover.

You can't see that I punctured it.

I put the bottle back, next to the other, full vials.

It looks exactly like the others.

After that I repeat the procedure with another two vials, so that I have replaced those that are in my pocket.

Surely this won't hurt zombie-Jonas? It's just water, and our bodies are seventy per cent water after all.

I take a deep breath, close the cabinet, lock it and put the key back where I found it.

As I do that I hear a dull thud.

I turn around and see Rachel in Jonas's room.

She is holding a shopping bag in her hand and her mouth is half open, as if she is trying to understand what she is looking at but can't quite. Her eyes look almost scared and the knuckles on the hand squeezing the bag are white.

'We ran out of hand cream,' I manage. 'I was just checking to see if there was more.'

Pernilla

When I have counted the money in the till and filled in the daily report I go into the office and knock on Stina's door.

'Come in,' she shouts.

I open the book and put the report on her desk.

Stina looks up over her reading glasses and smiles so that her blotchy skin folds like a dry old hide over her cheek bones.

'Thank you, dear,' she says. 'See you tomorrow.'

'Yes, see you,' I say and smile, turning around to leave.

'Wait,' Stina says, 'how did things go with your son?'

I freeze mid-step and consider my options.

How honest can I be?

Stina is nice and means well, I am sure of that. But she is also curious, like most people working here.

I decide to compromise. A halfway that doesn't make me seem too buttoned-up, but also won't supply her with juicy gossip for the staff room.

'He's gone,' I say. 'We had a disagreement and I threw him out. Well, that was Monday and now I can't get hold of him.'

'What are you saying?' Stina says and her eyes widen. 'That must be so hard for you. But I am sure he will be home soon. Björn disappears sometimes too. I guess it's part of being young.'

Even though Stina is past sixty she has a son Samuel's age.

I got started early, Stina started late.

She pauses. Takes her glasses off and lays them on the table next to the cash ledger. Then she continues: 'Was that why the cops were here?'

I hesitate.

'Yes,' I say. And manage to keep myself from elaborating even though the words are impatiently waiting at the tip of my tongue.

I feel my cheeks flush.

It is crazy that, at age thirty-six, I can't lie without feeling deeply ashamed. I can't manage even a little white lie without thinking of Jesus and the Final Judgement.

I can tell that Stina would like to know more, but instead of asking further questions she smiles again and says: 'It will all work out, you'll see. Now go home and get some rest.'

'I will,' I say, but end up standing on the floor in front of her unable to move.

I feel tears run down my cheeks and blink in surprise.

'Oh, sweetie.'

Stina gets up and comes over to me. Puts a hand on my back and assertively leads me over to the chair in front of her little desk.

'How are you?' she asks and resolutely pushes me into the broken wicker seat.

I look at the piles of paper on her desk. Catch the smell of cigarette butts in the ashtray.

Then it all comes out. All the words that have been waiting to be said rush out of me, unfiltered. I tell her about Samuel's disappearance, the bald man who scared me half to death in the stairwell, and what I have found out about Mother. I even tell her about the pastor: how he took advantage of my body in the congregation hall while Jesus watched from the cross.

'Oh, sweetie,' Stina says again and shakes her head. 'Oh, sweetie.'

And suddenly it feels good to hear her say that. As if her words alone could heal me.

'Let's deal with one thing at a time,' she says with authority.

She gets up, walks over to the worn old grey metal filing cabinet and pulls out one of the drawers.

I watch her broad back, see how her arms sort of overflow from her blouse, notice the frayed red hair that fans like a halo around her head.

The paper rustles as she digs around in the folders and the shiny synthetic sweater strains across her shoulders.

Then she closes the drawer again and returns with a flask and two small glasses.

'Are you kidding?' I say. 'Surely we can't sit here . . . ? I mean, technically this is working hours. Even though we're closed. But we're still getting paid. And we are *in* the shop. So. Even though there are no customers who . . . Well, what if someone . . . ?'

'Hush,' Stina says, raising her liver-spotted hand at me.

Then she unscrews the lid and pours the amber liquid into the glasses. Hands me one and gives a quick nod.

'Drink!'

I do what she tells me.

My throat burns as the alcohol makes its way down to my stomach.

'Now listen,' Stina says. 'It's terrible that your father denied your mother access to you, but there's nothing you can do about it n—'

'Father saved me,' I interrupt. 'He loved me even though I sinned and he helped me raise Samuel. I would never have made it without him.'

'It sounds to me like he was very controlling towards you,' Stina interjects, empties her glass in one swig and puts it on the table with a thud. 'That hit the spot,' she mumbles and inhales.

'But it was in my best interest—' I begin.

'Nonsense,' she growls. 'You should see yourself when you talk about your dad. You're like a dog afraid of being hit, scared and submissive. All men like that want is to control us women.'

I think of Father when we prayed for Mother's soul. How he laid his big dry hands against my cheeks and whispered: 'God created woman from a rib so that she would complement man. Not from the head, so that she would lord over him. Not from his feet so that he would step on her. No, from a rib, so that she would be protected. Close to his heart, to be loved.'

'There's nothing to gain by confronting him now,' Stina says. 'As for that pastor, I don't think you should be too upset that he revealed himself to be a horny old goat. It is just as well that you saw his true nature, don't you think? It might be time for you to re-evaluate him and the congregation too.'

'But he has helped me and Samuel so much.'

'How so?' Stina snorts.

'He has lent me money. And I have been given various re-sponsibilities in the church.'

'And you think that's a *coincidence*?'

My cheeks burn when I understand what she is saying. And she may be right because the pastor has always picked me first for all activities and often chose to speak with me in private. And when we spoke in private he would always touch me. Not in a sexual way, but still – a hand on mine, an arm around my shoulder when we went to the pantry to get coffee. Stroking my cheek with the back of his hand.

At the time I took his ministrations to be fatherly, but in light of his recent actions I too can see the pattern.

'Obviously he has been planning it for a long time,' she says as if she can read my mind. 'He's no dummy, that's for sure. He wanted to get close to you. And he wanted you to be indebted to him. But forget him.'

She waves her hand a little and continues: 'What we have to focus on is Samuel. It sounds as if he's running with a bad crowd. Have you spoken to his friends?'

'Not all of them.'

'Do it. Let's not get ahead of ourselves and assume you won't be able to find him, but I still think you should go to the police and report him missing. Because even though they came here asking about him they don't know he is missing. For real, that is.'

She pauses and looks me up and down.

'I'll go with you,' she says. In a way that leaves no room for argument.

'Perhaps we should wait a few days?'

Stina runs her index finger under her chin and looks pensive.

'Yes,' she says, hesitating. 'Let's wait a few days. But now you should go home and get some sleep, Pernilla. You need to rest. Call if you need anything. It doesn't matter if it's the middle of the night. You shouldn't have to deal with something like this on your own.'

'OK,' I say and get up.

The alcohol has made my legs soft and warm and my cheeks burn.

'And thank you,' I say.

Stina stands, comes up to me and gives me a long hug.

'We have to stick together against the odds,' she says briefly, with her mouth against my ear.

My eyes fall on the photo of Björn, her son, on her desk.

He has thick, strawberry blonde hair and freckles. His eyes are pale grey and his lips are full. The long hair and the generously proportioned mouth make him look like a young Liv Ullman.

Stina takes a step back and sees my gaze.

'It will work out, you'll see,' she says. 'It always works out.'

And for a moment I actually believe her.

I carry those words with me into the summer evening. But even as I walk towards the station the anxiety comes creeping and my thoughts start chasing each other at warp speed.

I think of Mother. Of that day she died on her way to our home. The tears come again, but now I am thinking of Samuel. I say a short prayer.

'God, watch over Samuel and show him the way. Let him come back to me and I promise I will do everything in my power to help him sort his life out. In Jesus' name. Amen.'

But God doesn't answer this time either.

God is as quiet as Samuel and the cool summer evening.

There is something else that is bothering me.

When Samuel was three years old Isaac showed up like Jack-in-a-box. As if everything were forgiven and forgotten.

I don't know what he had imagined – that he would just be able to waltz in and assume the role of Samuel's father?

Of course I explained that would not be possible, that I'd already told Samuel and all of our friends that his father was dead and that we had built ourselves a functional life in which there really was no space for him.

This upset Isaac and he nagged. At one point he even tried to kiss me at a café.

I was very close to giving in, because he was still just as handsome as when we were together, even though he had cut his hair and got a job and a record shop on Södermalm.

But this time I restrained myself. Surely I'd learned something?

Regardless, Isaac was very persistent and began talking about going to social services and demanding some kind of visitation rights.

That scared me.

After all, he was Samuel's biological father and who knew what could happen if he began to make trouble?

So we made an agreement.

I promised Isaac that he could come and visit Samuel every year on his birthday and on Boxing Day, and in return he promised not to reveal that he was Samuel's father.

And that's what we did.

I told Samuel that Isaac was an old friend of mine, who was very lonely and didn't have any family. And Isaac visited punc-tually, twice a year, from when Samuel was three until he turned fifteen. Then he moved to Gävle and his visits became more sporadic.

As far as I know he never married or had any other children.

They say it is important for boys to grow up with a male role model. I guess that is especially true for boys like Samuel – boys with problems. I can't help but wonder if he would have turned out differently had Isaac been more of a presence in his life.

But I was just doing what I thought was in Samuel's best interests – much like I assume my father did for me.

Maybe there really is an original sin in our family, but a completely different one than what I thought, one that has to do with denying our children contact with people who don't live up to the strict standards we have imposed upon ourselves.

One that robs our children of those closest to them.

The train rolls into the station, doors open and I step in. I sit down by the window and look out at the summer evening.

I could leave the congregation.

I don't know where the thought comes from, I have never thought that before and am immediately horrified.

I can't do that.

Why would I do that?

But the answer comes to me in the same instant I articulate the question: all these rules and the condemnation of those who don't measure up are one of the reasons that Samuel and I are where we are today. That, and my reluctance to accept that Samuel might have problems that are so big they can't be cured with prayer and fish oil.

And now there is nothing to keep me in the congregation anymore. Other than friends.

And God.

But surely there is nothing to say that I have to abandon God just because I leave the congregation?

I don't dare follow the thought further – I am far too afraid of where all those rebellious thoughts might lead me if I decide to go with them. So I take out my mobile and call Alexandra, Samuel's girlfriend, or whatever she is.

I don't really dare ask.

She answers after three rings. Her voice sounds happy, but when she hears who it is she immediately becomes subdued.

'I don't know where he is,' she says quickly. 'Haven't seen him since Monday.'

'Have you spoken with him on the phone?' I try.

There is a brief pause. The train slows down at Telefonplan and the woman sitting across from me gets up and leaves.

'No,' she says. 'We got into a bit of a fight so . . .'

She leaves the sentence unfinished and I can hear music in the background.

'Do you have any idea where he might be?'

'No. The police were here and asked the same thing. Apparently, they'd been to Liam's too. I have no idea what Samuel is involved in, but he might be lying low for a bit. If the cops are after him, that is.'

I ask her to tell Samuel to get in touch if he calls her and then we hang up.

My anxiety grows, my insides ache and I feel sick. Images of Samuel, Father and Mother play for my inner eye.

Dearest Samuel.

My little bumblebee.

Why does everything end up so wrong when all we want is to do right?

Manfred

Afsaneh brushes Nadja's tangled curls with a small pink brush. Then she settles down on the chair next to me.

'Shouldn't she be waking up soon?' she asks without meeting my gaze, as if she isn't asking me, but rather expressing a general frustration, or addressing some higher power.

'They said it could take a long time,' I answer.

'But it's been several days.'

'It could take weeks.'

Afsaneh squirms.

'I can't wait weeks.'

'Do we have any choice?'

The door opens and Dennis comes in.

Dennis is one of the doctors who has been responsible for Nadja since we got here. He is young, so young that I know Afsaneh has a hard time feeling any real confidence in him.

Personally, I have no problem with his age. In my experience the younger doctors – and police officers for that matter – are often well-educated and ambitious. Additionally, they haven't been broken down by the system yet; haven't had time to become cynical and indifferent to all the shit they have to deal with.

Afsaneh stands up and goes to meet him.

'Why isn't she waking up?' she asks, without saying hello, or softening the question in any way.

Dennis smiles uncertainly and glances at me.

'You'll probably have to wait another couple of days. And there isn't really any reason for you to be here all the time. We'll call you as soon as there is any change to her condition.'

'But I want to be *here* when she wakes up,' Afsaneh says.

'I understand. But we haven't fully phased out all the sedatives yet. This will take time. We will call you when—'

'Did you not hear me? I want to be *here* when my daughter wakes up. I don't want a bunch of strangers to be the first people she sees.'

I get up, walk up to Afsaneh and put my arm around her shoulders.

'Come, my love,' I say. 'Let's go and get some coffee.'

She frees herself from my grip with a strength that surprises me.

'I don't want coffee,' she says. 'I want Nadja to wake up.'

Dennis looks helplessly at me. I think he understands that it isn't possible to talk to Afsaneh right now, that she is in a place where words can't reach her.

'I want her to *wake up*,' Afsaneh repeats and starts to pace back and forth in the room with her arms folded across her chest.

Neither Dennis nor I say anything.

I simply sit on the chair by Nadja's bed again. Look at the little body resting peacefully between the hospital sheets.

Dennis leaves after a while.

Afsaneh ceases her pacing and sits next to me.

'I don't know how much more I can take,' she whispers.

I meet her gaze. Her eyes are black, her face pale. Her mouth pressed hard into a bloodless line.

'You can take it,' I say. 'We can take it. Because we must.'

An hour later I go to the station.

I smoke three cigarettes on my way there with the window down and silently pray Afsaneh won't notice the smell when I get home.

She didn't want to let me go, but Dennis and I managed to convince her I wasn't of any use at the hospital.

Dark clouds have rolled in and the first raindrops begin to fall right as the silhouette of the hospital disappears in the rear-view mirror.

When I drive across the bridge to Kungsholmen the rain is pouring down and I can hear the low rumble of thunder in the distance. Pedestrians run past on the pavement with newspapers and jackets over their heads in fruitless attempts to stay dry.

I can't help but feel the weather is symbolic somehow, despite knowing it is just my lizard brain searching for connections where there are none – because why would the weather have anything to do with my daughter?

And yet it creeps in, the magical thinking, the childish, naïve idea of causality.

As if the universe cared.

The investigative unit has expanded.

In addition to Malin and Letit two new people have joined. Next to Letit is Malik, whom I worked with during the investigation of the murders in Ormberg. He is wearing his black hair in a ponytail. Water is dripping from the wet ends and I conclude that he was not able to avoid the downpour. Malik has acquired a fashionable beard and is dressed in skinny, cuffed jeans and a plaid shirt. I would probably call him a hipster, but I am far too old to be able to discern the many fluid nuances of popular culture with any certainty.

The forensic pathologist, Samira, is standing in front of the whiteboard. She smiles and gives me a little wave, I wave back.

Malin stands up and clears her throat.

'Samira Khan, forensic pathologist in Solna, is here to brief us on the results of the autopsy of victim number two,' she says, and pauses.

It is unusual for the forensic pathologist to come here. Typically, we obtain his or her conclusions through a written report. My guess is that Samira has found something out of the ordinary, something that needs discussing and explaining.

'Please,' Malin says and nods at Samira.

Samira begins her review by showing photos of the body where it was found.

'The victim is a man between sixteen and eighteen years of age. Healthy and in good physical shape, though somewhat underweight.'

Malin looks at me and I sense what she is thinking.

Sixteen to eighteen years old: we are talking about a child.

Samira continues to systematically go over the injuries, from head to toe. She tells us about the fractures and the contusions inflicted post-mortem and about the long nail found in the victim's heel.

When she gets to that part Letit squirms a bit in his seat, hums and ploughs his fingers through his wild beard.

Not even the most experienced investigator can remain indifferent to what the boy has suffered.

'Have we been able to determine the identity?' I ask.

Samira meets my gaze.

'We have compared the DNA profile to three possible candidates whom you found in missing persons. The victim is Victor Carlgren, seventeen years old, from Saltsjöbaden. He disappeared after a fight with his sister on May 10th.'

'What do we know about this Victor?' Malin asks.

Letit clears his throat and pushes his glasses further up his nose with his index finger.

'Well-behaved. Good grades. No known issues with drugs or criminality. The parents have been informed and questioned. It would seem he took the parents' motorboat and left. That had happened before, so they weren't all that worried initially. But when he didn't come back after one day they reported him missing and the coastguard initiated a search operation. They feared he had been in an accident at sea.'

'What were he and his sister fighting about?' Malin asks.

Letit puts one synthetic-clad leg over the other.

'Netflix,' he answers. 'It seems they wanted to watch different things.'

The room falls silent as we ponder the absurdity of the situation.

The very thought that something so banal might have triggered the series of events that led to Victor Carlgren's death is enough to make anybody uneasy.

'Well, damn,' Letit sighs and pushes a strand of grey hair into place on top of his head.

'Johannes Ahonen disappeared in early March,' Malin says quietly. 'Victor Carlgren disappeared May 10th. Both bodies were found in the southern Stockholm archipelago. Both had been subjected to considerable violence and were wrapped in fabric and chains. Even if we can't prove these are murders, I think we can assume that they are, and that we are dealing with the same killer.'

The room is quiet. Only the rain can be heard, which keeps tapping on the window with undiminished force, along with the swoosh of the ventilation system.

'There is more,' Samira says and arranges her thick black braid on her shoulder. 'As you know we found skin particles under Johannes Ahonen's nails. The technicians at NFC have managed to extract a DNA profile. And . . .'

Samira pauses as if she doesn't really know how to proceed.

'The DNA results show the skin is from Victor Carlgren,' she says, curtly.

'What?' Malin says and drops her pen on the table. 'I'm sorry, but I don't quite follow.'

Letit looks up from his notes.

'The skin under Johannes Ahonen's nails, victim number one, came from Victor Carlgren, victim number two,' Samira says slowly, as if she wants the message to sink in. 'And there are half-healed scratches on Carlgren's lower arms that I would guess were inflicted by Ahonen. Which is to say the victims have met, and likely they were involved in some type of physical altercation just before Ahonen died. But Carlgren didn't die until much later.'

'Well, I'll be damned,' Letit whispers and strokes his synthetic-trousered legs, setting off crackles of static electricity. 'I'll be damned.'

Samuel

I read to zombie-Jonas, but can barely hear what I am saying. My thoughts are elsewhere, far from Stuvskär and Igor and Rachel, who almost caught me red-handed stealing Fentanyl yesterday.

I think of Mum, of that text she sent.

Come home. I love you.

Poor, poor Mum.

She really did her best.

Even though many of her attempts to save me from myself are misguided, she did try, nobody can say that she didn't.

I remember all the times she took me to church. Remember the stern looks from the elders and that crazy guy Stephen, who spoke in tongues and maintained the Final Judgement was nigh just because everyone uses credit cards these days.

More than anything I remember the pastor's voice.

The way they sound exactly the same: the pastor and that voice in my head, the one that tells me how *fucking* useless I am.

That is probably no coincidence.

Anyway.

They did everything to make me a good Christian – it was children's Bible school and Christian scouts and intercession and every other thing one can imagine. They sat on the floor in a ring around me praying for my soul.

I mean, how messed-up is that?

All it did was make me more anti. I even went through a phase when I was fourteen or fifteen when I really read up, just to be able to argue *against* Mum.

I explained that Christianity wasn't Jesus' creation at all, but that other guy's, Paul's, and that he – aside from being both Roman and Jewish and having actually persecuted loads of Christians – was a narrow-minded male chauvinist pig who sent a bunch of self-satisfied letters to Christian congregations around the world. Besides which he pretended that he was, like, best friends with Jesus, even though he wasn't even a disciple.

And I was pretty cunning, because I used the congregation's own methods on Mum when I quoted the Bible.

Mum cried and cried and said that I had the Devil in me. That my soul was lost.

That I was besmirched.

Yes, that was the word she used.

As if I was a piece of shat-on toilet paper.

I look at zombie-Jonas.

Where is his immortal soul?

His face is expressionless and his mouth half-open. The skin on his face is a bit shiny, as if he were sweating. His body lies motionless between the starched sheets and one lone drop of water glimmers on the long tube coming out of his nose.

Maybe he just ate, or whatever you want to call it when someone pumps grub straight down a tube into your stomach.

I think of Mum again.

She thinks it's her fault that everything turned out the way it did, that I never finished high school and work for Igor. That it is because I didn't grow up in a nice, Christian nuclear family in a semi-detached house in a good suburb.

That everything would have been different if only I'd been properly saved.

I wish I could explain to her it has nothing to do with any of that.

That everything is actually my fault.

Poor Mum – all her work in vain.

Sometimes I wonder if she's had some secret guy. I almost hope she has, because the thought of her doing nothing but struggling and taking care of me all these years is almost unbearable.

Maybe she had something with her friend – that creepy American guy, Isaac – who came every birthday and Christmas and made me sit on his lap.

I didn't dare protest, I basically just sat there while he stared at me with his moist eyes, as if he wanted to eat me up.

Or worse.

I only did it because Mum had made an effort – cooked and bought presents and the rest of it.

Because even if I had the Devil in me I was no monster.

Zombie-Jonas groans. A spasm goes through his body, his eyelids flutter a little and for a second I think he is about to wake up, but then he is still again.

I keep reading.

The protagonist is on his way to Spain to go fishing. Aside from the fact that he isn't fucking, he seems to have a pretty decent life. He coasts around Europe, hangs out at various bars and meets cool people.

Jonas groans again, and this time I put the book down on the bedside table, get up and bend over him.

'Are you OK?' I ask, even though I know he can't hear me.

He groans again and moves one hand. It trembles a bit as he reaches towards the bedside table.

'*Ahhhhrggg,*' he gargles.

I freeze in fear.

Is this one of the fits Rachel was talking about?

'*Uhhrrg.*'

His body stiffens and it almost looks like he is reaching for something on the bedside table. A foamy strand of saliva falls out of the corner of his mouth and makes its way down his cheek.

But the only thing on the table is the vase with the red rose that has begun to droop a bit and the book that I just put down.

Does he want me to start reading again? Is that what he is trying to tell me?

'Are you OK?' I ask.

'*Gaahhh.*'

He makes a fist, but the index finger is pointing straight out. It seems to be aiming for the bedside table, almost as if he is pointing *towards* it.

I look at the table but don't understand.

On the end closest to the bed there are some scratches in the wood, as if Jonas had scratched the hard surface with his nails.

Poor bastard.

'Wait here,' I say and run out to get Rachel.

First I run to her room, because she has been sitting at her computer working all morning. I could hear the tapping from all the way out into the hallway.

But she isn't there. The desk is neat and tidy and the laptop is closed on top of a stack of paper.

I run out into the hall and open the front door.

The warm summer air hits me like a wall. There is a scent of roses and honeysuckle and damp soil. Bumblebees buzz around the flower beds.

The flycatcher looks out of the bird house that is nailed to the wall. She has just fed her young and is on her way out to find new insects.

The male is nowhere to be seen. Perhaps he is off looking for a new territory – they do that. While the female hunts food for the chicks all day. She does everything in her power for them.

I think of Mum, which immediately puts me in a bad mood.

Rachel is kneeling in front of the young rose bushes in the raised bed with pruning shears in her hand. She is wearing a scarf on her head and yellow gardening gloves on her hands. The skin on her shoulders is red, as if she burned herself slightly in the sun. Next to her is a wicker basket where she has put cut stems and dead branches.

Her smile disappears when she sees my eyes.

'Something is wrong with Jonas,' I manage.

Rachel leaps up, drops the shears and runs toward me. She takes the yellow gloves off and throws them to the ground. They end up in the grass like giant chanterelles.

'Did he say anything?' she pants and I sense fear in her eyes, fear and something else.

Hope, maybe?

'No, he just sort of gargled.'

I follow Rachel as she runs into Jonas's room, sinks down next to him and strokes his hair. The scarf has slid off her head and is hanging loose on her back.

'Darling Jonas,' she says. 'Darling. How are you?'

'*Ahgg*,' Jonas says. '*Uaahhgg.*'

The body in the bed stiffens and then flexes, like a spring. There's a jolt underneath the sheets and the metal bed gives off an alarming squeak.

'Quick,' Rachel says. 'Give me the syringe and the vial on the shelf.'

I turn around and let my eyes wander across the shelves of plastic bags, nitrile exam gloves and medicine jars. And there, next to a stack of paper towels, is a syringe and needle packaged in plastic, next to a small glass vial.

I grab the needle and the vial and hand them to Rachel.

Rachel tears open the packaging, takes the syringe out, sticks the needle into the vial and withdraws some of the contents. Then she turns the needle upwards, flicks the syringe with her fingers and pushes out a drop of colourless fluid.

'Help me turn him a bit,' she says.

When I go up to Jonas I am so fucking scared I almost piss my pants, but at the same time I am determined to do what I can to help.

'Here,' she says. 'Grab his shoulder and I'll take his hip.'

With a joint effort we turn Jonas on his side.

Rachel pulls the sheet down and plunges the needle into one of his buttocks.

'*Aughh*,' Jonas gargles and his body goes taut under my grip. But seconds later he sighs deeply and relaxes. His shoulder softens under my grip, his head drops down towards the white cotton pillow and his facial expression relaxes.

Rachel sinks down onto the floor and ends up seated with her back to the bed. She lets out a quiet groan.

After a while she stands up, throws the syringe and the packaging in the bin and reaches for the scarf that has slid onto the floor.

'Thank you,' she says, with tears in her eyes. 'Thank you, Samuel. I don't know what I would have done without you.'

I nod without saying anything, but feel my cheeks grow red from pride and embarrassment.

'Come on,' she says. 'I'll make a cup of tea. He'll sleep for a while now.'

We drink tea in silence in the yellow kitchen.

Outside clouds have gathered and the branches on the bushes bend in the wind.

It looks like rain.

Rachel seems sad and tired. The wrinkles around her eyes have deepened and she is slouched forward with her teacup resting between the palms of her hands.

Once again I am reminded of how much she looks like my mum. It's not just her appearance, it is something about the look on her face.

She just looks so resigned.

'Things will get easier when Olle comes home,' she says. 'Everything will be easier then.'

'Where is he?'

She looks at me and seems surprised.

'Didn't I tell you? He is in Stockholm meeting with social services. That and a few other things. He will be back in a few days. But he has a novel to finish, so I don't think we will see a whole lot of him.'

I stretch a little and my phone almost falls out of my pocket. I take it out and put it next to my cup of tea.

Rachel glances at the screen.

'Can I see?' she says and reaches for it.

Reluctantly I show her the background image in which Mum and I are standing in front of the pastor's new red sports car.

'Your mum?'

I nod.

Rachel looks at me and then at the picture.

'You are alike,' she says. 'The same facial shape, the same . . .'

She goes quiet and stands up.

'Hold on,' she says and disappears towards Jonas's room.

A while later she returns with a couple of photo albums under her arm. She sits down on one of the dainty chairs and begins to leaf through one of them.

Her face softens and the deep furrow in her forehead disappears when her gaze falls on a boy who might be about five years old. He is sitting in a toy car, wearing a Spider-Man shirt. His bare legs are pale and have red marks that could be mosquito bites.

'I had one just like that,' I say, leaning forward to see better.

Rachel's scent of orange blossom and marzipan tickles my nose. My stomach tingles for some reason I can't quite identify.

As if a bumblebee just woke up and was tumbling around in there.

'The same toy car?' she asks and smiles.

'No, the Spider-Man shirt.'

'Ah. He loved that stupid shirt. He kept wearing it for at least a year longer than he should have; it had holes in it. I felt embarrassed at nursery.'

Rachel laughs and turns the page.

Jonas smiles at me from a portrait. He looks to be seven or eight years old. His skin is tanned and his hair bleached at the tips.

He looks so different from the zombie that's lying in the bed in the other room. It is almost impossible to grasp that it is the same person. Once again, I think that Jonas and I were probably pretty alike. That I could have been the one drooling in that bed, had life taken a different turn.

The thought makes the room move and I grab the table.

Rachel nods.

'Look at the eyes,' she says. 'Do you see?'

I look at the eyes. At the thin, sun-bleached brows and at the eyelids that look slightly heavy, even though he is just a child.

And I do see it.

I see Rachel in his face.

'You look alike,' I whisper.

She moves closer to me so that I will be able to see better. Her arm rests right next to mine, so close that I can feel the warmth radiating from her skin.

The bumblebee in the pit of my stomach wakes up again and my crotch tingles.

'We *looked* alike,' she corrects. 'After the accident, *he* . . . he has changed.'

Her face hardens and I have a sudden impulse to put my arm around her and comfort her, the way I do with Alexandra.

At the same time I am aware of all the other stuff: the rounded breasts underneath her tank top, the curve of her thin neck and the outline of her clavicles under her skin.

So messed-up.

She could be my mum, for fuck's sake.

'What happened to him?' I manage, even though my mouth feels as dry as the rocks baking in the sun outside.

'Car accident. A hit-and-run. He wasn't critically injured at all, but something happened at the hospital. Suddenly he took a turn for the worse. The doctors think it was oxygen deprivation or maybe a stroke.'

I don't know what to say.

'He had his whole life ahead of him,' Rachel adds and blinks quickly several times.

Then she draws a deep breath.

'And you?'

'Me?'

I don't understand what she means.

Rachel smiles and puts her hand on my arm.

My skin feels hot under her fingers, as if someone set it on fire. As if every single cell was aglow under her touch.

'Yes, *you*, Samuel. How are things with your family? Are you close to your mum and dad?'

'I . . .'

The words refuse to leave my mouth. They are pressing inside. Shy like waxwings or thrushes hiding in the canopy of a mountain ash.

I try again.

'I . . . my dad is dead.'

Rachel's eyes widen.

'I'm sorry,' she says and touches my arm again, just briefly this time, so that I sort of lose my train of thought.

'And your mum?'

Rachel gives me a warm and encouraging look.

'Mum is. She . . . I think she is disappointed in me.'

'Why do you think that?'

Rachel sounds genuinely surprised.

'Because . . . she . . . I was running with a bad crowd. And she . . . threw me out.'

Then I tell her.

It just happens. I'm not sure why.

Maybe because Rachel told me about Jonas.

Obviously, I don't tell her anything about shoplifting or dealing. But I tell her about the church, about Alexandra and even that I am being followed by a scary guy called Igor. And I explain that my mum isn't happy with me. That I am her greatest disappointment. That she might not actually love me.

But Rachel just smiles and shakes her head.

'Silly,' she says.

And then:

'Of course she loves you. You are her child. You love your child, that's just how it is.'

She pauses briefly and continues: 'You said you were on the run from that guy Igor?'

'Mhm.'

'Have you spoken to your mum since?'

Her face is hard now and she almost looks a bit strict.

'Well, no, I . . . she is always mad worried something will happen.'

Rachel smiles sadly.

'All mums worry.'

She pauses and then goes on.

'So you never worry?'

'No,' I say. 'I'm not that worried about something terrible happening. Or at least I wasn't before Igor . . . I was probably more worried about . . .'

'What?' Rachel asks and looks genuinely interested.

'That nothing would happen,' I say and know immediately that it is true.

My nightmare was always getting stuck in that room in Fruängen for the rest of my life. That everything would just keep on going. Mum's nagging, the nineteen-minute train ride to the city, the days imperceptibly adding up, becoming months and years. And next thing I know I'm sitting there and am, like, thirty years old and life is over.

Rachel looks both sad and amused. Then her gaze falls on the photo albums and her face contorts in pain.

'No,' she says. 'We can't sit around here all day.'

She stretches and the thin fabric of her singlet strains across her breasts.

I immediately look down at the table.

We work in the garden in the afternoon. The air is colder and a bit muggy, as if a thunderstorm is approaching. Dark, blueish-purple clouds have rolled in over the mainland, piling up like a giant wall to the west.

I have helped Rachel mend a big hole in the fence and she has raked pine cones from the lawn on the short end of the house.

Now she squints at the sky and goes over to pick up the gardening gloves and the shears that still lie discarded in the grass.

She stops for moment when she passes me.

'I know,' she says. 'Could you help me screw the security bars back on outside Jonas's window? They've come loose on the bottom.'

'Sure,' I say, shrugging slightly.

Rachel hurries away toward the storage cupboard.

A minute or so later she is back with screws and an electric screwdriver.

'There have been a few burglaries around here,' she says, nodding at the window bars. 'So better safe than sorry.'

I don't say anything but think that anyone who broke into this house would probably be disappointed.

Who would want to steal adult nappies and laxatives?

'It's probably the junkies over at the campsite,' Rachel mumbles and her mouth turns into a thin line. 'I guess they have to finance their habit somehow. But when you live this isolated, with a disabled child, the last thing you want is a visit from some high hippie in the middle of the night.'

The bars in front of the window are thick and rusted. Two screw holes gape emptily where the bottom attaches.

I lean forward to get a better look.

There are holes in the wood under the holes in the metal. Splintered holes – it almost looks like someone pulled the screws out.

I screw the bars back on and give them a tug to test. They don't budge.

'There,' I say. 'Now it should be solid.'

Rachel's face lights up.

'Thank you so much! You are so good at this stuff. The fence also turned out well!'

'Nooo,' I say, looking down at the grass.

'*Yes*,' Rachel insists and laughs. 'I would never have managed this without you. You're strong and technically minded.'

My cheeks burn and I hope she doesn't notice. Mum would never have said that. Even if she thought it, she would never have said it.

I turn my gaze away from Rachel, down toward the peonies growing underneath the window. The stalks shoot like spears out of the tall grass. The swollen deep red buds have freed themselves from the sepals and look ready to burst at any moment. A vine clings to the wall. The light green leaves seem to grow as I watch them.

There is a smell of grass and damp soil, and of Rachel's perfume. The insects buzz and hum around us. Birds sing. Butterflies flutter by. Everything is so verdant, so juicy, so full of vigour and life.

Rachel leans in. A strand of her dark hair falls across her face. She moistens her lips with her tongue and the saliva glistens at the corner of her mouth.

Now, I think.

Now.

Now I am about to die. Now it will happen.

She reaches her arm towards my face. But instead of stroking me she hits me hard in the face.

'A mosquito,' she says and shows me the palm of her hand.

I see a bloody smear, as big as a portion of snuff.

My skin burns like fire after the slap and from the fact that she actually touched me. That her pale hand met my cheek – OK, she hit me, but *still*.

Part of me wishes she'd do it again.

I'm lying in bed trying to sleep, but can't get my thoughts to shut up. They are doing their best to drown each other out in my head, like starving, blind chicks in a bird house.

I can't stay here.

Anything is better than sitting with zombie-Jonas in that room that smells like old farts.

And this thing with Rachel – her face and body that show up in my head at the weirdest moments. Despite her being at least forty years old and having a partner who is about to return from Stockholm.

Despite her looking like *Mum*.

Despite everything being so wrong I can't help but think of her. Of her pale skin, the heavy breasts and the fine lines that frame her eyes when she laughs. And of her smile when she said I was 'strong and technically minded'.

You're trying to look good in front of a forty-year-old bitch because you dream of fucking her. That's pathetic. And bloody perverted.

I turn over on my side and puff my pillow a bit under my head. The summer night is dusky and endlessly long, like one of those French films we watched in school. In the bluish half-light I can make out the silhouette of the wardrobe and the small chair next to it. My dirty clothes lie thrown across the seat.

Sooner or later I'll have to wash them, but I have nothing else to wear. And I can't spend a whole day naked while I wait for my clothes to dry.

But I have bigger problems than dirty clothes.

I try to assess my options.

Going to the cops is out of the question. First off, I don't want to end up in jail and second, that would make it necessary to snitch on Igor, which would be like signing my own death warrant.

Because they can't get at Igor.

I always thought that compared to Igor the cops were no more dangerous than a paper tiger, but now that they're after me, I'd certainly rather avoid them. The problem is – I can't reach out to Igor or Malte to explain that everything is a mistake. Too much time has passed for me to have any kind of credibility crawling back to apologise. I should have been in touch immediately, told them where I hid the money and that I borrowed the bike.

The money.

I sit up in bed and catch my breath violently. The pillow falls onto the floor with a rustle.

The money.

Why didn't I think of that sooner?

There is at least two hundred thou under that rock in the woods by the industrial area. If I borrow a little I can lie low for a while, at least until all of this has died down.

I know Igor has talked about moving to Miami.

If he does it'll just be Malte left and even if he is a real arsehole he isn't as insane as Igor. Plus, I have something over him. I *saw* him give Igor's money to a chick who was supposed to be due for a beating.

A chick we paid a second visit to.

I recall the words Malte hissed in my ear at the redhead's apartment.

Not a word about this to anyone, do you understand? I'd be dead. And you too.

My heart beats faster in my chest.

I pick the pillow off the floor, lie on my back and stare at the ceiling.

How to get hold of the money? I can hardly go home to Fruängen on Igor's bike and get it, the risk is too great that someone from the company will see me.

Could I ask Alexandra to get it?

No.

Not a chance in hell.

She hates everything to do with Igor. She would *refuse* to get involved in this mess.

I reach for my phone on the bedside table. Surely it can't hurt if I turn it on for a few seconds?

I wait for a second as the screen lights the room up.

I scroll through Instagram.

Jeanette has uploaded a backlit close-up. Her shiny lips are pouting and her eyes are open wide. The wind is catching her hair and the light from the sun is making a halo glow around her head. Her facial expression is both provocative and startled.

'So sad that we have buried my sister's hamster Snuff. Everyone was really upset,' reads the caption.

Four hundred and eleven likes.

Dead hamster combined with horny pouting lips is apparently just the thing on Instagram.

My mobile dings and I am so scared I almost drop it on the floor.

The message is from Liam.

Stop messaging me, for fuck's sake. The cops have let Igor go. There was no evidence. He wants to KILL you. Lie low. Don't call. I do NOT want to be fucking involved.

I close my eyes and let the phone fall onto my blanket.

Hopelessness grows inside until I feel like my chest is about to explode, as if someone or something is in there trying to claw its way out.

The tears come, even though I don't want them. They fall and fall as if I were a snot-nosed little kid who lost his security blanket and not a grown guy who put himself in this shit by being *so fucking retarded*.

You are nothing. You know nothing. You may as well lie down and just die, because nobody will care anyway.

I blow my nose into the sheet.

There is one person left to contact. Just one.

Pernilla

have just arrived at the congregation hall when I get the call.
I take off the backpack I packed for the hike with the congregation's child and youth group. The shift in weight almost makes me lose my footing.

I am so sure it will be Karl-Johan, the pastor, calling to check something off, that I don't even look at the screen.

I have been agonising about the hike for the past few days. Stina didn't think I should go. She felt everything the pastor had said was out of order and I should tell him to go hang himself and not show his hypocritical arse in church ever again.

But how could I do that?

After all, he is the pastor of the congregation, he has helped me countless times and he has supported Samuel. Besides, I have to think of the children. Because without me there will be no hike. No *real* hike anyway.

But when I answer it isn't the pastor. I hear *his* voice on the other end.

My heart skips a beat and I send a silent thanks to God.

'Samuel?'

My voice is so small that I'm not sure he can hear me.

'Hi, Mum. How are you?'

Words get stuck in my throat, but I feel a familiar warmth spread across my chest and my pulse quickens.

'Mum?'

It is a few seconds before I have gathered myself enough to answer.

'Where are you?' I ask and hear how curt I sound. 'Why haven't you been in touch? I've been so worried.'

I direct my gaze towards the group of children already gathered on the street.

The clouds have lifted and patches of pale blue are growing in the sky. The ground is still wet from the rain.

'Sorry,' Samuel says and then goes quiet again.

I can hear his breath through the phone.

Darling Samuel. Darling hopeless kid.

'Sorry,' he says again. 'You see, something really fucked-up happened.'

'Don't swear,' I say reflexively and immediately regret it.

I don't want to scare him off now that he has got in touch. But I also don't want my son to swear, at least not when he is talking to me.

'Sorry,' he says a third time. 'Something . . . happened. I had to stay away.'

'Does it have anything to do with those bags?' I ask, though I already suspect I know the answer.

'Yes. But . . . that wasn't my stuff, and when you threw them out the owner got really fucking, sorry, *very* mad at me.'

My stomach contracts when I recall how I pushed those strange little plastic bags into the rubbish. Not in my wildest imagination would I have thought that I was putting Samuel in mortal danger by doing so.

I thought I was helping him. That for once I was laying down a firm boundary.

'I-I didn't know,' I stutter.

'Of course you didn't. Listen, I have to go. Work starts at ten.'

Samuel's breath sounds laboured, like he is out for a walk.

'Work?'

'Long story. Found a job out on Stuvskär online.'

Samuel tells an incoherent story about how he found a job in the archipelago with a woman named Rachel and her partner, Olle, who apparently is an author. The woman's son, Jonas, is brain-damaged and needs company and supervision.

'The thing is, I can't stay here,' he says. 'I just can't take it. But I need to lie low for a while, until the guy who is out to get me leaves the country.'

When he tells me the last part, the bit about the guy who is out to get him, I remember the man who showed up in our stairwell.

I still have a red mark where he held onto my arm.

'That person,' I say. 'Does he have a shaved head and an accent that sounds like Polish or—?'

'Igor,' Samuel says quickly. 'His name is Igor. The stuff you threw out was his. How do you know what he looks like?'

'He came here asking for you.'

'Dammit.'

'But Samuel—'

'Fucking shit piss.'

'Please, Samuel!'

I can hear him pant between the swear words. It sounds almost like he is walking uphill.

'Mum, he is dangerous. I don't want you to talk to him.'

'But I didn't seek him out. He came here looking for you.'

'And what did you say?' Samuel asks.

'The truth. That I didn't know where you were.'

I lift my backpack up and take a step to the back of the pavement to let a woman with a pushchair and a dog pass. In front of the congregation hall some of the boys are playing football with what looks like a rubber boot. One of the girls is haplessly trying to get hold of it.

I really should go over to them and make sure they calm down, but I can't. Not now that Samuel has finally got in touch.

'Please, Mum, listen to me. There's something you need to help me with.'

'Of course I want to help you. If I can. I mean, I don't know what this is about. What you want help with, that is.'

'You know the small, wooded area – the one along the bike path between the industrial area and the plant nursery?'

'Yes?'

'There's a large rock a couple of yards to the right of the path. You can't miss it. It's kinda huge.'

I don't answer because I have an uneasy feeling about where this is going.

'Underneath the rock there is a cavity. You can get at it if you dig alongside the rock, on the side that faces the birch tree. There's a duffel bag in there. And in the bag—'

'Samuel,' I say using my strictest voice.

'There's money in there,' he continues, as if he hadn't heard me. 'Can you get me a couple of bundles of hundreds?'

'*Samuel!* Do you understand what you're asking? Money? In a bag in the woods? Stacks of hundred-kronor bills?

Where have they come from? Drug sales? Over my dead body will I get involved in something like that. You have to go to the police, Samuel. It's the only right thing to do. If you've done something illegal you must confess and accept your punishment.'

'You can forget that, for sure,' he mumbles.

'Why would you say that? The only right thing is to accept your punishment.'

'It's not that easy.'

'Easy? Are you joking? Who told you life was *easy*? And what makes you think the easy way is the right way?'

'Mum, listen to me—'

'No. I am done listening. I will not sit idly by as you ruin your life. And mine. I'm going to the police and asking for help. Yes, I am.'

'Please, listen. If I go anywhere near Stockholm again I'm dead. Do you understand? Dead, Mum. For real. And then it will be your fault.'

'But *Samuel*! How can you even say such a thing? After all I've done for you.'

'Because it's true!' he screams. 'Igor will find me and he *will* kill me. You have met him yourself. You saw what he was like, didn't you? What he *was*? He is a monster. He would not hesitate for an instant to kick my head in.'

I close my eyes.

Why can't he get it together? Why must he always get himself into trouble?

'You would have been welcome to borrow from me,' I say, struggling to maintain the calm I am already about to lose. 'But I don't have any money. I had to pay off some of your grandfather's bills and now I barely know how I'll make it through the month.'

'Get the money,' he says in a shrill voice. 'It's just lying rotting away.'

I glance over at the congregation hall.

'I couldn't help you if I wanted to,' I say. 'I am about to go on a hike with the congregation's youth group.'

'On a hike? Are you serious? Are you going to be grilling sausages and reading the Bible with a bunch of retarded Christian kids while Igor beats the crap out of me? *Seriously?*'

I can hear the tears in Samuel's voice, but I can't determine if he is telling the truth or if he is exaggerating.

He is always so dramatic.

But he is my child, my everything. The only person other than Father that I truly love.

'Help me, Mum,' Samuel whispers. 'You have to help me.'

'I-I . . .'

A hand lands on my shoulder and I turn around, still with the phone pressed against my ear.

'I'll call you right back,' I mumble and end the call.

Karl-Johan looks troubled and has a deep furrow in his brow.

'I couldn't help hearing,' he says. 'Pernilla, don't do anything you regret. You do remember your promise to me?'

I nod and lift the backpack.

'You didn't call him again, did you?' he continues.

I shake my head like an obedient child. Like a sheep.

'Good,' he says.

In his hand he has a small backpack.

'Where's your tent?' I ask.

'It's broken,' he says. 'I think it's best I use yours.'

My stomach contracts and a cold feeling spreads across my chest.

'No,' I say. 'That's not possible.'

But the pastor just scoffs.

'Don't be silly,' he says, and takes my arm, a bit too hard, pulling me over towards the congregation hall.

'Come now,' he says. 'We have to go.'

In that moment something inside me breaks.

I think about how obedient and compliant I have been all these years. How I first obeyed Father and then the congregation.

And the congregation is Karl-Johan, the man who is tugging at my arm as if I were a disobedient child. The man who doesn't think I should be alone anymore and thus probably would like to sleep with me even though he is married and a man of God.

Suddenly, I feel sick. I've had enough of my simple-minded compliance.

What good has it done me?

None. Absolutely none.

And the lies?

The image of Father's emaciated body and Mother's yellowed letters flicker past my inner eye. And I think of Isaac who was so keen to get to know his little boy. Who wanted so much and got so little – a couple of hours twice a year at most.

All those lies.

All the years we denied each other the closeness that was our right, the closeness we so badly needed.

I brace against the pavement with my feet and Karl-Johan looks at me in surprise. Out of the corner of my eye I see how some of the kids stop mid-play and watch us with wide eyes.

'Come on,' he says and pulls so hard it hurts.

But I resist, don't budge an inch.

'You are embarrassing us,' he hisses.

I look him in the eye. See the mix of frustration and anger in his face, but also genuine fear, as if my new-found strength frightens him.

That makes me even angrier.

'Come!' he insists and shoots a concerned glance at the group of children outside the congregation hall.

I twist my arm free and step back. Get the backpack onto my back.

'Never in a million years,' I say.

Manfred

Afsaneh reaches across and holds out her phone so that I can see the screen.

'Look!'

Alba, my oldest daughter who lives in Paris, smiles at me from the little picture. Her light brown hair flutters in the wind and in her hand she is holding a glass of white wine.

'But I want to get her pictures *too*,' I say.

Afsaneh rolls her eyes.

'Then download Instagram.'

'And how do you do that?'

'Oh my God!'

Afsaneh grabs my mobile on the bedside table and puts in the PIN, which she of course knows. Then she leans back against the pillow, kicks the thin blanket off and taps intently on the phone.

She looks like a savage, a forest nymph; her black hair is tousled and frizzy, her eyebrows growing wild, her nose shiny. Yet she is so beautiful that I am overcome by a sudden urge to touch her, as if to make sure she is real and not an apparition, conjured by my fantasy.

Afsaneh and I met four years ago, out in Sandhamn in the outer Stockholm archipelago. Contrary to common belief she was the one who picked me up, not the other way around.

I would never have dared make a move on such a young, talented and beautiful woman. At least not at the time, after the divorce from Beatrice had robbed me of all of my self-confidence.

But for some reason the beautiful psychology PhD student wanted to talk to me. And not just talk, as it soon turned out.

She invited me home to the little cabin she had borrowed from a friend. It lay embedded among pines and blueberry bushes on the south-western side of the island and had neither electricity nor indoor plumbing.

But what did that matter?

Of course I thought she was just playing with me, but I didn't mind being her toy. The days came and went, turned into a week. I called my boss and explained that I had contracted a bad case of strep throat. Afsaneh and I sunbathed on the rocks, ate long dinners at Dykarbaren down in the harbour and took walks around the small island. When it was time to go home she asked me for my phone number.

I hastily wrote it down on the back of a receipt and she told me she'd be in touch. All I could do was nod and emit a slightly embarrassed laugh, because I was convinced she'd never call. Besides the role reversal bothered me. She had made the first move, seduced me and invited me to her cabin. She had asked for my number and promised to call.

She had done all the things men do – men who don't have any intention of getting in touch.

But that same evening, as I came home to my empty apartment, the phone rang.

'There,' she says. 'Now you have to fill out your Instagram account.'

She helps me get started and then shows me how it all works.

'You can follow as many people as you want. If you like their posts you tap on this heart here. If you want to comment you tap the bubble. And you can post your own photos. Like this!'

I push her dark hair out of her face, lean over and kiss her cheek.

But Afsaneh, who seems deeply focused, recoils from my touch.

'Am I developmentally retarded?' I ask, my gaze still on my beautiful wife.

'Yes,' she answers truthfully, 'or at least digitally retarded.'

'Do you think I could learn?'

She is quiet for a while. Lifts her gaze from her phone and watches me silently.

'No,' she says.

'Don't get angry,' I say. 'But I just don't understand what it's about?'

'What do you mean? It's not *about* anything in particular. You can stay in touch with people. See what's going on in their lives. You can follow Alba, Alexander and Stella for instance.'

'But what about her?' I say and point at a young woman in cheap-looking expensive clothes. 'She has two thousand followers. Does she know all of them?'

Afsaneh lets out a deep sigh and laughs a little.

'Of course not. She is an *influencer*. She lives for likes. They are as important to her as going to work is to you.'

'Work,' I say looking at my watch. 'Dammit. I actually have to go.'

Afsaneh nods and sinks back down on the bed.

'See you at the hospital?'

'See you at the hospital,' I say and get up.

As usual when I step in through the entrance to the station I think of Peter.

I miss him so much.

Peter and I had worked together for more than ten years when the darkness of Ormberg lowered itself over him. The sight of his frozen body in the large deep freezer is forever etched into my memory. And I will never be able to stop examining my actions last winter, never stop asking myself if there was anything I could have done to save him.

Peter was one of the few truly close friends I have had in my life. I suppose Aron was the first, and perhaps also the very closest.

He taught me the pain of losing someone you love.

The image of Nadja's small body in the hospital bed flickers across my mind.

One might assume that I became depressed and isolated after Aron's death. That would have been the natural reaction.

Of course I grieved my brother and comforted myself with food, but in some strange way the tragedy also brought good things – for instance it gave me an elevated position among my friends.

Especially among the girls.

'There he is! The brother of the guy who died!'

I had just turned thirteen when Anna took me under her wing. She was a year older, had real breasts, knew how to kiss with tongues and was firmly dedicated to teaching me everything she knew about love in order to assuage my deep suffering.

And I was happy to be helped.

A rapid stream of girls followed Anna. There was Susi with the birthmark on her forehead and Elsa who had won the junior Swedish swim championships and Pirjo with the big tits. There was Marika who smoked weed, whose dad was in jail for white-collar crimes and whose mum took shopping trips to Paris and New York at weekends. And there was tall Stella and tall Sanna, sisters, who did not seem to mind sharing me with each other.

Then there was Beatrice, the beautiful upper-class girl who lived just two blocks away. The woman who became my wife and the mother of my three oldest children.

I don't think my friends ever understood what the girls saw in me. I wasn't particularly good-looking and was already carrying far too much weight.

What they didn't understand was that I – perhaps due to the tragic circumstances, or possibly to compensate for my lacklustre appearance – had developed other qualities.

I learned the hard art of listening. I cultivated what I myself considered to be an irresistible image, defined by cynicism and ennui. I cultivated a laconic sense of humour and began my life-long love affair with beautiful clothes.

Yes, I am not so stupid that I don't realise I channelled my vanity into my wardrobe, since I couldn't do anything about being overweight. Over time I have made friends with my body, as they say. Accepted the blubber, to put it plainly. From an aesthetic point of view, at least.

However the fear of my weight actually affecting my health, perhaps even shortening my lifespan, has grown.

I can't die. Not now.

I don't have the time.

Besides, it would be incredibly unfair to Afsaneh.

I am thinking of my poor wife.

I have always felt certain we would live together for the rest of our lives, but now I don't know anymore. We have invested so much of our love in Nadja that I honestly don't know what would remain if . . .

If she . . .

If she would . . .

I'm not able to follow the thought to its logical conclusion, because it seems unthinkable that the world would continue to exist without Nadja. That spring would come, that plants would return to life and send pale green tendrils through the cold dark earth in contempt of death. That new babies would be born and women be as full of hope for the future as Afsaneh once was.

Above all it seems unthinkable to contemplate Afsaneh and me without Nadja, because Nadja is the sum of us, of our love. Of our longing for life itself.

Without her we are nothing.

Without her we are like the dry dead leaves whirling around in the wind in the autumn. And just like them we would be scattered to the wind, without being able to do anything to stop it.

When I enter the small conference room Letit and Malin are already there.

Malin is dressed in a tight T-shirt that shows her rounded belly. She smiles when she sees my gaze. I smile too but it hurts inside because her belly makes me think of Afsaneh and Nadja.

Letit is sitting at the short end of the table. He is wearing a shirt in some kind of synthetic fabric. Through the transparent material I can see the outline of a string vest. His jeans have pleats, are high-waisted and an inch or so too short. His big toes, which are poking out of his sandals, have long yellow nails that curve towards the floor.

Jesus, I think. He looks like he just stepped out of his caravan at the campsite in Böda. It is a mystery how any woman would find that cantankerous, poorly groomed old man attractive.

'I've had a talk with the behavioural analysis unit about our case,' Malin says. 'They aren't formally involved, but they've shared some thoughts. I wanted to tell you what their conclusions were.'

She clears her throat and flips through her notepad.

'We have two murders,' she continues, 'or crimes against the exhumation law, in the unlikely event that these guys died of natural causes and were later dumped in the ocean. For simplicity's sake let's assume we're talking about murder. The theory that they died of natural causes is too much of a long shot. So, the typical killer is a man, but you know that already. In this case the profilers thought that was even more likely than in the average murder case, since the bodies have been subject to extreme physical violence and then dumped into the sea. Extreme physical violence indicates a male assailant. Further, dragging a body around is heavy work, which strengthens the hypothesis that we are dealing with a man. And these were young men. A person who was old or sick would in all likelihood not have been able to get at them. Therefore, they also believe the killer to be physically strong.'

Letit folds his arms across his chest and juts his lower jaw out.

'I don't believe that kind of mumbo-jumbo,' he scoffs. 'Civilians and shrinks in their fancy offices trying to get in touch with their insides. What do they know about real police work? I guess it's just a question of time before we hire psychics and crazies with divining rods too.'

Malin looks uncertain and shoots me a glance.

'Keep going,' I say.

'Furthermore, they believe this person is some kind of career criminal. Murder is rarely a first crime. There is a high likelihood that the suspect already has a criminal record or has been suspected of a crime – that he has gone a few rounds against the long arm of the law, maybe done time for some type of violent crime. For that reason they also think he is older than the victims. Probably somewhere between thirty and fifty.'

Letit stares pointedly out of the window.

'What about the way the killer treated the bodies *after* death?' I asked. 'The excessive violence they were subjected to post-mortem. What does that mean?'

Malin nods.

'We discussed that. It could have to do with a great rage, or ruthlessness.'

I lean further forward, lean my elbows on the table.

'The nail they found in Carlgren's heel? If the forensic pathologist is correct about it being driven in on purpose, and I am sure she is, then that brings to mind . . .'

Malin grimaces with discomfort and looks down at the table. Puts one hand on her belly.

'Torture,' she says and nods gravely. 'And that in turn could mean two things. Either we are dealing with a killer who is torturing his victims to extract information or to send a signal to others: this is what will happen if you cross me.'

Letit clears his throat and scratches his beard.

I note that his fingernails are also too long.

'Aren't we overcomplicating things now?' he says. 'Young guys. These murders are obviously drug-related. The good Carlgren may very well have used cocaine, for instance, even if he looks as pure as driven snow on the surface. We know how that goes on in the posh suburbs.'

I nod. Letit has a point.

'We will be speaking to Carlgren's sister tomorrow,' I say. 'If he was doing drugs she may know.'

There is another pause.

'You mention there are two main reasons for why a killer would use torture,' I say and turn to Malin. 'What is the other?'

'I'm sorry,' Malin says. 'But I'm sure you've already figured that one out. The other option is that we are dealing with a sadistic killer. Somebody who derives pleasure from causing pain. And, to be clear, one doesn't exclude the other in any way.'

PART III

Descent

Then the men were exceedingly afraid, and said to him, 'Why have you done this?' For the men knew that he was fleeing from the presence of the LORD, because He had told them.

Then said they to Him, 'What shall we do to you, that the sea may be calm for us?' – for the sea was growing more tempestuous.

And He said unto them, 'Pick me up, and throw me into the sea; then the sea will become calm for you. For I know that this great tempest *is* because of me.'

Jonah 1: 10–12

P A R T   I I I

Samuel

I t is warmer now.

My room on the top floor faces south, and even when I wake up at seven the air is hot and muggy and my sheets are sticky with sweat.

I get out of bed and turn my phone on. Promise myself I will be online for no more than one minute.

I scroll through the posts on Instagram, freeze when Alexandra's face appears above the rim of a disproportionately large cocktail glass. She smiles, winks and forms her thumb and index finger into an 'O'.

'And I'm single again,' reads the caption.

Fifty-two likes.

I slam my hand into the wall, grimace in pain and anger.

What does she mean 'single'? She can't write that. We were never together, for fuck's sake.

It's so damn hard sitting in this bloody house and not being able to communicate with anyone. I can't even comment. Can't send one message.

It's starting to feel like I don't exist anymore.

I take a couple of deep breaths and try to relax. Check my messages.

Nothing.

My heart rate calms down a bit.

Everything will be OK, I think. Even though she said she wouldn't, I know Mum will get the money. Then I can stay away until Igor has calmed down, or left the country.

And Alexandra can go to hell.

I turn my phone off again and put it on the bedside table. Go up to the window and pull the cord of the old, bleached blinds. It retracts with a flick and I open the window. Lean out, inhale the scent of heather and pine and look out over the sea, which spreads perfectly placidly beneath me. Little skerries look as if they're floating on the surface and the silhouette of the lighthouse is dark against the horizon. I can hear a boat departing in the distance and some seagulls crying.

Otherwise all is quiet and still.

I leave the window open, pull my jeans and T-shirt on and do my best to move through the house as quietly as I possibly can. I pad through the family room, down the spiral staircase and out towards the hall.

When I pass Jonas's room I hear something.

First I think he is whining a little, one of those many small sounds that escape him, completely involuntarily, but then I hear that somebody in there is crying.

Rachel.

Something about her sobs makes my stomach knot. There is so much grief and hopelessness in her crying. So much fuck-ing misery in every little sniffle that part of me just wants to rush out of the house, throw myself onto the bike and get as far the hell away from here as I possibly can.

Then I hear her say something, or mumble rather. Her voice is mushy from crying, but I can still make out the words.

'Jonas, my darling child, I miss you so.'

I swallow hard and rub the sweat off my forehead.

This is just too much.

Poor, poor Rachel.

I mean, it isn't exactly news that her son is a vegetable. But when I hear her despair; actually hear it straight through the door, of course it's going to give me a horribly bad conscience for not having considered how completely fucking wretched this whole situation must be for her.

And I wonder something else: is there anything I could do for her? Anything besides just sitting in that room with Jonas reading from that deathly boring book?

Is there anything that would make her, like, happier?

I hear a thud from Jonas's room and I quickly sneak over to the front door, pull my trainers on, unlock it and go outside.

I walk down the long wooden staircase towards the jetty. There are sixty-seven steps down to the sea, but it feels like an eternity to descend them.

On either side of me the cliff drops precipitously towards the water but the wooden structure seems stable – it clings to the granite and smoothly slithers along the rocks, like a giant snake.

The only visible vegetation is a few wind-beaten pines and some heather and moss growing in the deep, vertical crevices that cut through the rock like open wounds.

I slow down and take in the landscape. Poke a few rocks with my foot so that they roll off the cliff.

On the surface the rocks are barren, but if you look closely you can make out a swarm of life. Lichen spreads out like green and grey oceans across the stone. When I poke them with my foot they fall apart, become dry crumbs under the sole of my shoe only to be caught by the wind.

Grandpa Bernt used to say one shouldn't do that, because my little boy foot destroyed in a minute what it took the lichen hundreds of years to create.

Grandpa.

When I think of him my breath gets kind of heavy. Like there's a stone in my chest.

If I'm being completely fucking honest he's like a dad to me. Still, I can't deal with visiting him in that place they call a hospice – the place you go to die. It's like a concentration camp for cancer patients.

Grandpa has always taken care of me, watched me when Mum worked, scolded me when I did something stupid. If you disregard the religious shit I respect him one hundred per cent.

The problem is he lets the religious shit dictate his whole life.

I look out across the rocks. Lean forward to look really closely at the rough stone.

A myriad insects move in different directions: small black ants, big brownish-red ants and minute orange spiders with legs so small and so fast they appear to float across the rocks.

I kick another rock.

It rolls down the cliff with heavy thuds and finally hits the ground below with a sharp bang.

Several insects become visible in the indentation where the stone lay; shiny copper earwigs and matte black creepy-crawlies that rush around dazed by the sun.

I take a step back, suddenly worried a large furry spider will emerge.

I hate spiders.

Grandpa was the one who taught me all the names of the insects and plants. When I was little I got to come along to the congregation's summer camp on Ljusterö. Since I wasn't able to concentrate I didn't have to participate in Bible school and singing, but I tagged along for all the other activities.

We went sailing and camping and grilled sausages. And we learned about animals and plants.

Grandpa explained that spiders play an important role in the ecosystem and that they are definitely not dangerous to humans.

It didn't help.

Spiders are still the worst thing I know.

All that stuff with Grandpa seems so distant to me now, almost like it happened in another life, or was just something I saw on Netflix.

I keep going down to the water.

For each step the memory fades of the summers at camp and is replaced by the other shit, the shit that is my real life.

I remember Igor's expression when he realised that I didn't have the package of product samples, and Malte's skinny body and gleaming gold teeth.

I let them down.

Then I think about all the other people I have let down, like Grandpa Bernt and Liam whom I promised I would stop working for Igor. And Alexandra who stood there crying behind her front door and wouldn't let me in.

For fuck's sake, don't call me baby.

I guess she had a point.

But most of all I think of Mum.

All the things she nagged me about, that she has been there for me over the years etc., etc. – it's actually true. Without her I don't know what would have become of me. Now things have gone to hell anyway, but it would have happened a whole lot faster without her.

I hope she hurries up, that she gets the money soon, because I can't handle staying here for much longer. Zombie-Jonas gets on my nerves. Rachel, too, but in a completely different way.

It has been five days since I arrived and the day after tomorrow, Friday, it will be Midsummer.

I would like to be really far from here by then.

When I get down to the jetty I pull off my trainers and jeans. Take the T-shirt off and place it next to them.

The wood is warm and sticky under my feet. It smells of tar and seaweed. All I hear is a low, tinny lapping.

I look down into the water.

It looks deep.

All I can see is a wad of yellowish-brown seaweed floating past by the jetty and a couple of small fish darting past in the sunlit surface water.

I imagine what it's like further out, where the water is deep and cold. Where the Baltic herring swims and the eels slither along the bottom.

I stretch out and am just about to dive in when I turn around for some reason and look up toward the house.

There is a man standing outside Rachel's window. He is too far away for me to able to make out what he looks like, but it seems like this person is shading his eyes with his hand and looking in through the window.

I am guessing this is one of Rachel's friends and think of the sobbing from Jonas's room. For a second, I consider going back up but I decide to swim instead, so turn to the sea, take a deep breath and dive in.

It is colder than I thought it would be, but it is as if my entire body welcomes the cold, as if I am born again down there in the cold, greenish-blue stillness.

I open my eyes and squint at the surface. Bubbles rise, the sun crumbles into golden flakes that float on the waves, as if it were a Christmas tree ornament that fell from the sky and smashed into a thousand pieces.

When I come up to the surface I float on my back for a while and listen to all the sounds in the ocean, strange little snaps and thuds and the constant hum of all the invisible life that swims, crawls and floats in the water.

'You look like you're enjoying yourself.'

I turn to the jetty, treading water.

Rachel is standing at the very edge, dressed in a navy blue bikini. Her eyes are red and slightly swollen, but her smile is wide.

'Are you going to swim?' I ask and hear how fucking stupid that sounds.

Because she is standing there, on the jetty, in her bikini. Of course she is going to take a swim, not weed the bloody rose bed.

But Rachel just laughs.

She bends her knees slightly and dives into the water a short way to my right.

It is a near-perfect dive. There is barely a ripple on the surface. And just like the time I saw her from the window upstairs, she swims under water for a long time before she surfaces, at least twenty yards away.

Then she front crawls towards me with slow movements.

'God, that felt good,' she says and wipes her hair out of her eyes with one hand while treading water.

'Yes,' I answer.

She heaves herself up and sits on the jetty, but I stay in, suddenly very aware of the fact that I am only wearing boxers. White ones too, that are definitely see-through when wet.

Rachel watches me with amusement.

'Are you going to stay in long?'

'A while,' I say and feel my cheeks get hot even though the water is ice cold.

She shrugs slightly, closes her eyes and turns her face to the sun. The pale skin on her arms has goosebumps from the cold and I can see the outline of her nipples under her wet bikini top. She lets her feet swing slowly in the water and holds on to the edge of the jetty with her pale, slim fingers. Water is dripping from her long hair.

She is so damn fit.

I would give anything to touch her skin, run my hand through that hair, stroke her lips with my finger.

My legs feel like pieces of frozen meat in the cold water and I swim up to the edge of the jetty, at a safe distance from Rachel and grab on to the wood.

She looks at my hand and asks: 'What does your bracelet say?'

I meet her gaze.

'It's just something I did when I was a kid,' I say, feeling ashamed of the childish bracelet.

'I can see that. But what does it say?'

'"Mummy". It says, "Mummy". I made it for my mum.'

'So beautiful,' she whispers, reaching her hand out and stroking the bracelet lightly with her finger.

I'm not prepared for her touch. My hand jerks and I swallow hard.

There's a long silence. Rachel furrows her brow and looks like she is about to start crying again. She blinks a few times and turns her head away.

'Who came by?' I ask, mostly to say something.

She pulls her feet out of the water and turns to me again.

'Somebody came by just now,' I say.

'Did they?'

Without rushing she lifts her feet out of the water and stands up. Then she pushes her hands to the sky.

'Yeah, a guy. He was standing outside your window, I thought . . .'

'Outside my window? What did he look like?'

'Well, I couldn't really tell from here.'

Now I am trembling with cold. And not just because I am in the water, it is also because I am realising that if the man outside the window wasn't a friend of hers it may very well have been one of Igor's men.

'Shit,' I say. 'Shit, shit, shit!'

Rachel raises her eyebrows.

'What?'

'Well, it could be something to do with that guy I told you about.'

'The Russian? Surely you would have recognised him?'

'It wasn't him,' I say. 'But he might have sent someone else.'

Rachel cocks her head.

'Aren't you being a bit paranoid now, Samuel? Isn't it more likely that someone actually was looking for me? A neighbour, for instance? Or maybe you were mistaken. Maybe it was a deer. They like to stand there in the flower bed and feast on the flowers. If I had a gun I would shoot them.'

She looks up at the house on the rock.

'Show me where he was standing,' she says calmly.

I heave myself out of the water and quickly pull my jeans on.

But I needn't have worried.

Rachel is not looking at me at all, instead she is staring intently at the house with her hands on her hips.

We walk up the stairs in silence.

It gets warmer for every step we take and before we're all the way up I am sweating again. The sun is baking my shoulders and my heart is thumping in my chest from the effort.

When we get to the top we round the deck and walk over to the two windows with bars that face west on the ground floor – Rachel's and Jonas's bedrooms.

Below the windows there is a narrow flower bed with some kind of plant with large, round leaves.

Rachel sinks into a squat and I do the same.

With her hand she carefully pushes the juicy, shiny leaves aside, revealing large footprints in the moist dirt – prints that look like they come from a pair of heavy men's shoes.

Pernilla

What am I actually trying to do here?

I began to have second thoughts even as I left a speechless Karl-Johan on the pavement yesterday.

That percolating sense of triumph that came over me when I snubbed him was soon replaced by a growing doubt and an anxiety strong enough that it almost made me turn around, run back and retract and repent, like the good girl I have always been.

I look around.

The industrial area is cloaked in that ghostly blue light that only exists for a short time in early summer when the real darkness never dares emerge.

I hurry my steps, turn off on the bike path that leads to the plant nursery and take a shortcut across a small patch of grass.

It is unfathomable.

I – a hard-working, evangelical helicopter parent – am here retrieving *drug money* from under a *boulder* for my son.

I – who am so law-abiding that it would make a newborn look like a criminal, who has never even got a parking ticket or forgotten to return a book to the library.

What would Father say?

What would God say?

Instinctively I turn around, as if God were lying in wait for me in the dark bushes.

I can almost hear Father's deep voice as he reads from Hebrews:

'And no creature is hidden from His sight, but all are naked and exposed to the eyes of him to whom we must give account.'

But the bike path lies empty behind me.

Not a movement to be seen, not a sound to be heard.

But the street lights are sparsely distanced and some are broken. It would be easy to hide in the dark between the domes of light, if one really wanted to.

I shudder, even though the night is warm, at the thought of the bald man with an Eastern European accent in the stairwell. The man Samuel called Igor.

The man who is *a monster*.

I don't know if Samuel was right about Igor wanting to kill him, but I don't dare take the chance, because suddenly it is clear to me, everything is so liberatingly simple: Samuel is my only child and I must do what I can to help him.

It is entirely possible that this new insight is actually a subconscious attempt to compensate Samuel for having denied him a father all these years.

So be it, in that case.

But that Russian monster will not be allowed to lay hands on my son.

Besides, it was high time that I stood up to Karl-Johan. But it took me quite a while to realise that he was actually hitting on me.

It upended my world view actually – that the pastor, of all people, would do something so low.

Because if *he* can behave like that, who can one trust?

No person.

No congregation.

And what about God? How are things between us, Him and me?

I hurry my steps and look into the dark, trying to keep the theological quandaries at bay, but the pastor's face keeps intruding into my mind's eye.

Maybe he is right that I ought to meet someone.

Ever since Samuel was born I haven't had time for a real relationship.

Of course I have been on dates, I have even been in love a few times, but I always felt that Samuel's and my delicate relationship wouldn't withstand my letting a man into our lives in a significant way.

I think of Mario, the gym teacher at Huddinge high school, and feel a little butterfly in my stomach. What would happen if I called him and asked him over for dinner? If I really invited him into my life?

There is a sound behind me. Squeaking and clattering in the distance.

I step aside quickly, into the shadows next to the bike path. Stand behind a tree trunk and let my hand rest against the cold, rough bark.

The sound intensifies and a bike becomes visible fifty yards or so in the distance.

An older lady is bent over the handlebars, she seems to be struggling to keep the old bike moving. I realise something must have got stuck in the spokes, causing the clatter.

I press up against the trunk and wait until the woman has passed.

The noise dies away slowly in the direction of the plant nursery and I draw a sigh of relief.

I'm sure that Igor has heavies, but I strongly doubt he has old ladies on rickety bicycles working for him.

My eyes are getting accustomed to the twilight in the woods and the outlines of trees and bushes emerge more clearly now. I gaze into the sparse woods. Just as I make out the silhouette of something that might actually be a boulder, my phone rings.

I curse myself for forgetting to turn it off, but still pull it out of my pocket and look at the screen.

It is from Father's hospice.

After a few seconds of deliberation I pick up.

A woman, whose voice I don't recognise, introduces herself as Katja, a nurse. She calmly explains that Father has taken a turn for the worse.

'Can you come in?' she asks.

My heart sinks.

Not this too, not now.

And immediately the thought occurs: that this is God's punishment for my being rude to Karl-Johan and for leaving him alone with the kids when I knew that he would never manage the hike on his own.

'How bad is it?' I ask. 'I am in the middle of something important.'

The nurse patiently explains that it is impossible to say, but that Father hasn't been able to communicate since six o'clock and that his blood pressure has dropped. She says it could be hours or days and that it is obviously up to me to decide what to do.

I glimpse movement at the corner of my eye and turn toward the industrial area, but all is still.

Yet I am sure.

Someone or something moved, just within the nebulous fringes of the street light's glow, and disappeared into the dark woods, like a fish slides through a ray of sunlight in the water only to be swallowed again by shadows.

I take a few steps in among the trees so as not to be as visible. Explain to the nurse that I will do my best, but that I'm not sure I can come at once. I ask her to get in touch immediately if Father gets any worse and she promises to do so.

After I have hung up and turned the sound off on my phone I stand quietly looking into the dark for a long time, but all I see are silhouettes of low bushes and a few chalk-white, flecked birch trunks.

I take a few steps with my arms stretched in front of me in the dusk. And my hand grazes cold stone.

I have found Samuel's boulder.

Quickly I squat down and begin to dig with my hands at the side of the stone. Pine needles and leaves get stuck under my nails as I shovel last year's dry leaves and sticks to the side.

At first I think I might be looking in the wrong place, because despite my having dirt up to my elbows I haven't found anything. But then the ground gives way and my hands fumble in thin air, as if I've come upon a subterranean cave.

I bend down, tentatively stretch one arm in under the boulder. Feel around among roots and damp soil before I feel some sturdy canvas under my fingers.

*

Five minutes later I am back at the car. I toss the bag, which is surprisingly light, into the boot and look around one more time.

Everything is calm and dark. Nothing moves in the shadows, no sound can be heard. I sit in the driver's seat, close the door and sigh deeply with relief.

Then I look at my phone.

There are three missed calls.

They are all from Father's hospice.

Manfred

I wake up to the tapping from Afsaneh's laptop.

The blinds are still drawn and the room is dark. The air is stuffy and heavy, like inside a car that's sat in the sun for too long.

I glance at the clock on the nightstand.

Half past five.

What could be so important that you need to type it up at half past five in the morning?

'What are you doing?' I ask, perhaps a bit more aggressively than I had intended.

'Writing something.'

'I get that. But why right now? Do you know what time it is?'

'I can go and sit in the living room instead.'

I grunt and kick the blanket off. My skin is shiny with sweat and the sheets are heavy with moisture.

'Well, now I'm already awake.'

Afsaneh doesn't answer, but the tapping intensifies.

I turn on my side, towards her.

She is sitting up with the computer on her lap. On the screen I see a photo of a smiling bald child with a tortoiseshell cat in her arms.

'What the hell is *that*?'

Afsaneh's fingers freeze mid-movement and she turns her face to me. Her eyes are dark and guarded.

'*That* is Julia. A six-year-old girl with acute lymphatic leukaemia.'

'And why are you writing to her?'

Afsaneh sighs deeply and closes the laptop loudly.

'I'm not writing to her, I am writing to her mother. I met her in a forum for parents of seriously ill children.'

'So you still hang out in those types of places?'

Afsaneh places her laptop on the floor.

'Yes, I do. And you know what? Maybe you should too because talking to people in our situation actually helps. People who understand. Who really understand. I don't know what you do with all the anxiety, where you put it, but I actually have a need to talk about Nadja.'

I don't answer, because at once I feel so irredeemably less mature than my young wife.

Immature and tactless, and dying for a smoke.

Of course she must be allowed to communicate with these people if that makes her feel better. Nadja still hasn't woken up, and I assume that anything that can prevent us from losing our minds is worth a try.

'Sorry,' I say.

Afsaneh puts her hand against my cheek and strokes it tenderly.

'Would you mind explaining something?' I continue. 'None of that is reality.'

'What do you mean?' she asks sounding genuinely surprised – not angry, just astonished, as if she can't really understand my question.

'All I am saying is, these are people who you don't know nor have met and will likely never meet. You message or chat or mail or whatever you do. But they're not really flesh-and-blood humans.'

Afsaneh shakes her head slowly.

'I really don't get your point. That is exactly what they are, flesh-and-blood humans. With children who are as sick as Nadja, at the very least.'

'But you don't know them. Not *really*. You don't even know if they're telling the truth.'

'Why would they lie?'

I shrug.

'Why would they tell the truth? It's not really real.'

'Well, what is real to you?'

The question surprises me and I hesitate before answering. Philosophy has never been my strong suit.

'Things you can touch,' I suppose. 'Flesh-and-blood humans. Objects.'

'So when you see California wildfires on the news, that's not real?'

'Well, it is. But—'

'What's the difference?'

Her voice is deceptively soft, but I know she is getting seriously annoyed, because her hand is clenched and there are red blotches on her throat.

'Yes, but . . . television programmes, the news. There's some quality control there after all. Some sort of critical assessment. On the internet any idiot can say anything. There is no truth. It is bloody anarchy.'

'It's true to me,' Afsaneh says.

'It isn't the real world. It's the *internet*. It's . . . silicone and air.'

'It's the new world,' she continues, calmly but still with her fist clenched. 'Where everybody is connected. Where there are no limitations, no walls between humans.'

'It's ones and zeros,' I say. 'Electrical impulses generated by anonymous people whose intentions you don't know, not some fucking collective consciousness.'

'Must you always get so angry when there's something you don't understand?'

'OK,' I mumble. 'Sorry if I don't understand. I'm probably too old for that stuff.'

Afsaneh shakes her head. But then she relaxes, draws a deep breath and looks at me with that gaze that I know means I am hopeless, but that for some inexplicable reason she still loves me and that consequently I should be grateful.

'Yes,' she says, hesitating, 'you are probably too old.'

'A real old codger?'

She smiles but doesn't say anything.

The tapping intensifies again and I slowly get out of bed and go to shower.

Malin is supposed to pick me up a little after eight.

It is already oppressively hot and a thin film of sweat covers my skin. The smell of dusty tarmac and decomposing rubbish from the bin by the bus stop is so strong that I go and stand a bit further away to wait for her.

Malin, who is coming straight from the flat she has borrowed on Lidingö, brakes sharply in front of me and shoots me a smile when I open the front door and squeeze myself into the narrow seat.

'How are you doing?' I ask.

'I'm good,' she answers, turning right on Banérgatan and continuing down toward Narvavägen.

'Amélie Carlgren,' she continues, 'what do we know about her?'

'Older sister of victim number two, Victor Carlgren. Twenty-one years old. Studying at the Stockholm School of Economics and lives in a studio apartment on Luntmakargatan.'

'How can she afford that?' Malin asks, accelerates, overtakes a cyclist and then makes a right, onto Strandvägen.

In front of us the dock is spread out in the morning sun. Barges, restaurants and ferries to the archipelago lie in a line. People are already in line on Nybrokajen to take the boat out to Grinda or Sandhamn.

'Her family has money. They probably bought it for her.'

'Incredible,' Malin murmurs. 'Some people have it good.'

She shakes her head and turns toward Norrmalmstorg.

I don't say what I am thinking, that Amélie Carlgren would probably have gladly given up her expensive city apartment if it would give her back her brother. That money is only important until you actually have it, but sometimes a child has to fall out of the window, or a brother be murdered for you to understand that.

Amélie Carlgren opens her door slightly.

I get a glimpse of long blonde hair and a shiny, make-up-free face.

'Hi,' Malin says, flashing her ID. 'We're from the police. It was me who called you yesterday.'

The door closes, there's rustling from a chain and then it opens again, wide this time.

'Come in,' Amélie whispers.

She is dressed in grey sweatpants and a white T-shirt with a David Bowie motif. Her outfit and the fact that she isn't wearing any make-up makes her look much younger than she is.

We take our shoes off and pass the only room, which is furnished with a small sofa, a table and a bed.

'We will have to sit in the kitchen,' Amélie says, 'that's the only room with enough chairs. Would you like anything to drink?'

Malin shakes her head.

'I would love a glass of water,' I say.

The kitchen is spartan and looks out on a large courtyard. Next to the window is a small gate-legged table and three chairs. We sit down while Amélie fetches me some water.

Malin takes out her notepad at the same time as Amélie puts the water on the table and sits down at the short end, across from the window.

'First of all, I want to offer my condolences for what happened to your brother,' I say quietly. 'We will do everything we can to find out exactly what occurred and who is responsible.'

Amélie nods and lowers her gaze.

'We would like to ask you a few questions,' I continue.

'Sure,' she says. 'Ask away. I'll do anything to catch whoever killed my brother.'

She blinks a few times.

'My *little* brother,' she adds and then just sits with her eyes glued to the worn tabletop.

'As I am sure you are aware one of our colleagues has already spoken with your parents,' I continue. 'But we would like your thoughts on Victor and his last days too.'

Amélie sobs and stands up suddenly.

'I'm sorry,' she says. 'It is just all kind of too much.'

She goes over to the kitchen sink, tears off a sheet of paper towel and blows her nose. Then she returns to the table and sits down with her right hand tightly clenched around the paper towel.

'What was he like?' Malin asks.

Amélie shakes her head slowly.

'Ordinary. Kind. Good at school. Wanted to be a lawyer, like Mum.'

'Did he have any enemies that you know of?' Malin asks and makes a few notes in her pad.

'Definitely not. He was just . . . kind of completely innocuous, if you know what I mean. I don't think there is anyone who dislikes Victor.'

Amélie makes a face and corrects herself.

'*Disliked* Victor. Fucking hell. It is impossible to understand that he is gone. He was like my baby.'

She begins to cry again, takes the paper towel out and blows her nose one more time.

Malin looks at her and waits a while before going on:

'And what was his relationship with your parents like?'

Amélie inhales deeply and collects herself enough to be able to answer.

'Good. I mean, of course they argued at times. But it was nothing serious.'

'And that day?' I ask cautiously.

'We argued,' Amélie says quietly. 'About a fucking Netflix movie that I wanted to see and he didn't. It is completely insane, but that was how it was. And he left in the boat. Well, Victor could get pretty angry, so it wasn't the first time he'd left while we were having a fight.'

The room is quiet for a while.

'If I hadn't yelled at him he might still be alive,' she continues, in a quieter voice.

'What happened wasn't your fault,' I say, but Amélie doesn't answer.

'Do you have any theories about what might have happened to him?' Malin asks.

Amélie shakes her head forcefully so that a strand of her long hair catches in the corner of her mouth. She moves it out of the way with her middle finger. The nail is bitten so badly that the red quick is visible.

'No, he must have encountered a psycho. A fucking crazy person. Because *nobody* would want to hurt Victor.'

'OK,' Malin says and looks at me.

I can guess what she is thinking.

All these next of kin, the most innocent of victims – it is more rule than exception that they are unable to see their loved ones as having been anything but perfect.

Malin cocks her head a little and leans towards Amélie.

'What a beautiful earring,' she says.

'Thank you,' Amélie says, touching her earlobe with her hand. 'It's a ladybird. Victor has, or *had* one just like it. The earrings were our grandmother's and I inherited them when she died. So Victor got his ear pierced and my mum went crazy, but I gave him one. It was kind of like a sibling thing. We each had an earring.'

Malin nods and leans even further forward to see better.

The earring is small and indeed looks like a ladybird that seems to be crawling on the earlobe. It appears to feature some type of enamel.

'Did Victor wear the earring often?' I ask.

'Always,' Amélie answers quickly.

Malin nods, almost imperceptibly at me. We both know Victor wasn't wearing the earring when he was found.

'May I take a photo of your earring?' Malin asks.

Amélie shrugs.

'Sure.'

Malin brings out her phone and takes a few photos. Then she leans back in her chair and fixes Amélie with her gaze.

'One last question. Do you know if Victor or any of his friends used narcotics?'

Amélie's gaze wavers and she turns her head away.

'I have to ask you to be honest,' Malin goes on. 'It's not our intention to bust young people using recreational drugs, but it may be of importance to the investigation.'

Amélie is still silent. She pokes at a crumb with her finger, pushes it slowly across the surface of the table.

'Yes,' she says eventually.

'What did they take?' Malin asks.

'Coke. But only a few times, as far as I know. When they were partying.'

'Do you know how they got the cocaine?' I ask.

Amélie shakes her head.

'No. Or yes. I think one of Victor's friends bought it from someone named Måns, or maybe Malte. I don't really remember.'

'Which one of Victor's friends?' asks Malin, who has put her pen down and is completely focused.

Amélie sighs.

'I don't know. He never said.'

Malin looks at me. Here face is expressionless but her eyes say it all.

We need to find Malte Lindén.

Samuel

It is unbearably warm in zombie-Jonas's room, but it doesn't seem to bother him.

He is perfectly still, almost like a mannequin in the bed.

I also think he looks more gaunt. And his skin has become translucent – the bones and tendons are visible, like groceries in a thin plastic bag. His face is pale and his lips look dry and chapped.

I reach for the lip balm that is next to the vase with the rose on his bedside table.

It's quite touching. Rachel puts a fresh rose out for zombie-Jonas every morning, even though he has no idea it's there, even though he is a vegetable who would not have cared if there had been a turd in a bowl on the bedside table.

I lean over him and gently move the greasy white stick over his lips.

He doesn't react to my touch.

Then I go up to the window and open it, but it is only possible to open it a tiny way before the bars stop it.

When the window frame hits the rusty metal a pair of tree sparrows fly out of the bush that covers the window.

Passer montanus.

Mum could never learn the difference between tree sparrows and house sparrows.

Even though I explained that the tree sparrow has a black marking on its cheek, while the male house sparrow has a black bib.

I leave the window ajar, wipe the sweat off my brow and return to my worn-out sat-in chair.

I have a hard time focusing on reading aloud and consider putting some music on. I usually do that when I get tired of reading, which is often, since the book is so bloody slow. But today there is another reason I can't concentrate: I am thinking of the text from my mum that I read when I woke up, the one that must have come in sometime last night.

She got the money.

My mum – the world's most annoying, straight-laced, most anxious person – dug up Igor's money for me. Even though she can't so much as litter without being worried about going to hell or something, she went and got the money.

I can barely believe it's true.

We are going to meet in Stuvskär tomorrow, on Midsummer's Eve, and then it will be *bye-bye* zombie-Jonas.

It'll be so nice to get out of this place, even though I do like Rachel.

And Jonas?

I glance over at him.

He is lying still. His breathing is silent and shallow. The sheet has slid down and reveals his pale, hairless chest that slowly rises.

How can I have an opinion on him? You can neither like him nor dislike him. He sort of just is.

Like the creepy-crawlies and the earwigs under the rock.

I look down at the book in my lap. The pages are yellowed and wrinkled from moisture, as if it has been kept outdoors for a long time. I turn the pages and inhale the smell of damp paper and mould. At the back of the book, on the inside of the cover, I see something.

I turn until I get to the last page and inspect it. It's a stamp. It reads, 'Nacka High School, school library.'

Perhaps that's where Jonas went.

I close the book, let it rest in my hand and try to gauge the weight.

I would say fourteen ounces. Definitely more than eleven, but no more than sixteen. If the book were made of coke it would be worth about three hundred thou, but no one wants to pay that much for words.

The price per gram is nowhere near 800 kronor.

I open the book and make a new attempt to read, but stumble. The words get stuck in my mouth, tumble around, tangled up in each other and come out in the wrong order.

I have skipped a few chapters to see if the book gets more interesting at the end, but all that's happened is that the messed-up chick has hooked up with a nineteen-year-old matador named Romero. And to be honest I am not surprised, I actually saw that coming. But of course I feel for the protagonist, who seems to have a hard time understanding he should forget the bitch and move on.

Alexandra's face flickers across my mind. Her sad eyes look accusingly at me.

Yes, I regret treating her the way I did.

Yes, if I had thought about it a bit beforehand, used my brain, as Liam likes to say, I would've known what would happen if I hit

on Jeanette. I mean, you don't need to be a rocket scientist to understand what will happen if you put the moves on your girl's BFF.

*But thinking isn't your strong suit, is it, Samuel? That's why
nobody likes you, because you are a dumb, impulsive weirdo
who . . .*

'*Shut up!*' I say out loud.

I think about it.

Maybe Jonas would prefer some other book, something
more exciting. Maybe that would make him react, move his
hand a little, or grunt, the way he does sometimes.

Anything to make him a bit human.

There is a knock on the door and Rachel comes in.

'Hi,' she says in a soft voice, 'are things OK?'

I nod at her without answering.

She looks tired. Her hair is gathered in a messy ponytail
and the skin on her face and her cleavage is shiny with sweat.
She is dressed in a T-shirt and shorts and is wearing flip-flops
on her feet.

Still she is so very hot.

I can't help but wonder what it would be like to sleep with
her, what it would feel like to kiss those heavy breasts. It's
been so long since I fucked that I get hard the instant I think
about it.

I feel immediately ashamed and put the book in my lap.

'I was going to go and buy something,' she says, 'over by
the marina.'

'Down by that campsite?'

Her eyes darken.

'Have you been there?'

'No, I just . . .'

'Stay away,' she says. 'It's a real den. Drugs, stolen goods for sale and God-knows-what-else.'

Rachel has been stressed out and worried ever since we found those footprints in the flower bed. Even though she seemed cool when it happened, she has asked me several times if the man I saw in the garden might have been Igor. I repeatedly explained to her that it wasn't, because I would have recognised him.

I think she may be worried that it was one of the junkies from the campsite who came here to do reconnaissance. Somebody who wanted to break into the house.

'OK,' I say.

Rachel nods.

'I'll be back in an hour or so.'

Then her demeanour softens.

'You know, you're so good with Jonas. I'm so glad that you came to us. I just want you to know.'

I feel so self-conscious I don't know what to say.

Rachel waves her hand, then closes the door as she leaves me alone with zombie-Jonas. A minute later I hear the front door close. The car starts and soon after the sound of the engine fades into the distance.

'I'm going to go see if I can find a better book,' I tell Jonas.

I'm not sure why, but I've started to talk to him, as if he could understand what I was saying.

Maybe I'm going a bit loopy from living out here.

I leave the bedroom and carefully close the door behind me.

It's as if my feet know where to go, as if they're leading me to the spiral staircase and on up towards the top floor.

When I get there I end up standing in front of the door of what Rachel called Olle's study. The sun pours in through the large windows, cutting through the oppressively hot air. Through the windows I can see the expanse of the sea – seemingly infinite. There are only light ripples on the surface that glimmers in the sunlight.

I try the handle to the room.

The bloody door is locked.

But people are very predictable. And I guess there is no real reason to think Rachel would be any different.

I think of the key for her medicine cabinet, the one that lay on top of the cabinet, and walk over to the bookcase. Let my hand slide across the shelves at the very top.

It takes me less than a minute to find the key. It is at the far right on the top shelf, in front of a book about Swedish lighthouses.

The key slides easily into the lock and a few seconds later I am in the room.

It is pretty small, but has windows on two sides. The only furniture is a low shelf with books and a few folders, and a large, old-fashioned desk with an office chair. On the desk there is a printer and next to it is a stack of A4 paper. Next to that are a few framed photographs.

I go up to the desk, lean over and look at the pictures.

They are of Jonas as a child. In one picture he is smiling with a football under his arm and in the other he is posing in front of a moped.

I look around.

Next to the low shelf there is a navy blue duffle bag. It looks something like a gym bag, but a bit nicer. Like a bag you pack when you are going away for the weekend.

I go over and open it. Inside there are men's clothes – T-shirts, knitted sweaters and jeans. I dig around a bit among the clothes that seem clean and are neatly folded. At the bottom I notice a brown envelope.

I pull it out – no more than five ounces – and open it.

Inside there is a passport, belonging to Olle Berg, thirty-one years of age and five feet ten inches tall. Under the passport there is a credit card.

I look at the photo in the passport.

He doesn't look wholly dissimilar to me – the brown, tousled hair, the dark eyes.

Really it is only the beard that is different. And our ages, of course. He is thirteen years older than me, but if I grew a beard I might be able to pass for thirty.

Somewhere in the back of my mind a plan is coming together. It is still vague, loose around the edges like an egg over easy, but I know I am on to something.

The passport, the clothes. These are the puzzle pieces I have been missing.

Carefully I replace the envelope, pull the zipper shut and stand up. Go over to the desk again and reach for the thin stack of paper next to the printer.

At the top is a yellowed newspaper clipping.

A young man was found at midnight, badly injured, on road 53 by Sparreholm's castle. He was found by passers-by and it is not clear at present how his injuries occurred. The police are calling on any witnesses to get in touch with—

I put the clipping back down and pick up the papers underneath.

It is a printout titled 'Inertia'.

I leaf through it carefully. Under the cover there are a few pages of handwritten notes and a printout of what appears to be a long poem.

Olle is an author – he must have written it.

I think of zombie-Jonas down there, lying panting in the bedroom.

What would happen if I read something he recognised, or perhaps even had read before? Something Olle had written, for instance.

What if that would sort of set off some kind of reaction in his poor shutdown brain, like when you start a computer.

What if he were to wake up?

I close the door behind me and return to Jonas's room, sinking into the old chair beside him. It squeaks under my weight, but zombie-Jonas doesn't react.

I put the papers in my lap, clear my throat and begin to read.

You were the dove, I was the lamb
Paradise was our home,
our thorn-rimmed cemetery
Each day you flew further away

Like a storm you darkened the sun with your games,
like soot you befouled the air with your haughtiness,
like arrows your betrayal hurt

You were the dove, I was the lamb
You dismissed my warnings,

laughed at my words
You did not want to drink of my love
Your plumage quivered in excitement
Your mouth repeated 'no'
Your thoughts were everywhere,
but never here with me

I take a break.

What the hell is this shit?

I thought Olle wrote novels, not sick poems.

There's a noise from the bed.

Zombie-Jonas groans and his eyelids twitch. The bony fingers on one hand shake slightly and the muscles in his arm become taut.

His index finger lifts and he points toward the bedside table, just like the last time he woke up a little.

Does he understand what I am saying? Does he recognise the text?

Zombie-Jonas's arm reaches further and further, until it's just a few inches from the scratches in the varnish on the bedside table.

My heart beats faster and I continue to read.

You were the dove, I was the lamb
The rocks broke your wings,
the sun singed your feathers,
the lies blackened your beak
I fell, I died, I did not awake,
but in my greatest grief
a lion came to me

'Mahhrg . . .'

Zombie-Jonas gurgles from over in the bed and my pulse quickens.

> *You were the dove, I was the lamb*
> *I cared for your wounds*
> *I bid you to drink of my tears*
> *I carried you out of your inertia*
> *to the paradise that was ours*
> *Despite me saying that I forgive,*
> *you only wanted*
> *your wings back*

In the same instant I hear steps by the front door and a key in the lock.

I shoot up out of the chair and stash the papers under Jonas's mattress, but only have time to push them halfway in, one edge is still poking out.

Seconds later the door to the bedroom opens.

Rachel looks in.

'Hello, is everything all right?'

'Yes,' I say and glance over at Jonas who is lying still again.

Rachel goes up to the bed, bends forward and tucks him in. Gives him a light kiss on the forehead.

The papers rustle a bit and Rachel freezes mid-movement.

My heart stops and my stomach drops.

But Rachel's hesitation only lasts a second. She smiles and stands up.

'Would you like some food?'

Pernilla

I slept poorly; woke up several times and had a hard time going back to sleep. Listened to the blackbird who carried on in the cage in Samuel's room. Twisted and turned in the damp sheets. Cried and prayed alternately.

I cannot understand that Father is gone.

That his soul was called home by the Lord while I was digging up a bag full of drug money – because those bills hardly came from selling Brownie biscuits.

When I arrived at the hospice one of the nurses escorted me into his room.

There were fresh cut flowers on his bedside table and a candle was burning next to them. Father's hands were folded over the Bible on his chest. It was beautiful and terrible at the same time. Commonplace, even as it defied the imagination – that a beloved person can be here one second and gone the next.

And in the midst of sorrow I felt anger.

Father chose a very convenient time to die. Now I will never have any answers to why he didn't tell me that Mother wanted to see me.

We are alone now, Samuel and I.

I think of him. Remember the tiny body that the midwife placed on my chest and the joy in Father's eyes when he saw his grandchild for the first time, despite the unfathomable shame. Despite his unmarried teenage daughter having sinned and given birth to an illegitimate child.

And then the fat little two-year-old, with rolls on his legs and arms. The one who was always happy, as long as he got double portions of formula.

And now?

Money in a bag under a rock.

Tiny bags full of drugs, spread out like rose petals across the linoleum floor in the apartment.

Expensive designer clothes that I knew he couldn't afford.

And it is all my fault. It *has* to be, because of course Samuel was born perfect and innocent like all God's children.

I put the last of the cheese sandwich in my mouth and glance at the bag on the floor.

'Just do it,' it says.

I couldn't keep myself from looking inside the bag when I got home.

Samuel was right – it *was* full of money. And as soon as I'd seen the stacks of bills lying randomly the fear came creeping back in and I began thinking about the man in the stairwell again – Igor.

My body remembered too, because the place where he grabbed my arm ached and the skin stung as if I'd got sunburnt.

I had to get up several times. Check that the front door was locked and that the safety chain was on. And when I stood in the dark behind the thin curtain in the living room I thought I saw someone in the shadows outside – a dark figure hiding by the trees on the other side of the road.

But that had to have been my imagination?

In any case I do not intend to keep this money in my room a minute longer than necessary. I have made plans to meet Samuel by the dock in Stuvskär at five o'clock this afternoon, but I have decided to leave in the morning.

It is Midsummer's Eve.

I always spent Midsummer with Father. This will be my first time without him. Without pickled herring, sour cream and finely chopped chives. Without visiting the maypole. Without beer and aquavit and rain and sun and sun and rain.

I look out through the window.

The sun is shining down from a clear sky and the tree canopies don't appear to move an inch.

It is a beautiful day, as good a day as any to tell Samuel that his grandfather has passed away.

And to give him that godforsaken bag.

I still haven't unpacked the backpack I was supposed to bring on the hike. I decide to bring it to Stuvskär, in case Samuel needs to borrow something when he leaves.

I have a shower and brush my teeth. Put on a layer of mascara and pull a thin summer dress over my head. Then I take my backpack in one hand and the gym bag in the other and go out to the car.

Around the time I pass Länna I begin to get suspicious.

The black BMW that has been behind me since I got onto the Nynäs road is still there, even though I have tried slowing down as well as speeding up.

The vehicle is too far away for me to be able to see who is driving, but whoever it is, they are very concerned with maintaining distance.

A cold feeling spreads across my chest and my mouth goes dry. Despite the sunshine and the lush summer greenery surrounding me I feel unsafe.

I tell myself I am imagining things and turn the sound up on my stereo, so that I can hear the music through the roar from the open windows that are the closest my old banger comes to having AC.

The radio station plays 'Dancing Queen'.

ABBA was the only modern music group that Father would play when I was growing up. Really he preferred classical music and Christian bands, but I suspect he was so fond of ABBA that he just couldn't help listening to them.

The result was that we would play ABBA until the records were so worn that he was forced to buy new ones. And I knew every song by heart, despite not understanding the words.

The fact is that I would recount the names of the songs to myself if I got scared for some reason. Like a mantra.

'Dancing Queen'

'Mamma Mia'

'Chiquitita'

'The Winner Takes It All'

I adjust the rear-view mirror a bit and notice a white Volvo that has overtaken the black BMW and is now in the space between us.

My heart finds its normal rhythm and I draw a deep sigh of relief. Focus on the road in front of me. Loosen my white-knuckled grip on the steering wheel and wipe the sweat – first from the palm of one hand, then from the other – against the thin fabric of my skirt.

Then I raise the volume again and sing along to the lyrics.

But when I drive into Stuvskär a while later I see the black car again, maybe seventy-five yards behind me. It is rolling so slowly it is almost standing still.

The panic surfaces again.

My heart is beating out of my chest and sweat trickles between my breasts. Keeps running, like a small stream of anxiety, along the side of my belly.

What are my options?

Should I park, as if nothing has happened, and just go and lie down on a rock without worrying about the car, or should I try to shake off my shadow – *if* that is what it is.

Shake off my shadow?

That's a line straight out of a crime novel. Do I even know how to do such a thing?

Still I decide to try to do just that. Drive around the small roads in the area in the hope of losing the black BMW, as if it were an annoying insect crawling on my clothes.

I turn around by the ferry dock and drive back towards the black car. It immediately turns onto a forest road.

When I pass I slow down to try to get a glimpse of the driver, but it is impossible so I accelerate and continue a few hundred yards before I take a right on a small gravel road.

The road is terrible – there are large potholes here and there and I repeatedly have to dodge rocks.

I am surrounded by a forest of sparse, tall pines. The sun is filtering through the canopies and creating lace-like patterns on the roadway. Between the thin trees chubby slabs of granite poke through, partially overgrown with white moss. In the crevices I catch glimpses of ferns and blueberry bushes.

The air is cooler here in the shade. Cooler and saturated with the scent of conifers and rich soil.

I see fantastic villas from the last turn of the century and box-like summer homes from the 1950s. I see caravans and expensive sports cars parked on neat driveways, but I don't see any people.

Where is everyone? Have the Midsummer festivities already begun?

I glance in my rear-view mirror.

Nothing.

I slow down and continue winding along the narrow dirt roads around Stuvskär. Then I drive across a small bridge leading over glimmering water and onto one of the small islands.

There are fewer houses here. At one point I glimpse a driveway and I see one building a bit further into the woods, but generally speaking the area is oddly deserted.

Just as I am about to begin making my way back to the dock I discover the black car in my rear-view mirror.

I feel as if someone kicked me right in the gut.

Maybe it would be better to return to Stuvskär and go and lie on the rocks after all?

I slow down and drive around a large rock that has fallen onto the roadway. At the same time I see a narrow driveway on my right. There is a motorbike parked next to a black Volvo and something about the motorbike looks familiar. Something about the black paint and the flames on the petrol tank.

I look in among the pines. Glimpse the top floor and roof of a beautiful old wooden house.

I accelerate and look in the rear-view mirror again.

The car is still there and I say a prayer:

'Please, God. Help me get to Stuvskär safely. In Jesus' name. Amen.'

I squeeze the steering wheel as I whisper these words. Close my eyes for a moment trying to get in touch with Him.

When I open my eyes again I am blinded by a ray of sunlight. I squint and try to make out the contours of the road.

The forest has got denser. It is darker and in places there are fir trees growing among the pines.

I look in the rear-view mirror.

The car is gone.

Is it possible? Has my prayer been heard?

At first I don't dare believe it's true. I drive around the small roads for probably fifteen minutes before I realise that the BMW really *is* gone.

'Thank you, God,' I murmur and begin to find my way back to Stuvskär. 'Thank you, God, for hearing my prayer.'

Samuel

It is just after ten in the morning when I hear the front door close. Rachel has let me sleep in since I've been working so much overtime the last few days. Her guy, Olle, still isn't back from Stockholm and I haven't had as much time off as she promised.

I jump out of bed, step into my jeans, go out into the family room and draw a few deep breaths.

It has to be thirty *fucking* degrees in my room.

At least.

And you can't open the window without being eaten alive by mosquitoes.

The floorboards creak and sigh when I walk up to the window and look out across the water. Some sea birds glide high above and there is a sailing boat on the horizon.

Rachel jogs down the long wooden stairs towards the jetty dressed in her far-too-large navy blue bathrobe. Her long hair flutters behind her.

It seems she slept in too.

Maybe Jonas had a rough night, the kind that ends with him getting a shot in the bum cheek, making him high as a fucking kite.

I force myself to stop looking at Rachel and go over to the bookcase. The key is right where I left it – next to the book about lighthouses. And when I unlock the door to Olle's study, it opens without a sound.

The room is still in the shade and the air is pleasantly cool. There is a slight scent of dust and leather from the armchair in the corner.

I kneel down beside the navy blue canvas bag and pull out a pair of jeans, a T-shirt and a button-down shirt. Pick up the envelope containing the passport and the credit card.

Then I pull the zipper shut and make sure the bag looks like it did before.

It does – it is completely impossible to see that I've been digging around in there, unless someone opens the bag and notices that the clothes and the envelope are missing.

I sneak out of the room, lock the door behind me and put the key back in the same place as before. I put the clothes and the envelope in my backpack, next to the Fentanyl vials that I took from the medicine chest.

I make sure I have my other things too – the mobile, the charger and my keys – and slide my fingers across the key ring I got from Mum. A miniature book and a small plastic fish dangle on the stainless-steel ring. An idiotic Christian thing that the congregation bought to bribe the kids in the youth group.

The time has come to get out of here.

As soon as I am done for the day I am leaving to meet Mum by the dock.

And I don't intend to come back.

Once I have Igor's money I'll be able to stay away for a long time. And thanks to the passport I can even go abroad.

It's like, problem solved.

After I've showered I walk down the spiral staircase to the ground floor. There's a smell of freshly made pancakes.

That round, slightly burned scent arouses my hunger, but also something else: a nagging sense of guilt swells in my chest.

Poor Rachel – here she is making grub for me, even though she doesn't need to. She really deserves better than to run into a guy who steals from her and then takes off, leaving her alone with her vegetable kid.

I swallow hard and feel how tight my throat feels, as if an invisible ball was lodged there.

You don't know anything. You don't want anything. And now you are pissing on the only person who's helped you.

'Happy Midsummer! There are pancakes. I hope you're hungry.' Rachel smiles and pops a piece of pancake into her mouth with her index finger and her thumb.

She is wearing an apron over her white dress and I think of Mum again. She used to make pancakes for breakfast when I was little and she had an apron that looked almost the same.

The lump in my throat grows. I feel like my throat is about to explode and I can't speak.

I sit by the table, pour some juice into a glass and force down a few gulps.

Rachel comes up to me and places a plate of freshly made pancakes on the table.

'Here you are!'

'Thank you,' I manage, even as the lump in my throat threatens to explode.

'I need to go down to the shops for a bit,' she says, untying the apron at her back, pulling it over her head and hanging it on a hook by the stove. 'Will you keep an eye on Jonas?'

'Sure,' I say and feel myself slowly regaining control, the anxiety is fading and the hard lump shrinks like a punctured balloon.

I am not a bad person, I think.

I am just a guy like any other, who is in trouble and doing his best to get out of it.

I never had a choice.

Zombie-Jonas is lying motionless on his back.

The faint smell of urine that permeates the stuffy room mixes with the scent of the red rose in the vase on the table, like a lone exclamation point.

I lean over the bed and inspect his face carefully.

The skin in his nostril, where the cannula pokes out, is red and there is pus. Part of a scab has come loose, revealing raw flesh. His mouth seems even drier than yesterday and deep, vertical cracks criss-cross his lips.

'Hi,' I say, reaching for the lip balm. Take the cap off and carefully run the rounded tip across his lips.

He doesn't react, but a thin, viscous strand of saliva runs out of the corner of his mouth and onto the pillow.

I get up and fetch a paper towel from the shelf on the wall. Carefully wipe his mouth and place the towel next to the vase with the rose on the bedside table. Then I reach for the hand cream, squeeze out a blob and start to massage his thin, cold fingers.

'What do you think? Shall we finish reading that poem?'

Of course he doesn't answer, but the fact is that *I* am a bit curious as to what will happen to the lion, the lamb and that wounded dove that just wanted its wings back.

I lean across the bed and pull out the paper that is stuck under the mattress at the foot of the bed. Sit down in my armchair and begin to read.

> *You were the dove, I was the lamb*
> *The lion chastised you,*
> *Roared you have to stay*
> *But his teeth were so sharp,*
> *his claws so long*
> *He your body happened to crush*
> *in his attempt to catch you*
> *The dove was no more*
> *I cried myself a sea of tears*
> *and lay down to die*
> *on the soft tuft of grief*
> *But the lion emerged anew*
> *and in his giant maw he held*
> *an untarnished dove*

I lay the paper down in my lap. The poem continues on the next page, but something makes me stop.

I can't read any more.

Who would write this kind of messed-up shit?

Besides, this isn't just sick, it's sick in a way that is almost a bit *biblical*. And if anyone knows what that means, it is me, after having been forced to go to those fools at the Bible school in Mum's congregation.

I look at the text again. Reread the last lines.

But the lion emerged anew
and in his giant maw he held
an untarnished dove

There is something about this poem, the actual story, that makes the hairs on the back of my neck stand up. But I can't figure out what. It is as if some sort of epiphany is hatching in my subconscious, as if a big black animal is swimming down there, refusing to surface, even as I try to summon to it.

I fold up the papers with the poem, put them in the back pocket of my jeans and look at zombie-Jonas.

His whole body is shaking and his fists are clenched as if he is having a seizure.

Dammit!

He'd better not be about to die on my watch!

But just seconds later the pale hands relax and his body is still again. White foam is coming out of the corners of his mouth. It reminds me of the foam that gathers by the rocks when it's windy.

I reach for the bedside table, take the paper towel and wipe the drool off with a sense of growing unease.

'I have to go soon,' I say. 'Sorry. It's nothing personal, really, I just have to go.'

I think for a bit then say:

'Anyway, I hope you get better soon and all that.'

I'm out of words.

There is nothing more to say, nothing that can explain what I'm about to do.

After that I sit still in the armchair. Time has slowed to a crawl.

The door slams when Rachel comes home. I can hear her rustle with bags and opening the fridge. Then she disappears into her room.

I wait another half hour and then decide that it is time. I reach for Jonas's hand, take it in mine and squeeze it, but carefully so that he won't bruise.

'Bye. Get better.'

He lies there, immobile.

I go into the hall and knock on Rachel's door.

'Come on in!' she calls.

I crack the door open and see her sitting in front of her little desk, with the laptop open as usual.

She works a lot.

She takes her reading glasses off and closes the computer. Rests her arm on the table and looks at me.

'Everything OK?'

I nod.

'He is sleeping. I need to go to the shop to buy some stuff.'

'Sure,' she says. 'Could you get me a bike lock at the petrol station if you happen to pass it?'

'Absolutely,' I say and feel a bit ashamed as I think I will never buy her that lock. That I will soon be far away from here.

'Here, 200 should be enough?'

'Sure,' I say and put the money in my pocket.

The sun is shining in through the window, giving Rachel's hair a copper glow. She notices that I'm looking at her and smiles a little.

I swallow hard and resist the impulse to rush out of there, to get away from Rachel who is sitting there and like not really knowing how damn fit she is.

I merely smile back at her, like a really well brought-up lad.

She opens her laptop again, puts her glasses on and turns around, as if to signal that the conversation is over.

I go out into the hall, put on my shoes and backpack.

Just as I am about to open the door I hear steps behind me and turn around.

Rachel is standing in the hall behind me.

'Hey,' she says quietly. 'I just wanted to thank you again. You are so incredibly good with Jonas. I saw that you had moisturised his hands too. It means so much to me that you're here. Especially now when Olle is away. It is nice to have a man in the house.'

'Thanks,' I mumble.

It is nice to have a man in the house.

I can feel myself blush. At the same time I feel bad about being such a useless human. About being about to trick her and leave her very soon, like a straight-up conman.

I open the front door to Rachel's house for the last time and meet her gaze.

At that very moment Rachel's smile freezes, her eyes widen and her mouth becomes a little 'o'.

'*What?*' I ask and feel a little gust of warm, humid air gush in to caress my neck – it almost feels like standing in the breeze on a platform the seconds before the train rolls in.

Rachel doesn't answer.

Her mouth widens and she emits a scream so loud my heart feels like it stops for real. As if it freezes mid-beat and sort of dies on the spot, shrivelling into a dry little piece of cartilage in my chest.

Slowly I turn around towards the front door.

An enormous, dark figure towers on the doorstep. Muscles strain against his tight vest. His tattooed skin shines with sweat. His jaw is clenched and his eyes look dead, as if someone had gouged them out and replaced them with two lead marbles.

It is Igor.

Manfred

Sometimes I think things would have been easier if it hadn't been for the age difference between Afsaneh and me.

Sure, Nadja would still have been sick and I would have still been grappling with feelings of guilt.

But maybe not quite as much, or possibly not in the same way, because with Afsaneh it is as if I always start out in debt. As if she already did me an enormous favour in the first place by getting together with me, despite me being so much older and coming with the considerable baggage of a spoiled ex-wife, three grown children and a lot of excess weight.

The fact is that she didn't just accept my family, she liked them from the start. And the kids loved her. Yes, even Beatrice liked her, which is a bloody miracle, because there is scarcely a person alive that woman likes.

Maybe it's because Afsaneh doesn't have a family of her own that she bonded so quickly with mine. She was just a baby when her father and older brother were murdered in Iran in the early 1980s, a few years after the Islamists seized power under Ayatollah Khomeini. Her mother, who received notice of the deaths while she was at a market, fled the country with Afsaneh literally on her arm. Three months later they arrived in Stockholm and slowly began to build their life back up. It went pretty well, but when Afsaneh was seventeen her mother died in the aftermath of a massive myocardial infarction.

Afsaneh told me all of this the very first time we met. She was also clear that her main goal in life was to start a family. So the day she told me that she was pregnant I could hardly tell her that I already had three children and wasn't really interested in another.

I owed her more than that.

You might think I could have managed to protect our little family, the one Afsaneh had wanted for so long. That I could have prevented our child from falling from the third floor onto the hard tarmac below.

My stomach drops as I think of Nadja's little hand, sticky with butter, sliding out of mine, as the construction workers ran toward us on the street below.

If it hadn't been for Grzegorz Cybulski – a twenty-five-year-old Polish casual worker – Nadja would have been dead now. He tried to catch her and managed to break her fall.

Afsaneh and I visited Grzegorz a week or so after the accident to thank him and give him flowers. Despite having broken his arm he was in good spirits and seemed happy to see us.

We knew even then that Nadja's prognosis was uncertain, but we hadn't imagined that we'd be stuck in limbo, on the threshold of life and death, for an indeterminate period of time.

I look at Nadja.

She looks so peaceful in her hospital bed. The sun finds its way in through the window and falls across her right arm. Paints her skin golden and makes the fine hair on her skin shimmer.

I wonder what she is thinking as she lies there, sunk into the dormancy they call a coma. If she dreams, or perhaps even experiences moments when she is awake and floating just under the surface of consciousness. Perhaps she can hear us in those moments, in the manner that you can hear what's happening on the other side of a closed door if you put your ear against it.

Maybe the membrane that separates her sleep from our reality is actually paper-thin.

Maybe I can break through it, if only I want it badly enough, love her intensely enough.

If I atone sufficiently for my guilt.

And there it is again – that magical thinking. That doesn't lead anywhere but straight into the quagmire of self-pity and remorse.

Afsaneh gets up and goes over to Nadja. Bends over her.

'Why won't she wake up?' she asks.

'They did say she reacted to pain yesterday. That's a good sign.'

'I want her to wake up,' Afsaneh says. She is increasingly expressing herself in the straightforward manner of a child, completely without euphemism or pleasantries.

'You know that could take time.'

'I can't wait any longer. I want her to wake up now.'

Afsaneh pulls out her phone and takes a few steps back, squats.

'What are you doing?' I ask.

'Taking a photo.'

'I can see that. But why?'

She doesn't answer. Instead she sits down on the chair next to mine and begins to write something on her phone.

You're not really supposed to use mobile phones in here, but Afsaneh doesn't care. She says that her friend Lowe, who is working on a PhD in physics maintains that it cannot possibly interfere with the electronics in the ward.

I catch a glimpse of Nadja on the screen before Afsaneh's message is dispatched with a swishing noise.

'Why are you sending photos of Nadja?'

'It's for the forum.'

'For the forum? Are you *insane*? That is completely disrespectful to Nadja and to us.'

'You don't get it. We share our experiences. I wouldn't be able to go on without it. Besides I don't share any images where anyone might recognise her.'

Afsaneh puts her phone into her handbag and looks at me. If I didn't know she had given up smoking I could've sworn that she smelled like tobacco. Her eyes are swollen and red-rimmed. There is a crusty cold sore in the corner of her mouth. Her forehead is shiny and her lips pale.

For the first time in a long time I am uncertain as to which one of us is right.

Am I just an old fogey who doesn't understand her suffering, or is she the one who has lost her ability to maintain boundaries between public and private?

Just as we are about to go home and eat our humble Midsummer's lunch I get a text from Malin.

I read it and turn to Afsaneh.

'I need to go in to work for a bit.'

She looks at me with dark, empty eyes.

'It's Midsummer's Eve.'

'I'll be back as soon as I can.'

When I get to the station Malin is in the conference room waiting for me.

Being extremely pleased to have lost almost two stone, I hate these occasions when I have to confront my lack of self-discipline.

I look at the table.

She has bought chocolate croissants. The worst kind of calorie bomb, in other words. Nothing has been held back – sugar, fat and lightning-fast carbs ready to go, just waiting to sprint to the fat folds around my belly and set up camp there – it is all concentrated in the irresistibly crispy pastries that are crowding the greasy paper plate.

I take one and tell myself that it can't make much difference. One croissant does not a mountain of blubber make.

'What happened?' I ask.

Malin shrugs.

'No idea, but I hope this will be quick.'

Just as I am popping the last piece into my mouth, Letit enters the room, dressed in the same see-through shirt as the other day, this time without a string vest underneath.

'What would you say about a chat with Igor Ivanov's right-hand man?' he asks and sits down on one of the worn chairs.

Malin puts her paper cup down so hard that the coffee splashes onto the table.

'*What?* Did you find Malte Lindén?'

Letit leans forward, looks Malin in the eye and flashes a wide grin.

'The investigative unit located him last night and serious crimes pulled him in for questioning after a prosecutor's order this morning,' he says. 'I just went down there to look in on him.'

Malin nods and wipes the coffee up with a napkin with a faded Christmas print that has survived at least one winter in the recesses of the police building.

'Is he giving us a hard time?' I ask.

Letit shakes his head.

'No. He's not new to this. He's done time for possession and assault. He knows to pick his battles. But of course he did try to wangle his legal counsel into the questioning.'

'And what did you say?' Malin asks.

Letit smiles slyly.

'That he has no more right to a lawyer than a whore has to sick pay,' he says emphatically. 'You get a lawyer when you are reasonably suspected of a crime, according to the twenty-first chapter of Procedural Law – it follows that one must have been made party to such a suspicion according to chapter twenty-three.'

Malte Lindén is leaning back in his chair with his arms firmly folded across his chest.

He's wearing a white vest and a pair of baggy jeans. His body is thin, bordering on emaciated, thin light brown hair falls in greasy strips across his acne-scarred face. His facial expression is indifferent and his gaze bored, as if he were sitting on a train, rather than at the station being questioned by the police.

We introduce ourselves and sit down around the table.

Malte's face does not change, but he does raise one eyebrow when all three of us enter the room — normally there are two officers at a questioning.

Just as Malin is about to start the tape recorder there is a knock on the door and Malik pokes his head in.

'Letit, would you come with me for a bit?'

'Must I?' Letit asks, sounding like a cranky five-year-old.

'It's important.'

Letit sighs, gets up and leaves the room with deliberate slowness.

Malin starts the tape recorder and rattles off the formalities. Then turns to Malte and gets straight to the point.

'Did you know Johannes Ahonen and Victor Carlgren?'

There is a short pause before Malte replies.

'No,' he says, without looking at Malin.

'So you have never met either of them?'

'No.'

Malin takes out photos of Johannes and Victor and places them on the table in front of Malte.

'Do you recognise these men?'

'No,' Malte replies without looking at the pictures.

'I need to ask you to look at the pictures,' I say.

Reluctantly Malte's gaze makes its way down to the printouts. He shrugs.

'Do you recognise them?' Malin asks again.

'No.'

'Never seen them?'

'No.'

'And you are sure of that?'

'Mhm.'

'We have information indicating that both Johannes Ahonen and Victor Carlgren have bought cocaine from persons whom we can connect to you and Igor Ivanov. What do you have to say about that?'

'Nothing,' Malte answers sluggishly and in the cold glow of the fluorescent lights looks disinterestedly at the nails on one of his hands.

'So you have no comment on them having bought cocaine from your crew?'

'I didn't say that,' Malte says without raising his voice. 'I said I have no comment on your *allegation* that they bought cocaine from people you *allege* know me.'

Malin shoots me a resigned look and I shrug.

This is to be expected.

Hardened career criminals are not so easily shaken. There needs to be more than a couple of fragmented allegations during a questioning to get a guy like Malte to admit that he has done anything that even borders on illegal.

I try a different tactic. Take out the pictures taken by the forensic pathologist and put them on the table.

'The guys were likely murdered,' I say. 'They were young. Had their whole lives ahead of them. Someone took that from them and dumped them in the ocean, like rubbish.'

Malte glances at the pictures without altering his facial expression at all, apparently completely unaffected by the bloated bodies and the distended, split skin.

'That's too bad for them,' he mumbles in the same monoto-
nous voice.

Malin sighs, squirms and says: 'If you know anything at all
about this you would do well to tell us now.'

Malte doesn't answer.

'*Do* you know anything, Malte?' I ask.

Slowly the thin man's gaze meets mine and the hair at the
back of my neck stands up when I see his indifferent expression. A chill spreads through me, despite the interview room
being as hot as a sauna.

Something glistens inside Malte's mouth and only now do
I notice that his front teeth are gold.

'No,' he says. 'I don't know anything.'

The room is quiet.

'Malte, where is Igor?' I ask.

'Don't know.'

'You have no idea?'

'Maybe he went for a swim?'

'Went for a swim?'

Malte bends and pulls on his bony fingers so that the
knuckles pop, one by one, and I detect a smile on his skinny
face.

'Well, the weather is nice.'

On our way up the stairs we run into Letit who is on his way
down. He puffs and pants as if he has just run a 400-metre race
and I see large wet spots under his synthetic sleeves.

'Not a thing,' Malin answers the question that Letit hasn't
asked.

'What-did-I-tell-you?' Letit pants.

'But what if you were wrong?' Malin says.

'I'm never wrong,' Letit says, without a doubt. 'I have only been wrong once, and then I *thought* I was wrong. Although it turned out I was right.'

He laughs, grunting at his own hilarity.

'But don't mope, kids,' he continues and takes a step up the stairs. 'Because uncle Gunnar has a really nice bone for you to chew on. Come, let me show you!'

We follow him up the stairs to his office, where his laptop is open.

'Malik wanted me because we had a visitor from forensics,' Letit says, wiping sweat off his brow. 'And since I have worked a bit in this area he wanted me to be in on it.'

He says the last part emphatically and with poorly concealed pride.

He types something into the keyboard and the screen comes to life.

Then he clicks through a sequence of pictures.

'This is Victor Carlgren's body, neatly packaged in a sheet and wrapped in chains. What's not immediately apparent is that there is also some masking tape on the sheet, here by the neck.'

Letit points at the mummy-like figure.

'OK . . .?' Malin says hesitantly.

'The tape has protected the fabric under it from decomposition,' Letit continues. 'And right here . . .'

He points at a spot on the mummy's neck and continues:

'Right here a few hairs and corresponding follicles were found under the tape. The forensics team has managed to extract nuclear DNA, which means that we have a complete DNA profile of the person the hairs came from.'

He pauses and looks triumphantly at us.

'And it's neither one of the victims,' he adds.

'The *killer*?' Malin whispers.

'Could be,' Letit says, looking first at me, then at Malin. Then he flashes the biggest smile I have ever seen on him. His entire face, typically so morose, cracks and softens.

'But we know *whose* DNA it is!' he says. 'Because he has a criminal record.'

'Who?' Malin asks on an inhale.

Letit's grin gets even wider.

Malin boxes him tenderly on the shoulder.

'Dammit, Gunnar. Tell us!'

He nods slowly, strokes his beard and taps the keyboard again. A mugshot of a man with tangled brown hair and a beard appears.

'Olle Berg, thirty-one years old. Convicted of assault and unlawful threats.'

Pernilla

The ferry landing at Stuvskär is empty except for two ten-year-old boys sitting at the edge of the jetty fishing.

A muggy breeze ripples the water and makes my wide skirt flutter so that I have to hold it down. There is a strong smell of seaweed and fish from the small shiny perch that lie neatly lined up on a newspaper behind the boys. In the distance a white archipelago ferry is headed toward us. Foam is streaming around the bow and people are crowding at the gunwale for a place in the sun.

I'm supposed to meet Samuel in fifteen minutes.

I sit on the concrete bench and put the gym bag between my feet. I hope this has taught him a lesson and that he gets his life in order now. Because I can't always run to the rescue every time he's in a scrape.

At least, not if that involves breaking the law.

The boat is almost here now. I can see the passengers clearly. Those who are going to spend Midsummer in Stuvskär are already lining up at the bow with bags bursting with food, beer and aquavit.

The boys who were fishing on the dock get up. One of them takes out his phone and begins to photograph the perch. Then he picks up the paper and throws the fish in the water.

I feel immediately nauseous.

I know. These are just some fish. But why would you do that to another living creature? Catch it only to take a photo and throw it back in the ocean when you're done?

What's the point?

I watch the boys as they disappear in the direction of the harbour pub.

They walk side by side but do not seem to be talking to each other, instead they are so deeply immersed in their phones that one boy almost walks straight into a parked car.

The boat docks and passengers in their Midsummer best stream onto the jetty, walk towards the harbour and disappear in various directions. A flatbed moped starts and drives off with its cargo of people and luggage. Two dogs bark angrily at each other.

I press my ankles around the gym bag and glance at my watch – five minutes to go.

The landing is empty now.

The ferry disappears behind an island. Large dark clouds accumulate over the land and the wind picks up. The rusty semaphore tower squeaks a little and an old ice-cream wrapper flies past and lands in the water below me.

I look at my watch again.

Samuel is ten minutes late, but then that isn't unusual. Samuel is often late. Or early, but very rarely on time.

I look down at the bag between my feet.

It looks so ordinary, so quotidian and inoffensive. I would certainly not have suspected it of containing anything illegal if I'd seen someone carrying it about town.

My phone rings and I shiver, despite the heat.

It's Stina wondering if I will be able to work tomorrow. I say that I can and we talk for a while. When I tell her that Father has passed away she comforts me and promises that she will take care of me when we see each other. I suspect this means that she is going to fill me with alcohol again, but don't say that. Then we talk about Samuel. I hear genuine joy in her voice when I tell her I am waiting for him at Stuvskär.

'I am so very happy for you, my friend. So very happy.'

We agree to meet up as soon as I am back in town. Stina wants to make me dinner and I promise to come, if it's not too much trouble.

'Nonsense,' she exclaims. 'You're no trouble at all, sweetie. By the way, how did things go with that sanctimonious pastor? Has he left you alone?'

I tell her what happened when we were about to leave for that hike, how the pastor ordered me to come with and how I told him he could think again.

Stina wheezes with laughter and seems to drop her phone on the floor.

'I'm sorry,' she snorts when she has got hold of it again. 'Did you say that? In front of the kids? That's the funniest thing I have heard in a long time. You'll have to tell me more when you come over for dinner. And then I'll make sure to complain to you. It'll be my turn. I always meet the wrong men, have I told you that?'

I laugh and say no, she hasn't told me that. Then we hang up.

I don't tell her about the bag of money. I am far too ashamed.

The minutes pass, minutes become an hour. The sky gets even darker and I can hear thunder in the distance. Deep rumbling rolling across the islands like a giant rock.

I look out across the sea. I look out onto the land.

I check my phone every ten minutes.

I go up to the harbour pub and peer in through the un-washed windows. I go into the supermarket and buy the cheapest thing I can find – a ridiculously expensive carton of organic coconut water.

But still no Samuel.

Heavy rain begins to fall.

In the end I leave the dock and begin to walk aimlessly along the small gravel road along the water. I pass red cabins and small inlets where the water rests black and placid under the heavy clouds. The rain gathers force and I look around for some kind of shelter.

Next to a jetty, maybe thirty yards away there is a small boathouse. The roof extends beyond the door.

I jog over to the dilapidated wooden structure and press against the door.

I can hear the rain patter on the roof above me. The thunder rumbles and lightning is near constant. My dress is wet and cold and my hair hangs in wet strands down my back, but all I can think about is that my child is missing again. And suddenly I am seized by a completely irrational, yet entirely convincing sense that he is in danger.

That something terrible has happened.

Samuel

Igor is over me.

I am flat on my belly with my hands locked in an iron grip behind my back.

Strong arms lift me up and slam me against the floor.

Lift me up. Slam me.

Over and over, as if I were a rag doll or perhaps a coconut that he is trying to crack open.

I feel something in my face break; my nose crunches as he once again throws my head to the floor. Seconds later my mouth fills up with blood.

Igor's hold is so hard that I can barely breathe. All I can manage is to inhale teeny, tiny gasps.

Then he sits on me. A knee presses into my lower back. The grip on my hands becomes even harder and a sharp pain radiates through my already numb arms.

He leans over me and whispers in my ear.

'*Fucking. Bastard. Damn. Cunt.*'

Spit splashes across my cheek.

I can't answer, can't move. I can't breathe, but I can still detect his smell; a predator's acrid scent of sweat and rage.

And in the midst of all the chaos it is as if some part of my brain is still able to analyse the situation. Calculate the likelihood that he will crush my head against the floor or break my arms. Weigh my options with astonishing precision.

And that part of my brain dryly establishes that I am toast. That I stand no chance in hell against Igor. That he will mash me like an overripe banana.

I should be panicking. Perhaps I should be praying. But all I can do is think of her.

Mum.

'You thought you could get one over on me? You're going to *die*, do you understand?'

The words are more distant now, as if I am thinking them or maybe remembering them rather than hearing them.

'Your mum led me here. Isn't that comical? She . . .'

Igor's voice fades away and all that exists is the red-hot pain that pulsates through me in waves. As if I am drowning in a sea of pain.

Then everything is white and quiet.

The pain fades away and I can feel her presence. Know that she is standing there next to me, that she will not let me die. She places her cool hand on my forehead.

'Samuel.'

Her voice is a whisper, but it contains so much love.

'Samuel, how are you? *Please*, tell me that you are OK!'

The pain returns to my arm, my nose begins to throb and the world around me regains solid outlines. I recognise the shiny wooden floorboards against my cheek and become aware of the weight on my back.

She gives my shoulder a light shake.

'Samuel!'

I open an eye.

It's not Mum, it's Rachel.

And then I see the blood. It's oozing across the floor like a fucking lake. Covers almost the entire hallway.

I scream even though I suspect that I am dead. Surely nobody can bleed this much and live?

Rachel puffs and groans and a few seconds later the weight on my back is gone. The relief is immediate – I feel almost as if I am floating above the floor.

I manage to get up into a squat and look around. Slip on the blood and almost fall.

Igor is lying on his back on the floor next to me.

His arms have fallen out to the sides; his mouth is open, his eyes too and there is a gaping red hole in his temple. It looks like a predator took a large bite out of his head.

I look at Rachel.

She is standing next to Igor. On the floor beside her is a doorstop in the shape of a lamb.

It is covered in blood.

Rachel is distraught.

Tears stream down her cheeks and snot hangs in long strands from her nose.

'I. Didn't. Mean. To. Kill. Him.'

I can barely make out the words between her sobs as we move into the kitchen. I turn the tap off and wipe myself on the linen tea towel, but my hands are shaking so badly I drop it on the floor.

'*He's deeaaad*,' Rachel groans and begins to walk back and forth in the kitchen. She leaves sticky red footprints in her wake.

I glance out towards the hallway.

The large body is still lying in the puddle of blood.

Rachel sinks into a chair at the kitchen table, buries her face in her hands and rocks back and forth.

'What are we going to do?' she moans. 'What are we going to do? *What are we going to do? What are—?*'

'Maybe we should call the police?' I whisper.

Not because I really want the police to show up, but because this is too crazy for us to handle on our own. Not even I – who avoids the cops like the plague – have the faintest clue what to do when you have accidentally killed someone.

Rachel stops rocking, takes her hands off her face and looks at me. Suddenly she seems collected.

'We can't do that,' she says. 'I killed him. I can't go to prison, surely you understand? Jonas doesn't have anyone but me. He wouldn't make it, he would . . .'

Her voice cracks and she emits a barely audible sob.

'It was self-defence,' I say. 'You don't go to prison for that.'

Rachel slowly shakes her head.

'I can't risk that. No.'

And then:

'And you don't want the police on your tail, do you?'

I look at her.

Even though I have confided in Rachel I never told her anything about Igor's business, but maybe she figured that out on her own.

'But . . .' I say, feeling suddenly hopeless. 'What should we do?'

Rachel sighs.

'Maybe you are right. Maybe we have to call the police.'

Then, in the next second:

'No. We just can't. We *can't*.'

Then she begins to sob again and walks towards me with her hands raised. For each step she takes there is a smacking from the dried blood.

'Samuel,' she says. 'What have we done?'

She puts her arms around me and hugs me hard.

'Let's throw him into the sea,' I mumble with my mouth against her ear.

Rachel freezes, lets go of me and steps back.

'Are you crazy?' she whispers.

Then she furrows her brow and seems to be processing what I said.

'No,' she continues. 'We can't throw him in here. What if someone finds him?'

'But if we go further out to sea. You have a boat, don't you?'

Rachel shakes her head and wipes a tear.

'In this weather?'

She turns her face to the window. The rain is pouring down outside and the thunder rumbles.

'Besides,' she murmurs. 'Something is wrong with the boat. It stops all the time. No. That wouldn't work. What if our engine stalls with him on board?'

She nods in Igor's direction. Seconds later she puts her hand to her mouth, as if she is feeling sick.

I push the wheelbarrow down the narrow path. Rachel is walking in front of me, guiding me.

The rain lashes the back of my neck and the thunderclaps come hard and fast. My head is throbbing, my nose feels as swollen as a fucking balloon and every once in a while I feel so nauseous I want to throw up, but I keep walking because I don't want to let Rachel down.

I think that in some sense we are lucky, that it is probably less likely we'll run into anyone in this weather.

Igor's body is covered by a blanket, but a bloody hand pokes out from beneath the fringed hem.

The situation is so messed up.

We have actually killed a person, even if it was in self-defence and the person in question was a monster, a real arsehole who was trying to do the same to me.

We have taken a life and that is incomprehensible – that Igor, who was recently breathing and reeking of sweat and slamming my head into the floor like some kind of psycho, is now squeezed into the wheelbarrow, covered with a tartan blanket.

When I think about it that way I get nauseous and have to close my eyes. And when I close my eyes I need to stop and steady myself against a tree so as not to fall over.

Rachel turns around and looks at me with concern.

'Come,' she says and looks around quickly.

I grab the wheelbarrow and keep going. Count the steps, like I always do.

We walk along the road and up a small hill – 147 steps from the gate. Then we turn left onto something that looks like an abandoned lot – 197.

Rachel's wet dress clings to her back and her bra is clearly visible under the wet fabric.

Two hundred and ten.

She turns around.

'Here!' she says, pointing into the bushes.

I can make out the outline of a dilapidated building, partially covered with weeds and saplings.

She waits for me to catch up.

I gather momentum and force the wheelbarrow over a small bump. Then I stop next to her.

Two hundred and fifty.

'There used to be an old paint factory here,' she says, nodding towards the ruin. 'It closed fifty years ago but the ground is still poisoned by the chemicals and the council and the government can't agree on who should fund the clean-up. By the way, that is the reason there are so few houses on the island. Nobody wants to build on toxic waste. Anyway, the ruin here is the old foreman's quarters.'

I look around.

Next to the ruin I can make out an old well and beside that there is a pile of rocks overgrown with vines.

'Nobody—'

Rachel's voice is drowned out by a thunderclap.

'Nobody ever comes here,' she says emphatically. 'Nobody.'

She gives me a serious look with her dark eyes and once again I think of Mum.

In the next instant I remember that I was supposed to meet her at Stuvskär. That must have been at least an hour ago. She has probably been standing on the dock in the rain waiting. Got angry, got sad and ultimately disappointed.

As usual.

Rachel points to the old well.

'There!' she says.

She walks up to the lid and grabs the rusty handle.

'Can you help me?' she asks.

Manfred

Evening.

The thunderstorm has abated but a light rain is falling over Stockholm. Steam rises from the still-warm tarmac. The sky is dark and the air that streams in through the small crack in the conference room window is heavy with humidity and the many scents of summer. The angry wail of a car alarm set off by the storm is coming in off the street.

I get up, walk over to the window and close it. Adjust my bow tie, the one I wear when I'm in the mood – dotted, silk of course, just like Churchill's.

I think of Afsaneh, who was left to eat Midsummer's lunch alone, even though I had promised I'd be home. I think of Alba, Alexander and Stella, whom I have not had time to call. And I look at my colleagues; we all want to get out of here. We all have people waiting for us somewhere, people who want to celebrate the most Swedish of holidays with us.

Malin sits leaning forward with her elbows on the table. Though she is trying to summon a façade of enthusiasm the tiredness shines through. Letit is standing by the whiteboard with his hands jammed deep into the pockets of his hopelessly unfashionable jeans with pleats.

Malin gets up and stretches.

'Olle Berg,' she says, attaching a couple of photos to the whiteboard using small, round magnets and wiping sweat off her brow. 'Also known as "Bullen". Thirty-one years old and from Flemingsberg, south of Stockholm. Convicted of aggravated assault and gross violation of a woman's privacy. Did eighteen months and got out just over a year ago.'

'Tell us about the assault and the violation of privacy,' I say, massaging my knee with my left hand.

'The assault happened at a party in Tumba. Berg got into a fight and repeatedly beat the host over the head with an unopened can of beer. The host sustained a busted lip and needed three stitches to his right eyebrow. Appears to have been a drunken brawl. But the violation of a woman's privacy . . .'

Malin falls silent and blinks a couple of times.

'That was pretty disgusting,' she says after a while. 'He threatened and badly assaulted his former partner. Seems she lost the use of one eye. Besides that, he violated his restraining order repeatedly and vandalised her car. A real pig.'

'I'm sure he's had a hard time,' Letit says dryly. 'Those guys always have. Have you spoken to the ex?'

'Yes,' Malin says. 'She's not in touch with him anymore, but they have a few friends in common, so she has some insight into his life. Or she did until about six months ago.'

'And what happened six months ago?' I ask, glancing at my mobile to see if Afsaneh has texted, but my screen is empty apart from the picture of Nadja in a yellow swimsuit and armbands that I took last summer.

'He met a new girl and apparently went all in on that relationship,' Malin says. 'He all but stopped seeing his old friends. It seems they live together now. Before that he was staying with a friend.'

'*Where* do they live?' I ask.

'That's exactly it,' Malin says. 'Nobody knows where Bullen is or where this woman lives.'

'So, what's her name?' I ask.

'We don't know that either. All we know is that the ex-girlfriend described it as "vaguely Old-Testament". We also know she has a disabled teenage son named Jonas. Apparently, he has some kind of brain damage after an accident.'

'But . . .' Letit mumbles, stroking his beard with both hands. '*Somebody* has to know *something* about her. Have you spoken to the friend he lived with previously?'

'Yes,' Malin says patiently. 'We've spoken to him, but he doesn't know anything either.'

'Oh, for fuck's sake,' Letit says. 'This just gets weirder and weirder.'

Malin glances discreetly at her wristwatch. When she notices that I am looking at her she immediately lowers her gaze.

'Are there any other threads for us to follow?' I continue. 'Does this Bullen have a job? Relatives? Have we checked mobile history and credit card transactions?'

Malin nods.

'He hasn't used his phone or his credit card since he disappeared. As far as jobs go he worked as a delivery driver until eight months ago. But apparently he messed about, wasn't on time in the morning and so on, so his contract wasn't extended. Both his parents are dead and he has no siblings.'

'Don't we know anything else?' Letit growls.

'Sure,' Malin says. 'Lots. But nothing of interest. He is left-handed. He is an Arsenal supporter. He played computer games in his free time. He liked romantic comedies, but apparently preferred to beat his women in real life.'

Letit, who seems to have worked up a rage against the suspect, hisses: 'But surely someone can't just disappear? Somebody has to know where he is.'

Malin doesn't answer, but she leans against the whiteboard and closes her eyes, as if she wished herself far away. Then she begins packing up her stuff.

'I'm sorry,' she says. 'I really do have to leave.'

I give her a sympathetic nod.

'Can we reach out to all local police stations in southern Stockholm and request information on this Olle Berg?' I ask. 'And make sure to mention that he is living with a woman who has a disabled teenage son named Jonas. People remember that kind of thing.'

Malin nods, pulls her notepad out of her bag again and makes a note.

'I'm leaving now,' she mumbles. 'Andreas is in Stockholm.'

I follow her with my eyes. Consider the lanky body, the large belly and the resigned facial expression.

I know how she feels.

I remember very well what it was like being a young police officer, wanting so much. Passionately wanting to solve those cases that couldn't be solved.

All the nights, all the weekends spent at work combing through interrogation transcripts and forensic reports. All the friends, girlfriends – and eventually children – waiting in vain at home in front of the TV.

Was it really worth it?

'See you tomorrow,' Malin says over her shoulder as she walks towards the door. Before she's put her hand on the handle the door flies wide open and Malik looks in.

He is wearing his black hair in a bun, making him look like a drag version of the character Little My from the Moomins. His clothes are wrinkled and he has several thin leather straps around his wrist.

Of course it looks awful, but I would never tell him that.

I leave people to their own embarrassment; they don't need my intervention.

Malik raises his hand at Malin, as if he wanted to physically stop her from leaving the room.

'*Wehaveanewvictim*,' he says so fast that I have to make a real effort to discern the words.

Now I hear how short of breath he is. He must have run up the stairs to get here.

'A body has been found in the water east of Gålö beach,' he continues. 'Can you go to forensic medicine now?'

Samuel

The rain is pouring down when I jog out of Rachel's house. The lawn grabs at my trainers, as if it wanted to keep me there.

All I want is to get far away from here.

Away from the house on the cliff and Rachel and Jonas, who drools and reeks of piss. Away from the hallway – which still has dark stains from Igor's blood on the floorboards, despite smelling of tar soap and chlorine. Away from the smell of pancakes and Rachel's thin summer blouses that strain across her tits.

Rachel lay down a while ago to rest, so I decided to sneak out. Even though I doubt Mum is still at the harbour, I want to look. And if I find her I will leave this place and never come back.

I close the gate behind me and continue down the road.

It looks like someone moved the motorbike.

I'm certain I parked it right by the car, but now it's closer to the side of the road.

It takes me a couple of seconds to realise it was probably Igor.

Maybe the bike was what tipped him off to my hiding place. That and Mum leading Igor to Stuvskär.

I should have hidden the bike better.

You should have. Now you've got yourself into a worse mess, you little shit.

I ignore the voice, start the bike up and give it full throttle. My jeans, that I have rinsed, are wet and strain across my thighs. When I get to the bridge I have to stop. My head aches and nausea lurks just beneath my ribs.

I park the bike by the side of the road and stagger down to the water. Go out onto a rock and sink into a squat. Then I pull my backpack off and lie down on my stomach on the wet, rounded rock. Cup my hands, fill them with water and rinse my face. The salt in the water makes my broken nose sting.

I roll onto my back and remain lying there, without being able to get up. The rain falls across my face like tears.

What the hell am I going to do? Where do you go when you've accidentally killed someone? What do I do if Mum isn't in Stuvskär anymore?

Should I go home to Fruängen?

Do that, Igor's guys will beat the crap out of you.

Should I go to some friend and hide out?

You don't have friends anymore.

I can't be sure, but I think Igor came to Stuvskär alone. Otherwise Malte and the others would already have found me. Maybe he thought I was so harmless he could take care of me himself. Or he hated me so much that he *wanted* to take care of me himself. In any case, it's probably best to lie low.

I take my phone out of my backpack and turn it on.

Mum has sent five messages. First she writes that she is waiting at the dock, then she wonders where I am and in the three latest texts she is pissed off.

I turn it off and walk over to the motorbike.

Maybe she is still at the harbour. Maybe she is waiting for me.

But when I get down to Stuvskär the dock is empty. There are no cars parked by the harbour and Mum is nowhere to be found.

The rain is pouring down when I park the bike and run up to the supermarket to peek in through the window.

Closed.

I continue to the harbour pub. Lean against the glass and peer in through the curtains, but Mum is not there either.

The nausea returns.

On unsteady legs I go out onto the dock and sink down onto the bench. It is even windier here – the waves break across the rocks and white foam fills the crevices.

It is over, Samuel. You can't run anymore.

Fucking bullshit, of course I can run.

The tears come. They stream across my face, blending with the salt water and the rain. Make their way into my mouth and down my throat.

The cruel voice is right this time.

Even if I were to go to Thailand or Marbella or Miami, I'll still be the same worthless guy. It would be better if I disappeared. If I let the sea take me.

But . . .

Mum wouldn't survive that. It's like her whole life is about me. I can't do that to her.

The rain intensifies. Grey veils sweep across the sea, erase the outline of the lighthouse and the islets. There is the rumble of thunder in the distance.

I force myself to think of all the people I have let down again.

Can you see what you have done?

And I do see.

For the first time in my life I actually see how much damage I have caused, even if I never meant to. Even if the last thing I wanted was to hurt anyone. And it's not a pretty vision, because I don't want to be that hopeless guy who makes everyone sad.

I want to be nice, I really do. Someone Mum can be proud of. Someone she can rely on.

What's stopping me, anyway?

I look across the sea. Stand up, open the backpack and take the vials of Fentanyl out.

They clank dully in my hands.

'The killer drug', they call it in the tabloids.

Without hesitation I throw the little vials, one by one, as far into the ocean as I can. Then I turn around and walk towards the motorbike.

Halfway to the car park I pass a bin.

I press Olle's passport and credit card into the empty cans, nappies and dog shit bags.

I'm going to straighten out my life. And I am starting by going back to Rachel, who actually saved me from Igor.

I can't just leave her here with Jonas. It's not right. No, I'm going to go back, give notice like an ordinary Joe and help her with Jonas until she has found a replacement. Perhaps we can go to the police together, too – explain what happened with Igor.

Fuck it, I am going to buy her the bike lock she wanted from the petrol station – just like any decent guy would have.

And in that moment the weirdest thing happens: the weight on my chest lifts and the voice in my head goes silent. The air feels easier to breathe and the cramp in my neck and shoulders subsides.

Just as I am about to start the bike I catch sight of something red poking out from behind the supermarket.

I go closer.

Mum's car is parked in the empty courtyard behind the shop.

It is empty, but the window on the driver's side is open an inch or so as usual – Mum doesn't have AC and insists on driving around with the window down.

I think. I don't want to use the phone again and risk being located by Igor's accomplices, but maybe I can find Mum.

If Mum was here in Stuvskär she should have sought shelter from the rain in the shop, or maybe at the harbour pub. Alternatively she would've been sitting in the car now but there isn't a soul here.

Could she have gone home and left the car here?

The damn thing has broken down at least three times in the last six months. One time she had to take the bus all the way from Norrtälje.

It is possible, but not very likely.

It could also be that she is hiding under some tree somewhere, but I don't really want to drive around all of Stuvskär looking for her since it can't be ruled out that Igor's cronies might be here.

It would be best if I could meet up with her a bit later, somewhere close by.

I look at the open window and think. Then I open the backpack, pull a piece of paper out of my back pocket and unfold it.

It's Olle's sick poem. I read the last stanza.

I cried myself a sea of tears
and lay down to die
on the soft tuft of grief
But the lion emerged anew
and in his giant maw he held
an untarnished dove

There is plenty of space under the poem.

I squat down, take out my pen, put the paper on my knee and write.

It has almost stopped raining by the time I park the bike next to Rachel's car.

Large puddles have formed along the gravel path and the tall grass is flat and wet against the ground in soft whorls, like newly washed hair.

The house looks as idyllic as always. Above all it does not look like a place in which somebody was just beaten to death with a wrought-iron lamb.

My stomach drops when I think of Igor's weight on my back, the pain in my arms and the crunching sound from my nose. Reflexively I bring my hand up to my face and feel across my tender skin.

It feels swollen, but at least I can breathe without any difficulty.

The thunder rumbles in the distance and I turn around. Dark purple clouds hover over the mainland, brooding over the road to Stockholm.

I walk towards the entrance, take my key out and unlock the door.

The wrought-iron lamb is once again in its place by the wall. It gleams a bit in the light from the ceiling. The room smells like detergent and a swimming pool.

I take my wet trainers off and the thin jacket I borrowed out of Olle's wardrobe. Then I take out the bike lock I bought at the petrol station.

The lock – which is extra long – consists of a thick chain covered in red plastic. The guy behind the counter assured me it was the best they had. He said takes a lot longer to saw or cut it open than a regular lock.

I hear steps from Jonas's room. Seconds later Rachel shows up in the doorway.

She looks pale and her eyes are swollen and red-rimmed.

'Samuel,' she says, walking toward me.

She threads her thin arms around me and holds me tight.

'I just went to the shop,' I say.

Her warm skin rests against mine, the long hair tickles my arm a little. I hear her heartbeat – fast and light, like a bird – and feel her rib cage heave against me with each breath.

It is arousing, even as my tears burn under my eyelids.

'Jonas,' Rachel murmurs, running her hand through my hair.

'What?' I say, trying to not press myself against her body.

She lets go of me, taking my hands in hers. Looks at me with a solemnity I haven't seen before.

'Come,' she whispers so quietly I almost don't hear her.

'I bought the bike lock,' I mumble, holding it up.

Rachel stops for a moment, turns around and looks a bit confused.

I immediately regret it.

Why did I say that? Why did I ruin this magic moment by blathering about a dumb bike lock that nobody gives a shit about?

She reaches out and takes the lock. Weighs it in her hand as if she were wondering something, puts it on the bench and turns her back to me.

'Thank you,' she says, continuing into Jonas's room.

I follow her.

The room is dark. A lone candle is burning next to the rose on Jonas's bedside table. The flame flutters when we sit down: Rachel on the chair, me in the old armchair.

A few lonely raindrops fall on the windowsill.

Rachel clasps her hands and points her gaze at Jonas.

I look at her, the lit candle, and then at zombie-Jonas who is lying perfectly still in his bed. His skin looks translucent and his mouth is open as if he were about to scream.

'Really it is ironic that we named him Jonas,' Rachel says with a thin voice.

'It is?'

'Do you know the story of Jonah and the whale?'

'Yes,' I say without elaborating, because I have absolutely no inclination to tell her how Mum forced me to go to Bible school when I was little.

Rachel gives me a quick look.

'My father was a priest in the church of Sweden,' she says. 'I know all those stories. Anyway, Jonah was fleeing God when he was surprised by a violent storm at sea. He told the sailors to throw him overboard, since God was angry with him. They did and he was swallowed by a whale, or if you are to believe the older translations, a fish, plain and simple. He was prisoner in the belly of the fish for three days and three nights. He repented and prayed, and in the end the fish spat him back onto land.'

'OK . . .' I say, wondering what her point is.

'When Jonas got sick I used to think it was as if he were imprisoned in the belly of the whale. He couldn't communicate, he was cut off from the world, like a foetus still in the womb.'

I don't say anything.

'And how I prayed,' Rachel continues. 'But God didn't keep his side of the bargain, Jonas never came back out of his coma. He remained in the belly of the whale. But I took care of him. I was there. Did a good job. God should have let me keep him, because he was all I had left. Do you understand?'

Rachel gets up and walks toward me. Stands behind the armchair and puts her hands on my shoulders.

But I don't understand anything.

Absolutely nothing.

'I am sorry,' she whispers and the grip of her hands hardens a little.

I turn around and look up at her. But her gaze is fixed on Jonas.

And then I see.

Jonas.

My stomach knots up and I shudder. There is a rushing sound in my ears and the walls close in, as if they were on wheels. The dripping on the windowsill intensifies until it sounds like deafening bangs on a giant drum.

He isn't breathing.

Zombie-Jonas isn't breathing.

Pernilla

gaze across the dark sea trying to understand.

Father is gone, Samuel is gone.

Aside from the immediate grief and fear of what might have happened to Samuel, a feeling of detachment is beginning to grow, as if I were a tree without roots, or maybe a very small boat adrift on an enormous sea.

Without Samuel and Father I am not anchored in the past or future. Who am I without them? Do I even exist?

I think the thought again, force myself to process the painful truth: Father is gone, Samuel is gone.

Or is he?

I am clear on Father not coming back, but with Samuel you never really know.

Disappearing has always been one of Samuel's special talents.

I remember that time in May when we were supposed to meet up outside the shop in the square to visit Father for his birthday. How I waited and waited for more than an hour, until I was convinced he had been either mugged, beaten up or run over. And just as I was about to leave he came sauntering across the pavement, completely unhurried, with that baby blackbird in one hand, that he claimed to have saved out of a large bin.

Other times he got the day wrong, couldn't get out of bed or was distracted by the TV, something that happened on the street, or perhaps his own muddled thoughts.

Samuel is unreliable, impulsive and has the attention span of a puppy dog. But he isn't evil.

He is just . . .

I search for the word and find it: *hopeless*. Yes, I do have to admit he is hopeless.

The wind grabs hold of my dress, lifts it above my knees, but I don't react, don't care if anybody happens to see.

I think about Father.

About how it can be that I loved him, despite him being so controlling and also taking Mother away from me.

And then I think about the pastor, about his betrayal – which is equally grave. Of how he deceives his flock of credulous sheep into thinking he is God's deputy on earth, when he is actually a completely ordinary, somewhat horny, middle-aged man.

Other thoughts come knocking.

All these men who have been ruling my life, where do they come from anyway?

And who gave them the right to hold power over me?

But I already know the answer to that question.

I gave them the right. It was me and no one else.

I lean against the car, sobbing uncontrollably and fight the impulse to scream out loud. Then I open the door and sink into the driver's seat. Inhale the smell of plastic and damp fabric. Turn the ignition and press my foot on the accelerator.

But something is in the way. There's a bit of a rustle when I press down, as if there were an empty bag of crisps there.

I lift my foot and feel along the floor with my hand, find a piece of paper and pull it out.

I carefully unfold the page and spread it out on the dashboard. Lean forward to see better.

It looks like a printout of some kind.

'"Inertia",' I read.

Then there is a poem about a lion and a dove. The last stanza pierces my heart.

> *I cried myself a sea of tears*
> *and lay down to die*
> *on the soft tuft of grief*
> *But the lion emerged anew*
> *and in his giant maw he held*
> *an untarnished dove*

What is this, and why is it in my car?

The poem makes me vaguely uncomfortable. There is something familiar about the lion and the lamb, but just as I try to catch the elusive thought I see that somebody has written a message in ink at the bottom of the page.

I immediately recognise the sprawling, sloping handwriting. The messy letters that look as if they are falling over each other.

A warm feeling spreads in my chest, as if I had drunk a cup of hot tea.

*Can we meet at the petrol station at 10 p.m., some really
weird shit happened, so I had to fix some stuff. Love, S.*

Under the message Samuel has drawn a small map and marked
the petrol station in question with a thick 'X'.

I toss the sheet of paper with the poem onto the passenger
seat and squeeze my eyes shut. Father's face floats through my
mind's eye and I hear his voice when he told me not to meet
Samuel.

No!

I will not repeat Father's mistake.

I look at my watch.

I can still make it.

Manfred

Samira gestures to us to sit down in front of her desk.

Letit and I each take a seat on two ugly chairs with plastic seats. Mine buckles under my weight and I am immediately concerned the puny chair will collapse under my voluminous body.

We let Malin go to her Midsummer's dinner with Andreas. It's enough that the two of us have our evening ruined.

'I don't think there is any point in you taking a look at the remains,' Samira Khan says matter-of-factly and tosses her black braid across her shoulder as if it were a long scarf. 'There isn't much left, to be honest. The body has been in the water for at least four or five months. It seems a family with children out sailing found it.'

'So it was floating in the water?' Letit asks.

'No,' the forensic pathologist sighs. 'They were anchored in a bay for the day, to swim, and when they were about to move on . . .'

'Oh, fuck,' slips out of me. 'You don't mean to say . . .'

Samira nods and looks at me with those beautiful, dark eyes that have seen so much pain.

'Yes. The anchor was stuck in the chains wrapped around the body, so when they pulled it up . . .'

'. . . the body came up with it?' Letit fills in making a face of distaste.

We fall silent for a while, as we consider this.

'What can you tell us about the victim?' I ask.

Samira nods, flipping through her papers.

'You'll have to speak with the forensic technicians later, but the victim was wrapped in chains, just like Johannes Ahonen and Victor Carlgren. However, we didn't find any fabric, so either that disappeared, or the killer never used any. I have made a preliminary assessment of the body, but I won't perform a post-mortem until tomorrow.'

'Him?' I say.

Samira nods, looking at her notes.

'It is a man, likely between thirty and forty years old, but I can't confirm that until after the post-mortem. I can't tell you anything about the cause of death either right now, but the victim has typical contusions and multiple fractures on his legs, arms and pelvis, which indicates that the body has been subject to heavy force.'

'High-energy impact?' I ask.

'Exactly.'

'And that was post-mortem?' Letit asks.

'Can't say yet,' Samira answers. 'I don't even know if I will be able to determine that at the autopsy. Considering the condition of the body it will be challenging to even determine the precise cause of death.'

'And identification?' I say.

'I'm actually more optimistic when it comes to that. I'm pretty sure we will be able to extract DNA. Additionally, the victim has a very unusual bite. We'll have to see what the forensic odontologist says, but it looks like a serious crossbite.'

Samira draws on a piece of paper to illustrate and then turns it around so that we can see her sketch.

When I arrive at the hospital Afsaneh has already been home, eaten, showered and come back.

Contrary to what I expected she isn't angry.

She just looks up at me from her laptop and smiles.

'I'm sorry, darling,' I say, hurrying up and giving her a kiss on the cheek.

'Mhm,' she says, lingering. 'It's fine.'

She looks me over.

'You look so good in a bow tie,' she says.

I smile, fumble with my hand over my tie and continue over to Nadja. I bend over her little body and place a careful kiss on her cheek.

Her skin is warm and slightly moist under my lips, as if she'd just been running around playing the way all children ought to be allowed to.

I turn to Afsaneh again. She types something on her computer and smiles.

'How is she doing?' I ask.

'Who?' Afsaneh says without taking her eyes off the screen.

Her reply surprises me. This is the first time since the accident that she is not completely absorbed in Nadja.

Maybe it's a good thing she can focus on something else, I think, before she automatically corrects herself.

'Oh, I'm sorry. Like before. She is doing just like before.'

I sit on the chair next to Afsaneh's, so close that I can smell her perfume and the cigarette that she must have snuck before going into the hospital.

There is something almost touching about our sneaking cigarettes – me hiding my smoking from her and she hers from me.

I glance at her laptop. There is a picture of a girl in a wheelchair on the screen.

Even though she is wearing a cap I can see that she is bald. She is smiling widely, but her posture reveals that she isn't feeling well – her head is drooping to one side, her body is reclined and hunched over.

'Amelia, three weeks into the new chemotherapy,' the caption reads.

Under the caption there is a long list of comments.

Sending you hugs and strength!
Most beautiful Amelia! you can do this!
<3 <3 <3
   Have you tried colloidal silver? If not, please do. It really does work! See the link in my profile!
Nadja and I are keeping our fingers crossed for you!

Afsaneh turns toward me.

Her face isn't sad anymore, rather it is focused, but also a bit confrontational. Her eyes are gleaming and her lips have their colour back.

'Yes?' she says. 'I am keeping my fingers crossed for her. Do you have an issue with that?'

Pernilla

Sunlight shimmers over the bay. A thin mist floats above the water, like smoke from a distant fire.

There is no sign of yesterday's storm; the rainwater has receded, rocks have dried and the tall grass has stood back up during the night and is once again reaching for the rising sun.

I stand next to my little VW Golf, brushing my teeth with the toothbrush that was in my backpack.

Sometimes being outdoorsy pays off – even if you are playing hooky from the hike. It turns out your kit can come in handy at the most unexpected moments.

I spit into the grass and put the toothbrush back in its case.

My head aches and my eyes sting. I feel as if I haven't slept a wink. But then again an almost ten-year-old Golf isn't very comfortable, no matter how much you twist and turn. But I'd rather sleep in it than in my tent because I forgot my sleeping mat.

Samuel didn't come yesterday.

I had no problem finding the little inlet that Samuel had marked on the map and I actually made it before the designated time.

But he never showed up.

I sit down in the grass and shut my eyes against the sun. Think about what Samuel wrote under the poem.

'Messed-up shit'. What did he mean by that? Messed-up as in dangerous, or just a bit crazy?

Messed-up as in being chased by a murderous drug dealer, or messed-up as in dropping your phone in your coffee cup?

I massage my temples with my index fingers, trying to think clearly. Brush off a shiny blackish-green beetle crawling across my dress. Then I look at my watch.

Quarter to eight.

I should go home. The damn blackbird needs food and water. And in a little over an hour I am supposed to be at work. But how can I work when my child is in danger? How can I stand there ringing up cans of peas and corn for old ladies when my son – the only living person I truly love – has encountered 'some messed-up shit' and has disappeared?

The question is what to do.

I don't even know where Samuel is.

I take my phone with me and go out onto the rocks. Sit down and find Stina's number. She answers on the third ring and sounds just as happy as ever. As if she just won the lottery or became a grandmother or maybe both. As if the world weren't an evil and dangerous place where 'messed-up shit' happens all the time.

I explain. Tell her about Samuel who seems to have vanished into thin air.

As expected Stina isn't annoyed with me at all for being forced to call someone else to fill in for me at work, she is full of empathy and offers to help if there is anything – 'anything, anything at all, sweetie' – that she can do.

'That is so nice of you,' I say. But I don't know where to start.

'It's time for you to go to the police now,' she says sounding absolutely certain. As if her children and friends disappear all the time and she knows exactly how long you ought to wait before getting the authorities involved.

'Yes, I guess so. But I don't even know where he's been living lately.'

'Didn't you say he was working for a family?'

'Yes, he's been working for a family who have a disabled son. They live somewhere around Stuvskär, but I don't know exactly *where*.'

'So how did Samuel find the job?' Stina asks and I can hear the rustling of paper and a scratching sound, as if she is taking notes.

I search my memory, try to recall what Samuel has told me.

'I think he found some kind of ad online.'

'Hmm,' Stina says, then there is more scratching. 'And he didn't tell you the name of the family?'

'No. Only that the mother's name is Rachel and that the son, who has some kind of brain damage, is called Jonas. Oh, and the dad, or Rachel's partner, is apparently an author. I think his name is Olle, or something like that. But that's all. I don't have a surname.'

Stina pauses, as if she is considering what I just told her. Then she continues, in a quieter voice: 'And he didn't send you any photos from there?'

'Nothing. And now his mobile is off again and I don't know what to do. We were supposed to meet at ten o'clock last night, but he never came.'

'Go to the police,' Stina says in an authoritative voice. 'Go straight to the police and then get back to me. Of course we will find him. Do you hear that, sweetie? We will find him!'

I drive past maypoles dressed in grass and flowers that have already dried in the heat. Beer cans and wine bottles strewn along the side of the road are testament to the party that was happening in parts of the archipelago during the night.

It only takes twenty minutes to drive to the nearest police station, but the further I get from Stuvskär, the more reluctant my body becomes. It is as if every cell can feel how the invisible band that ties me to Samuel is being stretched to the limit.

When I finally park I am drenched in sweat and my heart feels like it's beating out of my chest.

The police officer who takes down my report is called Anna and doesn't look to be a day over seventeen. I almost wonder if she stole the uniform somewhere or if she is actually an intern.

'So. You want to report your son missing?' she says and purses her oddly swollen lips a bit.

'Yes. He is gone. Samuel. My son, that is. Well, that is his name. Samuel. Per Samuel Joel.'

The teenage police officer looks at me with a bored expression.

'And how long has he been missing?'

'We were supposed to meet yesterday, at ten in the evening at Stuvskär, but he never showed up. And it's been twelve hours now. Although he has been gone longer than that. Or —what I'm saying is that he hasn't been home for a few weeks. So obviously I have been very worried. But then he sent a text, so one can't really say he was missing, I guess. But now he is.'

I stop and then add:

'Missing, that is.'

I immediately regret not simply answering her question. When will I learn to shut up?

'Twelve hours?' she says.

A furrow deepens between her brows, making me realise, first off, that she probably thinks I am crazy, and second, she is probably not as young as I thought. This hypothesis is strengthened by a bump poking out under her shirt.

I missed that earlier. She must be six months pregnant, at least.

You have no idea what it is like to have a child, I think.

You know nothing about how much it hurts when they suffer, the super-human strength you feel when they need help, or how absolutely terrified you are when they're in danger.

You're sitting there with your mouth shining with lip gloss and thinking you know something about life, even though it actually hasn't started yet.

'Maybe we should take this from the top?' she says.

I start telling her about Samuel and the family he works for in Stuvskär – about Rachel, Olle and Jonas. And I explain that even though Samuel is careless he always shows up. I show his note too, the one that is written on the page with the strange poem.

But before she has time to read it there is a loud crash in the corridor. The crash is followed by a sharp bang and a furious howl.

'Don't touch me, you fucking cunt. Do you hear me?'

The teenage police officer sighs and rolls her eyes to show just how annoyed she is.

'*Sorry*,' she says. 'I've got to help my colleagues. Be back in a minute.'

But a minute can be pretty long, and as time passes and the howling and banging outside slowly but surely moves in the direction of the exit I get increasingly uneasy.

Even though the female police officer didn't straight-up insult me it was obvious that there would be no talk of any real police intervention at this point.

It seems Samuel hasn't been gone long enough.

I wonder how long one has to be missing before the police care – a day? A week?

Besides, what would Samuel say if he knew that I was sitting here?

Other questions pop up in my already confused mind.

Should I tell her that her colleagues are looking for Samuel?

I start to sweat at the temples and my heart picks up speed when I begin to realise what I have started.

And the gym bag full of hundred-kronor bills, what should I say about that?

My heart skips a beat and I swallow hard.

No, this just won't do.

I get up so suddenly that I almost knock the chair over and reach for my handbag. Then I sneak out the way I came in.

The teenage officer and her colleagues are busy calming the violent man who is currently stretched out on the floor of the corridor. He has a firm grip on the calf of a female police officer while sobbing loudly.

I leave the police station with a liberating sense of relief. Open the door to my car and sit on the boiling-hot seat.

My skin smarts from the heat, but I barely feel it. All I can think is that I got away in the nick of time and that I have to come up with some other means of finding Samuel. A way that *doesn't* necessitate me needing to account for mine and Samuel's involvement in criminal activity.

First off I am going to go back to Stuvskär – because he has to be there somewhere. *Someone* must have seen him.

It isn't until I have driven almost all the way to Stuvskär that I realise that I left the poem with Samuel's handwritten note on the teen cop's desk.

Manfred

Yet another glorious morning that in no way reflects my state of mind. Because sunshine does not necessarily make for a sunny personality, a sunny disposition, or a sunny outlook.

Still I decide to make the best of the day and put on my pink shirt and the grey suit. With it I don a magenta silk handkerchief that I carefully fold into my breast pocket. I top it all off with a few drops of Aqua di Parma on my neck, take a few steps back and contemplate the large strawberry blond man who is looking out at me from the mirror.

Afsaneh looks at me and smiles.

'You are so handsome,' she says and lingers on the last word, as if she is tasting it.

'Thank you,' I say. 'You don't look too shabby yourself.'

Afsaneh is wearing a bright yellow fitted dress in shiny cotton chintz. She is radiant in it, but then she would have been in a dirty T-shirt too.

She is beautiful in everything, but I'm not such a fool that I don't realise that my love for her is what makes me think that.

We leave the apartment together.

The parade along Karlavägen lies almost abandoned in the quivering summer heat. The air around us is filled with some kind of downy seeds. They stick to everything: our hair, our mouths, the soles of our shoes. They lie in droves along the kerb. Like snow.

Summer snow.

We stop for a moment on the pavement outside our front door. Afsaneh laughs and plucks a few seeds off my face. Then we give each other a quick kiss – like any couple in love – before we each disappear in different directions.

I know it would be closer for Afsaneh to walk with me to Karlaplan, but she can't handle passing the spot where Nadja fell and thus chooses to make a detour.

As for me I tend to hurry up when I pass that place, sometimes I cross the street so as not to have to step on those specific stones, on that tarmac, on that cursed pavement, that threw itself at my defenceless child.

I inhale deeply and try not to think of Nadja. I think of that yellow dress, of how it fluttered around Afsaneh's slender calves when she turned away from me and walked off. About how the wind lifted the hair from her shoulders and the ease in her step.

Are her friends on the internet what's making her feel that much better? Is that where she is getting the support I haven't been able to give?

I don't know.

I spend the morning going through the old notes from the preliminary investigation for the assault and gross violation of privacy that Olle Berg, aka 'Bullen', was found guilty of, both in the magistrates' court and in the courts of appeal.

The image of an impulsive and misogynistic person emerges – a man who in many aspects is so immature that one would do better to call him a boy.

Among the documents I find a statement from a psychologist who has examined Berg. The psychologist also IQ-tested him and concluded that he has an intelligence quota of about seventy-five.

That means that he is considered to be above the line for what would formally be considered an intellectual disability, but not by much.

Olle Berg was simply not very well-equipped in the head.

Right after lunch I go to the coffee maker as usual to collect my government-financed hopelessly watery coffee.

As I approach I see Letit and Malin standing close together next to the grey metal beast. They gesticulate eagerly. When they see me they both start walking towards me at the same time.

'We need to talk,' Malin says.

'May I have some coffee first?' I ask.

'What kind of monsters do you think we are?' Letit grunts.

I get coffee and we sit down in the conference room.

'I'm listening,' I say.

'Yesterday you asked me to check with our colleagues south of the city to see if they have any information about Olle Berg, or his girlfriend and her son,' Letit says.

'And now, today, a colleague with the police in Haninge got in touch,' Malin fills in. 'A trainee, Anna Andersson, received a report of a missing person this morning.'

'The trainee thinks the missing person works for the family in Stuvskär,' Letit says and leans toward me. 'She is on her way over here so that we can talk to her.'

'And,' Malin says as she inhales, 'both Victor Carlgren and Johannes Ahonen have made calls to unregistered prepaid phones.'

'Have they called the *same* number?' I ask.

Malin shakes her head.

'No, but through the operator we could link both prepaid cards to the same IMEI number. So it belongs to an iPhone that has been used for all the calls. Both the phone and the prepaid cards were bought in a shop in Haninge Centrum, although at different points in time. The calls were also made from there. The colleagues in Haninge are going to check to see if there is video surveillance in the shop and if the person who made the calls has been caught on camera.'

'Stuvskär,' I say. 'That's close to Haninge Centrum, isn't it?'

'It's probably twenty-odd miles,' Letit murmurs.

'I'm sorry,' says Malin, 'but I don't know Stockholm that well – what kind of place is Stuvskär?'

I think about it for a few seconds.

'It's like Ormberg only the other way around. Just as small. An old fishing village that has become completely gentrified. There are mostly summer houses for rich people from Stockholm. Almost nobody lives there year-round.'

'OK,' Malin says. 'Then let's talk to the trainee.'

'There's just one problem,' Letit says. 'The woman who wanted to make the report disappeared before the trainee could take her information.'

*

Anna Andersson is muscular and as obviously pregnant as
Malin. Her mousy-blonde hair falls in soft curls around her
cute, slightly too made-up face.

'So she just took off?' Malin asks making a note in her pad.
Anna squirms.

'We had a rowdy guy in the corridor outside. A frequent
flyer. I went out to help my colleagues and when I got back she
was gone.'

'Any idea why she disappeared?' Malin asks and looks
genuinely confused.

Anna's cheeks turn pink and she looks at the floor.

'Well . . . I told her that since Samuel, her son that is, had
only been missing for a few hours it would probably be a while
before we . . . *uhm* . . . took any concrete action.'

'So you scared her off?' Letit asks, jutting out his bearded
jaw.

Anna, who looks terrified, doesn't answer.

'He's joking,' Malin smooths things over, but Letit isn't
smiling. He is looking straight at the trainee while slowly
chewing on a toothpick.

'Oh,' Anna says, but still looks like she is about to wet
herself any second.

'So, exactly *what* did she tell you before she disappeared?'
I ask.

Anna pulls out her notepad and flips through it until she
finds a few sloppy notes she's jotted down.

'That she was supposed to meet her eighteen-year-old son,
Samuel, at Stuvskär at ten o'clock the night before, but he
never showed up. That he was working with a family that had
a brain-damaged son, somewhere in the vicinity of Stuvskär.

The mum was named Rachel and the son Jonas. And the mum had a boyfriend too. A writer named Olle or something like that. I wrote it all down as soon as I realised she'd left.'

'Nothing else?' I ask.

Anna's gaze wanders up toward the ceiling, as if she is searching her memory.

'No. Actually, yes. One more thing. She said that her son had disappeared once before, but come back. Honestly, she seemed pretty confused. Besides it was Midsummer's Day, so I figured the guy was probably sleeping it off somewhere. So I—'

'Oh, for fuck's sake,' Letit says and inspects the chewed-up toothpick. 'I don't know what you're reading at the police academy these days – gender power dynamics? Diversity policy? Foundational values? Regardless, some good old-fashioned common sense wouldn't hurt.'

Anna doesn't say anything but looks, if possible, even more wounded.

Letit lets his gaze wander between Anna and Malin.

'And maybe some counselling on contraceptives too,' he mumbles and spits a small wood splinter from the toothpick into his hand.

I clear my throat.

'And you said she left something behind?' I ask.

The trainee, who looks like she is about to start to cry at any moment, nods and presents a piece of paper, inserted into a transparent plastic pocket.

It looks like a poem of some kind.

Instinctively all three of us lean over the table and read it in silence.

'What the hell *is* this?' Letit mumbles.

I look at the poem again.

For some reason the last stanza gives me the chills. I read it out loud because I feel like I need to hear it.

I cried myself a sea of tears
and lay down to die
on the soft tuft of grief
But the lion emerged anew
and in his giant maw he held
an untarnished dove

'What in the *hell* are we supposed do with this?' Letit growls. 'Send it on to the poetry unit? Try to find a forensic lyricist? Or should we ask the clowns in communications to help us?'

'Read this handwritten text underneath,' the trainee with the red cheeks says.

And we read:

Can we meet at the petrol station at 10 p.m., some really weird shit happened, so I had to fix some stuff. Love, S.

'OK,' I say. 'There can't be that many people named Rachel in the area who also have a disabled son named Jonas?'

Malin nods and stands up.

'And this poem,' I continue. 'Can you check where it comes from?'

'I will look into that,' says Malin, who has stopped in the doorway. 'What are our thoughts on this Samuel guy – is he in danger?'

'I don't know,' I say honestly. 'But we need to get hold of him bloody fast.'

None of us say anything. We don't need to.

Then I look down, read the poem again.

and in his giant maw he held
an untarnished dove

'I think we should visit our friend in Ormberg,' I say.

'Ormberg?' Letit says.

'Hanne Lagerlind-Schön lives there,' Malin says quietly.

'The witch?' Letit snorts.

'Call her whatever you like,' I say. 'Without her we would never have solved the murders in Ormberg. She is special, I don't think I have ever met a person with that ability to get into the minds of criminals. I actually understand why they call her the Witch, because she is by far the best profiler I have ever come across.'

I pause, adding: 'Or at least she was before.'

Letit wrinkles his eyebrows and strokes his large nose with his pointer finger and his thumb.

'Before what?' he asks.

'Before she developed dementia,' Malin says quietly.

Pernilla

I sit on a rock looking out over the sea. Follow the undulating movements with my eyes and listen to the peaceful shushing when the little waves wash over the granite tongue that stretches out into the water.

The afternoon sun burns my bare shoulders and the soft breeze feels hot against my skin.

I have spent the day walking around Stuvskär showing pictures of Samuel from my phone to the people who work at the supermarket, the petrol station and the harbour pub. Passers-by didn't escape my attentions either.

But nobody recognised him.

I can't help but think that's pretty strange. He had to have been to the harbour several times.

Do we not see each other anymore? Are we so busy tapping at our phones and taking selfies that we aren't even interested in our neighbour?

I think of the boys fishing at the steamboat landing, only to photograph the fish and throw them back into the sea, like rubbish.

I bury my face in my hands and inhale deeply.

The pastor was probably right the time he said there is something wrong with the times we are living in, that we are headed toward replacing the true faith with narcissism and materialism. Although I'm not sure I agree with him that this means we are living in the end times. That credit cards, the internet and the United States recognising Jerusalem as the capital of Israel are signs that the second coming is nigh. That the antichrist is lurking behind every corner and that we are well on our way to building the tower of Babel.

I'm actually not sure I trust anything he said anymore.

He has sent me several text messages since I insulted him in front of the children outside the congregation hall.

The last one arrived this morning, as I was on my way back to Stuvskär from the police. It said that he was worried for my 'immortal soul'.

I was so angry I almost threw the phone out the window of my car.

Seriously?

My immortal soul?

The only part of me that Karl-Johan is interested in is the part that is between my thighs. And from what I gather that is not my soul.

I consider texting him that and the thought makes me laugh out loud, despite everything being so miserable.

I lie down on my back on the rock and close my eyes. Feel the rough heat of the stone against my back, like a barren but reliable embrace.

Like Father.

Oh, how I miss him!

It makes my chest ache, my entire body aches, when I think of his thin, daffodil-yellow body, at once fragile and irrepressible. Even my skin hurts. As if the grief and fear is on the outside of my body, like an invisible costume of pain.

'Samuel.'

I say his name out loud, into the summer.

But of course nobody answers.

There has to be something I have seen or heard but not understood the importance of. Something that can help me find him.

I say a brief prayer as I take the suncream out of my bag and rub it into my sweaty face.

Yes, I am able to multitask like that – pray and apply cream, pray and drive, or for instance pray and mark down bread that's past its sell-by date with neon-orange sale tags while smiling politely at everybody who passes by.

Prayer is good like that.

Prayer is like casual exercise – one can fit it in here and there during the day; it does not demand any specially designated time.

I open my eyes and look straight up at the blue sky. See the seagulls float on the breeze like tiny, tiny dots. So free, so unaware of all the human struggle. I put the suncream back in my bag and look at the rock, rounded by the millennia. It is shot through with cracks and lines, reminiscent of a very old person's skin.

Stina's wrinkled, sun-damaged face appears in my mind and at once her words echo through my ears, drowning out my own thoughts.

So how did Samuel get the job?

I freeze mid-movement just as I am about to close the bag and hit my elbow hard against the stone.

Why didn't I think of that earlier?

'Thanks,' I murmur, as I glance quickly up at the sky.

Manfred

'Should we drive via Nyköping or Gnesta?'

Malin gives me a quick look.

'Gnesta,' I answer, and look out through the window where fields are glowing yellow with blooming rapeseed.

'This feels really strange,' Malin says, squeezing the steering wheel so that her knuckles go white. 'What if I run into Mum?'

'If that happens, we'll deal with it,' I answer.

Malin curses quietly and brakes for a tractor pulling onto the road.

'Do you know how Hanne is doing now?' she asks.

'No,' I say. 'But last time I saw her she was doing pretty well.'

Malin changes gear, accelerates suddenly and veers slightly left to overtake the tractor. As the car speeds up I am pushed back, instinctively grabbing onto my seat. A few seconds later we smoothly glide in front of the tractor and I let go, drawing a deep breath.

Malin shifts up again, glancing at me.

'And her memory?'

'So far it's mainly her short-term memory that is giving her trouble,' I say. 'When we meet her I will explain where we are in our investigation, show her the poem and so on. Then she can give us her immediate thoughts, because her cognitive capacity is basically intact. And she remembers everything that happened up until about a year ago. So she can still make use of her entire professional experience. But if we were to return to Ormberg tomorrow or next week, she will likely have forgotten all about it. I would have to explain the whole thing all over again.'

'What hell it must be to live like that,' Malin murmurs.

I don't reply but think that she is only partially right about that, that there are probably advantages too.

Hanne isn't plagued by memories of what happened in Ormberg, for one.

I look out across the fields that undulate towards the horizon like a green and yellow sea, where slow, mighty swells roll in. The wooded areas, towering here and there, throw long, ghostly shadows across the fields.

'By the way, I couldn't find that poem online,' Malin says. 'So it was probably written by an enthusiastic amateur.'

'Mhm.'

'That woman, the trainee,' Malin begins, biting into a plum.

'Anna Andersson?'

'Exactly,' Malin says, popping what's left of the plum into her mouth. 'She said something about Olle, who we can probably assume to be Olle Berg, being a writer.'

'He is as bloody far from being a writer as it is possible to be,' I say. 'But what do I know, every Tom, Dick and Harry calls himself a writer these days.'

Malin cracks the window open, fishes the plum stone out of her mouth and flicks it away with her thumb and her index finger.

A smell of cow manure and grass spreads through the car.

'Thanks,' she says. 'I too have read the file. All I am saying is that maybe he did some writing, that poem for instance.'

'Sure, that's possible. I also do some writing. Most of it is shit, frankly.'

'Speaking of writing,' Malin says slowly. 'I spoke to a colleague who worked on the street-dealing unit on Södermalm. Well, before it disappeared in the restructuring, that is. She knows all the addicts and they know all the dealers and they . . . well, you get it. Anyway. Igor Ivanov has written two books. Poetry collections.'

'You're kidding.'

'No. They're sold on Amazon and it seems he makes pretty good money from them. I ordered one. We'll have to take a look at it. We can't rule out that the poem is from Igor's book.'

'I wouldn't bet money on it,' I say, roll down the window and pull out a cigarette. I light it and inhale deeply.

Malin looks at me with wide eyes but doesn't say anything. Then she turns off towards Ormberg.

The road is worse here – there are large gashes in the asphalt and the patchwork of repairs covering the roadway is reminiscent of those ghastly patched jeans my friends used to wear in high school.

As for me, I would never have worn such a thing, not even as a teenager.

A deer dashes across the road, maybe fifty yards ahead of us. Malin brakes suddenly. I crush the butt against the paintwork, let it fall to the ground and wait for Malin to accelerate again. Instead she slows down and stops on the hard shoulder. Her fingers are desperately gripping the wheel and her gaze is pinned on a tall fir tree.

'I'm not sure I can do this,' she mumbles.

'It'll be fine,' I say and think about the murder investigation in Ormberg last winter that changed Malin's life forever. She said she would never go back there, and now I'm forcing her to do just that.

She shakes her head slowly.

'Nothing will be fine.'

'Shall I drive?' I say and immediately feel bad about making her come along.

Malin shakes her head and begins to drive again.

We continue slowly towards Ormberg. The forest around us is denser now and the road narrower and darker. It cuts through the tall firs, like a ravine through a mountain pass.

I glance at my phone but Afsaneh hasn't texted.

When I told her I had to work tonight she wasn't even angry. She just sort of hummed. As if she was busy doing something else and not really listening to what I said.

She is so changed and I'm not sure whether to be concerned or glad.

When we roll into Ormberg it is almost eight in the evening. The sun has set behind Orm mountain, but the sky is still light teal with golden streaks, like a Rococo painting.

But that is where the similarities to sixteenth-century art end.

To be fair, the community is embedded in deep greenery. But the few houses that are popularly called the centre are just as ugly as I recall.

When we pass the old shop – the one that we used as our temporary office during the murder investigation – I note that the space is being renovated. Outside there is a cement mixer and a couple of large bags of construction debris. Above the window somebody has put up a sign.

'Hassan's Grocery,' I say. 'Well, I'll be damned.'

This sleepy industrial town was now starting to prosper after years of decline.

Malin doesn't answer.

We pass the church. It sits ominous and dark in the field, a monolith and a reminder of better times, when the community and the congregation flourished. Tall grass is growing around the building and bushes obstruct the entrance. The rendering has fallen off the façade, revealing large, brick-coloured wounds.

For the last bit of the way to Berit Sund's house our drive slows to a crawl.

The giant, watchful figures of the firs close in around us again. Winter has been unkind to the old gravel road which is covered in potholes. In several places the shoulder appears to have collapsed into the ditch, as if the soil under it is marshy.

And then the forest thins out and Berit's little cabin appears.

There is a welcoming light from the windows and smoke is rising up towards the light summer sky.

We park outside and get out of the car.

'So Berit Sund is still going strong,' Malin notes quietly.

Berit is an older lady who has lived in the area since forever. She has worked for the council and for social services and now she is helping take care of Hanne. I assume she is some combination of friend, caretaker and domestic help.

'It looks like it,' I say.

'There are worse ways to end one's days,' Malin says and lets her eyes travel across the small red cabin with white trim.

The colour has returned to her face and she seems relieved to have made it through the little community without running into anyone she knows.

Fruit trees grow on the well-kept lawn and there is a lush flower bed all the way around the house where catnip is vying for space with tall hollyhocks poised to burst into bloom. In the damp evening air the scent of smoke mixes with the sweet, heavy scent from the large mock-orange bush that is spreading out from the left of the front door.

Berit opens almost immediately when we knock.

She is wearing a shapeless floral dress of the kind that my grandmother used to call a house dress and a pair of wool socks on her feet. Her fringe is combed to one side and pinned down with a childish hairpin with a star that gleams and glistens from the light inside. Her wrinkles have deepened into sharp furrows. In the light of the ceiling lamp they look like axe cuts running this way and that across her skin, making her face look like an old chopping block.

Behind her Joppe stands with his head lowered, cautiously waving his tail.

Berit smiles when she sees me and gives me a surprisingly hard hug.

'Manfred, it's been a while.'

Her body feels smaller and thinner than I remember it, as if parts of her have melted away along with the thick snow cover.

Then she embraces Malin.

'My dear child, it's so nice to see you.'

She puts her hand on Malin's belly.

'And congratulations, what a blessing! Well, you can't stand around here all night. Come in, come in!'

Inside the cabin everything looks like it used to; clothes hang neatly on their hooks, shoes stand just as neatly on the shelf underneath and the geraniums in the window look exactly as sad as they did last winter.

A fire is crackling in the kitchen.

We take our shoes off and follow Berit inside. Hanne is sitting by the table.

As soon as I enter the room she stands up and smiles.

She looks radiant.

Her red hair is longer and has more grey streaks, her arms might be a bit thinner, but other than that she is her old self when she takes my hands and fixes me with her gaze.

'*You* I have missed,' she says, giving my hands a hard squeeze.

'It is mutual,' I answer.

Then she takes me into her arms and holds me for so long that I almost feel embarrassed.

Finally she lets go and turns to Malin.

'Hanne,' she says reaching her hand out.

Malin gives me a quick look.

'Malin Brundin,' she says, taking Hanne's hand. 'We've met before, actually. We worked together for a bit on the murder investigation here in Ormberg.'

'I'm so sorry,' Hanne says, looking embarrassed. 'I must have forgotten.'

'No worries,' Malin says.

We sit down at the kitchen table.

'How are you?' I ask.

'I can't complain,' Hanne says, smiling. 'How about you? How are Afsaneh and Nadja?'

My heart skips a beat and I have to catch my breath. I have told Hanne what happened to Nadja, but she has obviously forgotten.

Berit looks noticeably nervous.

'We talked about that, Hanne,' she mumbles. 'Nadja was in an accident and is in the hospital.'

'*Oh*,' Hanne says bringing her hand to her mouth as if she wanted to stuff the words back in. 'Oh. I am so sorry.'

'Don't worry about it,' I say and force a smile.

'Is it serious?' Hanne asks, with her hand still over her mouth.

I hesitate, and then answer:

'Hopefully not.'

Hanne remains sitting with her gaze fixed to her lap for a long while.

Berit does her best to lighten the mood by waiting on us. She serves coffee out of her old floral china pot, offers us home-baked biscuits and talks about the weather while Hanne slowly but surely recovers.

'I'm going to take Joppe out for a bit,' Berit says over her shoulder as she fixes the hair clip in her fringe.

Then she limps out of her kitchen followed by her limping dog.

We talk to Hanne about Ormberg for a while. About the old shop that is going to open back up.

And we talk about the long winter, the one that almost killed an elderly couple a few miles away – apparently they were snowed in for weeks and had to use some of their furniture for kindling because they couldn't get to their woodshed.

Hanne becomes noticeably more assured when we approach the reason we're here.

She looks at us, gazes first at me and then at Malin.

There is a calm about her, a sort of dignity, but at the same time I sense a smile on her face and get the distinct feeling she is very pleased that we have come all the way to Ormberg to consult her.

'But you didn't come here to gossip about Ormberg?' she asks.

'No,' I admit.

'Tell me!' she says, leaning in.

Hanne has listened patiently to our account of the three victims who have been found in the waters of the southern Stockholm archipelago and about the woman who was going to report her son missing, but was likely scared off by an insensitive trainee.

She has a pad in front of her and jots down notes, hums and asks brief questions while her pen dances across the paper.

After about forty minutes Berit returns with the dog. She offers us more coffee, but quickly disappears to the top floor when we decline.

Outside the summer evening grows darker.

A blueish-grey haze falls like a blanket across the meadow and the forest behind it, where giant firs stand to attention. A large moth lands on the windowpane, perhaps lured in by the ceiling light.

'And you haven't identified this third victim yet?'

'Right,' I say. 'But he is significantly older than the first two. The forensic pathologist thought he was between thirty and forty. He has been dead longer than the others too.'

'Hmm,' Hanne says. 'He does break the pattern a bit.'

'Correct,' I say.

'But your theory is that Olle "Bullen" Berg is involved in these crimes one way or another, or may even be our killer?'

'His DNA was found on the sheet wrapped around Victor Carlgren's body. Besides, he is known to be a violent criminal and has recently gone underground.'

'And this missing boy . . .'

'Samuel,' Malin fills in.

'That's right. So you think he is working for Olle Berg and his partner . . .'

Hanne searches through her notes, then adds: 'Rachel?'

'Yes. They fit the description. Olle Berg's friends have said that he was together with a woman who had a disabled son.'

'Hmm,' Hanne says again, puts a scarf over her shoulders and strokes her freckled cheek.

'And this poem comes from the missing boy, who *could* have got it from Berg and his partner?'

Malin nods.

Hanne puts her reading glasses on and reaches for the copy of the poem with Samuel's handwritten message for his mother. Then she turns on the light on the table and begins to read.

She reads through all of it, looks up at the ceiling as if she is thinking, and then reads the text yet another time. After that she takes her glasses off and rubs her temples with her fingertips, leaning back in the spindle chair with her eyes closed.

'Well, it's not exactly great poetry,' she begins. 'But there's something . . .'

And then:

'Rachel. Rachel. Jonas. Jonah. Rachel and Jonah.'

Malin shoots me a questioning glance and I shake my head at her slightly so that she won't interrupt.

Hanne puts her glasses on. Her eyes are sparkling and she has that excited expression again, the one that almost makes her look like a mischievous child.

'So,' she says and pauses briefly before going on. 'The dove and the lamb lived in harmony until the dove began making longer and longer excursions. Listen to this: *Each day you flew further away. Like a storm you darkened the sun with your games, like soot you befouled the air with your haughtiness, like arrows your betrayal stung.*'

Neither Malin nor I say anything.

Hanne pushes her reading glasses further down her nose and looks seriously at us over the frames.

'Do you follow?'

'Yes, but . . .?' I say uncertainly.

Hanne raises her hand at me and goes on: 'The lamb loved the dove, but the dove rejected the lamb's expressions of tenderness. I quote: *Your mouth repeated "no". Your thoughts were everywhere, but never here with me.*'

'OK,' Malin says and I can see her eyes wandering toward the cuckoo clock on the wall.

'Then the dove was in an accident,' Hanne continues. 'The lamb is distraught and ran into a lion. That accidentally killed the dove. Which is described as follows: *But his teeth were so sharp, and his claws so long, he your body happened to crush, in his attempt to catch you.*'

Malin squirms in her chair.

'The lamb grieved,' Hanne says, furrowing her brow and cocking her head. 'The lamb grieved, but the lion got her a new dove. Listen: *I cried myself a sea of tears, and lay down to die, on the soft tuft of grief, But the lion emerged anew, and in his giant maw he held, an untarnished dove.*'

'I'm sorry,' Malin interrupts Hanne. 'I don't want to be impolite or anything, but I really don't understand where this is going.'

'Wait,' I say and lean so far forward that the flame from the live candle on the table almost laps at my cheek. 'Why do you say that the lion gets *her* a new dove? How do you know that the lamb is a . . . she?'

Hanne breaks into a wide smile. Reaches for the pad and flips to a blank page. Then she places it so that all of us can see what she is writing.

'Rachel is an Old Testament name, as you may know?'

'That's not really my department,' Malin mumbles, repressing a yawn.

'Rachel means lamb, or ewe, in Hebrew,' Hanne says and writes on her pad:

The lamb = Rachel

Malin looks at me, her mouth open.

Hanne smiles and continues:

'And guess what Jonas means in Hebrew?'

Malin shakes her head without saying anything. I detect fascination as well as worry in her face.

'Jonas is a Swedish form of the name Jonah, meaning dove. It is also a name that shows up in the Bible, as I am sure you know.'

The pen scratches against the thin paper as Hanne writes yet another line:

The dove = Jonas

'*Jesus fucking Christ*,' I whisper. 'You're not saying . . .?'

'So the author of the poem is describing Rachel's relationship to her son, telling of his accident and his . . . *death*?'

Malin's voice is so weak it is almost inaudible.

'But the dove was killed by the lion,' I say. 'Who is the lion?'

Hanne's face turns serious. Her smile fades and her eyes seem to darken in the fluttering light of the candle. She grasps the pen and writes four letters on the paper:

Olle =

'And what do we get if we get rid of an "l" and switch the "o" and "l" around?' she asks rhetorically.

The paper creases a bit under the nib of the pen as she fills in the bottom line without waiting for our reply:

Olle = Leo

'And Leo is Latin for . . .'

'. . . *lion*,' I say.

Hanne nods, writing down the last word:

Olle = Leo = Lion

Then she stretches a bit and carefully places her pen next to the pad.

Malin stands up suddenly and begins to pace back and forth across the kitchen floor while pounding her right fist into her left palm.

'Damn it,' she hisses. 'Fucking hell. Why did we not see this before?'

Neither Hanne or I say anything.

'Read those last lines again,' I tell Hanne.

Hanne reaches for the poem and reads out loud: '*I cried myself a sea of tears, and lay down to die, on the soft tuft of grief, But the lion emerged anew, and in his giant maw he held, an untarnished dove.*'

'And how the *hell* should we interpret that?' I ask.

PART IV

In the Belly of the Whale

Now the LORD had prepared a great fish to swallow up Jonah. And Jonah was in the belly of the fish three days and three nights.

Then Jonah prayed unto the LORD his God out of the fish's belly.

Jonah 1: 17–2.1

Samuel

'm flying around the dark cave.

Round and round – carried by the cool, damp air. My wings are strong and my body endures, but sometimes I hit the wall. Then I lie down and let my beak fall to the side. Rest against the ground as my little bird heart ticks feverishly inside my chest.

I cock my head. Look at my grey plumage. My tail and wings have black markings and my chest is pinkish. My legs are short, sturdy and pink.

Without being one hundred per cent certain I'd say pigeon.

Columba palumbus.

Occasionally fragments of conversation, of human voices, penetrate the thick rock into the cave, like water trickling down through cracks in a mountain.

Sometimes I recognise the voices, even understand what they are saying.

For instance I heard Rachel. She sounded scared and said: *What have you done with him?* Then she said: *If you as much as touch a hair on his head him I will . . .* And then: *. . . will call the police if you don't leave my house NOW, do you hear me?*

The man she was talking to answered in such a strong southern Swedish dialect that I couldn't understand what he was saying, but he sounded angry, very fucking angry.

My brain was slow and tired, but I could still articulate the question: was it Olle she was talking to? Had he come home at last?

But the voices always fade away.

They crack, crumble and become dust that spreads across the damp floor of the cave.

Sometimes there is light.

The light is harsh and hard and cuts my sensitive eyes like a sharp knife. I close my eyes, longing for the dark of the cave, but the light pulls at me. Pulls and tugs as if I were a wet towel that had to be wrung out. I am stretched out and my beak burns like fire.

In the end I land in my body again, the *other* body – the one that has arms rather than wings, fingers and toes rather than talons.

But that never lasts very long, because then there's the sting in my buttock and the next instant the warmth spreads inside of me.

Then I fall again.

I fall and fall, straight through the floor, through the ground and through the rock. I fall all the way down into the cave again. Ruffle my feathers, coo a bit and let my beak sink into the soft down that covers my chest.

The cave isn't too bad by the way.

There is no pain here, no hunger, no anxiety.

Everything is predictable, has its own rhythm, like waves or heartbeats. At regular intervals the darkness hands me over to the light, which in turns hands me back over to the darkness.

Until.

Until.

Somewhere above me I sense that the colour of the cave's ceiling has shifted. The black is sort of less black. Outlines emerge more distinctly and the air is clearer.

The light is coming and it is stronger than ever before. It intensifies, becomes a sun and finally wrests me out of the cave, as if I were a carrot being harvested.

Everything becomes sharp and hard and hurts like hell.

And I can feel my arms, legs, yes, even my toes resting under something soft and warm. I can feel my heart too – which isn't really a bird heart at all, but a much bigger one beating heavily in my chest. And I can feel the weight of my head and the blood rushing through my veins.

But I feel other things too, unpleasant things, like how dry my mouth is – it is as if my tongue is glued to my palate – and the odd burning pain in my nose.

'*Gaahh aarrgghh.*'

The sounds are coming from my body.

The words that aren't words, just grunting sounds, pig sounds, are coming from *me*.

I squint at the light, even though it cuts and stings my eyes.

Above me a giant spider is hanging from its web in the ceiling.

The body is as large as that of a human. The belly, head and the long jutting jaws are blue, but the legs are long and black.

I try to scream, but all that happens is that warm saliva spills out of the corner of my mouth and down my cheek.

The spider's legs come closer, so close that I can see the long, bristle-like hairs growing on them and the claws at the ends of the limbs.

On the intensely blue head there are several pairs of shiny metallic eyes. They gleam dully in the sharp light.

I scream again and again, and in the end I must have actually scared the giant arachnid because it sort of freezes and shifts shape before my eyes.

The legs shrink and become black nylon straps. The claws become plastic buckles and the blue body shifts shape and becomes rectangular. The eyes ossify into metal buttons.

I blink, trying to comprehend.

What the hell?

It isn't a spider. It is Jonas's fucking retard-harness. The one that Rachel uses when she needs to move him.

I am lying in the bed, under the seat sling.

In Jonas's fucking bed!

The realisation is like a kick to my gut.

What the hell am I doing in Jonas's bed? Am I sick?

And where is Jonas?

I try calling for Rachel, because surely she knows what happened? Surely she can explain why I, and not he, am lying here in bed like a clubbed seal without being able to lift a finger.

But my mouth won't obey, it refuses to shape the words and the only thing I can get out is more saliva.

And then I remember how Jonas was lying there in the bed – skinny as a fucking junkie with skin as white and smooth as polished marble – and wasn't *breathing* anymore.

A chill creeps up my spine.

Is Jonas *dead*?

I try turning my head so that I can see the bedside table better, but I can't. I tell my body, no, I shout at it to turn my head, but it refuses, as if it were still down there, in the cave.

I make a new attempt and this time my head actually does turn a bit, just not enough to see the bedside table that I know is right next to me.

I give it another try. Close my eyes, concentrate as much as I possibly can and visualise my head moving on the pillow. How it slides to the side, as if it were the easiest thing in the world.

One more inch.

I open my eyes.

On the bedside table there is a vase with a fresh-cut rose. Next to it is the tube of hand cream and the lip balm. I can see a glimpse of the calendar on the wall above the bedside table.

June 24th.

That can't be right, it is the 22nd, Midsummer's Eve.

Because surely I haven't been lying here for two days?

The thought makes the room spin and my ears rush.

'*Gaahhrraa.*'

The grunt just comes. I'm not even trying to scream this time. The sound just sort of slips out of my chest, as if it too wanted to escape this place.

I look at the bedside table again, and at the rose in its little vase, just as usual. Then my eyes are drawn to the scratches in the veneer, the ones Jonas tried to reach with his hand.

And I see.

From my new vantage point in bed I see that they aren't scratches.

They are letters.

Inscribed, or maybe rather *scratched* into the veneer, with crooked, sprawling letters, is a lone word.

HELP.

Pernilla

'Of course we will help you! I've said so all along. You shouldn't be so scared of asking for help. Next time I will be the one in need of help, Pernilla, and then I will come to you.'

Stina's voice is firm and the hand squeezing my back is warm and secure.

'Next time I will have met some hopeless man again and be in need of a good cry,' she adds, with a hoarse laugh.

We are sitting on a blanket on a rock a couple of hundred yards from Stuvskär harbour.

The sun is low over the skerries and the rock under us has just started to cool off. Stina's flaming red hair glows in the warm light and her leathery skin is the colour of copper. She is wearing a bright pink singlet that is so low-cut that I can see almost all of her bra.

'Isn't that right, Björn?' Stina adds and looks encouragingly at her son, a skinny boy in his late teens with strawberry-blond hair and a beautiful, almost feminine face that I recognise from the photo on Stina's desk.

'Yeah,' Björn says and immediately looks very uncertain. 'But it will probably be mad awkward.'

'Nonsense,' Stina says, waving a mosquito away with her hand, setting the loose flesh under her arm in motion. 'Nobody can see that you feel awkward over the phone.'

Björn shrugs his thin shoulders and prods a bit at a large pimple on the side of his chin.

'Let's go then,' I say and give Björn the prepaid mobile I've bought.

Björn takes the phone in one hand and the paper with the notes and the pen in the other.

'It was half past eight, wasn't it?' Stina asks.

I nod. 'That's correct, but I can't promise she will call exactly then.'

Rachel is cautious. After I found the ad online and answered it via email she has sent me two messages: the first to ask follow-up questions, the second to book a time when she can call me.

She has not given any contact information.

The minutes pass and the sun descends into the water that lies perfectly placid in front of us. Only a few small waves nip, almost silently, in the green seaweed growing at the water's edge, the slippery mess that one always slips on when one is going to swim.

Somewhere in the distance there is a motorboat and the sound rises and sinks as it bounces between the islets.

Stina takes her out her flask that I recognise from the shop and raises it at me.

'Would you like a drink?' she asks, pouring the amber liquid into two limp plastic cups without waiting for me to answer.

'Why not?' I sigh.

Then she opens a bottle of Coke for Björn, who raises his hand and shakes his head.

He looks nervous, twiddling his pale hands in his lap.

As for me, I think of Samuel. Of how ironic it is that his name actually means 'God heeds prayer'.

Because Samuel in the Bible got his name because his mother, Hannah, had him after she prayed to God for a son.

God heeds prayer.

But who's listening now?

It has been three days since Samuel was supposed to meet me in the harbour – three days without me hearing a word from him. Not a text message, not a phone call.

Just silence.

I suppose I ought to go to the police again, but that arrogant girl sitting there being cheeky made me lose my nerve.

I promise myself that I will go back if we get hold of this woman now, because then I will at least have something concrete to show them. Something to make them act, rather than sit there and stare at me as if I were truly crazy.

The phone rings and Björn picks up with a resigned look.

He looks at me and I nod encouragingly, raising a thumb in the air.

'Uhm, hi?' Björn says and his voice breaks.

Stina looks at me and nods, smiling; I can tell that she is proud of her son.

'OK,' Björn continues.

And then: 'No, well not specifically, but I have had a part-time job at an old people's home. But that was mostly cleaning. And of course I couldn't give them any medicine or injections or anything.'

He is silent and nods several times.

'Nineteen. In three months.'

He is silent again and I hold my breath, saying a prayer that it will work.

'The thing is, I dropped out,' Björn says, managing to sound exactly as embarrassed as I have instructed him to. 'I was pretty sick of school and just wanted to work. I mean, I haven't been truant or anything I just like . . .'

He goes quiet again, looking at me.

'Yes,' he says, hesitantly. 'That works.'

Then he writes something on the paper as he nods.

'OK, see you there.'

He hangs up.

I don't dare ask, but Björn's face, which cracks a broad Colgate smile, betrays him.

'Stuvskär harbour, the day after tomorrow, at eleven o'clock,' he says triumphantly, holding up his hand so that Stina can give him a high five.

I do as Stina does, slapping my palm against his and draw a deep sigh of relief.

'What did she say?' I whisper.

'That she would love to meet me and talk a bit. That it was hard to find good people. That she hoped we would get along.'

Stina looks at me and her green eyes gleam.

'I *told* you it would work out,' she says and smiles so that I see all the fillings in her nicotine-stained teeth.

'Thank you,' I say, with tears in my eyes, nodding first at Stina and then at her son. 'Thank you so much. I don't know how I will ever be able to repay you.'

Manfred

My mother used to say that time heals all wounds. As if time were a nurse in a starched white uniform, with lily-white hands, going around serving hot dinners, rather than a grim reaper lurking behind every corner. Just waiting for you to commit that fateful mistake that will cost you your life.

Or somebody else's life – your child's, for instance.

I taste the wine and smile at Afsaneh and Martin, her colleague at the university.

They laugh at something that Martin is saying – something I don't catch, but smile at anyway, because I have neither the energy nor inclination to share my dark ruminations. Besides, I cannot stop thinking of what Hanne said about the lamb, the dove and the lion.

The lion who is Olle Berg.

We have to find him and we have to do it fast. Because although the poem likely won't hold up as evidence in court, we can tie him to at least one of the victims via DNA. Besides, he has a documented history of violence, so the likelihood that his DNA ended up there by chance should be negligible.

Anyway, I don't believe in chance.

I let my gaze wander across to Martin.

He is the same age as Afsaneh and has a pale, long, thin face with a disproportionately large nose. His hair is light brown and curly and appears to defy gravity. The impression is enhanced by the cut, which makes him look like a poodle.

Martin looks at me and nods, as if he is waiting for me to comment on something he just said.

I hurriedly guide the conversation to a different subject so that he won't notice how distracted I am.

'Afsaneh says your thesis is going well,' I say.

Martin smiles and glances quickly at Afsaneh.

'Well,' as I was saying, 'I will be getting my PhD in October, unless something goes terribly wrong. Of course you have to assume it will. And my old professor at the psychology department has gone and slipped a disc, so we shall see.'

'Sorry,' I say. 'My thoughts were somewhere else entirely.'

Martin raises his hand. 'No worries. God knows you have other things to worry about than my dusty old thesis.'

There is a pause and I look down at the kitchen table. Study the dents in the wood that Nadja made last spring. I remember how angry I was with her and promise myself that will never happen again.

As long as she gets well. As long as everything goes back to normal.

Afsaneh clears her throat. 'I would hardly call it dusty,' she says. 'It paints a pretty good picture of our time.'

'What are you writing about?' I ask.

Martin runs his hand through his curls and cocks his head a bit so that his hair almost touches his plate and his large nose gleams in the glow of the ceiling light.

'Narcissism, or to be more specific, why the prevalence of narcissistic personality traits is increasing so dramatically.'

'Is it?' I ask. 'Increasing, I mean.'

Martin leans forward and places his elbows on the table.

'It is actually. Two American researchers, Twenge and Campbell, have shown that the prevalence of narcissistic personality traits has increased as much as obesity since the 1980s. And that is especially true of women.'

Martin winks at Afsaneh and pours more wine into their glasses, before continuing: 'And several other studies confirm this,' he says.

'Could you call it an epidemic?' Afsaneh asks, emptying her glass in one gulp.

'We are doing exactly that,' Martin says quickly. 'Because it *is* an epidemic.'

'But why?' I ask. 'Why should we have become more narcissistic?'

Martin smiles a crooked smile.

'Society has changed. Social structures have dissolved, the smallest unit is no longer the family, but the individual. Add to that the emergence of social media. More than a billion people use Facebook each month. A *billion*, you hear me? And other social platforms are growing exponentially. And there's a strong link between social media and narcissistic behaviour. It is actually clinically proven. And really it's not that strange, because everything is about presenting a façade that gets you the maximum amount of followers, likes, comments, or whatever it is you're looking for.'

'We're looking at this in the Project too,' Afsaneh says, suppressing a yawn.

'But haven't people always been dependent on social approval?' I ask.

'Yes,' Martin says, lowering his voice. 'But technology has taken hostage our natural quest for social approval and acceptance. There are people now who don't go out. All they do is photograph themselves or film themselves in different situations in different clothes and post the pictures to social media. And all their friends are online. It's sort of like they have become one with technology.'

Afsaneh leans forward, pouring more wine into her glass. Her movement is clumsy and the bottle hits the table hard when she puts it down dangerously close to the edge.

'It's a bit like Chinese weddings,' she says, giggling.

'Chinese weddings?' I ask, moving the bottle to the middle of the table.

'Well, I heard from a Chinese guest researcher at SU that it is common not to have a wedding celebration when you get married. Instead you go to the photographer and take lots of photos with props. You get champagne glasses to hold in your hands, you cut a fake wedding cake. You kiss in front of a set and so on. All so that you can show off the album to your family and friends afterwards. And in Japan you can apparently rent wedding guests, so that it looks better in the photos.'

'Exactly,' Martin says. 'It's the same mechanism. It's like it is more important to be able to show off the pictures than to actually have experienced your wedding with friends and family. That's precisely what I'm looking at. But you don't put pictures in an album, you post them on some kind of social media platform. Online, the opportunity for validation is endless. I was at Auschwitz last winter. Do you have any idea how many people are there taking *selfies*? As if it's more important to show off having been there than digesting what actually happened.'

Afsaneh grimaces.

'Are you serious? I'd have thrown up if I had seen someone gurning in front of the gas chambers.'

'And yet that's exactly what they were doing.'

Martin leans back in his chair, looking resigned.

He goes on: 'We've only seen the beginning. The internet has changed the social contract. The one that regulates how often it is acceptable to say "look at me!". And real life doesn't offer nearly as many or as frequent opportunities for positive validation as the internet does. So why focus on real life?'

'So Facebook has won?' I say, mostly joking.

But Martin doesn't smile.

'Did you know that Facebook virtually exploded when they invented the like button? A woman named Leah Pearlman came up with that, if I don't misremember. In any case that was almost ten years ago. And that little icon, the thumbs-up, would change the entire internet. It has changed human be-haviour, it has helped companies succeed or caused them to perish. It has made and broken presidents.'

'Aren't you exaggerating just a little?' I ask.

Martin shakes his head vehemently.

'Social media will fundamentally change society. It will fundamentally change *us*. And not necessarily for the better. Beyond our addiction to likes, there is the risk that we're ren-dered passive. How does the world change when we access everything second-hand rather than take part ourselves? It is a bit like reading about the colour blue, but never seeing it.

Internet separates us from real reality. We live our lives through a camera lens, where there is always a layer between the individual and reality. A film. So I think there is a risk that the new technology makes us dumber. That it brainwashes us and puts us into some kind of . . .'

'Inertia?' I ask.

Martin nods enthusiastically.

'Come on,' Afsaneh says. 'I don't think we need to worry. Not in the longer term, anyway. Of course we will continue to interact. Interacting with only technology is not sustainable in the long term. We wouldn't even be able to reproduce.'

'Now you are talking like a biologist,' Martin says, making it sound like a severe insult. 'Besides there are other problems. For instance, it is impossible to know what's true on the internet.'

'Do people even care what's true anymore?' I ask.

'Interesting question!' Martin exclaims and I immediately regret posing it, because I can feel my eyelids growing heavy. 'I think we are on our way towards a society in which our model of explanation is primarily phenomenological.'

'Phenomenowhat?'

'Sorry,' Martin says running his hand through his curls. 'When I talk about a model of explanation I mean how we explain our reality. For instance, there are religious models of explanation. Imagine that you don't feel good and you wonder why. Based on a religious model of explanation you might draw the conclusion that you have distanced yourself from God. So the cure is to . . . well, pray for example. And then there are scientific models of explanation. You may draw the conclusion that you aren't feeling well because you are deficient in iron.

The cure is a pill. A phenomenological model of explanation is based on the individual's own experience, like, I feel bad because I have experienced this trauma, or because I am the way I am. I have the right to my own experience, my own trauma. What I feel is true and cannot be questioned. That is exactly how it is online today. Besides, there is so much information online but only that which supports your own point of view and goes viral penetrates the noise.'

I get up and begin to clear the table hoping that Martin will get the hint.

'What makes something go viral?' Afsaneh asks.

'Extreme things go viral,' Martin whispers, as if he were revealing a big secret. 'The quotidian lifestyle is dead! You need to be more of a Dostoevsky than a Tolstoy online, if you follow me.'

There is a brief pause and I look Afsaneh in the eyes.

'*Um* . . .' I begin.

'Tolstoy wrote about the quotidian,' Martin continues without waiting for my answer. 'People don't give a *shit* about the everyday on social media, unless you are super famous. They don't care about your geraniums, your puppy, or the salad you just made. They don't give a flying fuck about your new couch or how many miles you jogged this weekend. If you want to make it big on social media you have to be extreme. Dostoevsky wrote about lunatics. *That* works very well online. Feel free to quote me on that.'

Martin makes a theatrical gesture of thanks with his hands, as if he is bowing in front of a large audience.

A mobile rings and Afsaneh gets up. Goes over to the countertop, picks up the phone and looks at it. Then she hands it over to me.

'For you,' she says.

I reluctantly take the phone.

It's Letit.

'We have him,' he says. 'We've found Olle Berg. You need to come in.'

Samuel

The darkness is cool and odourless.

I walk around on what might be a floor, pecking a bit. Not because I am hungry, but because that's what pigeons do. They fly and peck food and coo and groom their feathers and do other bird stuff.

Somewhere in the distance I hear human voices, but the words blur into a strange cackle that is impossible to comprehend.

Then something happens.

It is the exact same feeling as when the light pulls me out, only there is no light. Everything is just darkness.

Still I land in my body again.

Everything tingles and prickles and I slowly become aware of my arms and legs. Feel my hands resting against the smooth surface of the blanket. Notice the bitter taste in my mouth, the throbbing in my head and the burning pain in my nose, as if I had been snorting coke non-stop for weeks.

I try to scream, but my mouth and my vocal cords won't obey me. The roar becomes a weak puff that leaves my lungs with a faint hiss.

I remain immobile in bed, panic clawing at my chest.

Minutes pass, maybe they become hours, it's hard to say, because I have no real sense of time. But it's still dark, except for the thin streak of moonlight creeping in through the window and curling up on the floor like a sleepy pet.

What if this is it? What if this is death?

Tears burn under my eyelids and a knot grows in my throat.

What have I done with my life really? What has become of Samuel Stenberg?

Not a damn thing, but I could have told you that long ago, if you had taken the time to listen.

I think of the only person I miss right now, the only one I would give anything to meet again.

Mum.

And suddenly it is almost as if she is standing by the bed, as if I can feel the warmth from her body and the scent of her lavender soap. For a moment I even think I can see the gold cross she wears around her neck gleam in the dark. But in the next instant I understand that I have imagined it all.

The tears come.

They roll slowly down my cheeks, like a gentle summer rain, as the night slowly lightens into a blue-grey dawn. And as the sky grows pale outside the window my body comes to life.

I try clenching my fist and the muscle does what I want it to – it clenches my fist over and over again. Then I wiggle my foot a bit under the blanket and my limbs continue to do as I say, as if I were in charge and not the other way around.

I turn my head, brace my arms against the mattress and heave myself up.

My head aches and the nausea lurks just under my ribs, but I *can* move.

Mysteriously I have triumphed over my body. Whatever disease I've had it's over now, and I am not going to stay here a minute longer than I have to.

Outside the window an early bird sings, and soon another one chimes in.

Carefully, I touch my face and feel surgical tape on my cheek. It is attached across something long and thin that feels like a soft straw. Without hesitation I pull the tape off and pull at the straw.

It stings and I realise that I am holding a tube that runs through my nose and into my stomach.

I recall Rachel's words.

Jonas is tube-fed. But you don't need to worry about it. I take care of all that.

Panic explodes in my chest and I tear the tube out without regard for the consequences. Pull violently, as if it were a tapeworm that had crawled into my stomach. Inch after inch of slimy tube slides out of my sore nostril.

I cough and have the urge to vomit, but just as the vomit is on its way up my throat the tube is out. I toss it away, stumble over to the window and open it.

The next instant it hits metal.

I reach my hand out through the crack and feel the bars that I screwed on, testing them.

Like rock.

I inhale deeply.

The night air is humid and smells like grass and soil. The birdsong is deafening, so loud that I am afraid someone will wake up and force me back down into Jonas's bed.

The room is at ground level and it would have been easy *fucking* peasy to climb out if it weren't for the bloody bars. I am locked into a giant cage now, because I've been so bloody helpful.

I pull the window shut and continue to the hallway.

Everything is quiet and still.

The only sounds are the hum from the fridge and the birds.

The floorboards creak under my weight. Creak and pop, as if they were calling to Rachel to come.

I stop. Listen, but can't hear anything out of Rachel's room, so I take another step and grab the handle on the front door. It rests cold in my hand when I turn the lock.

But the door doesn't open, the deadbolt must be locked.

I try again, but the door won't budge. It might as well be made out of stone.

Disappointment washes over me like an icy wave. Slowly I slide down into a sitting position with my back to the fucking door.

Tears come again. I don't even notice, but this time they are virtually gushing out. They wash over my cheeks and pour into my mouth. There is a sting when a tear settles by my raw nostril.

What the hell is going on?

My thoughts are like wild dogs, chasing each other aimlessly and fiercely without making me any wiser.

There must be a way out of this fucking house; after all it's only a house, not a prison. I draw a deep breath and try to see the shit logically.

All windows on the ground floor have bars, so I can't get out that way. The front door is locked with a hell of a lot of safety locks, so I can forget that too. The terrace doors are probably locked too, and even if they're not I can't climb down from there since the terrace is built over the cliff. Unless I want to risk falling sixty feet and being crushed against the rocks below, that is.

The top floor – that is the only alternative.

I can sneak up the stairs, go into my room, open the window and jump out. That should work, it's not that high. Eleven, twelve feet tops and there is grass underneath, so I will land softly.

My legs tremble as I walk into the living room. Through the large windows I see the ocean stretch out in the dawn, like a giant leaden quilt reaching all the way to the horizon.

I take the stairs in five quick steps – the wrought-iron structure is solid and doesn't emit any sounds to give me away.

The door to my room is open and I go in.

The bed is freshly made. The pillows are just as hotel-fluffy as they were when I arrived. My bag is gone and the wardrobe, which is ajar, is empty. There is a slight scent of pine tar soap in the air.

It is as if I was never even here, as if someone washed away every trace of me.

I go up to the window, open it and look down at the ground.

I feel a tug at the pit of my stomach – it's higher up than I thought and here and there are rocks in the grass that I definitely don't want to land on. Besides: Rachel's room is directly under mine. If there is a thud, or I scream when I jump, she might wake up. So whatever happens, no matter how I fall, I have to be as quiet as a mouse.

I climb up carefully and sit in the window. Think about how to do this.

Shall I grab on to the windowsill with my hands, so that I hang straight down, and then let go?

No.

That would reduce the height of my fall, but I can't choose where I land. The risk is high that I'll end up too close to the wall, hit it, wake Rachel up and maybe that Olle guy, if he's here now.

I decide to jump from a seated position and push off as far as I can so that I don't end up too close to the building wall.

Then I close my eyes and send someone a thought, not sure who, not God in any case. I push off with my feet and hands and sail through the summer night. The ground hits me hard like a clenched fist, knocking the air out of me. A sharp pain in my ankle spreads through my entire leg and I have to summon every ounce of self-discipline to not scream out loud.

I sit in the grass and look at my foot, scared shitless that I'll see broken bones poking out of my skin.

But my foot looks like it always does.

It has to be a sprain, I tell myself, and get up on all fours. I try to stand up, but the pain in my foot is too severe, so I begin to crawl through the grass towards the front of the house instead.

My left wrist hurts so much that I don't dare put any weight on it.

I'm slow, far too slow, but neither my foot nor my hand is much use, so I have no choice but to make my way like a fucking one-year-old.

When I round the corner of the house the numbing heavy scent of roses from Rachel's flower bed hits me. The delicate, dark red flowers with their thorny stems strive toward the lightening sky. There is a fine layer of dew on their petals.

I crawl around the flower bed and on to the gate in the fence.

Just another twenty yards.

My hands scrape against stones and pinecones in the grass. I have lost sensation in my knees, my foot throbs with pain.

In the distance the seagulls join the choir of birds.

Ten.

Hand, knee. Hand, knee.

I feel something slimy against my hand. When I look into the grass I see a crushed snail.

I keep going.

Five.

Hand, knee. Hand, knee.

The fence appears in front of me, from my perspective it feels as tall as a wall.

I support myself on the splintered boards, pull myself onto one leg and hold onto the gate.

A light falls across the ground. I turn around and look quickly at the house.

A light is on in Rachel's room.

I try to open the gate, but can't, it almost feels as if it is locked.

Fucking hell!

Noise is coming from the house; someone gives a shrill scream.

I think.

The fence is pretty high. If I hadn't patched the hole I could have crawled through it now. If I hadn't needed to look so bloody helpful to Rachel, I would've been free by now.

As if that made any difference.

What was I thinking, anyway? That I'd get to fuck her?

I look up at the fence and the realisation hits me: I'm the one who screwed on the bars and fixed the fence that is keeping me prisoner in this insane asylum.

You stupid fuck; you built your own prison.

And now?

There is only one option: I have to climb over the fence. Normally this would not have been a problem. But now, when both my foot and my hand hurt like hell, I don't know if I am able to.

I grab onto the top of the fence with both hands and try to pull myself up. It shouldn't be harder than doing a push-up, but my body is weak, so damn weak. My body is a hundred years old and would prefer to just lie down in the grass and die like an old elephant.

I hear a window open and hit the bars with a dull, metallic thud.

This will be my only chance. If I want to get out of here I need to get over the fence now.

I grab hold of the top again, look up at the sky and use all the strength I have. I pull until my back, shoulders and biceps feel like they are on fire with pain. Until I black out and the darkness pulls me down towards the cave again. Until the quills push through the skin on my arms and my nose becomes a beak.

You will never pull this off. You may as well give up.

But I get up. I pull it off.

I end up hanging off the fence, like a sock left to dry, panting and unable to move even an inch.

Slowly I land in my body again.

The front door opens and I can hear heavy steps on the stairs.

With one last enormous effort I heave myself over the fence and fall headlong down onto the other side.

My cheek hits the ground and I feel crunching in my shoulder, but I don't care anymore. All I can think about is how to get to Igor's bike which is parked next to the road.

I manage to stand up and begin to run. My foot hurts like hell, but the fear is worse than the pain.

I hear steps on the gravel path, then there's the clinking of keys and the squeak as the gate swings open. But in the same instant I straddle the bike and fumble the wires for the ignition.

I will make it!

There is no chance anyone will catch up with me on the bike. Not even by car.

The steps approach from behind as I start the bike with a roar. I let go of the ignition and feel the thrill in my chest – that intoxicating feeling of freedom and triumph, of having cheated death itself.

The bike jerks, flies away from its spot by the pine, but stops mid-air, as if it were a duck that had just been shot.

And me, I keep going.

I fly headlong over the handlebars and land on the gravel path with a bang. The taste of blood spreads in my mouth and I spit out gravel, or is it teeth?

I don't know.

I don't know anything anymore.

But my brain wants answers. My brain keeps working even though my body is completely fucking out of it.

I remember the vials of Fentanyl that I stole out of the medicine cabinet. Remember the dull clink when I took them out of my backpack and threw them into the foaming waves. Above all I remember replacing the contents of three of the bottles with water and putting them back in the cabinet.

Is that why I woke up? Did someone keep me drugged until tonight?

Until I was given water instead of drugs?

Was it the man I heard, the one from Southern Sweden who Rachel was arguing with?

I recall her words:

. . . *if you so much as touch a hair on his head I will call the police unless you leave my house NOW, do you hear me?*

The darkness pulls at me, carefully this time, almost benevolently. Tempts with its promise of freedom from pain and fear.

But I don't want to. Not yet.

I need to understand. There is so much I have to understand, like for instance, why I am lying here on the road and not sitting on the bike on my way back to Stockholm.

The darkness pulls at me. My field of vision is shrinking, fading away. The throbbing pain is receding.

I search with my gaze, let it sweep across the motorbike that lies smoking on its side in the tall grass by my feet.

And I see.

I see something red wrapped around the back wheel and the pine like a long snake.

The big, red bike lock I bought for Rachel.

PART V

The waters surrounded me, even to my soul;
the deep closed around me;
Weeds were wrapped around my head.
I went down to the moorings of the mountains;
the earth with its bars closed behind me forever.

Jonah 2: 5-6

Manfred

I arrive at the station in a taxi just after midnight, still a bit tipsy after my liquid dinner with Martin and Afsaneh earlier in the evening, but it doesn't matter. I feel expectant and my steps across the dewy grass are lighter than they have been in a long time when I make a shortcut through the park.

Malin is in the small conference room where we have gathered all the information about the investigation. The photos of Johannes Ahonen and Victor Carlgren are hanging on the whiteboard. Next to them someone has taped up the poem and written in large letters:

THE LAMB = RACHEL, THE DOVE = JONAS, THE LION = OLLE BERG

Next to this hangs the mugshot of Olle Berg. His gaze into the camera seems empty.

'How are you doing?' Malin asks.

'I'm OK,' I answer. 'Tell me, where did we find Olle Berg?'

'Somewhere in the archipelago,' Malin says. 'Letit has all the information. He'll be here soon to brief us. I think he worked all evening.'

'Well, I'll be damned. I thought Letit went home at five every day to air his polyester shirt.'

Malin flashes a crooked smile.

'Actually, I didn't go home either,' she says. 'I'm sort of trying to construct a hypothesis on how this happened, but I just can't.'

I shrug. 'Why complicate it? Berg killed Johannes Ahonen, Victor Carlgren and the unknown victim.'

Malin clasps her hands at the back of her neck and looks at the ceiling.

'That's too easy,' she says.

'It usually is easy.'

'But why?'

'Who the hell knows?' I say. 'Likely drug-related, like everything else these days.'

But Malin, whose gaze is still pinned to the ceiling, does not seem convinced.

'Victor Carlgren doesn't exactly appear to have been a junkie.'

'His sister told us his friends had bought drugs from someone named Måns or Malte,' I say. 'It had to have been Malte Lindén.'

Malin shakes her head slowly.

'That connection is very weak, you know that too. And who is victim number three? The guy with the weird bite.'

'Probably another junkie,' I say and hear how certain I sound, even though I'm not actually all that convinced.

Malin squirms in her seat and sighs. Scrunches up a small piece of paper into a ball and throws it into the bin over by the door.

The ball lands on the floor next to the bin, but Malin remains seated with a deep furrow in her forehead.

'So why was Ahonen's DNA under Carlgren's nails?' she asks.

'They probably got in a fight before Ahonen went and got himself beaten to death by Olle Berg.'

'Hmm,' Malin says. 'Skin under the nails. When would you scratch someone? Other than during sex, that is.'

'Speak for yourself. I don't scratch my bedmates. But generally speaking I would say people do that when they're at a disadvantage. When everything has gone to hell. When someone has their hands around your neck, or has buried a knife halfway into your stomach. When you can't breathe and are bleeding out.'

Malin stretches a bit so that her belly pokes out.

'The victims' injuries,' she continues. 'The high-impact violence inflicted post-mortem. They had broken almost every bloody bone that can be broken. What the *hell* did Berg do to them?'

'Maybe they were hit by a boat when they were in the water. The forensic pathologist did say—'

Malin interrupts me: 'All three of them? Seems unlikely. And why did so much time pass between the murders, or the deaths, if they weren't murdered? If this was a reckoning in the crime world, surely they would have died at the same time?'

'Not necessarily,' I say.

Steps approach in the corridor and Letit shows up in the doorway. He has some papers in one hand, the other is resting on his hip with the thumb inside the waist of his shiny, worn trousers with crooked pleats. The shirt is unbuttoned at the neck, revealing a grey tuft of hair.

He sinks onto the chair next to Malin without saying hi.

I look at Malin who is wearing a pair of worn maternity jeans and a T-shirt that must have been white once upon a time, but which is now grey like dishwater in good used condition.

People just don't want to look good anymore, I think. They want to look interesting, dangerous or perhaps rebellious. They want to look like they've travelled the world, smoked weed all night, or are coming to work straight from the brothel.

I look down at my discreetly patterned suit trousers and the well-polished shoes sticking out beneath my protruding belly.

Letit clears his throat. 'Olle "Bullen" Berg was located on a campsite just west of Stuvskär,' he says. 'He bought food for 340 kronor there yesterday.'

'And how do we know this? Malin asks.

'The bank got in touch,' Letit says quietly. 'He used his credit card at 15.36 yesterday. Note that this was the first time he's used it since disappearing. And we're lucky. The shop he went to has a surveillance camera. They caught him on film. Our colleagues from Haninge were there and picked it up.'

Letit slides over three blurry black-and-white pictures of a man in a cap and sunglasses. In the first he is entering through a door. In the next he is standing in front of a counter on which food items are displayed. He is leaning against the counter with his left hand while signing the receipt with his right. The third image looks identical to the second, other than the clerk having moved.

I clear my throat. 'Nice work.'

Letit nods. 'I mean, this is a bit of a special interest. Film, that is,' he says, there is a dreamy aspect to his voice which hints that there is a lot I don't know about him.

Then he furrows his brow. 'There's one thing that is strange. It takes him a very long time to sign that receipt.'

'What?' Malin asks, leaning over the printouts.

'Look at the time stamps.'

'I don't follow,' Malin says, shaking her head.

'Olle is in the exact same position, with the pen against the receipt, in the second and third image,' Letit says quietly.

'And?' Malin asks.

'The pictures are thirty seconds apart. Not even the slow fuckers at the lost property office take thirty seconds to sign a receipt. And I have gone over the original recording with the technicians, there's nothing wrong with the time stamp.'

Letit's eyes gleam behind the heavy lids and I recall the time he helped a colleague go through the video of the car explosions. How he was immediately transformed from grumpy old man into a sharp analyst.

I don't doubt that he knows this like the back of his hand.

'How do you interpret this?' I ask him.

He shakes his head slightly, scratching his beard.

'Hmm. That's a hard one . . . that's what she said.'

Malin shoots me a disgusted look.

'Perhaps he was distracted by something in the shop,' Letit says thoughtfully.

We consider the grainy images in silence.

'You can't see his face,' I say.

Letit nods.

'True. But the man in the shop recognised him. He's apparently well-known there. Or infamous, rather. He lives in a tent just *outside* the campsite, which they obviously don't like. They also said he'd never used a card there before and didn't know the PIN, so he had to present ID. And guess what?'

I shrug at the rhetorical question.

Letit lowers his voice, pulling out one of his toothpicks. 'He's still there. The *stupid* fucker is still in his tent. All we need to do is go there and nab him.'

Malin and I drive toward Stuvskär. In the grey van a couple of hundred yards ahead of us are Letit and four guys from the Reinforced Regional Task Force, the unit formerly known as the SWAT team.

I follow them at a distance while trying to prepare mentally for the strike. Malin and I are going to wait by the cars while Letit and the guys from the regional task force arrest Olle Berg. It is probably not necessary to assign five people the task of arresting one camping man, but we aren't taking any risks.

'It's fine by me if you have a cigarette,' Malin says, glancing at the pack wedged between the seats. 'As long as you open the window.'

'I don't smoke,' I say.

Malin sits silently for a while, then says: 'We'll get him today.'

I nod but don't answer, I know from experience that it isn't over until the lady who is as fat as me sings.

And as we know she is in the habit of being late.

The road winds between lush fields and dusty paddocks. Red cottages are strewn out like Lego bricks across the greenery. A lone cloud floats on the clear blue sky.

'Why did he go by "Bullen" anyway?' I ask, slowing down behind a horse trailer pulling out from a farm.

'Olle Berg? No idea. But I can check.'

'No rush,' I say. 'We can deal with that later.'

But Malin has already got her phone out.

'No worries,' she says. 'I have the number for Berg's old girlfriend on my mobile, I'll text her.'

'The girlfriend he beat black and blue?' I ask.

Malin doesn't answer. She simply taps at the phone with her slim fingers and then puts it back in her pocket.

We pass an inlet on the sea.

The sun is shining on the glimmering waves; a few sails peak out on the horizon, like sharp teeth protruding from the ocean.

Right before Stuvskär the van takes a right and Malin glances at the map.

'Here,' she says. 'Let's keep our fingers crossed that he hasn't disappeared.'

I slowly follow the grey van onto a narrow gravel road and then stop on the hard shoulder.

The men from the task force jump out of the van, followed by Letit.

They're all dressed in leisurewear, like campers. Or, if we're being honest, like the police's *idea* of how campers dress, which is apparently Bermuda shorts and polo shirts.

A couple of hundred yards further down the road I can see the campsite spread out along the beach. Caravans and RVs are neatly lined up. Colourful tents and collapsible furniture can be seen here and there. A Swedish flag is flying in the wind next to the entrance.

I park and open the front door. The scent of hay hits me. The wind has picked up and I squint so as not to get dust in my eyes.

Malin's phone buzzes and she takes it out of her pocket. Positions herself with the sun at her back and looks at the screen. Then she turns her head and looks at me.

'"Bullen" is short for "The Bulldog",' she says.

'So why do they call him "The Bulldog"?'

Malin shrugs.

'I'll ask,' she says briefly and writes something.

We begin walking across a field with stubby grass, towards the group of men in silly knee-length shorts and colourful shirts standing around Letit. The ground between the tufts of grass is bone dry and each time we take a step a small cloud of dust is stirred up.

'OK,' says Letit, who seems to be done with his briefing. 'You can assume your positions now. Let's go in ten. Questions?'

The men shake their heads, then disappear in different directions.

I watch Letit's squat figure disappear across the field in front of us and I look at Malin who is standing still with her arms folded across her chest.

And in that instant I feel it, that familiar sense of discomfort – the hairs going up at the back of my neck and my mouth going dry.

Something is wrong.

I just know.

There's no way for me to explain how I know, because it is as if the knowledge is in my bones. In my muscle fibres, in my arteries, in the sensitive skin at the tips of my fingers.

The body knows.

The body knows long before the brain understands, and the brain realises and accepts that the body has an advantage. It doesn't jump to conclusions, it doesn't try to convince.

Instead it patiently awaits the body's conclusion.

I follow the colleagues from the task force with my eyes. They have left the car park and fanned out across the field surrounding the campsite. Two of them are walking towards the water with a confident air, carrying fishing rods. One is talking on his phone, yet another is jogging toward the water, dressed in active wear.

In a few minutes they will be by Olle Berg's tent. They will arrest him without any major problems since that is what they do best.

But something is wrong.

I look at Malin again. She squints at the sun, wipes the sweat off her forehead and raises her eyebrows inquisitively.

'What?' she says.

'Something is wrong.'

She laughs uncertainly, shaking her head.

'What do you mean, *wrong*?' she asks, looking at Letit who is doing his best to keep up with one of the very fit police officers carrying fishing rods.

Then she looks at her watch and says: 'Five minutes.'

I walk round and around in the dry grass, trying to sort out my thoughts. Kick a tuft, making the dirt fly around the bone-dry straws.

'One minute,' Malin says.

Sweat streams down my forehead and in under the collar of my shirt. Insects buzz above my head and seagulls cry.

Malin puts her phone in her left hand and digs around for something in her pocket with her right. The phone buzzes and when she tries to open the message with her left hand, she drops it in the grass.

When she tries to open the message with the wrong hand she drops it in the grass.

And suddenly I know.

Suddenly I recall the images of Berg from the surveillance camera in the shop at the campsite. How he stood bent over the counter writing his signature on the receipt. And Letit's comment that something wasn't right about the pictures.

'Letit was right,' I say. 'The guy in the surveillance footage hesitated. He hesitated because he wasn't sure what to do when writing Berg's name.'

'What are you *talking* about?' says Malin, still looking for her phone on the ground.

'And when he did sign he wrote with his right hand. But Olle Berg is left-handed.'

Malin freezes mid-movement.

'That's not Berg in the pictures,' I say. 'Berg is left-handed.'

Malin pulls the mobile up from between two shaggy tufts of grass. At the same moment her phone rings.

Arduously she straightens out. Puts one hand on the small of her back and makes a face. Then she gives me a long, inquisitive look and answers her phone.

'Yes. OK.'

Then she is quiet. Strokes her big belly with her hand and looks up at the sky.

'Eighteen? *How the hell . . .?*'

Malin turns toward the car, leaning on her elbows against the body, as if all strength drained out of her in an instant and she can no longer stand upright.

'That's fucked up,' she snaps. 'So where did he find it?'

And then: 'OK, see you later.'

I look at her as she hangs up.

'I cannot fucking believe this,' she says. 'It wasn't him. This guy is eighteen. But he *had* used Berg's credit card. Says he found it and Berg's passport in a bin in Stuvskär. Well, that doesn't sound very likely, so they're bringing him in.'

She sighs, resting the entire weight of her body against the car.

She looks so young, despite the big belly. So young and so distraught that I have the impulse to hold her in my arms and comfort her.

'You were right,' she adds.

'That's not much help now.'

'One more thing,' she says. 'That book Igor Ivanov wrote.'

'Yes?'

'Malik just texted me. We got our hands on a copy.'

'And?' I say.

Malin shakes her head slowly.

'There are only two words in the book. *Lorem ipsum*. Page after page, the same thing.'

I consider this, the words sound familiar.

'*Lorem ipsum*, isn't that . . .?'

'Yes, those are the words typically found at the start of sample texts for print production. If you want to show what something with a text will look like, but you don't have the actual text yet.'

Malin slides down along the car and ends up seated on a tuft of grass.

'Money laundering,' she says, answering the question I haven't had time to pose. 'Welcome to the twenty-first century. Forget money laundering through takeaway pizza, or winning bets on horses. Everything is digital now; that's where it's at. And this is a pretty creative example. Books are put up for sale online. Books that sometimes completely lack content. And the price is set sky-high, Igor's book for instance cost 900 kronor. Then you get bots – that is to say computer programs – to place orders for them and pay for them with dirty money.'

'And then you make a healthy profit that you can put on your tax return?'

'Exactly, the money becomes as clean as a whistle. And one gets to call oneself an author.'

Malin lets out a loud sigh.

'Igor has nothing to do with our poem,' I say.

Malin's phone buzzes again and she reads the message. Seconds later she is furrowing her brow.

'What?' I ask.

'It's Olle Berg's old girlfriend,' she begins. 'Olle was called "The Bulldog" because he . . .'

She looks at me and shakes her head in disbelief. The she goes on:

'Because he had weird teeth,' she says. 'Like a bulldog. He had a crossbite. Just like . . .'

'. . . victim number three,' I fill in. 'Bloody hell. Bloody *hell*! Victim number three is Olle Berg.'

Malin looks at me and her eyes darken.

'But if Berg is dead, then who is our killer?'

Samuel

've been in the cave for a long time now, so long that the light is just a distant memory, a whisper from a past that has long since faded and lost its relevance.

So when the light tugs at me, pulls me out of the ground, I am surprised at first and then a bit scared, because I have begun to feel comfortable in the cave. My wings have got stronger, my eyes sharper and better accustomed to the dark. I need nobody, and nobody needs me.

In many ways it is perfect.

But the light tugs at me. Pulls me upwards, through the ground and almost up to the surface. I'm not in my body, but I'm not in the cave either. I am floating helplessly somewhere in between, as if I am stuck between two dimensions – it is a bit like standing between two train carriages and being able to look in through the windows to both, but not open the door to either one of them.

Finally I land in my body even though I don't want to. I immediately feel every cell and every cubic inch of flesh and blood.

And what I feel is pain.

But in the midst of the chaos, in the midst of the pain, there is also the everyday; the fly intrepidly bouncing against the windowpane, the slight scent of detergent from the sheets and the scent of the freshly picked rose in the vase on the bedside table.

I hear noises too – somebody is moving in the room – but I don't have the energy to open my eyelids; they seem to weigh at least a hundred pounds.

The panic starts up and a scream wants to form in my chest, but the sound gets stuck somewhere in my throat, like a piece of potato lodged there.

'Jonas?'

It is Rachel's voice, but it sounds different, as if I'm lying under water in a bathtub listening to her.

A hand strokes my hair, soft lips press against my cheek.

'*Darling* Jonas!'

I turn around and give her a hard slap.

But only in my mind because my body is as immobile as a Sunday steak in the refrigerated counter in the supermarket.

'My poor darling,' she whispers. 'Now you are in the belly of the whale.' She is crazy, I think, with detached interest, I have the sensation of watching a movie – a really messed-up movie, but still just a movie.

'I will take care of you,' she continues.

She puts her warm hand over mine and continues in a slightly harsher tone of voice.

'But first I need to make sure that you don't do that again, Jonas. It was a very stupid thing to do. You aren't strong enough to go out yet. Anything could have happened. You could have tripped on a rock and hurt yourself, or fallen into the sea or . . .'

There is a long drawn-out sob, and Rachel's hand disappears as she moves towards the foot of the bed.

'I can't handle losing you again, do you understand?'

There is a sound of metal against metal. As if she is rattling coins in a tin can. Then there are duller sounds. Also from metal but these sounds are from larger, heavier objects.

Maybe tools of some kind.

The blanket disappears from over my legs. Cool air whispers against my shins.

'I know you can hear me,' she says. 'And I know that you can't move. I'm not a monster but I can't let you run away. This is for your own good.'

There is a hand on my foot and I can feel something sharp against my heel. Then I hear a bang and my heel explodes into unfathomable pain. My whole leg is on fire and even though I am numbed and not really entirely in my body, I scream in pain and kick with both my legs, sending her flying into the wall.

But only in my mind.

Because in the *real* reality I am lying still in Jonas's bed while she strikes and strikes and strikes and the pain explodes inside of me, over and over.

When the darkness pulls me down I am thankful.

I don't want to be in the light anymore, I don't want to be in my body.

Before I sink through the bed I still manage to analyse what happened and formulate a hypothesis. But it seems so sick, so fucking messed-up, that I can hardly believe it.

Did she really do that?

Did she drive a *nail* into my heel?

Manfred

I get home late.

The disappointment over Olle Berg not being our killer has drained me of energy and I feel depressed and despondent.

Yes, I know.

Berg can still be the lion, he could still have killed Rachel's son, if we are to believe the poem. But he could hardly have killed Ahonen and Carlgren because his body was in the water considerably longer than theirs.

No, either the lion isn't Olle Berg, or the lion is not involved in the deaths of Ahonen and Carlberg.

When I get into the hall I carefully close the door so as not to wake Afsaneh, but she comes from the kitchen to meet me. Wraps her arms around my neck and gives me a light kiss. Then she announces that she has made my favourite dish – chicken with saffron rice – and decided to stay awake and wait for me.

We eat and make small talk about our days.

I don't tell her about Olle Berg. I don't have the energy to dwell more on that today.

We talk about silly, shallow things for the first time in forever. We open a ridiculously expensive bottle of wine, that we really should be saving for a special occasion, and quickly drain the bottle.

Then we make love, tipsy on the living-room floor. As if we were clueless teenagers without responsibilities.

As if our daughter had never fallen onto the hard tarmac.

Afterwards I take a shower.

I let the hot water stream across my body. Wash away the frustration lingering in the dust from the campsite. Head off the thoughts of Igor's so-called book, the one that only contains two words – *Lorem ipsum* – the only purpose of which is to launder drug money.

When I come out of the bathroom Afsaneh is standing outside, naked.

'I think I need one too,' she says and squeezes past me into the bathroom.

I go into the bedroom and sit on the bed. Glance out through the window, where the sky is getting dark behind the sheer curtain.

Afsaneh's computer is open next to her pillow. My eyes fall on a photo of a young man in a bed. The picture is both scary and beautiful at the same time and I can't help but look.

I reach for the laptop and pull it closer. The headline is written in blue, old-fashioned cursive: STRUGGLE FOR LIFE. My gaze moves further down, I let it slide across the page.

It catches on a stanza of a poem at the beginning of the latest post.

I cried myself a sea of tears
and lay down to die
on the soft tuft of grief
But the lion emerged anew
and in his giant maw he held
an untarnished dove

My body freezes and my heart skips a beat.

It isn't possible.

It is not bloody possible.

Afsaneh comes in with a towel wrapped around her hips.

'What's this?' I ask and turn the laptop so that she can see the screen.

She wrinkles her eyebrows.

'A blog, why?'

'Who wrote it?'

Afsaneh takes her towel off and hangs it over the back of a chair. Then she puts on one of my old T-shirts.

'Not a clue. She has a brain-damaged son. That's all I know. And she is quite active on the forum too. Posts a lot of stuff.'

Afsaneh sits on the bed and strokes my cheek.

'I'm tired,' she says, yawning.

I don't answer. I pull the laptop back towards myself. Scroll down the page.

Photos of the guy in the bed flicker past. There are close-ups of a hand, a face that is turned away, and a lone rose in a vase with drops of dew on its petals. And pictures of nature where one can see the ocean, smooth rocks and a lighthouse.

There is no face to be found anywhere, but in a few places I can see a side-view of a woman's face. The pictures are blurry and the long hair fluttering in the wind partially obscures her features.

'Is she big?' I ask.

'What do you mean, *big*?'

Afsaneh crawls into bed next to me.

'Can we turn out the lights?' she mumbles sleepily and puts her hand on my thigh.

'Do a lot of people read her blog?' I clarify.

'A hundred thousand at least. You can see for yourself how many comments the posts get. Honey, I am sorry, but I have to get some sleep.'

'Can I borrow your computer?'

'Sure,' she says, turning off the light.

I sit in the living room reading the blog for a long time, despite my head aching with tiredness and my body crying for sleep. The posts deal with everything from the grief over her son's accident, to the daily trials and tribulations involved in caring for a brain-damaged person in the home.

At three in the morning I call Malin. It rings five times before she picks up.

'Can you come into the station now?' I ask.

It takes her a few seconds to answer.

'Do you know what time it is?'

'I know what time it is.'

She sighs.

'Is it important?'

'It's very important.'

A few hours later Malin and I have gone through the blog in detail, comparing it to our own timeline. We have inspected

the pictures and read countless posts and comments from
followers.

The sun has risen and the station has come to life. Doors
have been walked through and stairs run up and down. A scent
of freshly brewed coffee has spread across our floor. Letit has
arrived, listened to our conclusions, hummed and lumbered
off again.

'Show me the introduction again,' Malin says and I do
what she tells me.

> *My name is Rachel. My son Jonas was a completely
> normal teenager when he was in a traffic accident. I was
> over the moon when I realised he would survive. I didn't
> understand at the time that the battle for a decent life had
> just begun, because after the accident my son was badly
> brain-damaged and fell into a deep coma. But I decided
> to NEVER give up! Now I care for my son at home. Follow
> our struggle on this blog.*

'According to the poem the lion killed the son,' Malin says.
'But the son is still alive.'

She nods at the computer where we can see the picture of
the young man in bed.

'I know,' I say. 'Perhaps we shouldn't take the poem literally.
Maybe it's symbolic. Perhaps it feels as if he is dead, although
he's really just completely out of it.'

The door opens and Letit comes in.

'We've found her,' he says. 'I spoke to the prosecutor. And
with forensics. The IT forensics are going to over it all in detail,
but they have traced the blog to Susanne Bergdorff.'

The room falls silent.

'*Susanne?*' I ask.

'It appears that she goes by Rachel,' Letit grunts. 'Susanne Bergdorff was born and raised in Flen, in Sörmland. She was a promising swimmer well into her teens. She is a widow and has a disabled son, Jonas. Her husband suffered from MS and died after a bout of pneumonia four years ago. Susanne worked as a pharmacist until her son's accident. He was in a hit-and-run. Her parents are long dead and their family estate has been sold. Her father was a pastor in the church of Sweden and her mother was a housewife. They divorced when Susanne was little.'

'How do you know all this?' Malin asks.

'I got the name of Susanne Bergdorff's therapist from one of her friends. Apparently, she was in some kind of therapy.'

'Where is Susanne now?' I ask.

'That's the problem,' Letit says, exhaling loudly as he sinks into the chair next to mine. 'We can't find her anywhere. It seems she is still getting mail at her old address, where she is still registered, but that house has been empty for over a year. She's been collecting the money she gets from social security and her private insurance every month. The withdrawals have been made at an ATM in Haninge Centrum. We are going to get the film from the surveillance camera there.'

'Well,' I say, and go up to the whiteboard. Pick up a pen and begin to write. 'We can link our three victims to one another through DNA.'

I write 'Johannes Ahonen', 'Victor Carlgren' and 'Olle Berg' on the board and circle each name.

'And Olle Berg can be connected to Rachel, also known as Susanne, thanks to a witness statement,' I continue, writing

'Susanne/Rachel', circle that too and draw a line to Olle Berg's circle.

'The bodies were found in the southern archipelago. They could very well have been killed in Stuvskär, where the woman who wanted to report a missing person claimed that Rachel lived.'

'The one who was scared off by the pregnant bimbo with the trout pout?' Letit asks.

'Yes. She did say that her son worked in or in the vicinity of Stuvskär. And that's not too far from Haninge where the cash was withdrawn?'

'Definitely,' Letit nods. 'But Susanne and Jonas Bergdorff aren't registered there. That was the first thing I looked into.'

'There's no Rachel either. I've already checked,' Malin says.

'They could be living in Stuvskär without being registered there,' I say.

Letit's gaze fastens on Olle Berg's mugshot. He sticks a toothpick in his mouth and his jaws begin to grind mechanically.

I draw a circle next to Rachel's name, write 'The Lion' inside of it and draw a line to Rachel.

'Susanne is the key to all of this. If we find her we'll also find the man she calls the lion.'

'If he exists,' Letit snorts.

'The forensic psychologists believe the killer to be male,' Malin says. 'The extreme violence, moving the bodies. It all points to that.'

'In any case,' I say, 'we've got to find Susanne.'

I go back to the computer, scroll down so that an image becomes visible.

Dark sea, foam washing across shiny worn rocks. A lighthouse, illuminated from the side by the sun that is low in the sky. Silhouettes of thin pines reaching for the sky.

'I will try to find that therapist,' I say. 'Gunnar, can you see if Malik can find out where those photos on the blog might be taken?'

'The lighthouse,' Letit nods, leaning closer into the computer and taking the broken toothpick out of his mouth. 'I think he should focus on the lighthouse.'

'Right,' I say. 'It's visible in several of the photos. There can't be that many lighthouses in the vicinity of Stuvskär. Ask Malik to see if it is possible to determine where the photos were taken. And check with some of the colleagues if they can go out to Stuvskär and knock on some doors. Somebody has to know her.'

Letit nods, flicks the toothpick toward the bin and ambles off down the hallway.

Pernilla

We drive into the Stuvskär harbour.

Stina is wringing her sun-damaged hands and looking intently at the dock. I glance at the back seat where Björn is biting his dirty nails.

It is just after ten o'clock.

The straits glimmer. The surface looks so smooth and innocent, so polished and restrained. But the water still carries the memory of the wind and the waves out on the open sea. They are still imprinted on it – in the heavy swell that slowly heaves over the sunken skerries, then rolls in and washes over the rocks with surprising force.

The sky is clear blue, the air is warm and a thin haze grazes the outlines of the skerries and the islets that lie spread out in a row, like bits of crushed granite on the horizon. The scent of seaweed and tar blends with freshly brewed coffee from the jetty behind the harbour pub. Scattered laughter and fragments of conversation carry from the moored boats.

In less than an hour Rachel will be here to meet Theo, almost nineteen, who has dropped out of high school and is looking for a part-time job.

Theo – who is really Björn, but may as well be Samuel.

I look across the harbour, trying to decide where to park. Stina and I must be able to sit in the car while keeping an eye on Björn. And Rachel mustn't see us.

'What about over there?' Stina suggests, pointing to the shop. 'There are two cars parked there already, so we won't draw unnecessary attention. Besides, we can clearly see the dock and easily follow a person leaving by car.'

'You're right,' I say.

Björn sits quietly, but I can hear small, popping noises as he bites his way through his nails.

I park and then we go into the supermarket and buy a wildly expensive coffee with milk made out of some type of Indian nut, and sit in the car and wait.

'How do they stay afloat?' Stina says nodding toward the shop. 'Their stock is ridiculous. Just a bunch of obscure things and that vegan rubbish. Who buys that? Not our customers anyway, I know that much. The floor was dirty too. And the staff were looking at their phones instead of helping the customers. And what's the point of their fancy linen aprons?'

She snorts, taking her sunglasses off.

The minutes crawl by.

I look at my phone to see if I have any messages, but the screen is empty. All I see is the lock screen photo of Samuel and me last Christmas.

It is crazy how much he looks like Isaac in this photo – the thin, expressive face, the large dark eyes, the cheekbones and the curve of the upper lip.

I promise you will have your father back, I think, stroking the picture with my index finger. Just as long as you come home. Just come home, and I will do anything.

The clock on my mobile says a quarter to eleven and I turn toward Björn.

'Are you ready?' I ask. 'Because if you're not we can go over this one more time. It never hurts to rehearse an extra time. If you aren't. Ready, I mean.'

Björn takes his ring finger out of his mouth and looks at me.

'It's cool,' he says. 'I'll talk to her and then you follow her when she goes home. How hard can it be?'

'And you're not going to give her any personal information,' Stina adds. 'Not your real name, not your mobile number. Not—'

'*Please*,' Björn interrupts her with a sigh. 'Why *would* I?'

I look up at the sky, at the almost unreal blue dome that separates us from Him. Then I tuck my phone down beside the gear stick, take a gulp of the coffee that tastes like mould and look out over the harbour. Study the sailors who are driving jerrycans of water, ice packs and grocery bags on little wagons and women parking their expensive cars next to the supermarket to replenish their stores of pomegranate juice, juniper-cured trout, tahini, or perhaps egg-and-anchovy salad.

The dock is empty except for a lady in her sixties who is sitting by the semaphore tower reading a newspaper. She has unbuttoned her blouse, hitched up her skirt, taken her shoes off and put her feet on her suitcase.

Could that be Rachel?

'Well, that's not her for sure,' Stina murmurs as if she read my thoughts. 'She's way too old. Rachel is probably younger, maybe between forty and fifty.'

A white Mercedes SUV parks next to the harbour pub and a buxom blonde in her thirties jumps out. Her bust defies gravity and her nails are long and pink, reminiscent of talons. She takes a few steps onto the dock, looks around uncertainly and then goes over to the ferry schedule on the message board. Then she pushes her rhinestone-encrusted sunglasses up onto her forehead and studies the schedule very carefully.

I look at her car where two children, about five years old, are wrestling in the back seat.

'It's not her either,' Stina says, with absolute certainty. 'Rachel didn't have preschoolers, did she? Besides: there's no way she could care for a brain-damaged child with those nails. She probably has trouble wiping her own butt.'

Stina sends herself into a snorting laughing fit with that comment.

I turn my head away from the dock, letting my gaze sweep the turning space in front of the supermarket and the harbour pub.

A black Volvo saloon parks just behind the white SUV. A few seconds later a woman with long, dark hair steps out. She is dressed in denim shorts, a thin white blouse and flip-flops.

She looks around and then goes to the dock. Sits down next to the woman sunning herself and waits.

I look at the woman's car again.

It looks new. Expensive but not flashy. On the windscreen I can see the disability parking permit with the wheelchair symbol.

'There!' I whisper although she obviously can't hear us.

Stina nods.

'Yes, that could be her,' she murmurs.

Björn opens the door.

'Be careful,' Stina cautions.

'Stop nagging me,' Björn hisses and begins to walk towards the dock with gangly steps.

The woman, who might be Rachel, is sitting still on the bench with her hands folded in her lap. When Björn comes up to her, she gets up and shakes his hand. Then they both sit down and begin to talk.

Rachel gestures and Björn laughs.

'How long do you think they're going to talk?' Stina asks.

'I don't know,' I say. 'How long does a job interview take?'

Stina doesn't answer.

I turn the radio on, because I suspect Rachel's and Björn's conversation could take a while.

The news anchor explains that the heatwave could last for at least another week and that the incidence of drownings has increased sharply due to the warm weather. Yesterday a pair of siblings – three and four years old – drowned on a beach outside Norrtälje. The children's mother, who was with them at the time, was on her phone while the accident happened, according to witnesses.

'My God, how awful,' Stina says, turning the radio off. 'What is wrong with people these days? Playing with your phone while your young children are swimming. That ought to be a crime.'

I am about to answer her when I see Rachel get up.

Seconds later Björn does the same. They begin to walk towards the car park, side by side.

'What are they doing?' I ask.

'Well, I have no idea,' Stina says.

Rachel and Björn go up to Rachel's Volvo.

'They're about to say goodbye,' Stina whispers.

But instead Björn walks around the car and gets in on the passenger side.

'Sweet Jesus,' Stina says. 'What is he *doing*? I told him not go with her whatever happens. Why doesn't he ever listen to me?'

The black car takes off, leaving a cloud of dust in its wake.

'Hurry!' Stina says and I hurry. Start the car, put it in gear, and press down on the accelerator to follow the Volvo.

But my old banger sputters and is left standing still.

'Sorry,' I say. 'You just have to . . . there's something . . . when you start . . . something is wrong. I mean. But only sometimes. It can start without a hitch, even if it's winter and freezing. Well, sometimes I wonder how—'

'Please, will you just *drive*, woman?' Stina interrupts.

I start the car again. The gear box gives off a piercing sound, but the car jumps and is on its way.

We follow the black car and we're in luck. A large military-green SUV gets in between us and the Volvo, lessening our chances of being discovered.

But the SUV stops and we're stuck behind it.

'Overtake it!' Stina commands.

'I can't,' I yell, pointing at the cars coming at us in the other lane.

'Overtake it anyway!'

'But I can't.'

Two young girls jump out of the SUV which is parked in front of us. They walk towards the boot at a leisurely pace, open it and begin to pull out bags.

'Good grief,' Stina huffs.

I put my foot on the accelerator and overtake the SUV. It's a dangerous manoeuvre and I just have time to turn before a large truck passes from the other direction.

It honks loudly.

I slow down and look ahead.

'What?' Stina says.

And then: '*What the . . .?*'

I look at the country road stretching out ahead of us like a long snake. At the thin pine trees next to the road and at the little rocks poking up out of the vegetation here and there.

The black Volvo is gone.

Samuel

don't know how long I have been in the darkness when the light pulls me up again.

I can hear steps approaching, voices, laughter.

Rachel's laugh.

I am in my body again.

The pain in my foot is excruciating. I want to cry, but there are no tears. All that happens is that sweat starts to break out at my temples and my heart beats fast.

The door opens and Rachel and a thin guy with long blond hair come in.

I can't open my eyes enough to see them clearly, and as soon as they come toward me they disappear from the narrow field of vision I have through the crack between my eyelids.

'You can sit there,' Rachel says, and moments later I hear creaking from the grandma chair as the guy takes a seat. Then the scraping of the stool against the floor as Rachel pulls it out to sit on it.

There is a warm hand on mine.

'This is Theo,' Rachel, says, squeezing my hand a little. 'He's visiting today. He might begin working for us, to keep you company. Read to you and play music.'

Her lips graze my cheek. The light touch burns like fire and I feel nauseous.

The guy says something about my nose and Rachel answers.

'Oh that. Jonas is tube-fed. But you don't need to worry about it. I take care of all that.'

I want to scream at them to get the bloody tube out of my nose, but I can't. I want to speak with them, tell them about the pain in my foot, but I don't have words. The pain is speaking to *me*, it shouts and screams, so that I can't hear my own thoughts.

'Did he fall?' The guy asks.

'Yes, he had an epileptic fit a few days ago. But it looks much worse than it is. It'll heal well.'

A drop of sweat runs down my temple and makes its way behind one ear. I hear a smacking sound and a click. Seconds later I feel something slippery and cold on my hand.

Rachel's fingers are massaging me. Rubbing the sticky stuff in slowly and methodically.

'His hands get so terribly dry,' she says. 'I usually moisturise them once a day or so. It's a good idea to put some balm on his lips too. There's a stick on the bedside table.'

There is another smacking sound, Rachel begins to massage my other hand.

'*Uhh*,' I manage, but it sounds more like a groan than a word.

'He knows you're here,' Rachel pants theatrically sounding at once elated and surprised. 'You know what, I think this will work out really well!'

'I'm not sure,' the guy says. 'I mean, I don't know anything about diseases and stuff.'

'All you need to do is keep Jonas company. Read to him, play music. He is almost always calm, but sometimes he gets restless or has seizures. If that happens I want you to come and get me immediately. He can end up hurting himself.'

'OK.'

'You can read a bit now. Begin where the bookmark is.'

'*Now?*'

'Of course,' Rachel says.

The guy clears his throat and begins to read:

'*You don't like Paris? No. Why don't you go somewhere else? There isn't anywhere else.*'

Rachel laughs.

'I was just joking. You don't need to read right now. You're just here visiting today.'

'Uhm, OK.'

The guy clears his throat.

'Nice bracelet.'

Rachel's hands stop mid-movement and my wrist is lifted up. Someone fingers my mum's glass-bead bracelet.

I want to cry, even though I don't have any tears left.

'Isn't it pretty?' Rachel murmurs with feeling and a bit of a tremble to her voice. 'He made it for me in Year One, but after his accident I put it on him so that it would always be with him. Look at the beads.'

The guy leans in. I can't see it, but I can feel his breath against my cheek. It comes in regular, warm puffs that smell of snuff.

'M-U-M-M-Y,' he sounds out like a fucking six-year-old. And when he does that – when he takes the word he shouldn't be allowed to say into his mouth – something inside of me stirs and my whole body stiffens into spasms.

I want to hit him. I want to punch him, a straight punch to his face to send him straight into the wall head-first.

I test moving my fingers, expecting resistance but it's not there. The sedative must be wearing off.

My arm flies up to his face, but not fast enough to knock him out. My fingers bend and I scratch him across the face. I can feel my nails cut through his skin before he yelps and jumps back.

'*Jonas*,' Rachel gasps.

And then: 'I don't understand what happened. He has never . . .'

'Don't worry about it,' the guy says.

'Wait here and I'll get some Neosporin,' Rachel says.

I hear steps and glimpse Rachel's silhouette as she leaves the room.

It is quiet.

The guy breathes heavily. A few seconds later I hear a snap. He is taking a *photo* of me.

Why is he doing that?

A moment later I hear steps. Rachel is on her way back.

I try forming my lips into words, try to warn the guy. Because even though I didn't like him messing with Mum's bracelet I don't want Rachel to get her hands on him.

But no sound passes my lips. My mouth won't form itself around the words. My lungs are powerless. My vocal cords won't obey me.

'What are you doing?'

Rachel's voice is calm, but I can hear the fear and anger under the surface.

'I just wanted to . . .'

Rachel takes a few steps into the room.

'Why are you photographing my son?'

'I . . . didn't mean. I . . .'

'Give me your phone!' Rachel screams.

No, I bellow. *No, no, no!*

But only in my head.

Manfred

Ulla Waldén is in her sixties and greets us in her apartment on Gärdet, where she just moved in. She is an elegant woman with thick salt-and-pepper hair swept back into a ponytail and a tight red cotton top that does her petite body justice. Large silver earrings dangle from her ears and around her neck she wears a simple pearl necklace of the kind that is probably more expensive than it looks.

Her handshake is firm, even though her hand is small and thin.

When Letit takes her hand he lights up and fires off one of his rare smiles. He sucks his gut in and stands up tall. His face softens and his eyes acquire a mischievous sparkle. For a second he almost looks like a roguish boy, rather than the curmudgeonly old man we are accustomed to.

'Gunnar,' he says, shakes her hand enthusiastically and shoots her another wolf-like grin.

They end up standing like that, in the hall, a few seconds too long and Malin gives me a meaningful look. This is exactly like when we met with Tuula Ahonen, I think. There's a sort of charge in the air, some kind of energy between Letit and the slender woman.

'Oh,' Ulla says and smiles coyly. Looks at her hand that is still holding Letit's and lets go hesitantly.

'Welcome, Gunnar,' she adds, emphatically.

In the next instant the moment has passed and Ulla shows us into her small, but cosily decorated living room.

The furniture has a patina. There are rag carpets on the floor and colourful paintings on the walls. The window is open and summer is flooding in through the small rooms.

'Please have a seat,' says Ulla, whose cheeks are now rosy. 'Coffee?'

'No thanks,' I say. 'We won't stay long.'

'I'd love some,' says Letit, stretching himself.

Ulla smiles and disappears into the kitchen.

Malin and I sit down on the couch and Letit sits down in an armchair. His face is almost serene. Malin looks at me again and I nod slightly to confirm that I noted the small but very strange occurrence in the hall.

Ulla comes back with coffee and cinnamon buns for all of us on a silver tray. She places the tray on the coffee table and moves a vase of pink peonies and a few newspapers to make room. Then she sits on a stool. Puts on a pair of glasses with red frames and looks at me.

'So, you wanted to talk about Susanne Bergdorff?'

'Yes,' I say. 'And of course I realise there is client confidentiality, but since we are investigating a murder you are no longer bound by it.'

'I know,' Ulla says calmly. 'How can I help you? Is Susanne suspected of anything?'

I avoid answering her question directly.

'Could you tell us a bit about her?' I say instead.

Ulla nods, smoothing her skirt across her lap.

'Susanne was one of the ones you remember,' she says. 'She came to me because she was depressed. The doctor at the medical centre recommended she speak to a therapist.'

She pauses, looks across the room and then continues:

'She'd had a hard time. She was bullied as a child. Had difficulties with social interactions. Her parents died early on; I think they both got cancer. And then her husband fell sick and died – MS. You'd think that would be enough, that she'd already suffered plenty. Not so. Then her son was in that terrible accident.'

Ulla goes quiet and looks at the ceiling.

'She cared for her husband herself, in their home. To the very end. And now she is apparently caring for her son at home. She made sacrifices, first for her husband and then for their son. A lot of people probably think that's a beautiful thing, but I don't. I think she might have bothered to think of herself a bit. And I told her as much.'

'Do you know how her husband died?' Malin asks.

Ulla shakes her head.

'I don't have any details on that, but I do recall that everyone was surprised. Sure, he had MS, but he wasn't all that sick, as I understood it. Then one day suddenly he was dead. It was a big shock to Susanne.'

A clock on the wall chimes.

I clear my throat.

'Are you in touch with Susanne at all now?'

Ulla smiles sadly and pushes her glasses up the bridge of her nose. Then shakes her head.

'No, I've stopped working. I don't see patients anymore. I moved to Stockholm to be close to my daughter, Greta, after my divorce.'

When she mentions her divorce her eyes quickly wander over Letit, who smiles again, and holds up a half-eaten cinnamon bun.

'These are *fantastic*,' he says, sounding so enraptured that you'd be forgiven for thinking Ulla had made a unicorn, rather than completely ordinary – and truth be told, rather dry – cinnamon buns.

Ulla smiles sheepishly and the colour on her cheeks deepens.

'Why th-thank you,' she stutters.

'Do you know if Susanne had any boyfriends after her husband died?' I ask.

'No,' Ulla says.

'Does the name Rachel mean anything to you?' Malin asks.

'*Rachel?* No, I don't think so. It sounds a bit biblical. Not exactly my area of expertise.'

I look down at the rag carpet. I'm beginning to wonder if this conversation is going to yield anything, because no matter how sympathetic an impression this nice-looking therapist gives, she does not seem to know anything that could further the investigation.

'Was Susanne interested in biblical matters?' Malin asks, making a note on her pad.

Ulla raises her well-groomed eyebrows slightly.

'Well, I don't know that she was especially religious, if that is what you mean. But her father was a priest, so she knew a lot about the Bible and often referred to Bible stories.'

'Do you remember which ones?' I ask.

She shakes her head.

'No, I've forgotten that a long time ago. Or . . . wait! Actually, I do remember! How silly of me. She spoke of Jonah in the belly of the whale. She felt her son was trapped in the belly of the whale, just like Jonah. That his illness sort of held him prisoner.'

There is a pause. Malin gives me a quick look before she continues:

'Were you able to help her?'

'I think so. She didn't have any close friends and at least she could talk to me. I tried to help her build a social base, a network that she could interact with, both at her home in Flen and on the internet. Well, there are lots of forums and the like on the internet for people in her situation. I encouraged her to be active there.'

Malin stops writing, her gaze still on her pad.

'Was she?' I ask.

Ulla shrugs slightly.

'Yes, absolutely. Especially after her husband died. Susanne made many friends online and they helped her through her grief. I could tell by looking at her that the support from those people sort of carried her through that period. And she helped them too, that was the beauty of it. But then her son was in that terrible accident. After that she became more introverted. Came to me increasingly rarely. At first I was worried about her, but then I came to understand that she spoke to her other friends about all that – her friends online, that is.'

'Do you think Susanne might pose a danger to herself or others?' I ask.

'A *danger*?'

Ulla looks confused, as if she doesn't understand the question.

She continues: 'I can't imagine Susanne would hurt anyone,' she says emphatically. 'No. She was definitely not violent in any way, if that's what you mean. Her big problem was that she was so shut off, that she couldn't talk about stuff.'

Malin's phone buzzes.

She picks it up and looks at her screen, then holds it up for me to read.

It's a message from Malik.

Susanne Bergdorff lives on Marholmen outside Stuvskär. Meet me at the station in 15.

'It must be hard,' I say, turning to Ulla to wrap up the conversation in a reasonably nice way. 'Not being able to talk about what hurts the most. Then there's not much to—'

'Oh, there is always a way forward,' Ulla interrupts and smiles. Her eyes are shining and for the first time during our conversation I sense real enthusiasm in her.

'It's not always necessary to talk,' she says. 'I have talked my whole life. My entire career. One can write instead. What cannot be spoken can perhaps be written. And Susanne found her voice in that, in writing. Yes, she wrote poems. Really nice poems, I think.'

Samuel

' 'm sorry,' Rachel says, stroking my cheek. 'I don't know who that guy Theo was, or why he was taking photos of you, but you can't stay here.'

The door closes. Rachel's steps fade away and I am alone with my pain and uncertainty.

You can't stay here.

What does she mean by that?

A while later the door closes and the steps disappear.

My thoughts are clearer and my body has come back to life. I can move my fingers, but not my arms or legs.

I've understood that she is keeping me drugged.

What I don't understand is *why* – why is she doing this? What kind of sick kick does she get out of having me here in this bed, massaging my hands with cream and sticking a fucking tube up my nose?

Steps approach from the outside, but I hear something else too, something that rattles on the steps and a hollow metallic bang, like from a tin bucket hitting something.

The steps enter the room.

'We've got to hurry,' Rachel murmurs, without further clarification.

One hand grabs on to my right upper arm, another takes the right leg, dragging me towards the edge of the bed.

I fight to open my eyelids but don't succeed. But my hands have come to life – I spread my fingers and clench my fists, over and over again. Try to pump some life into my lower arms. I do my best to grab on to the mattress, to stop her from pulling me onto the floor, but don't succeed.

The next instant the edge of the bed disappears from below my right shoulder.

I slide helplessly off the mattress, but not onto the floor. Instead I land in something hard that feels like a big box.

Rachel lays me on my side, takes a hold of one leg, bends it and puts it inside the edge of the box. Then she does the same with my other leg, then folds both my arms against my chest so that I am in a foetal position.

Steps leave the room. My cheek rests against cold tin.

I put my hands against each other and feel around. Feel the dry, cracked skin and the warm glass beads on the bracelet. My body wants to start to cry again, but whatever drug she shot me up with has made me as dry as the fucking desert.

Steps approach from the hallway.

Seconds later something soft lands over me – maybe a tablecloth or a blanket.

Rachel tips the whole tin box – my head is raised and my feet are lowered. The box shakes and I understand.

I'm in the wheelbarrow.

The fucking lunatic has put me in the wheelbarrow, just like we did with Igor.

*

She wheels me out of the door and down the ramp. Then she continues straight ahead and I hear the sound of gravel crunching under the wheel, which must mean that she is headed towards the road.

The wheelbarrow jolts and my head bounces against the bottom over and over, while I am unable to do anything about it. I smell soil and grass. Tiny rocks make their way into my mouth.

I think of Mum and of Alexandra. Of how I would do anything to have them back, to have my life back. And I think of how messed up it is that I thought that I was the one who was going to trick Rachel, steal from her, when in reality she was the bad guy.

Nice Rachel who is always so understanding. Who makes pancakes and looks like my mum. Who likes roses and takes morning swims and actually saved my life. Is she wheeling me off in a wheelbarrow?

This is so messed up; it has to be a punishment from God.

But even now I can't believe in God.

Even now I can't believe in heavenly salvation. Because if there was a God I don't think He would have let Rachel do something so sick. No, he would have crushed her like a bug between his fingers before she could say hand cream.

Rachel wheels me over a bump and my hands end up outside the edge of the wheelbarrow.

Why doesn't she say anything? Can't she explain why she is doing this?

What does it matter? You're going to die now either way, you little shit.

My eyes burn and it actually feels like real tears. Maybe the drugs are loosening their grip on me, maybe the tears will come after all.

Something is poking into my cheek, something sharp. It almost feels like a pin, or a small twig. With effort I manage to open one eyelid, try to see what it is, but the object is too close.

And then the wheelbarrow jolts and a small orange object rolls over a bit, so that it ends up an inch or so from my face.

It's a ladybird, but not a real ladybird. It almost looks like an earring.

The wheelbarrow stops, my head is lowered and my feet are suddenly elevated.

There are a few seconds of silence, then I hear the rattling of keys and the squeak of the gate.

My head is raised again and I roll on.

After a while I feel as if Rachel is turning. The fabric that she has laid over me tickles my cheek and I have the impulse to scratch myself but I can't move.

It is a few seconds before I realise where she is taking me.

My stomach contracts and my heart thumps in my chest, like a rabbit scared out of its mind. The only thought I can hold on to is that I need to get out of here somehow, that I have to stop her. But my arms and legs still won't obey me. I'm lying helplessly on my side with my hands resting over the edge of the wheelbarrow.

I feel around for something to grab on to – anything, a stick or a rock – but around me is nothing but air, nothing but the teasing caress of the summer breeze.

I'm going to die today and nothing I do can stop it.

I'm going to die today, Mum.

I clasp my hands in desperation and suddenly I have an idea.

Suddenly the thought appears.

I don't know if it'll work, but it is worth a shot, after all it's just a simple math problem.

There are 252 steps where she is going and she can't have walked more than ten steps from the gate.

I put my right hand against my left and make a quick estimate. Then I begin to count Rachel's steps.

One. Two. Three . . .

Pernilla

We're standing in the harbour when Björn comes running along the road.

He runs as if he were chased by wolves. The long, gangly legs fly over the dusty dirty road. His face is an angry red and his blond hair stands out like a mane.

'We're over here!' Stina calls, waving both her arms above her head so that her bangles rattle against each other.

We begin to run too, around the local history museum till we reach Björn.

He throws himself into Stina's arms and pants, without getting a word out.

Stina scolds him.

'I told you not to go with her, but you never listen to what I say. How many times do I have to—'

'*Please*,' Björn manages between the gasps. 'Otherwise we wouldn't know where she lives. She said she was going to go shopping, unless I wanted to come with her and say hi to Jonas.'

'And what happened to your face? You're all bloody.'

'Maybe we should let him catch his breath first,' I suggest and hand Björn a water bottle.

He takes it without a word and drains it in one swig. Then he bends forward and steadies himself with his hands against his shins, spits into the dry gravel.

'Everything checks out,' he says and gets up. 'She has a disabled son. I saw him. I even got a photo of him. And he scratched me. I don't know why because he seemed unconscious. But she, Rachel, is weird. She tried to stop me when I left.'

'*My God*,' Stina says, raising her hands to her mouth.

'Whatever,' Björn says, giving Stina a dismissive look. 'I ran away from her. But it was like a couple of miles, and I was scared the whole time that she would come after me with the car, so I ran in the woods next to the road. Do you know how hard that is? Try running in the woods some time and you'll see.'

Stina looks at me, rolls her eyes and shakes her head.

'Why can you never do what you're told? How can it be that you, who have such good grades, can't follow the simplest instruction?'

'Can I see the photos you took?' I ask.

'Sure,' Björn says, gets his mobile out of his pocket, punches in the code, taps at the screen a few times and then hands me the phone.

I examine the photos.

A young man in a hospital bed. The man's face is turned away and also in the shade, so you can't see what he looks like. But he is thin, almost emaciated. His face looks swollen and is full of scabs. One of his hands is resting on the cover and around his wrist . . .

Jesus.

Around his wrist he is wearing a bracelet.

I put my thumb and index finger on the screen and zoom in. See the glass beads, can even make out a few of the letters.

There is no doubt.

The man in the bed is wearing the bracelet Samuel made me.

'You have to show me where she lives,' I whisper.

'No,' Stina says with authority. 'We are taking this to the police.'

'How about we *call* the police?' Björn suggests.

'OK,' I say, 'but then you have to drive me to that woman Rachel. She must know where Samuel is.'

Half an hour later I am standing on the gravel road beneath Rachel's house looking up at the beautiful whitewashed wooden building with green windows.

Stina and Björn have gone to meet the police officer we just spoke to, the one we were transferred to when we called.

There is something strange about the fence, the height; it reaches almost to my chest.

Why would you build such a tall fence around a summer house in a neighbourhood that is so peaceful that the police are probably only ever called to rescue cats out of trees?

Who are you trying to keep out?

Or is it the opposite? Are you trying to keep someone in the house? Like livestock in a pen?

The thought gives me the shivers and Samuel's face shows up in my mind's eye.

'How I have let you down,' I mumble. 'How I have let you get hurt. All the times you needed help, all I did was pray and give you fish oil. But that's over now. Now I am coming to get you.'

My phone buzzes and I look at the screen. Read the message that is from a police officer named Manfred.

What he told me over the phone about Rachel and that poem I handed over to the police was the strangest, most hair-raising story I have ever heard. The fact is, it is so unbelievable that I am actually inclined to believe it is true.

Nobody could make up a story like that.

I can recall the sad stanzas that I read so many times that I know them by heart.

I fell, I died, I did not wake
but in my greatest grief
a lion came to me

So Rachel may have written the poem. And she, or more likely, a male accomplice, could be linked to several violent crimes.

The lion.

I think about this.

Something doesn't add up.

First of all Rachel's son isn't dead, like the poem says. I saw him in the photo Björn took.

Second, Rachel and Jonah are Hebrew names, but surely Leo is Latin? Besides you need to rearrange the letters in Olle and subtract an 'l' to make it Leo.

Isn't that a bit odd?

I try to tell myself that I'm only getting stuck on this because I have been to Bible school. That the police, with all their experts with their fancy training and titles, probably know what they're doing.

Still, there is something about Manfred's interpretation of the poem that bothers me.

The lion and the lamb.

The lamb and the lion.

The image of the Pastor's self-satisfied face shows up in my mind. He is in the assembly hall, in front of the pictures with illustrations from the holy scripture.

I shudder involuntarily, despite the heat, and stomp my foot in the dry grass in frustration when the memory fades without my understanding what it means.

I look down at my phone again.

Read Manfred's message one more time.

It says we can't go into, or even approach, the house where Rachel and her son live. It says we need to wait for them in Stuvskär.

I let go of the phone.

It lands with a soft thud on the grass. The tissue I was holding in my other hand flutters away in the soft breeze and is caught seconds later by a dry little pine sapling that has managed to survive in a crevice in a large rock next to the road, against all odds.

Then I turn my back to the road and begin walking towards the high fence.

To heck with the church and all the holiness, I think.

To heck with the pastor and the congregation.

To heck with my father and his lies. And to heck with the storytelling police officer who wanted to stop me from finding my son.

'Samuel, I'm coming,' I whisper. 'I don't care what they say. You have waited long enough. I'm coming now.'

Manfred

The car flies across the speed bumps in the road. If my bad knee is suffering from the motion I don't notice, I am far too focused on getting us out through the city as fast as humanly possible.

We have just left Letit and Malik, who have taken another car to meet Stina and Björn Svensson, and Pernilla Stenberg in the Stuvskär harbour.

Malin and I drive straight to Susanne's house.

Malik has done a solid job: the lighthouse that could be seen in Susanne's blog is called Klockaren. It is one of the oldest lighthouses on the east coast and there is no other lighthouse that looks like it.

Based on what was visible of the open sea, other islands and the position of the sun in relation to the lighthouse, Malik drew the conclusion that the photo was taken on Marholmen, which is a few miles east of Stuvskär. There are only two properties on Marholmen. Malik asked around and found out that one of them is owned by an older lady named Mai-Lis Wennström, who has rented out her house over the last year. She is the daughter of the last lighthouse keeper on Klockaren, but moved into an assisted living facility last year. At the time the house was partially wheelchair-accessible, which likely suited Susanne, aka Rachel, perfectly. Letit spoke to the other person who lives on Marholmen as well, and he could confirm that a woman named Rachel was living there with her son.

'Malik did a good job,' I say to Malin. 'And even though I dislike the fact that Pernilla Stenberg has played private investigator, that does mean we do have two independent sources pointing to this property now.'

Malin looks at her watch.

'Are you sure it isn't better to wait for our colleagues from Haninge?'

I don't answer. I just manoeuvre onto Nynäsvägen and put my foot down.

'Shall I?' Malin asks.

I nod and Malin turns on the blue lights and the siren.

'Why the hurry?'

'I don't know exactly how it is all connected,' I say, 'but something doesn't add up.'

I shift down, accelerate and overtake an eighteen-wheeler struggling to make its way up a long, flat hill.

Malin sits quiet and still and then continues: 'Why did you tell Pernilla Stenberg about that poem?'

'I wanted to know if she knew anything else about it, if she had interpreted it the same way we had.'

'And?'

'It hadn't occurred to her at all that the animals might symbolise real people. But she did know that Rachel means lamb, or ewe rather, and that Jonah means dove in Hebrew. She seemed pretty well acquainted with . . . biblical matters.'

I think for a minute, then go on: 'But she was confused.'

'What do you mean confused?'

'Talked incessantly about completely unrelated matters. Like how her neck hurt because she'd slept in her car. And that she had a bunch of scouting paraphernalia with her because she was really supposed to be on a hike. But that she never went on the hike because she got in a disagreement with the pastor whom she had trusted her entire life, but now she'd discovered that he was a real creep. Well, as you can tell . . . a few sandwiches short of a picnic.'

Malin considers this silently. Then she says: 'I called my mum.'

At first I'm so surprised I can't think of a word to say. Since the investigation in Ormberg last winter, Malin has not been on good terms with her mother. In fact, she said she would have nothing more to do with her.

'I don't know,' Malin says. 'All these dead and disappeared boys and their distraught loved ones. I just thought that – I don't know, but I don't really want Mum and me to lose touch completely. Despite all that happened. She still . . .'

Malin inhales deeply and continues in a quiet voice:

'. . . raised me. Loved me. All of that.'

'Good,' I say, fighting to keep my voice calm. 'Are you going to meet?'

'I think I want to take it slowly.'

The traffic ahead of us gets denser and I slow down.

'*Damn it*,' I say.

'Accident,' Malin notes without moving.

We end up sitting behind a red Volvo that is loaded to the brim with luggage, kids and a dog that appears to be drooling uncontrollably.

A few cars are honking further down the queue. A motorcyclist passes us at high speed on our left.

I look at my watch and at the queue that isn't moving an inch. Pull out my phone and punch in Pernilla Stenberg's number to double-check that she is waiting for Malik and Letit in Stuvskär. But the signals go through, one after another, without anyone answering.

In the end I get her voicemail.

'*Hi, this is Pernilla. Stenberg. Please leave a message and we'll talk. I mean, I will get back. To you. Later.*'

'*Damn it!*' I say again and look at the queue.

'Should I radio and ask what happened?' Malin asks.

'Let's drive to the front and see what it is,' I answer, as I turn left and begin to pass the long queue.

I drive deliberately cautiously in the opposite lane, but there are no cars, which does point to there being a complete jam somewhere further down.

After a mile or so I see blue lights and seconds later an ambulance and two police cars parked in the middle of the road. I note that the cars in the queue to the right are empty and that several doors are open, as if the passengers had left the vehicles in a hurry.

I turn off the siren and the lights, open my window and drive up to a police officer who is talking to a woman with a young child on her hip.

'Hi,' I say and flash my badge. 'Accident?'

The young police officer with a dark complexion nods.

'A van hit someone on horseback. It's fucking chaos here.'

I gaze ahead but all I can see is a crowd of curious rubberneckers. It looks as if everyone has a mobile in their hand and is either filming or taking photos. Some have lifted their children onto their shoulders so that they can get a better look.

'What the hell,' Malin murmurs. 'What is *wrong* with people?'

The young olive-skinned colleague nods.

'The paramedics could barely get through all of the people taking pictures. But not a soul helped the man who'd fallen off the horse.'

'Can we get through? This is an urgent matter,' I ask and purposefully use the term that indicates that we basically can drive as fast as we want and also break all traffic rules.

'I'll see what I can do,' my colleague says and goes over to another uniformed police officer.

They talk for a while and then one of them shouts something. In an instant people start to scatter.

The olive-skinned officer beckons us forward and I drive slowly through the sea of curious people and first responders. I catch a glimpse of a horse lying on its side on the roadway. It isn't moving and the ground around it is covered in fresh blood. A fireman is attaching a chain around the horse's belly. I'm guessing that they're about to pull it off the roadway so that traffic can resume.

At the edge of the road there is a white van and next to it lies an older gentleman in an old-fashioned tweed riding coat. A medic is crouched next to the man, talking to him.

As soon as we've passed the accident site I turn into the empty right lane and accelerate so hard that I am pushed back into my seat.

'We should be there in fifteen minutes,' I say. 'Let's hope it isn't too late.'

Pernilla

The palms of my hands are scraped and full of splinters. I pull them out, one by one, then look at the tall fence behind me.

Father would have been proud of me now. He was always so disappointed that I didn't do well at school gymnastics – although my grade in religious studies did compensate, to some degree.

I begin walking towards the entrance on the narrow gravel path that runs across the lawn. The gravel crunches under my feet and I step to the side, walking through the soft, lush grass.

There are fruit trees around me and on my right I pass an abundant bed of red roses. The scent of the exquisitely shaped flowers lingers sweet and heavy in the muggy air.

When I get to the house I walk up the steps. I stop halfway.

There is a suitcase on the landing and the door is open.

I hesitate. Should I ring the bell or just sneak in?

What if the woman named Rachel has nothing to do with Samuel's disappearance? If so, it would be incredibly embarrassing if I was caught sneaking into the home of Samuel's employer and her disabled son. It might even be illegal.

And I can't do anything illegal.

Besides: what if the man the police officer told me about is hiding in the house – the accomplice, *the lion*.

But then I think of Samuel, of how much I miss him. Of all that never was said and never done. Of how I am the only person searching for him right now, the only one he can trust.

You'd do anything for your child, anything and then more.

'If I find you I promise I will give you your father back,' I whisper to myself. 'And I will become a better person.'

I think for a minute.

'And lose two stone,' I add.

I step into the hallway and pull the door behind me so that the wind won't catch it and slam it shut. A second later it slides closed behind me with a low sigh, as if it were made out of metal.

My heart skips a beat. I freeze, mid-step and listen, but can't hear anything. No footsteps approach. Nobody calls. No lion with sharp teeth jumps out.

I look around.

The hallway is like something straight out of an Arts and Crafts movement painting.

The walls are covered in blue wainscoting and an old-fashioned floral edging runs along them. Men's clothes hang on hooks – hoodies, a parka and a thin down jacket. A small grey console table with trendily scuffed paint stands by the wall. On the table is a glass vase with fresh red roses.

Further down the hallway I see two black suitcases.

Someone just arrived or is just about to leave.

I take a few, probing steps, then I stop and take my shoes off. Through a doorway I see an empty hospital bed with a metal headboard. A couple of yards away there is a large metal frame. A blue harness with black straps and buckles hangs from the frame.

The harness sways slowly back and forth, as if someone recently gave it a little nudge.

Next to the bed there is a small table with a lone rose in a vase and a jar of some sort of cream. There is yet another suitcase on the floor. The walls are covered in pieces of tape, as if someone has taken down posters that had been put up there. On the floor next to the suitcase there is an old pair of football boots.

Jonas's room?

But if that's the case, where is he? Björn met him here less than an hour ago. And where is Rachel?

A slight scent of detergent and something else, chlorine maybe, tickles my nose. A squeaking sound comes from somewhere inside the house.

My heart skips again. Sweat streams down my forehead and between my breasts. My hands tremble so badly that I instinctively look around, afraid of unintentionally knocking something over.

The room seems to shrink and my field of vision narrows as fear grips my body. Invades every part of me until my legs no longer obey me and my arms hang down by my sides like weak-willed lumps of flesh. My hands and feet tingle and my mouth goes dry.

The fear is so strong that I am thrown back to childhood. To lonely, anxiety-filled hours with a monster lurking under my bed. To walks through dark wooded areas, where wolves were waiting in the bushes. And right then the words come out of my mouth on their own:

'Dancing Queen'

'Mamma Mia'

'Chiquitita'

'The Winner Takes It All'

My heart finds its rhythm and sensation returns to my limbs. The room regains its outlines.

'Fernando'

'Waterloo'

'When I Kissed the Teacher'

I turn my head slightly and look straight ahead, into a living room where the sun flows in through large casement windows. One of the windows is open; it sways slowly in the light breeze.

That must have been where the squeak came from.

I shake my head at my own imagination. Inhale deeply and begin to walk towards the living room.

'Head Over Heels'

'Name of the Game'

My steps are calm now. Determined. They are steps that know what they want and will not budge for imaginary monsters. But the wide floorboards groan alarmingly under my weight and I am forced to stop.

I let my gaze wander across the room.

Outside the window the sea stretches lazily in the afternoon sun, doomed to forever strive for the heavens, but never reach beyond the horizon. White sofas and armchairs are positioned across the floor. There are bookshelves along the walls. Spines in all sizes and colours of the rainbow fill the shelves, but also photos and ornaments.

Next to a photo of a woman and a little boy there is a cobalt-blue glass bowl on a stem that reminds me of my old cake platter back home in Fruängen that I inherited from my grandmother.

I step closer.

There is a man's watch with a canvas strap in the bowl, a mobile phone case with a hemp leaf pattern and . . .

And . . .

The window squeaks again and thumps as it swings open and hits a flowerpot. A warm gust of wind caresses my back and the hairs at the back of my neck stand on end.

I look at the blue bowl uncomprehendingly.

Next to the phone case there is a keychain. A tiny fish and an equally small plastic book dangle from the key ring.

That is Samuel's key ring – I gave it to him myself. We ordered those for all the kids in the congregation's youth programme. Of course it was cheap Chinese tat. But the important thing was what it meant – obviously the fish symbolised Christianity and the little book was the Bible, the holy scripture.

But why are Samuel's keys here, in the blue bowl, if he isn't here anymore? I reach out to touch the key chain, as if it could help me understand what happened. As if the cheapest plastic might transmit some kind of hidden message.

Thud.

Instinctively I turn around. Expect to see the window hit the flowerpot again. But I am face to face with a woman.

She is dressed in jeans shorts and a thin, white blouse. Her dark, almost black hair, hangs over her shoulders. No, it doesn't hang, it flows, like a river, down her shoulders, along the pale marble skin of her neck.

She is beautiful, very beautiful.

Beautiful in a way that I have never come close to being. And even as the panic comes roaring back, I register that we look alike – kind of like sisters, where one turned out beautiful and the other ugly.

Rachel.

'Who are you and what are you doing in my house?' she says in a shrill voice, squeezing hard an object that she is holding in her hand. I can't see what it is, but it is small and when she moves it reflects the sunlight.

I open my mouth to answer but no words come out.

Rachel takes a step towards me and I step back, knocking my elbow into the blue bowl. It rocks a couple of times, but remains on the shelf.

'Who are you?' she screams.

'I . . .'

My voice doesn't carry.

I back a few steps out towards the hallway. Trip on the threshold and almost fall, but manage to grab on to the door frame at the last second. But my sweaty hands slide across the painted surface and I lose my balance again:

'Honey Honey'

'When All is Said and Done'

'Samuel,' I whisper. 'I am Samuel's mother. Where is he?'

Rachel begins to walk towards me and I keep backing into the hallway. I trip again and fall against the grey side table. The vase topples over with a crash. Glass shards and roses scatter across the floor like spillikins. Cold water runs down my calves.

'Samuel quit,' Rachel says.

'No,' I say. 'I saw his keys. He has to be here.'

'He quit,' she says again, taking yet another step towards me. 'He found another, more ambitious job. Just like the others.'

Rachel stops and for a second she looks endlessly sad. And the sadness somehow seems to take the edge off her anger, at least for a moment, so I decide to keep talking. Just talking.

When it comes down to it, that is what I am best at.

'I miss him terribly,' I say and to my surprise I hear that my voice carries.

She knits her brow and lets her eyes wander across the roses on the floor. Then she slowly shakes her head.

'I know all about missing someone,' she says after a short pause.

I nod and follow her gaze. Next to my foot there is a door stopper of wrought iron, shaped like a little lamb.

A thought crystallises. A thought so terrible that I almost don't want to follow it all the way to the horrific conclusion.

I think of the poem. I look at the wrought-iron lamb.

And at that very moment the image of the self-satisfied pastor shows up in my mind again, but I also see one of the framed illustrations on the wall behind him in the congregation hall. It shows a lamb resting safely next to a giant lion.

The Lion of Judah.

The sacrificial lamb.

It is so ridiculously simple that I can't believe I didn't think of it earlier. Or that those clever police officers didn't crack the riddle sooner.

'It was you,' I whisper. 'You are *both* the lion and the lamb. The atonement and the battle, just like Jesus. There is no accomplice.'

'I don't know what you're talking about,' Rachel says, but she doesn't look at me. Her eyes are fixed on the floor.

'You assumed the right to play with God,' I say.

In the same instant I realise my mistake:

'Oh. Sorry. *To play* God, I mean.'

But my mistake completely passes Rachel by. There's a twitch in one of her eyes and she is bracing herself against the wall with one hand.

'I read the poem,' I say. 'Samuel wrote me a message on it. On the poem, that is. And put it in the car. My car. So that I found it.'

'My partner is a writer—' she begins.

'You know your Bible,' I interrupt. 'Just like I do. The lion and the lamb are one and the same. They are both symbols of Jesus. The sacrificial lamb who died for our sake and the lion, the king, the messiah. They are Jesus in two different guises. That is how you see yourself, isn't it? As God? And just like God you believe you have the right to take lives.'

'I just want my son back,' Rachel murmurs. 'Just like you.' She is crying now. Big tears roll down the pale cheeks and I see real grief and pain in her face. And in that instant yet another piece of the puzzle falls into place.

She didn't choose the name Rachel just because it meant lamb.

I recall the words from the gospel of Matthew clearly, can almost hear Father's voice as he reads out loud from his old well-worn Bible:

'*In Rama was there a voice heard, lamentation, and weeping, and great mourning, Rachel weeping for her children, and would not be comforted, because they are not.*'

Rachel raises her eyes, taking a few steps towards me. There is crackling and crunching as she walks across the broken glass with her bare feet, but her face is as expressionless as stone.

She leaves bloody footsteps as she walks across the wooden floorboards. They glisten in the sunlight that is making its way in from the living room.

'Where is Samuel?' I ask again, backing towards the front door. Feel with my hand for the doorknob and find it.

She shakes her head slowly.

'He is gone,' she whispers. 'He is gone. Everyone is gone.'

'*No!*' I say with tears in my throat. 'He isn't gone, do you understand? You know where he is and you are going to tell me.'

The handle rests cold in my hand when I push it down, but it doesn't move one inch.

I look around, search with my gaze for the keys, that have to be somewhere.

Rachel shakes her head slowly. A large puddle of blood has spread around one of her feet, but she doesn't seem to notice.

'Are you looking for this?' she asks and holds up a bunch of keys.

Manfred

'No chance I can make it over that fence,' I say, looking down at my gut protruding over my waistband.

'Yes, there is,' says Malin who has already climbed over to the other side. 'If I can climb it in my condition, then so can you.'

I follow her, hesitantly.

It ends up being a humiliating experience.

I get stuck halfway up and my expensive English suit trousers acquire a long tear before I clumsily roll over the fence and fall into the grass on the other side like overripe fruit in the autumn. I land on my side and feel a stab in my bad knee. Slowly I get up, end up on all fours like a dog till I recover my dignity and manage to stand.

Once I'm on my feet my phone buzzes in my pocket. I pull it out and read a message from Afsaneh.

Come to the hospital now!

A cold hand squeezes my heart as I reply.

What's happened?

Then I run after Malin as fast as my knee will allow. She has already made it to the house and is standing on the stoop, gazing up at the whitewashed exterior. She turns around and looks at me. Then she puts her hand on the handle and tries to open the front door.

I catch up with her, panting. Stop, put my hands on my knees and take a few deep breaths.

Malin looks at me quizzically, then knocks very carefully on the door and inspects the locks.

'Safety door,' she says. 'We're not getting in this way.'

'Perhaps we should try ringing the bell,' I suggest. 'Like normal people.'

'You do that. I'll check the windows.'

Malin disappears down the steps at the same time I get up and wipe the sweat off my forehead.

I push the brass button. Hear the signal cut through the silence, then wait.

Nothing.

I ring again, and then again, but nobody opens. No steps approach from inside the house. Rachel doesn't open the door and my sense that something is wrong grows stronger.

Malin comes back, shakes her head.

'I heard something from inside the house; it sounded like a scream. Perhaps we should wait here and call for back-up.'

I look at my pregnant colleague and know she is right. Going into the house on our own is against all rules and common sense. You're not allowed to even carry a gun when pregnant, much less discharge one. At the same time my conviction that time is of the essence grows stronger.

'We have to go in,' I say.

'There are thick bars on all the windows on the ground floor. She must really have been scared of burglaries. And there's a deck facing the ocean, but you can't get up onto it. It's at the edge of a cliff.'

I lean back and let my eyes wander across the white house, absorb the gingerbread work, the bars in front of the windows and the security door.

'Do we still have that long wire in the car?' I ask.

'I think so, why? Do you think we should climb up? We aren't exactly the most agile in the force, you and I.'

Malin smiles, as if the thought of the two of us hanging from a wire is comical.

'No. We're going in through that window.'

I point to one of the gables and then look at Malin's questioning gaze.

A few minutes later I have secured the wire and give it a light tug.

'Ready?' Malin calls from down the road.

'Ready,' I answer.

It is quiet for a bit. Then I hear the bang of the car door closing and the sound of the engine starting.

The metal wire goes taut. There are groans and little cracks become visible in the wood around the attachments for the safety bars. The cracks deepen, the wood fibres snap and long splinters poke out of the wood.

Malin accelerates and I hear the wheels spin on the dry gravel road. A second later the bars come off with a crash, fly off and end up in the grass a bit further away.

I wrap my jacket around my fist, break the window, stick my hand in and open it from the inside.

Malin comes running across the lawn.

'I'll do it,' she says, and climbs in the open window with surprising agility.

A second later she reaches her hand out. I grab it and climb after her into the house. We are in a bedroom furnished with a hospital bed and some sort of metal frame with a harness attached. The room has two doors: to the right I look into what must be the hall.

The floor is covered in blood. Broken glass and red roses are scattered all over the place. Malin takes her gun out and cocks it. I do the same and follow her into the hallway.

'There,' Malin says and points to tracks of blood that continue into a living room with large windows facing the water.

A white armchair has been knocked over and there are smudged bloodstains around it. A flowerpot lies broken on the floor.

Through the large windows there is a deck, surrounded by a white wooden railing. A section is missing from the middle of the railing, it looks almost as if someone has kicked it in. Sharp pieces of wood jut out from the hole, and right next to one of them, someone is clinging to the actual railing.

My heart picks up speed and I run for the doors. In that instant I am no longer here, in Rachel's house in Stuvskär. In that instant I am at home on Karlavägen and it is spring and Nadja still hasn't . . .

And I run.

I run because it is the only thing I can do. I run because I have to, because I must. You cannot let your child, fall, die. It is the one thing you cannot do in life.

'*Nadja!*' I bellow when I get out onto the deck and see the hands with their white-knuckled hold on the railing.

'Nadja!'

And I am so afraid. So very afraid, because I already know how it ends. But I throw myself towards her because that is what you do. You throw yourself at your child, you walk through fire and water.

You do everything and then more.

And I get a hold of her, I make it. But the hand is slowly sliding out of mine.

'I'm losing her!' I scream and in the next instant Malin is by my side and I am transported back to reality – to Stuvskär and a time in which Nadja is already lost.

To the reality in which it is already too late.

But this woman won't fall. I can save this woman.

Malin gets a firm grip on her lower arm and braces against a board.

I look down at the woman whose hand I am holding – the woman who is Rachel, aka Susanne Bergdorff. I can see the precipice over her shoulder and my stomach drops. It has to be at least fifty feet down to the ground, covered with rocks and boulders. Beyond them is a jetty and a boathouse.

Then nothing but sea.

Rachel's long hair flaps in the wind and she groans heavily. Her arms are bloody and her eyes half-closed.

There is a crash and another part of the fence breaks. A foot-and-a-half long piece of wood falls off, bounces down the rocks and then floats to the ground where it lands with a sharp bang.

'*Now!*' Malin says and with a joint effort we get the woman onto the deck.

*

Ten minutes later Susanne Bergdorff is lying prone on the deck in handcuffs, because although we don't know if she is our killer we aren't taking any risks. We have searched the house, established that it is empty and called for back-up.

Susanne murmurs something inaudible.

'*Uehl.*'

'Either she got hit or she is under the influence of something,' Malin pants and stands up with much effort. 'I let them know that we will need an ambulance as well.'

She goes into the living room to contact central command.

'*Muehl,*' Susanne groans again.

My gaze wanders away from her, past the enclosure and on down the paving to the jetty.

If she'd fallen from the deck she would have died instantaneously. She would have broken every bone in her body.

High-energy impact, I think.

And in the next moment the logical conclusion emerges: could that be what happened? Dead bodies are difficult to drag, but even a child could roll them off a cliff. And once down there it would be relatively easy to transport them out to sea.

The realisation makes my stomach turn.

Malin comes out again.

'We have a neighbour here,' she says. 'Can you have a few words with him? I'll stay in touch with our colleagues and keep an eye on her in the meantime.'

The neighbour, a man in his forties, introduces himself and takes my hand. He would have looked ordinary had it not been for the large disfiguring scar running from one temple down to the corner of his mouth.

'She is renting from Mai-Lis Wennström,' he says in such a broad Southern Swedish dialect that he is hard to understand. 'I spoke to a police officer earlier today, on the phone. And I told her something isn't right here.'

'OK?'

'What happened by the way?'

The man looks inquisitively towards the house and then at the three cars that are parked by the side of the road.

'We can't talk about it right now,' I say. 'What do you mean something isn't right?'

The man makes a face, turns his head and spits, as if he'd just bitten into something sour.

'Young boys. New ones every time I came. And then the sick son. In the end I went in to find out what she was doing. But then she asked me what *I'd* done to the boy, even though I hadn't even touched him. But I have seen her photographing him in there.'

'She was *photographing* him?'

The man nods and turns his disfigured cheek away so that he is watching me from the side.

'Did you ask her what she was doing?'

'I spoke with her several times,' the man says, nodding. 'But she was slippery, like a snake. And she threatened to call the police unless I got off her property. *Her* property? What bullshit. I wish Mai-Lis would've heard that. Then the bitch would have been thrown out head-first.'

When I get back out onto the deck Malin is kneeling next to Susanne.

'I don't understand what she is saying.'

'*Muehl*,' Susanne mumbles, '*Muehl*.'

'Wait a minute,' I say.

I lean over Susanne.

There is another stab in my knee and I grimace in pain.

'What are you saying?' I ask.

'*Muehl*,' Susanne repeats.

I go completely cold, even though the sun is shining and the breeze is hot.

'That neighbour,' I say. 'Did he come by car?'

Malin shakes her head and looks at me quizzically.

'So why are there three cars outside? If one is ours and one is Susanne Bergdorff's.'

'*Ahmuel*,' Susanne grunts again.

A small, dark puddle of saliva has spread on the wood under her cheek.

Malin looks at me and at that very moment we both understand.

'She is saying *Samuel*,' Malin whispers.

Carefully we turn the woman on her back so that we can see her face clearly.

Her long brown hair is matted and has broad streaks of silver. Her skin is freckled. Her eyes are half shut and a foamy strand of saliva is coming out of the corner of her mouth. In her décolletage is a golden cross.

'What is your name?' I ask.

'*Nilla*,' she whispers.

'Oh my God,' Malin says. 'This is her. The mum of the guy who disappeared. Pernilla Stenberg.'

I get up. The world is spinning and I have to hold onto the railing so as not to lose my balance.

'*Damn it!* How could we miss that?'

'But,' Malin says suspiciously, 'wasn't she supposed to meet Letit and Malik in Stuvskär?'

I don't answer, but think to myself that I would probably also have gone looking for my child rather than obediently waited for the police.

Malin unlocks the handcuffs and puts Pernilla in the recovery position. Then she gets up and looks down across the edge.

'There,' she whispers.

And I see it.

In a crooked little pine growing out of the side of the rock, maybe six feet below, something glistens.

It is a hypodermic needle.

My mobile rings and I take it out of my pocket.

'I'm in the middle of a bust,' I say. 'What's happening?'

I hear muffled sobbing in the background.

'Afsaneh? *Hello?*'

That cold hand grips my heart again. Squeezes and tugs at it as if it wanted to pull it out of my chest.

'Manfred?'

Her voice is fragile like night-old ice and I am so scared I cannot breathe.

'Nadja has woken up,' Afsaneh says. 'Can you come?'

'Yes,' I say, but then I can't. Then no more words come out of me.

I look at Malin without managing a single word.

But Malin doesn't appear to have noted my reaction. Her eyes are fixed on a point just below the horizon.

'There,' she says, pointing out to sea.

Quite far west of us there is a small dot.

A dot that is a human being, swimming with calm crawl strokes.

Rachel

I stop, tread water and look back, towards the house that clings, like an eagle's nest, to the rock.

Nothing.

No boats, no people can be seen on the jetty, so I keep swimming, fall into the rhythm.

Arm, arm, breathe.

Arm, arm, breathe.

I pass a skerry on my right. The rocks that protrude above the surface are covered in a thick layer of cormorant droppings. The waves are high out here and the water is cold. The sea tugs and whispers. Lures me down, towards the black void.

I get water in my airways and stop. Cough, throw up some seawater and then continue, though my arms and legs feel like logs.

I think of Samuel's mother whom I left dangling by the fence on the deck. Of what she said about missing her son. When she said that I actually felt some kind of affinity with her. I almost told her everything.

But how could I explain?

She would never have understood. Nobody can understand.

I see Birger's old leaky motorboat now. It is bouncing on the pointy waves next to the buoy.

The boat lies moored here inside the islet of Klockaren, waiting to be transported to the shipyard on Kornholmen.

If I'm lucky I will make it to the boat before anyone discovers me. Then I can hide in it and swim to the shore once it gets dark. I can't take the boat and flee out to sea, it is almost out of fuel. Besides it takes in far too much water, as I learned the hard way when I borrowed it to transport the boys' bodies.

Arm, arm, breathe.

Arm, arm, breathe.

I raise my head above the water to look.

Perhaps another fifty yards.

The woman who is Samuel's mother must have fallen down onto the rocks. Her body has probably been crushed and become soft and lifeless like the boys' did. As if they were made out jelly.

The thought makes me feel sick again. I never wanted to kill anyone, it just happened, the way autumn follows the heat of summer. It was an inescapable consequence, but never, ever my intention.

I grab on to the boat, pull myself along the hull to the little ladder in the aft. Heave myself up and end up standing, panting, with my heart thumping in my chest.

I look in the direction of my house, squint at the sun and try to see.

A speedboat is headed my way.

Yes. It is my boat. Or Victor Carlgren's boat, if I'm being precise.

Victor wasn't like those others; he wasn't looking for a job as a caretaker. He just stood there one day, at the dock for small boats in Stuvskär, with his motor that was acting up.

I assured him that we could fix it. That Olle loved tinkering with boat motors. And that was actually partly true: Olle was good with motors, before he began to question how I cared for Jonas. Before he became violent and I was forced to defend myself.

I chose to ignore the boat for a bit longer, thinking that maybe the motor will stall like it usually does.

If I am lucky I will get away.

My thoughts go to you, Jonas. They always land with you, regardless of where they start.

I miss you so desperately, the absence hurts so much. It cuts and pierces my chest until I feel like I am going insane.

Those boys – I don't think I ever seriously believed they were you, although I wished it so much it almost became true.

But at least they made me feel like a mother again. Like *somebody*'s mother.

Because they lay there, completely helpless and dependent on me. At the mercy of my love and care. And as they got worse, lost weight, got bed sores and suffered other complications, I began to think about the next boy. Of how it would be perfect then, that it had to be perfect.

But nobody was like you.

I gaze across the sea. Look at the approaching boat. It skips across the waves like a pinball and leaves a white trail of foaming water in its wake.

There is nowhere for me to hide.

I open the aft hatch and take out the anchor.

It is so heavy that I can barely lift it. The chain rattles dully when I wind it around my waist. I loop it a turn around my neck too and then sit on the railing with the anchor in my lap and my back to the water.

The sea is calling me.

Come! it says. *Here is oblivion and understanding. Here is all that you have been missing.*

Here is your son.

In the small motorboat that is drawing closer there is a young woman with long brown hair. It flutters behind her, but settles over her shoulders when she stops a few yards from me.

'Police!' she shouts. 'Lie down face down in the boat!'

I don't answer.

The woman continues to talk, calmer now, with her eyes on the chain around my neck. She says that everything will be OK, as long as I lie down in the boat. That there is a solution to everything. That no problem is so big it can't be fixed. That there is so much left to live for.

I look at her silently and my gaze catches on the protruding belly.

She has life ahead of her. It is growing inside of her.

My life lies behind me. I drag it behind me, like a tail. My life is a train filled with stones. A load of timber. I pull and I pull but I don't get anywhere, never free of my past. Just walk around in the same circles.

'Lie down in the boat!' the police officer bellows.

Perhaps she is tired of luring and coaxing.

But I turn my face to the sun and close my eyes. Feel the warmth spread through my body. Notice how my skin, which has goosebumps from the swim, becomes smooth again.

Then I let go of the railing and fall back, down into the water with a firm grip on the anchor.

PART VI

Atonement

Those who regard worthless idols
forsake their own mercy.
But I will sacrifice to You with the voice of thanksgiving;
I will pay what I have vowed.
Salvation *is* of the LORD.

Jonah 2: 8–9

Manfred

Berit pours more tea for me, Malin and Hanne. Outside the window the sun is lowering itself over Ormberg, making space for the shadows, the darkness.

'I am so happy for you,' Hanne says again, laying her hand over mine.

'Yes,' I say. 'Although she's only been awake for two days, so we don't really know to what extent she will recover. What we do know is that there is a lot of hard work left. Physical therapy, speech therapy and so on.'

I think of my visit to the hospital this morning. How I looked straight into Nadja's brown eyes and she into mine.

She opened her mouth as if she wanted to say something, but there were no words, even though the tube in her throat is gone and the little hole has been stitched up.

But she blinked.

My child can blink again. Blink and look me in the eye. And in her gaze I could clearly see that she was still in there, that she wasn't just a shell.

The doctors say that the first examinations indicate problems with speech and with motor skills on the right side of the body.

But that hardly matters.

I don't care if Nadja ends up deaf, mute, or disabled.

All I care about is that she is alive. That my child, who fell out of the window, onto the hard tarmac, is actually alive.

That we – who were a normal family up until that morning that separated then from now as with the cut of an axe – will have our life back.

I see Pernilla Stenberg's distraught face in my mind's eye.

Not everyone is as lucky as I am. Not everyone gets their child back.

Though my colleagues have searched Marholmen for almost two days by now, Samuel Stenberg has not been found. And though I haven't said it out loud to Pernilla I am certain: Samuel is gone. He's lying somewhere on the bottom of the ocean, wrapped in chains just like those we found in the boathouse.

It's a strange coincidence, a sort of poetic justice maybe, that the woman who called herself Rachel also drowned, wrapped in chains. Because when the divers brought her body to the surface it was too late, far too late.

Susanne Bergdorff was gone.

By the way, the boat that Malin took, the one that was in Susanne's boathouse, belonged to Victor Carlgren, or more accurately the Carlgren family. We don't know why Susanne didn't use it to escape, but likely she thought it would be easier to escape unnoticed if she swam.

With the help of Susanne's email, messages and notes we have made ourselves a pretty clear picture of what happened.

Young men were lured in by Susanne with promises of work, but instead they ended up drugged. They likely died from malnutrition and dehydration. The forensic toxicology report also showed that the victims had high levels of opioids and other drugs in their tissue.

The forensics team also found hair and traces of blood in the wheelbarrow, so we have drawn the conclusion that Susanne Bergdorff wheeled the bodies from Jonas's room to the deck in the wheelbarrow. After that she rolled them over the edge – which resulted in severe contusions. Once down on the jetty she wrapped them in fabric and chains. Then she transported the bodies out to sea where she sank them.

She likely used Birger Jämtmark's old boat, the same boat that she swam to before taking her own life. That Johannes Ahonen had Victor Carlgren's DNA under his nails was likely due to Ahonen scratching him at some point when they were both at Rachel's. We still don't know who the boy Samuel was taking care of was, but if we're lucky we will find the body, which will aid us in identifying him.

When it comes to Olle Berg the picture is less clear.

He was, as far as we know, Rachel's boyfriend.

Perhaps he tried to stop her and paid with his life, perhaps he was the first victim, before Rachel realised she could target young male aides.

'So, you want help understanding?' Hanne says hesitantly, bringing both her hands to her head, taming the long unruly curls with nimble fingers, shaping her hair into a loose bun at her neck.

And then: 'That's what everyone wants. To understand. Every time an unfathomable terrible crime has happened people want to understand. But sometimes that isn't possible. Sometimes there is no logic to explain the horrors that we humans subject each other to.'

'But if you were to try?' I say, because I know that Hanne loves it when I draw her hypotheses out of her.

'Show me those diary entries,' Hanne says.

I take out the folder of papers and find the copies from Rachel's diary that we found in the house. Mainly it contains short notes on what medicines she gave the boys, how they were doing and trends in the numbers of followers on her blog. But in a couple of places she has written personal reflections.

'Here,' I say and give Hanne a copy of a page from the diary.

We read it in silence.

Last night I dreamed of Skrållan – our grey speckled cat that we got when I was eight. And it was JUST like being back that day when it all happened. It was as if it all happened again, but in my dream. I sat with Skrållan in my lap. Wanted her to stay there so that I could pet that furry little body for a while longer. But when I did, when I grabbed the thin little cat leg, something went wrong. There was a sound like pulling a cork out of a small bottle and the leg ended up at a strange angle.

I ran to get Dad. Said that Skrållan had caught her leg when she was jumping off the bookshelf.

Dad examined Skrållan and after he had determined that something really WAS wrong we took her to the vet. The nurse patted me on the head and said that I was a really

*good young owner to have discovered what was wrong with
Skrållan. She got me ice cream and held my hand while the
vet examined the cat.*

*The vet also nodded appreciatively when I told her what
had happened. Said that she wished all owners of animals
were like me. That they noticed when their animals weren't
feeling well and sought care immediately. If they did a lot of
suffering could be avoided.*

In school I told the story over and over again.

*My schoolmates stood in a ring around me. Nobody
called me ugly or fat anymore. The teacher also wanted to
hear the story and in the end I drew several drawings that
illustrated what had happened. The teacher put them up on
the wall and they must have hung there for several years,
because I recall that they were still there when I left primary
school.*

'Very interesting,' Hanne says, making some notes on her
pad.

'Would you agree that she was a sadistic psychopath?' Malin
asks.

Hanne hesitates before answering.

'I'm not so sure about that.'

'There is one more passage I think you should read,' I say
and dig out the other page.

*A girl who follows my blog emailed me and wanted to send
me a pie! Really, a PIE! It's just like with André. Every last*

neighbour showed up on our doorstep with a pie or a bag of buns when he got sick. They mowed our lawn, shovelled snow, pruned our trees.

It was like standing in the sun.

But after a while that passed.

I guess people found other tragedies to take an interest in – cancer-stricken mothers of young children, children in wheelchairs. The crippled and maimed. The childless. The paralysed. The dying. All those who STOLE attention from André and me – because NOBODY was interested in some-one with 'a bit of MS' anymore when the neighbour had liver cancer and two months left to live.

All I wanted was to stand in the sun again, for a little while. Feel that warmth and love that shone on me.

Hanne takes her reading glasses off and wipes a sweaty strand of hair from her forehead. Nods slowly and puts the paper down on the worn wooden table. Her gaze makes its way out of the window, towards the lush vegetable garden. Her expression is focused and a bit sad and at once I think she looks old.

'André – was that her husband?' she asks.

I nod and put the sheet back in my folder.

'Can I have another look at the blog?'

'Sure,' I say, pushing the laptop over to her.

Hanne spends a long time scrolling through the posts again. Once in a while she hums and nods slowly.

'Just like I suspected,' she mumbles.

'What?' I ask.

'Susanne Bergdorff started her blog after her son was in the accident. She quickly acquired a large number of followers. A seriously injured child against the backdrop of the archipelago was apparently an irresistible concept. This is what I find interesting.'

She points at the numbers that show how many likes and comments the various posts have.

Malin and I lean in to see better.

'Initially she wrote that her son was recovering,' Hanne says. 'That he was showing clear signs of waking up. And then what happens? The number of comments and likes *decrease* drastically. Nobody wants to read about a regular, healthy boy. It looks like what people wanted was the grief, the disease, the misery. And then he gets worse, as if by chance, and the blog's following explodes. And then . . .'

'*What?*' Malin asks.

'Then Susanne is the centre of attention,' Hanne says and smiles sadly. 'The sun is shining on her again, just like she described in her diary entries.'

None of us say anything.

'I think we have to consider the possibility that Susanne was driven by getting more and more followers and likes,' Hanne says quietly. 'And that people at home really liked what she had to offer, that her . . . misery sustained them. And in that game, the dance that emerged between her and her followers, a number of people had to pay with their lives.'

A cold chill runs down my spine and I remember Malin's comment about that group of rubberneckers who were photographing the accident.

What the hell is wrong with people?

Then I think of Afsaneh, who photographed Nadja and posted the pictures on a forum for parents of sick children. And of Martin, Afsaneh's old colleague, who claimed with absolute certainty that the incidence of narcissistic personality traits had increased exponentially since the 1980s. That people were prepared to do anything for digital validation.

'What are you saying?' I ask. 'Do you think Susanne hurt her son *on purpose*?'

'Yes,' Hanne says calmly. 'Her son and probably her husband too. And after that she began to seek out new victims. She was the lion and the lamb. She cared for her victims and hurt them too, just like in the poem. It all checks out. And it all began with the cat. That incident planted a seed in her. Then her parents fell ill and died. Perhaps she cared for them too. Perhaps that enhanced these tendencies. Much later her husband became sick and Susanne helped care for him. She was motivated as well as competent, by dint of her degree in pharmacy. And once again she got a lot of validation, from healthcare workers as well as friends, both online and in real life. So she hurt him so she could stay there in the sunshine. I don't think she meant to kill him but that is what happened.'

'And then the pattern repeated with her son,' Malin whispers.

'Yes,' Hanne says. 'With the difference that Susanne had created a blog and accounts on several social media platforms. And the sicker her son is, the more likes and followers she gets. So she takes matters into her own hands. Makes sure he gets a bit worse. We can probably assume he died eventually, as a result of her . . . *treatment*.'

Hanne pauses.

'That is so fucking horrible,' Malin murmurs, buries her head in her hands and lets out a sob.

'When Jonas died she felt a void so great it couldn't be contained,' Hanne continues without taking any note of Malin's reaction. 'For reasons we may never know she replaced her son with his home aide. And after that she began to repeat the behaviour.'

'Hey, look at this!'

She scrolls to a post from seven months ago.

Now the council has decided that we will only get three hours of home help a day. Due to this neither I nor my partner can work full-time anymore. Help us by sending us money via the link below. No contribution is too small! Thanks in advance to all the amazing people who will help us cope!!

'She asked for money online and defrauded the authorities by cashing in various types of subsidies,' Hanne murmurs. 'I guess we will see what kinds of sums were involved, but that may have been an incentive for her to find new boys to play the role of Jonas.'

Malin lifts her head and wipes a few tears off her cheek.

'I'm sorry,' she whispers. 'But what kind of a person does that?'

'Someone who is disturbed,' Hanne says calmly, smiles and sips her hot tea. 'Someone *deeply* disturbed. She was extremely manipulative too. Lied about almost everything, as I understand it. That indicates that she had antisocial traits.'

None of us say anything. The idea of hurting people, your own child even, in order to achieve online fame is so extreme that it is almost impossible to understand.

'If you want a diagnosis I can give you one,' Hanne says and taps her pen lightly against the table.

I nod.

'Münchausen by proxy,' she continues, looking pleased. 'Well, that's when someone hurts a person, often one's child, and then seeks help in order to appear as the saviour. The killer is validated by the attention he or she gets. This perpetuates and enhances the pathological behaviour. I imagine this is also true of attention one gets online. Perhaps we have just seen the first case of Münchausen by proxy online, or whatever you would like to call it. But not the last, because we are on our way into a completely new era, that much I know although I am old.'

She pauses and her gaze wanders to the ceiling.

Malin's phone rings.

'Sorry,' she says, gets up and goes into the next room to answer.

'It is too bad that she died,' Hanne says, almost to herself. 'It would have been very interesting to meet her.'

Malin comes back with her phone in her hand.

'They found another body.'

'Samuel?' I say and feel my last hope fade.

But Malin shakes her head.

'No, this person died many months ago.'

'Jonas?'

Malin nods.

'They think so. And guess where they found him?'

I shake my head.

'Under the fucking rose garden. She buried him under her flower bed, or grew flowers on his grave. Regardless I guess she wanted to keep him close.'

Pernilla

have been wandering Marholmen for two days. I have walked along the rocky beaches, climbed the rocks. I have searched among verdant ferns and austere pines. I have looked under firs and fallen trees. Methodically gone over plots and wandered aimlessly in the woods.

But he is nowhere to be found, my Samuel.

The fat police officer, Manfred, was here last night and tried to convince me to go home. He said there was nothing I could do. That they had gone over Marholmen with a fine-toothed comb and that Samuel wasn't there.

That he was gone.

And when he said it I could no longer control myself. The tears gushed out of me and I collapsed next to my car. Felt the rough grass against my cheek and the coldness emanating from the ground, like a portent of the grief to come.

I couldn't explain to him, actually I didn't even try to explain why I wanted to stay here on Marholmen.

What would I have said?

That Samuel is my child? That I have carried him in my body, but that despite that I have let him down more times than I can count?

No.

So I went home. Showered. Tried to eat something.

I made the mistake of turning on the TV too. They were talking about the murders and about Samuel. And they interviewed Bianca Diaz, the girlfriend of one of the victims. Something about the young pregnant woman's restrained despair woke me out of my own grief and compelled me to act. I know only too well how hard it is to raise a child alone.

I found her on the internet and drove out to her apartment in Jordbro. Hung the duffle bag full of money on her door, rang the bell and then hurried out.

I suppose I was paying penance, as if that would give me Samuel back.

Then I returned to Marholmen, because what is there for me at home without my child?

I close my eyes and open the wafer chocolate bar in my pocket. Break off a piece and put it in my mouth. Peek through the half-open door at the blackbird sitting in the cage in the grass next to the car. The wind catches a piece of the torn-up newspaper that covers the floor of the cage. Flaps it against the bars, where it gets stuck.

He's not a chick anymore, but an almost full-grown bird that shouldn't be imprisoned in a cage. I know Samuel would have wanted to be the one to let him out. But now that he can't I want to do him the favour.

I look up at the house that Rachel rented from the old light-house keeper's daughter who lived here her whole life. It lies quiet and still behind the blue-and-white crime scene tape.

'Where did you go, Samuel?' I whisper, slamming the car door. Then I take the birdcage in my hand and begin walking down the gravel path and think of the strange dream I had last night.

I dreamed of the wise king Solomon in the Book of Kings, the one who was going to settle the dispute between the two women who both claimed the right to the same child.

Solomon asks for a sword, and when it has been fetched he says:

'Cut the living child in half and give the women half each.'

In the dream the women were Rachel and I, the child was Samuel.

Once again I think this cannot be true. He cannot be gone.

Two days. Nobody can survive for that long in the water, Manfred said.

But what if she didn't throw him in the water?

Then we would have found him.

Manfred's words echo in my ears.

Dusk lowers itself over the island, but the real darkness is still in its infancy, waiting patiently for summer to retreat and make way for autumn. The sky lies heavy above, bruised in shades of blue and purple. Mosquitoes and gnats buzz around me, but I wave them away. Distractedly scratch the bites I have already got and look in between the copper-glowing, scaly trunks of the pines. The ditch is frothy with cow parsley and here and there the yellow flowers of St John's wort glow.

It is so beautiful it makes my heart ache.

The scent of Labrador tea and yellow bedstraw – lady's bedstraw – permeates the air.

I think of Father, who knew everything about flora and fauna. He never wanted to call the plant by that name, our lady, the real Virgin Mary, lay on a bed of straw, not yellow bedstraw.

That was just something that ignorant peasants had come up with.

This will do, I think, placing the cage on the ground. Open the little door and wait for the blackbird to fly out.

But it just sits there, still and looking at me with its little yellow-rimmed button eyes.

In the end I put my hand in the cage and push it out.

'There you go, good bird. Now fly!'

The blackbird hops out but then sits next to the high grass by the side of the road. I step toward it to force it to fly away and enjoy all of this freedom. The summer, the woods, the cool evening air.

Life, that is so short and unpredictable.

The blackbird flies up, passes in front of my face and lands on a branch just a few yards from me. Then it turns to me. Cocks its little head and looks at me again.

'Samuel should see you now!' I say out loud.

And at that moment.

At that moment it hits me that he really is gone. That Samuel will never come back again and that the fat police officer was right.

My body contracts in a spasm, forces me onto my knees and presses my forehead against the gravel. My body drains me of tears and forces me into submission. And I let it happen. I shout out my pain, on my knees on the roadway, as if I were a woman in labour.

After a while the tears dry up and my breath calms down. I become aware of the forest sounds again; hear the birds sing, the wind whispering and rustling the canopies. The creaking and squawking from a heavy branch somewhere above me. The rattle of a woodpecker working his way into a tree trunk.

Just as I am about to get up, brush the gravel off my dirty dress that smells of sweat, I see the blackbird again.

It is sitting next to the shoulder of the road.

But I see something else too – wedged between two rocks next to the blackbird.

I take a few steps, squat down, reach out my hand and grasp the blue glass bead between my thumb and my index finger.

I look around. Scan the long shadows, search among dry leaves and rocks.

But all I see is the gravelly, light brown roadway disappearing in among the pines.

Then I sense something very small, but intensely red, in the middle of the road, a few yards further down. I gasp for air, run there, sink into a squat and pick up yet another glass bead. Turn it over and see a letter.

'M'

The tears come again, but this time they are tears of joy.

My energy returns when I understand what I need to do, I begin to look along the road.

I find more beads. A blue one, a yellow one, a brown one. They appear to be scattered at regular intervals along the side of the road. Almost as if they were placed there on purpose.

I cup my hand and hold it up. Move the beads around with my index finger to form the word. 'MUMMY'.

'*Samuel*,' I whisper. 'I'm coming!'

I keep looking for the small glass beads, find another three, but then there are no more.

Right when I am about to give up I see the small path veering off to the left.

The light is dim under the large trees, so I pull out my phone, turn the torch on and shine it in among the branches. An enormous pine partially obscures my view, but behind its needle-less pinafore I glimpse some kind of ruin, almost completely overgrown by saplings and bushes.

I duck, bend under the dry branches and walk toward the dilapidated building. Halfway there I stop, bend over and pick up a white bead gleaming on the bed of dry pine needles and moss. Then I stand up and look around.

The door to the collapsed building is askew and the plants form a green wall in front of the bared bricks.

'*Samuel?*' I whisper.

But all I can hear is the low rustle of the canopies and the mosquitoes buzzing around my head.

I sweep the phone torch around me.

To the right of the ruin there is an old well and next to it . . .

Wait a minute.

A fresh twig with drooping leaves sticks out, squeezed between the well and the lid, as if someone had recently opened the well and the branch had got stuck there when it was closed.

I go over to the well and bend down. Next to the rough stone there is something orange. The small item glistens in the light from my phone.

It is a ladybird. Or rather, an enamel earring shaped like a little ladybird.

I put the beads and the earring in my pocket and pull tentatively at the rusted handle on the old lid. It is heavy and I need to use all of my body weight to move it.

The lid gives off a scraping noise and moves a few inches to the right.

I let go and gasp for breath. Pant and brace against the well.

It is heavy, really heavy.

A second later I hear it.

A knocking sounds from the well makes me jump. I scream, but then there is a spark of hope inside my chest.

I knock so hard on the lid of the well that my knuckles start to bleed.

Knock-knock-knock

I grab on to the rusted handle again. Pull until I black out. I pull and pull and all I can think is that I need to remove the lid. That I have to open this hellhole before it is too late.

Each time I lean back and brace with my legs the lid moves a few inches. In the end a crescent of darkness gapes at me from the underground.

I pick up my phone and shine the flashlight into the black hole.

And there he is.

My child.

He looks straight up at me and blinks several times.

Under him there is a body lowered into the water. The surface is partially covered with some sort of plant with tiny, tiny green leaves, but I can see a hand stick out in one spot.

'I knew you would come,' Samuel says.

Manfred

Three weeks later

It is night. A light blue summer night.
But the hospital is awake, as always.

A low clatter from the corridor, muffled voices from the nurses' office. An alarm beeping somewhere.

Nadja is sleeping.

I am holding her little hand in mine. The same hand that slid out of my grip, lubricated with butter.

Her face is wet from tears, it takes me a few moments to realise they are my tears, not Nadja's.

The nurse, who enters our room, laughs a little, and tousles Afsaneh's hair.

'Go home now,' she says. 'It's late.'

I look at the clock, confirm that it's already morning and that she is right. I have a meeting with Letit at the station at nine o'clock and should try to get some sleep.

We have grown close, those of us on the investigative team. Even Letit, who was such a curmudgeon in the beginning, has softened and become social. He whistles on his way to the coffee machine, holds doors open and hasn't uttered a single sexist or homophobic insult in weeks. He has even cut his toenails and stopped wearing that terrible string vest.

It almost makes me wonder if he's gone and fallen in love. And the fact is that Malin told me that she suspects he is dating one of the witnesses in our investigation, Stina Svensson, the manager at the shop where Pernilla Stenberg works and thus a highly unsuitable match for our good Letit.

But I'm not going to point that out to him.

I'm just glad to have Nadja back. And that Pernilla Stenberg found her son alive, against all odds.

Samuel was badly injured and dehydrated after lying in the well for two days. Apparently, he survived by licking the wet concrete walls, sitting on the dead drug lord.

He hovered between life and death for several days, but we now know that he will make it, that he will fully recover. Physically at least. I don't even dare imagine what he might see in his dreams at night.

'Sleep for a few hours!' the nurse says. 'You need it. After all, tomorrow you get to bring your daughter home.'

Afsaneh nods and I reluctantly let go of Nadja's small, damp hand.

We leave the hospital together.

Outside the entrance the humid night air hits me like a wall. My tears begin to flow again and I let out a small sob. There's a stabbing pain in my knee but I couldn't care less.

Three women in green surgical scrubs are standing by the wall. They smoke in silence and stare down at their phones. A man comes walking from over by the car park. He is pushing a pram with one hand. The child is moaning and squirming like a snake, but the man is focusing his full attention on the phone in his other hand. The pram slips off track and one front wheel rolls off the kerb. The child jolts and screams. The man straightens the pram out without taking his eyes off the screen on his phone for a moment.

Over by the taxi stand there's a lone car. The driver has opened the door and has one foot on the ground, as if he is about to get up and go. But he is sitting perfectly still. His face is illuminated by the light from the phone in his lap.

Afsaneh sees my gaze and nods.

'What is wrong with people?' I ask.

She doesn't answer but sneaks her hand into mine.

I squeeze it hard and wipe away my tears with my other hand. Then I rummage through my pocket, pull out a pack of cigarettes and hand it to her.

'Would you like one?'

Afsaneh laughs quietly.

'I knew you were sneaking smokes.'

'Right back at you,' I say, lighting the cigarette she's just placed between her lips.

We sit on a concrete step barrier. My knee hurts like hell and apparently humanity is going to hell too, right down a spiral of escalating narcissism.

But what does it matter?

I look at Afsaneh.

She smiles, inhales the smoke deeply, tilts her head back and lustily blows the smoke out into the brightening summer sky.

We are a pretty ordinary family. It is a morning like any other.

And even though nothing is as it used to be, we have our life back.

Acknowledgements

I would like to extend a big thank you to everyone who has been part of and contributed to my work on *The Hideout*, especially my editor Katarina, and my publisher Sara at Wahlström & Widstrand, as well as my agent, Christine, and her colleagues at Ahlander Agency.

I would also like to thank Åsa Torlöf, who has contributed important insight into police matters, and Martina Nilsson, who has shared her knowledge on DNA analysis.

Finally I would like to thank my family and my friends for their understanding and encouraging words during my work with this book. Without your love and patience there would not have been a book!